AUTHORS LOVE HIM

"Amazing."
—Michael Connelly

"Thrilling."
—Louise Penny

"Brilliant."
—Jeffery Deaver

"Watch for those twists—they'll get you every time."
—Ian Rankin

"Edge-of-your-seat, heart-in-your-throat suspense."
—Tess Gerritsen

"The novels of Peter Robinson are chilling,
evocative, deeply nuanced works of art."
—Dennis Lehane

CRITICS LOVE HIM

"Devilishly good."
—*New York Times Book Review*

"Superb."
—*Wall Street Journal*

"First-rate."
—*Washington Post*

"Atmospheric."
—*Los Angeles Times*

"Exquisite."
—*USA Today*

"Rewarding."
—*Seattle Times*

"The equal of . . . P. D. James."
—*St. Louis Post-Dispatch*

YOU'LL LOVE HIM

One of the world's most popular and acclaimed writers, **PETER ROBINSON** grew up in the United Kingdom, and now divides his time between Toronto and England. The bestselling, award-winning author of the Inspector Banks series, he has also written two short-story collections and three standalone novels, which combined have sold more than ten million copies around the world. Among his many honors and prizes are the Edgar Award, the CWA (UK) Dagger in the Library Award, and Sweden's Martin Beck Award.

THE PRICE
OF LOVE
AND OTHER STORIES

Peter Robinson

wm
WILLIAM MORROW
An Imprint of HarperCollins*Publishers*

For Sheila

HarperCollins
PUBLISHERS
Since 1817

Page 357 serves as an extension of the copyright page.

THE PRICE OF LOVE AND OTHER STORIES. Compilation copyright © 2009 by Eastvale Enterprises Inc. All rights reserved. Printed in the United States of America. No part of this book may be used or reproduced in any manner whatsoever without written permission except in the case of brief quotations embodied in critical articles and reviews. For information address HarperCollins Publishers, 195 Broadway, New York, NY 10007.

HarperCollins books may be purchased for educational, business, or sales promotional use. For information please e-mail the Special Markets Department at SPsales@harpercollins.com.

A hardcover edition of this book was published in 2009 by William Morrow, an imprint of HarperCollins Publishers.

FIRST HAPER PAPERBACK EDITION PUBLISHED 2010.
FIRST WILLIAM MORROW PAPERBACK EDITION PUBLISHED 2017.

The Library of Congress has catalogued the hardcover edition as follows:

Robinson, Peter, 1950–
    The price of love and other stories / Peter Robinson.—1st ed.
        p.   cm
    ISBN 978-0-06-180948-4
    1. Detective and mystery stories, English. 2. Banks, Alan (Fictitious character)—Fiction. 3. Police—England—Yorkshire—Fiction.
    I. Title.
PR6068.O1964P75   2010
823'.914—dc22   2009011265

ISBN 978-0-06-180949-1 (pbk.)
17 18 19 20 21 OV/LSC 10 9 8 7 6 5 4 3

Contents

Introduction

For someone who considers himself primarily a novelist, I seem to have written rather a lot of short stories. I have also been very fortunate in that my publishers want to publish them in collection form, which induces a retrospective frame of mind in me as I gather these tales together and prepare them for publication.

Most of the stories in this collection were written at the request of one editor or another. I know that sounds rather mercenary, and that, in the Romantic view of art, the writer is supposed to work from pure inspiration. But I think of the stories as challenges, and sometimes a challenge can bring out the best in a person, or at least it can bring to the surface something he didn't know he had, something he hadn't explored before. And that is very much the case in this collection.

I'm not going to go into details here about the content or origins of any of these stories. I'm saving that for the afternotes because I don't want to spoil anything for those readers who, like me, want to know as little as possible about a story or novel they are about to read. I will say, though, that some of these requests for stories opened up new directions for me, took me places I would not normally have gone, and forced me to dig deep into areas where I might never have ventured left to my own devices.

In some cases, I simply set off into the dark without even a light to guide my way, moving from one word to the next and letting the story find itself. In others, I thought and fretted about the story for months, shaped it in my mind, despaired over it, scrapped it, started again, and when I was finally driven by the demands of a deadline to put fingers to keyboard, it came out as something different, often something better than I could ever have hoped for.

I have said before that I find short stories difficult to write, and that is still the case. The discipline is exacting and the amount of space in which I sometimes feel I have to maneuver feels quite claustrophobic. The bits I have to leave out would probably make a novel. But the satisfaction level is high. I remember when I used to write mostly poetry, I would sometimes work for weeks trying to get a poem right, especially when I began to value form and structure as much as, if not more than, Romantic self-expression or postmodernist confessional. Everyone who has ever written a poem knows that to make it work you sometimes have to sacrifice your best line or image, and working on a short story is far more akin to that process than is writing a novel, which in some ways is a constant search for more things to put in.

So here are the stories. I hope you enjoy them. People often ask me whether they should start with the first Inspector Banks novel or with one of the later ones, and I usually answer that it doesn't matter unless you are the kind of person who *has to* start at the beginning. The stories are not presented chronologically, and nor did I agonize over their order according to some secret code or system of symbolism known only to me. Please feel free to jump in wherever you wish.

PETER ROBINSON
Toronto, January 2009

Going Back

An Inspector Banks Novella

I

Banks pulled up outside his parents' council house and parked his Renault by the side of the road. He wondered if it would be safe left out overnight. The estate had a bad reputation, even when he grew up there in the sixties, and it had only gotten worse over recent years. Not that there was any alternative, he realized, as he made sure it was locked and the security system was working; his parents didn't own a garage.

He couldn't very well remove the CD player for the weekend, but to be on the safe side, he stuffed the CDs themselves into his overnight bag. He didn't think any young joyriders would want to steal Thelonious Monk, Cecilia Bartoli or the Grateful Dead, but you couldn't be too careful. Besides, he had a portable disc player now, and he liked to listen to music in bed as he drifted off to sleep.

Banks's parents' house stood near the western edge of the estate, close to the arterial road, across from an abandoned factory and a row of shops. Banks paused for a moment and took in the redbrick terrace houses—rows of five, each with a little garden, low wall and privet hedge. His family had moved here from the tiny, grim back-to-back when he was twelve, when the houses were new.

It was a Friday afternoon near the end of October, and Banks was home for the weekend for his parents' golden wedding anniversary that Sunday, only his second overnight stay since he had left home at the age of eighteen to study business at London Polytechnic. When that didn't work out, and when the sixties lost their allure in the early seventies, he joined the police. Since then long hours, hard work, and his parents' overt disapproval of his career choice had kept him away. Visiting home was always a bit of a trial, but they *were* his mother and father, Banks reminded himself; he owed them more than he could ever repay, he had certainly neglected them over the years and he knew they loved him in their way. They weren't getting any younger, either.

He took a deep breath, opened the gate, walked up the path and knocked at the scratched red door, a little surprised by the loud music coming from the next house. He saw his mother approach through the frosted glass pane. She opened the door, rubbed her hands together as if drying them and said, "Alan, lovely to see you. Come on in, love, come in."

Banks dropped his overnight bag in the hall and followed his mother through to the living room. It stretched from the front of the house to the back, and the back area, next to the kitchen, was permanently laid out as a dining room. The wallpaper was a wispy brown autumn-leaves pattern, the three-piece suite a matching brown velveteen and a sentimental autumn landscape hung over the electric fire.

His father was sitting in his usual armchair, the one with the best straight-on view of the television. He didn't get up, just grunted, "Son, nice of you to come."

"Hello, Dad. How are you doing?"

"Mustn't complain." Arthur Banks had been suffering from mild angina for years, ever since he'd been made redundant from the sheet-metal factory, and it seemed to get neither better nor worse as the years went on. He took pills for the pain and didn't even need an inhaler. Other than that, and the damage booze and fags had wreaked on his liver and lungs over the years, he had always been fit as a fiddle. Hollow chested and skinny, he still sported a head of thick dark hair with hardly a trace of gray. He wore it slicked back with lashings of Brylcreem.

Banks's mother, Ida, plump and nervy, fussed a little more about how thin Banks was looking, then the kitchen door opened and a stranger walked into the room.

"Kettle's on, Mrs. B. Now, who have we got here? Let me guess."

"This is our son, Geoff. We told you he was coming. For the party, like."

"So this is the lad who's done so well for himself, is it? The Porsche and the mews house in South Kensington?"

"No, that's the other one, Roy. He's not coming till Sunday afternoon. He's got important business. No, this is our eldest: Alan. I'm sure I told you about him. The one in that picture."

The photograph she pointed to, half-hidden by a pile of women's magazines on one of the cabinet shelves, showed Banks at age sixteen, when he captained the school rugby team for a season. There he stood in his purple and yellow strip, holding the ball, looking proud. It was the only photograph of him they had ever put on display.

"This is Geoff Salisbury," said Ida Banks. "Geoff lives up the street at number fifty-five."

Geoff moved forward, hand stretched out like a weapon. He was a small, compact man, with lively, slightly watery eyes and cropped gray hair, about Banks's age. His smile revealed what looked to Banks like a set of perfect false teeth. His handshake was firm, and his hands were calloused and ingrained with oil or grease from manual labor.

"Pleased to meet you, Alan," he said. "I'd love to stay and chat, but I can't just now." He turned to Banks's mother. "Have you got that shopping list, Mrs. B? I'll be off to Asda now."

"Only if you're sure it's no trouble."

"Nothing's too much trouble for you. You know that. Besides, I have to go there myself."

Banks's mother picked up her handbag, took out her purse and gave Geoffrey a handwritten list and a twenty-pound note. "Will that cover it?"

"Easily, Mrs. B. Easily. I'll be back in a tick. Coach and Horses tonight, Arthur?"

"Maybe. We'll see how I feel," said Banks's father. On closer examination, he did look tired and drawn, Banks thought. More so since he had last seen him in the summer. His eyes had the look of milky marbles and his skin was the color of porridge. It could be the strain of the preparing for the upcoming party—Arthur Banks, while gregarious enough in the pub, had never liked a house full of relatives—but most of the organization, Banks guessed, would have fallen to his mother. Perhaps it was simple old age catching up fast.

Geoff Salisbury left, and Banks saw him go up to the red Fiesta with the rusted chassis, parked behind Banks's Renault. Geoff paused and looked Banks's car over before getting into his own and driving off.

"Who's that?" Banks asked his mother.

"I told you. Geoff Salisbury. He's a neighbor."

"He seems at home here."

"I don't know what we'd do without him," said Mrs. Banks. "He's just like a son to us. Anyway, son, sit yourself down. Have a cuppa."

Banks sat and his mother poured. "So Roy's not coming till Sunday, then?" he said.

"No. He rang us last night, didn't he, Arthur?" She said it as if it were some momentous event. Arthur Banks nodded. "He's got an important business meeting all day Saturday," she went on. "Something to do with some Yanks flying in, and they have to be back in New York by evening . . . I don't know. Anyway, he says he should be here by Sunday lunchtime."

"Good of him to bother," Banks muttered.

His mother cast him a long-suffering glance. Banks knew she had been used to the brothers' bickering when they both lived at home, and it was no surprise whose side she usually took. "What time are you planning on starting the party?" Banks asked.

"We told everyone to come about six o'clock. That'll give us time to clear up and get things ready after lunch. By the way, I don't suppose you've heard yet, but Mrs. Summerville passed away just last week." She announced it in the sort of soft and solemn tones generally reserved for those who had *passed away*.

"I'm sorry to hear it," said Banks. Mrs. Summerville was the mother of the first girl he had ever slept with, though he had always believed that neither the late Mrs. Summerville nor his own mother knew that. "What did she die of?"

"It wasn't anything suspicious, if that's what you're thinking."

"Perish the thought."

His mother studied him, frowning. "Yes . . . well, it was a blessing really. She'd been very poorly. Died in her sleep, according to Alice Green."

"Still . . ." said Banks, uncertain what to say. He sipped some tea. As usual, it was milky and sweet, though he had stopped taking milk and sugar twenty years ago.

"And how are the Marshalls?" Banks asked. The Marshalls were the parents of Banks's school friend Graham, who had disappeared at the age of fourteen and whose body had been discovered the previous summer. Banks had come down to help the locals work on the case and the solution hadn't pleased anyone. It was during that time Banks had met Detective Inspector Michelle Hart, whom he had been seeing on and off ever since. Pity she wasn't around this weekend, he thought.

"Same as ever, I suppose," said Mrs. Banks. "We don't see much of them, do we, Arthur?"

Arthur Banks shook his head.

"It's as if they've shut themselves away since you were last down." Banks's mother cast him an accusing glance, as if their becoming recluses were his fault. And maybe it was, in a way. The truth is rarely as liberating as people would have us believe; it often binds more than it frees.

"I'm sorry to hear that," he said.

"You know," his mother went on, "while you're here, you ought to go and see Mrs. Green. She keeps asking about you, you know, and she was very put out you didn't drop by and see her in the summer. She still thinks very fondly of you, though I can't see why, the noise you lot used to make at her house."

Banks smiled. He remembered Mrs. Green fondly, too. She was the mother of an old school friend, Tony Green, whom Banks hadn't seen since he left home. Tony hadn't been one of the real in-crowd, but he had been on the rugby team with Banks, and Banks had always liked Mrs. Green. Most of the kids did. She didn't stop them from smoking in her house, and she didn't mind them playing the sort of music—the Beatles and the Rolling Stones mostly—that most adults hated. Once or twice, she had given Banks and Tony half a crown apiece and sent them off to the pictures out of her way. She had also been very pretty, with the kind of bosom young boys dream about, and she certainly had a mouth on her. Mrs. Green had a reputation for speaking her mind, and nobody ruffled her feathers and got away with it. Tony had gone off to Canada, Banks remembered. Also, Mr. Green had died of emphysema a year or two ago. His mother had told him over the telephone, and he had sent a sympathy card. Yes, he would pay Mrs. Green a visit.

II

So Banks sipped tea with his mother and father, catching up on the local gossip. The usual stuff: another school friend had emigrated to Australia, an old neighbor who had moved into a home a year ago had died, and the Venables lad from number sixty-six had been sent to Borstal for mugging a pensioner. Banks didn't bother telling his mother that it wasn't called "Borstal" anymore but "detention center" or "youth custody center." They weren't much interested in what he'd been doing, outside of the divorce from Sandra. They were more interested in Brian and Tracy, and they expressed regret that neither could come to the party on Sunday: Brian's band was playing an important series of gigs in Germany, and Tracy had the flu. Not entirely convinced this wasn't some excuse, Banks had dropped by and offered to drive her from her university residence in Leeds, but when he saw her, he took pity on her and said he'd look in again on his way back. Fortunately, she had friends there who would feed her chicken noodle soup and Lemsip in the meantime.

"Have you seen who's moved in next door?" Mrs. Banks asked.

"No," said Banks. "But I heard them."

"Not that side. The other. A Paki family, that's who. I must say, though," she went on, "they seem really nice. Very quiet, they are, even the kids, aren't they, Arthur? And polite. Always say good morning and ask how you're doing. Talk just like us, they do. Makes a change from that lot on the other side."

"Who are they?" Banks asked.

She shook her head. "I don't even know their name. They moved in about two weeks ago. They're not very friendly neighbors. Don't know how many of them live there, either. Shifty-looking lot. Comings and goings all hours of the day and night. Noise. And the place is a pigsty."

It sounded like a drug house. Banks made a mental note to keep his eyes open. If he noticed anything suspicious, he'd get on to the local police.

Banks's father picked up the remote control and turned the television on at half-past five, as Banks remembered he did every weekday. "Is that the time?" said Ida Banks. "I'd better get the tea on. Pork chops, peas and chips all right?"

"Fine," said Banks, his stomach sinking. As if there was a choice.

"And a nice bit of steamed pudding and custard for sweet."

"I'll help." Banks followed her into the kitchen.

True to his word, Geoff Salisbury came back from Asda with a bag of groceries. He dumped it on the kitchen table and handed Ida Banks two pound coins in change, then they went through to the living room. Banks, peeling potatoes at the time, started to unload the groceries. As he did so, he came across the printed receipt stuck by condensation to the side of a bottle of chilled apple juice.

The print was a little blurred, but even so he could see that the total came to £16.08, which left a discrepancy of £1.92, between that and the two pounds Geoff had handed his mother. Holding the receipt, Banks went through into the living room.

"I think you've got the change wrong," he said, holding out the receipt for Geoff to see.

Banks mother frowned. "Alan! Must you?" Then she turned to Geoff. "I'm so sorry. Our Alan's in the police and he can't seem to let us forget it," she said, with a dismissive sniff.

"One of the boys in blue, eh?"

"CID, actually," said Banks.

"Ah. All that Sherlock Holmes stuff."

"Something like that."

"Let's see, then." Geoff took a pair of bifocals from his shirt pocket and squinted at the list. "Bloody hell, you're right," he admitted, blushing. He showed the receipt to Ida Banks. "It's a fair cop. See there, Mrs. B? It looks like an eight to me but it's really a six. That's what comes of being too vain to wear my glasses in the supermarket."

Ida Banks laughed and slapped him on the arm playfully. "Oh, get away with you, Geoff. Anyone could make a mistake like that."

Geoff counted out the rest of the change into her hand. He glanced sideways at Banks, still slightly red with embarrassment. "I can see I'll have to watch myself now there's a copper around," he joked.

"Yes," said Banks, not laughing. "I think you better had."

III

"There was no need for that, Alan," Banks's mother said after Geoff Salisbury had left. "Embarrassing us all."

"I wasn't embarrassed," Banks said. "Besides, he tried to cheat you."

"Don't be silly. It's like he said. He couldn't see the figures properly."

"Does he do this often?"

"Do what?"

"Go shopping for you."

"Yes. We can't get around like we used to, you know, what with your dad's angina and my legs and feet."

"Legs and feet?"

"My varicose veins and bunions. Getting old is no treat, Alan, I can tell you that much. You'll find out, yourself, one day. Anyway, he's been good to us, has Geoff, and now you've gone and upset him."

"I don't think he's upset at all."

"Only here five minutes, and there's trouble already."

"Mum, I really don't think I upset him. Maybe he'll just be more careful in the future."

"And maybe we'll have to find *someone else* who'll do our shopping for us and give the place a good dust and a vacuum every now and then. Fat chance of that."

"I'm sure he'll be fine."

"Well, I just hope you'll apologize to him next time you see him."

"Apologize?"

"Yes. You as good as called the man a thief."

"Fine," said Banks, raising his hands in surrender. "I'll apologize."

His mother gave another disapproving little sniff. "I'd better see to those pork chops." Then she strode off into the kitchen and shut the door behind her.

IV

The Coach and Horses, about a hundred yards away, on the main road, was one of those pubs that had hardly changed at all in the past forty years or so. True, they'd got in a jukebox and a few video machines, and the brewery had forked out for a minor facelift sometime in the eighties, hoping to pull in a younger, freer-spending crowd. But it didn't take. The people who drank at the Coach and Horses had, for the most part, been drinking there most of their lives. And their fathers had supped there before them.

Though there were few young people to be seen, it still managed to be a warm and lively pub, Banks noticed as he walked in with his father just after eight o'clock that night, the steamed pudding and custard still weighing heavy in his stomach. His father had managed the walk without too much puffing and wheezing, which he put down to having stopped smoking two years ago. Banks, who had only stopped that summer, still felt frequent and powerful urges.

"Arthur! Arthur! Come on, lad, come on over."

It was Geoff Salisbury. He was sitting at a table with an elderly couple Banks didn't recognize and two other men in their sixties he remembered from his previous visit. They cleared a little space when Banks and his father walked over to join them.

"My shout," said Geoff. "Name your poison."

"No," said Banks, still standing. "I'm the visitor. Let me buy the first round."

That got no argument, so Banks wandered off to the bar. He hardly had to fight his way through the crowds of impatient drinkers. The bartender, the same one Banks remembered when he had last been in the Coach that summer, nodded a curt greeting and proceeded to pull the pints. When Banks carried the tray back to the table, his father was already talking football with one of his old pals, Harry Finnegan.

Harry looked up and said hello to Banks, asked him how he was doing.

"Fine," said Banks. "You're looking well yourself."

"Fair to middling. Sorry to hear about you and that young lass of yours splitting up."

Sandra. No secrets here. He wondered if they also knew about Sean and the imminent baby. "Well," said Banks, "these things happen." More to his generation than theirs, he realized. Theirs tended to stick at marriage, even when all the love had gone out of it. He didn't know if that was better or worse than changing wives every decade. Probably best not to get married at all, he suspected.

But his mother and father still loved each other, or so he believed. Fifty years together meant they probably didn't have much new to say to each another anymore, and the passion may have disappeared from their relationship years ago, but they were comfortable together. Besides, passion is transitory and infinitely transferable anyway, Banks believed. What his parents had was stronger, deeper, more permanent; it was what he would never get to experience with Sandra: growing old together. He was used to the loss by now, but every now and then he still felt a pang of regret for what might have been, and a lump came to his throat.

Harry introduced Banks to the couple at the table, Dick and Mavis Conroy. The other man, Jock McFall, said hello and shook hands.

"I hear you're a Leeds United supporter these days, Alan," said Harry, a twinkle in his eye.

Banks nodded. "For my sins. Not that I get the chance to go to Elland Road very often. *Match of the Day* is usually the closest I get."

"*Elland Road*," his father said. "You'd not be able to bloody afford it on what a copper earns, son." They all laughed.

Banks laughed with them. "Too true."

As the conversations went on in that vein, people started to pair off: Dick and Mavis talking to Jock McFall about the latest supermarket price wars; Harry and Arthur Banks discussing Peterborough United's miserable performance that season. Banks edged his chair closer to Geoff Salisbury's.

"Sorry about that business with the change," said Geoff. "My eyesight's not what it used to be. Honest mistake."

Banks nodded. "Honest mistake. No offense," he said, though he still wasn't convinced. It was the closest he was willing to get to an apology, so it would just have to do. There was certainly no point in antagonizing Geoff and upsetting his mother even more. After all, he was only down for the weekend; these people had to live close to one another day in, day out. And if Banks couldn't be around to help his parents with their shopping and housecleaning, then it was a good thing Geoffrey Salisbury was.

"How long have you lived on the estate, Geoff?" Banks asked.

"Six months now."

"Where did you live before?"

"Oh, here and there. Bit of a wanderer, really."

"What made you settle down?"

Geoff laughed and shrugged. "My age, I suppose. I don't know. Wandering lost its appeal."

"Well, there's something to be said for knowing you've always got a roof over your head."

"There is that." Geoff took a stick of chewing gum from his pocket. When he had unwrapped it and put it in his mouth, he folded the silver paper time and time again until it was just a tiny square, which he set down in the ashtray. He noticed Banks watching him and laughed. "Habit," he said. "Stopped smoking five years ago and got addicted to this bloody stuff. Wish I'd stuck with cigarettes sometimes."

"You're probably better off as you are," Banks said. "What line of work are you in?"

"Odd jobs, mostly."

"What? Fixing things? Carpentry?"

"Cars, mostly. Tinkering with engines. I used to be a mechanic."

"Not anymore?"

"Got made redundant from the last garage I worked at, and I just couldn't seem to get taken on anywhere else. My age, I suppose. Again. They can get young kids still wet behind the ears and pay them bugger all to do the same job."

"I suppose so," Banks said. "So you work for yourself now?"

"Odd jobs. I don't need much, just enough to keep the wolf from the door."

"And you help out Mum and Dad?"

"Grand folk, Arthur and Ida," Geoff said. "Been like a mother and father to me, they have."

If there was any irony intended in the remark, Geoff didn't seem aware of it. "How long have you known them?" Banks asked.

"Since not long after you'd left this summer. They told me about that business with the missing lad. Terrible. Anyway, they always said hello right from the start, you know, like, when they saw me in the street. Invited me in for a cup of tea. That sort of thing. And with them not being . . . well, you know what I mean, not as able to get around as well as they used to do, I started doing little favors. Just little things, washing, cleaning, shopping and the like, helping them out with their finances. I like to help people."

"Finances?"

"Paying bills on time, that sort of thing. They do get a bit forgetful sometimes, just between you and me. And taking the rent down to the council office. It's an awful bother for them."

"I'm sure they appreciate it, Geoff."

"I think they do." He nodded. "Another?"

Banks looked at his empty glass. "Yes," he said. "Go on, then. One more." He looked over at his father. "All right, Dad?"

Arthur Banks nodded and went back to his conversation with Harry Finnegan. The pub had filled up in the last half hour or so, and Banks thought he recognized some of the faces. One or two people looked at him as if they knew him, then decided perhaps they didn't, or didn't want to. Banks watched Geoff Salisbury at the bar. He seemed to know everyone; he was shaking more hands and patting more backs than a politician on election day. Popular fellow.

Geoff came back with the drinks and excused himself to talk to someone else. Banks chatted with Dick and Mavis for a while—they wanted to know if he'd helped catch the Yorkshire Ripper—then, after his second drink, his father said he was tired and would like to go home. "You can stay if you like," he said to Banks.

"No, I'll walk back with you. I'm feeling a bit tired myself."

"Suit yourself."

They said their good-byes and walked out into the cool autumn night. It was mild for the time of year, Banks thought: light jacket weather rather than overcoats, but the leaves were changing color, winter was in the air and the weather forecast said they had a shower or two in store. Neither Banks nor his father had anything to say on the way home, but then Arthur Banks needed all his breath for walking.

V

Banks's bedroom, he had been amazed to discover that summer, was almost exactly as it had been when he first left home. Only the wallpaper, curtains and bedding had been changed. The bed itself was also the same one he had had since he was about twelve.

As he squeezed himself between the tightly tucked sheets in his narrow bed, he remembered how he used to hold the old transistor radio to his ear under the sheets, listening to Radio Luxembourg amid the whistles and crackles. First, Jimmy Saville playing the latest top-ten hit from "member number 11321," Elvis Presley. Then, a few years later, came the pirate stations, with even more static and interference: John Peel playing the Mothers of Invention, the Jefferson Airplane and Country Joe and the Fish, names from another world, music so startling and raw it transcended even the poor radio reception.

Banks's eyes were too tired and scratchy from the smoky pub to read his Graham Greene, so he put on the Cecilia Bartoli CD of Gluck arias and listened as he drifted toward sleep.

As he lay there, he couldn't help but think about Geoff Salisbury. Something about the man put Banks on his guard. It wasn't just the wrong change—that *could* have been an honest mistake—but the manner in which he seemed to have insinuated himself into the lives of Banks's parents, the ease with which he breezed in and out of the house. Banks wouldn't be surprised if Geoff had a key. He switched off the CD and turned on his side, trying to shake off the uneasy feeling, telling himself he was being too mistrusting, and that he probably only felt this way because he felt guilty he wasn't taking care of his aging parents himself. He knew he ought to be glad that *someone* was doing the job; he only wished that someone wasn't Geoff Salisbury.

VI

Banks awoke with a start the following morning and experienced a moment's absolute panic and terror when he had no idea who or where he was. It was as if he had woken from a coma after many years, all memory gone and the world around him totally changed, or as if he had been abducted and had woken up in an alien spaceship.

But it only lasted a second or two, thank God, and after that he managed to orient himself and his heartbeat slowed to normal. He was in his old bedroom, of course, the room he had slept in between the ages of twelve and eighteen. It was at the back of the house and looked over backyards, an alleyway and a stretch of waste ground to the north, where he and his friends used to play. When Banks looked out of his window, he noticed that the builders had moved in since his last visit and laid the foundations for yet more houses. As if Peterborough needed to grow any more. Since the midsixties, when the developers decided to make it a catchment area for London's overcrowded suburbs, it had done nothing but grow, swamping outlying villages with housing estates and business parks. The planners and promoters said it blended old and new in unique and interesting ways. Even so, Banks thought, King Paeda, who founded the city, would turn in his grave.

On a Saturday morning, the building site was deserted; concrete mixers sat idle and quiet, and the thick sheets of polythene covering pallets of bricks or boards flapped in the wind. It was another grand autumn morning: sunshine, bright blue sky and a cool wind to make everything look and feel fresh. Banks checked his watch. It was after nine o'clock, and he was surprised he had slept so long and so deeply; he couldn't remember having any dreams at all. He listened for sounds of life from downstairs and thought he could hear talking on the radio and dishes rattling in the sink. They were up.

Desperate for tea or coffee, Banks dressed quickly and made his way downstairs. In the living room, his father looked up from his paper and grunted, "Morning, son."

"Morning, Dad," Banks replied, glancing out of the window to make sure his car was still there. It was. His father's newspaper rustled back into position, and the local radio station, according to the

DJ, was about to play a request for "Memories Are Made of This" by Val Doonican, for Mrs. Patricia Gaitskell, of 43 Wisteria Drive, Stamford. Jesus, thought Banks, he could have been caught in a time warp while he slept, back to the B-side of 1967. Perhaps that was why he had felt so disoriented the minute he awoke?

He walked through to the kitchen where his mother, washing the breakfast dishes, gave him a cursory glance and said, "Well, you've decided to get up at last, have you?" It was exactly what she used to say when he was a teenager and liked to lie in bed most of the morning. The only thing that saved him from seriously doubting his sanity was the little television on the kitchen table showing a breakfast program. That hadn't been there all those years ago, nor had breakfast television.

Banks made some comment about having had a long drive and put on the kettle. "Want a cup of tea?" he asked his mother.

"No, thanks. We had ours ages ago."

"Well, you could have another."

She gave him a withering look, and he busied himself looking for the tea bags, telling himself that his parents really weren't being especially nasty to him. They had their routine; it just took a little getting used to.

"They're where they've always been," his mother told him.

That didn't help much, as he couldn't remember where they'd always been. A terra-cotta jar in the cupboard with TEA engraved on the front looked promising, but it turned out to be empty. Beside it, however, Banks found a jar of instant coffee. Might as well, he thought. As long as you convince yourself it's a different drink, not really coffee at all, then it doesn't taste too bad. The kettle boiled and Banks made himself a cup of instant coffee. Specks of undissolved powder floated on the surface no matter how much he stirred it.

"Don't you want any breakfast?" his mother asked, drying her hands on her pinafore. "We got some Sugar Puffs in for you specially. You always used to like Sugar Puffs."

When I was about twelve, thought Banks. "I'll give it a miss this morning," he said. "Maybe tomorrow."

He wandered into the living room again, his mother not far behind. Val Doonican had given way to the Searchers singing "Someday We're Gonna Love Again." An improvement, Banks thought. Funny how the Searchers were exactly the kind of "pop rubbish" his parents dismissed thirty-five years ago, but now they were as acceptable as Val Doonican.

Banks needed a newspaper to complete his morning ritual. His father was still buried deep in the *Daily Mail,* which, being a Labour man, he only read so he could find things to complain about. The *Mail* wasn't Banks's kind of paper anyway. No real meat on its bones. Especially on the weekend. He needed something with a bit more writing and fewer pictures, like the *Independent* or the *Guardian.*

"I'm off to the newsagent's for a paper," he announced. "Anything I can get for you?"

"You'll be lucky if they've got any left at this time," his mother said. His father just grunted.

Banks took their responses as a no and set off. In the house next door, the upstairs windows were all open and music thudded out. It definitely wasn't Val Doonican or the Searchers; more like Nine Inch Nails or Metallica. Banks studied the house. There were no curtains on the windows, and the front door was wide open. As he was looking, a scruffy couple walked out on to the overgrown path. They looked like Fred and Rosemary West on acid. The man's eyes, in particular, reminded Banks of the opening of *Vertigo.*

"Morning," said Banks. "Lovely day, isn't it?"

They looked at him as if he were from Mars—or as if they were *on* it—so he shrugged and walked down to the newsagent's across the main road. The short strip of shops there, set back from the road by a stretch of tarmac, had gone through dozens of changes over the years. When he first moved to the estate, Banks remembered, there had been a fish and chip shop, a ladies' hairdresser, a butcher's, a greengrocer's and a launderette; now there was a video rental shop, a takeaway pizza and tandoori place called Caesar's Taj Mahal, a mini-mart and a uni-sex hair salon. The only constants were the fish and chip shop, which now sold takeaway Chinese food, too, Banks noticed; and Walker's, the newsagent's.

Banks waited to cross the busy road. On the other side, lower down from the shops, stood the remains of the old ball-bearing factory. The gates were chained and padlocked shut and it was surrounded by high wire mesh fencing with barbed wire on top, the windows beyond covered by rusty grilles. Despite these security precautions, most of them were broken anyway, and the front of the blackened brick building was covered in colorful graffiti.

Banks remembered when the place was in production, lorries coming and going, factory whistle blowing and crowds of workers waiting at the bus stop. A lot of them were young women, or girls scarcely out of school, and he had a crush on one of them. Called Mandy by her friends, she used to stand at the bus stop smoking, a faraway look in her eyes, scarf done up like a turban on her head. She had pale smooth skin and lips like Julie Christie, whom Banks had gone to see in *Darling* with a couple of school friends because she did a nude scene in it. They had only been fourteen or fifteen at the time, but the bored woman in the ticket box at the local fleapit hardly even looked at them before issuing their one and threepennies. The nude scene was wonderful, but he didn't understand much about the rest of the film; it didn't make the same sense as *Billy Liar* did for him when he saw it only a few months later. Escaping a boring environment was something he could easily relate to.

One day, Mandy started wearing an engagement ring, and a few weeks later she no longer stood at the bus stop with the others, and he never saw her again. He spent ages in his room moping, and even a few years later, when he bought *Beggars Banquet* and listened to "Factory Girl," he thought of her.

Banks went into the newsagent's. Mrs. Walker moved much more slowly now, and the joints on her left hand were swollen. Arthritis by the looks of it. There was still a small pile of *Independent*s under the magazine rack, so Banks picked one up and took it to the counter.

"You're the Banks lad back again, aren't you?" she said.

"That's me," said Banks.

"I thought so. My body might be falling to pieces but my mind's still all right. Haven't seen you since that business in the summer. How are you doing?"

"Fine, thanks. I see you're still soldiering on."

"I'll be here till I drop."

"I'm surprised you can manage all by yourself."

"Oh, I've got help. Some local lads help with the papers, and there's Geoff helps with going to wholesalers, stocktaking and whatnot."

"Geoff?"

"Geoff Salisbury. Nice lad. Well, I say 'lad,' but he's probably your age or older. Always there when you need him, is Geoff. And with a smile on his face, too. There's not too many folk you can say that about these days."

"True enough," Banks agreed. So the ubiquitous Geoff Salisbury had his feet under Mrs. Walker's table, too. Still, he did say he did odd jobs, and Banks assumed Mrs. Walker paid him for his "help." He had to make a living somehow. It didn't seem that one could go far around the estate, though, without finding some traces of its patron saint, Geoff bloody Salisbury.

The bell jangled and someone else walked into the shop. Banks half-expected it to be Salisbury himself, but when he turned he was gob-smacked by what he saw. It was Kay Summerville. And looking hardly a day older than when he had last seen her thirty years ago. That was an exaggeration, of course—her eyes had gathered a few crow's-feet, and the long blond hair that still cascaded over her shoulders now showed evidence of dark roots—but she still had her figure and her looks.

A hoarse "Kay" was about all he could manage.

She seemed equally stunned. "Alan."

"Are you two going to stand there gawping at each other all afternoon or are you going to step aside, young man, and let the lady get what she's come for?" said Mrs. Walker.

"Of course." Banks moved aside.

Kay smiled. She was wearing a thin white T-shirt under a blue denim jacket, and hip-hugging blue jeans. The hips looked as if they were worth hugging. She caught him looking at her and gave him a shy smile.

"Packet of Polo mints, please, Mrs. Walker, and"—she turned to the magazine rack and picked out a copy of *Marie Claire*—"and I'll take this, too."

Banks stood by the door and loitered, pretending to be looking at a display of anniversary cards. When Kay had finished, she walked toward him.

"Walk back with you?" he said.

She did a little curtsy. "Why, thank you, kind sir."

Banks laughed. He had been sixteen when he had first met Kay, and just about to go into the lower sixth. Kay had been fifteen, about to enter her O-level year. Her family had just moved up from North London, and Banks had seen her walking along the street in her blue jeans and orange jacket, or in her school uniform—white blouse, maroon jacket, gray skirt probably just a couple of inches too short for the principal's liking—pouty lips, pale skin, head in the air, and her long blond hair trailing halfway down her back.

She had seemed unobtainable, ethereal, like Mandy from the factory and, if truth be told, like most of the women or girls Banks lusted after, but one day they met in the newsagent's, just like today, both wanting the latest issue of *New Musical Express.* There was only one copy left, so Banks, being the gentleman, let Kay take it. They walked back to the estate together chatting about pop music. Both were Cream fans, upset about the band's splitting up that summer. Both loved Canned Heat's "On the Road Again" and hated Mary Hopkin's "Those Were the Days." Kay said she would lend her *NME* to Banks when she had finished with it. He asked her when that would be, and she said probably Saturday. Emboldened, he went on and asked if she'd like to go to the pictures with him on Saturday night. He could have dropped in his tracks when she said yes.

They went to see *Here We Go Round the Mulberry Bush,* on a double bill with *I'll Never Forget What's 'isname*, and that was it, the start of Banks's first serious relationship.

"I heard about your mother," Banks said, holding the door for her. "I'm sorry."

Kay pushed a stray tress of hair from her forehead. "Thank you. She'd been ill for a long time. She was riddled with cancer and her heart wasn't strong. I know it's a cliché, but in this case it really was a blessing."

"Is that why you're up here?"

"Yes. I've got to deal with the house before the council relets it. The rent's paid up till the end of the month, so I thought I'd take a few days and get it all sorted. You?"

"It's Mum and Dad's golden wedding tomorrow."

"That's marvelous."

"It is pretty remarkable, isn't it? Fifty years. What kind of work do you do?"

"Investment banking."

"Oh."

Kay laughed. "Yes, that's usually the reaction. Quite a conversation stopper."

"I'm sorry, it's just . . . I don't . . ."

She smiled at him. "It's okay. Most people don't. Even the ones who *do* it. What about you? I seem to remember Mum saying you had something to do with the police."

"True. Detective chief inspector, CID, Major Crimes."

"Well, well, well. I *am* impressed. Just like Morse."

It was Banks's turn to laugh. "Except I'm not on telly. I'm real. And I'm still alive. Like your job, it's usually a conversation stopper. You must be the first person who hasn't jumped a mile when I told them what I do for a living. No skeletons in your closet?"

She wiggled her eyebrows. "That's for me to know and you to find out."

They reached Banks's parents' house and stopped on the pavement, both a little awkward, embarrassed. It was one of those moments, Banks felt, like the one thirty years ago when he had asked her out for the first time. "Look," he said, "seeing as we're both up here this weekend, would you like to go out tonight, maybe find a country pub, have a bite to eat or a drink, do a bit of catching up? I mean, bring your husband, by all means, you know . . ."

Kay smiled at his discomfort. "Sorry, there's only me," she said. "And yes, I'd love to. Pick me up at half past seven?"

"Good. Great, I mean." Banks grinned. "Okay, then, see you this evening."

Banks watched Kay walk away, and he could have sworn she had a bit of a spring in her step. He definitely had one in his, and it couldn't be dampened even by the sight of Geoff Salisbury talking to his mother in the hall when he opened the front door.

"Morning, Alan," Geoff said. "Have a good time last night?"

"Fine," said Banks.

"That the Summerville girl you were talking to?"

"Yes," said Banks. "We're old friends."

Geoff frowned. "I was sorry to hear about her poor mother. Anyway, must dash. Just a passing visit." He turned back to Ida Banks. "Right, then, Mrs. B, don't you fret. I'll pick up everything we need for tomorrow, and I'll pop around in the morning and do a bit of tidying and vacuuming for you. How's that?"

"It's all right," said Banks. "I can do that."

"Don't be silly," his mother chided him. "You don't know one end of a vacuum cleaner from the other." Which might have been true at one time but certainly wasn't any more. "That'll be just dandy, Geoff," she said, handing him a plastic card, which he put quickly in his pocket. "I know we can always rely on you."

It was too late to argue. With a smile and a wave, Geoff Salisbury was halfway down the path, whistling "Colonel Bogey" as he went.

"I mean it," said Banks. "Anything needs doing, just ask me."

His mother patted his arm. "I know, son," she said. "You mean well. But Geoff's . . . well we're *used* to having him around. He knows where everything is."

Does he, indeed? thought Banks. "By the way," he asked, "what was that you just gave him?"

"What?"

"You know. The card."

"Oh, yes. That's the Abbey card. He'll need some cash, won't he, if he's going to get the food and drink in for tomorrow?"

Banks almost choked. "You mean he knows your PIN number?"

"Well, of course he does, silly. A fat lot of use the card would be to him without it." Shaking her head, she edged past Banks toward the living room. "And what's this about you and Kay Summerville?" she asked, turning. "Didn't you two used to go out together?"

"That was a long time ago. Actually, we're going to have dinner together tonight."

His mother's face dropped. "But I was going to make us toad-in-the-hole. Your favorite."

True, Banks had once expressed an enthusiasm for toad-in-the-hole when he was about fourteen. "I'm sorry," he said, "but it's the only chance we've got to catch up."

"Well," his mother said, that familiar, hurt, hard-done-by tone in her voice. "I suppose if that's really what you want to do. I must say, she always seemed like a nice lass. Her mother and me weren't close at all, just to say hello to in passing, like, but you tell her she's welcome to drop by tomorrow, for the party. I'd like to offer her my condolences."

"I'll ask her," said Banks, then he took his coffee and hurried upstairs.

VII

With his bedroom window open, Banks could hear the polythene from the building site flapping in the breeze and hear the cars whoosh by on the main road. He could also hear a dull bass rumbling from next door, along with the occasional shout and bang. Their back garden, he noticed, was full of rubbish, like a tip: broken furniture, rocks, a dismantled bicycle. Maybe there was even a body or two buried there.

His knees cracked as he squatted to read the spines of the books in the old glass-fronted bookcase. There they were, a cross section of his early years' reading, starting with the large, illustrated *Black Beauty*, which his mother read to him when he was small; old *Beano*, *Dandy* and *Rupert* annuals; and *Noddy* books—the originals, where Noddy and Big Ears slept together, hung out with Golliwog, and "gay" meant "cheerful." He must have kept Enid Blyton in luxury almost single-handed, he thought, as he had moved on to the Famous Five and the Secret Seven.

Then came his high school reading: Billy Bunter, Jennings and William, followed by war stories such as Biggles, *The Wooden Horse*, *The Guns of Navarone* and *Camp on Blood Island*. Next to these were several *Pan Books of Horror Stories*, from a phase he went through in his teens, along with some H. P. Lovecraft and M. R. James. There wasn't much crime fiction, but he did still have a few dog-eared old Saint paperbacks, the Father Brown stories and a complete Sherlock Holmes. The James Bond books were all there, too, of course, and a few Sexton Blakes.

There were also history books, the kind with lots of illustrations, some Oxford and Penguin anthologies of poetry and those children's illustrated encyclopedias that came out with a letter a week, none of which he'd got beyond C or D.

In addition, on the bottom shelf, there were books about his many hobbies, including photography, coins, birds, stamps and astronomy, and several old *Observer's* books of cars, aircraft, geology, trees, music and pond life. He'd seen these old editions in secondhand bookshops and some of them were worth a bit now. Maybe he should take them back up to Yorkshire with him, he mused. Would that upset his parents? Were his books and his room some sort of virtual umbilical cord that was all that tied him to them now? It was a depressing thought.

One book stood out. Sitting between Enid Blyton's *River of Adventure* and *Mountain of Adventure* was a used orange-spined Penguin edition of *Lady Chatterley's Lover,* a 1966 reprint with Richard Hoggart's introduction. Curious, Banks picked it out. He didn't remember buying it and was surprised when he opened it up and saw written on the flyleaf: "Kay Summerville, London, 7th June, 1969." Banks remembered that day well. Smiling, he put it aside. He would give it back to her tonight.

The more he thought about his "date" with Kay, the more he looked forward to it. Not only was she an extremely attractive woman, she was also intelligent and she shared some of his past with him. He didn't imagine the date would lead to anything of a sexual nature—he certainly wasn't out to seduce her—but you never knew. He wondered how he would feel about that. Michelle Hart was on holiday in Tuscany. Besides, they had made no commitments, and Michelle always seemed to be holding back, on the verge of ending what tenuous relationship they did have. Banks didn't know why, but he sensed deep and painful secrets she didn't want to share. It seemed that all the women he had met since parting with Sandra—including Annie Cabbot back up in Yorkshire—shied away from intimacy.

Banks stood up and looked down at the books. Well, there they all were, for what they were worth, like those strata of different colored rock or the layers of antiquities at an archaeological dig. His mother called up: "Alan, are you coming down? Lunch is on the table. It's potted meat sandwiches."

Banks sighed. "Coming," he shouted. "I just have to wash my hands. I'll be right there." True, he had once loved potted meat, the same way he had liked Sugar Puffs and toad-in-the-hole, when he was a teenager, but he hadn't touched the stuff in years.

VIII

The people next door were out in force, Banks noticed on his way to see Mrs. Green after lunch. There was an unmarked delivery van outside their house, and two strapping young lads were carrying what looked like a fifty-inch television set up the path. It hardly looked as if it would fit through the door. Fred and Rosemary stood on the lawn, rubbing their hands together in glee, practically salivating at the sight, and their various children, aged between about five and fifteen, milled about beside them. Banks hadn't seen so many shaved heads since the nit nurse had visited his school. He tried wishing them a good morning again, but everyone was far too intent on the imminent television to even notice him. He bet a pound to a penny it was stolen.

The wind had picked up even more, Banks noticed, bringing a few fast-flying clouds and a chill with it, and there was a smell of rain in the air. Banks zipped his leather jacket all the way up and walked the short distance to the close, where Mrs. Green lived. She answered Banks's knock and expressed delight at seeing him again. She had certainly aged—thickened at the waist, drooped at the bosom—but she had lost none of her sprightliness, and she fussed around making tea and bringing out a plate of scones. Her living room was sparsely decorated—plain cream wallpaper, no prints or paintings—and a few framed family photographs stood on the mantelpiece.

"How's Tony doing?" Banks asked. "I've always regretted we never managed to stay in touch."

"These things happen," said Mrs. Green. "People drift apart over the years. It's only natural. It doesn't mean they don't share good memories, though."

"I suppose not."

"Anyway, Tony's doing fine. He lives in Vancouver now, you know. He's a tax lawyer. This is him about two years ago." She picked up one of the photographs and handed it to Banks. It showed the smile he remembered, the mischief in the eyes, surrounded by a bald head on a pudgy body in brightly colored shorts and a red T-shirt. Tony stood with a relaxed, smiling woman Banks took to be his wife, and two bored and/or cool-looking teenage children. They were on a beach, and there were cloud-topped mountains in the background. "I'll let him know you were asking about him," Mrs. Green said.

"Please do." Banks replaced the photo on the mantelpiece. "I've been to Toronto but never Vancouver."

"You should go if you get a chance. Bill and I visited him there five years ago. It's a lovely city. I'm sure Tony and Carol would be happy to have you stop with them. They've got a big house."

"Maybe I will," said Banks.

"We don't see you down here very often, do we?"

"Well," said Banks, feeling guilty he hadn't made time for Mrs. Green on his previous visit, "I keep pretty busy up north. You know how it is." He sipped some tea.

"Your parents are really very proud of you, you know."

Banks almost choked on his tea. Where had that come from?

Mrs. Green considered him through her tortoiseshell glasses. "You might not think so," she said, "and they might not admit it, but they are. Especially since that business last summer."

"What makes you say that?"

"Oh, don't think I don't know about your differences. They never did approve of what you chose to do with your life, did they? Your dad thought you'd joined the enemy, and your mother thought you'd let her down. That was clear enough to anyone who knew them."

"Was it?"

"Oh, yes. And I knew where they were coming from, of course."

"What do you mean?"

She smiled. "Oh, don't be so obtuse, Alan. You always did have that infuriating habit of pretending not to see the obvious. You wouldn't have gotten far in your chosen career if you couldn't even add together the basics. You had all the opportunities; they had none. They had to settle for their lot in life. And the Thatcher years were pretty tough around here. How do you think your dad felt when he saw coppers laying into workers on the news? Miners, whatever they were, they were still workingmen, like himself. How do you think he felt when he saw the police in riot gear waving their overtime pay in the faces of men who'd lost everything? Do you think he actually enjoyed working at that factory every day of his life? I'd say it was a cause for celebration when they made him redundant, but for him it was a blow to his pride. And your mother, cleaning up other folks' messes? They made a lot of sacrifices for you, so you could do better than they had. And what did you do? You joined the police force. You must have known how people around here felt about the police."

"I'd say they expect us to make sure their cars are safe and keep the muggings and gang fights to a minimum."

"You always were a cheeky young beggar, Alan Banks. Perhaps now they do. But not back then."

"I know what you mean," said Banks.

"But what I'm telling you is they know you've done well for yourself now. Every time you got a promotion they told me, and you should have heard the pride in their voices. 'Our Alan's a detective *sergeant* now,' they'd say. Or 'They've made Alan detective *chief* inspector now!' I got sick of hearing about you. It just took them a long time to work it out, and they don't find it easy to express. It also helped that you came down on the right side last time you were here. Of course, they always did dote on that useless brother of yours."

"Roy."

"Yes. I'm sorry, but you know I've always spoken my mind, and I can't say I ever took to him. Sly, he seemed to me, two-faced, always up to something behind your back. You were no angel, mind, but you weren't sly."

Banks smiled as he buttered his scone, thinking about the time he had orchestrated going to bed with Kay while his parents were visiting his granny, and the time he and Tony Green had drunk some of Mr. Green's whiskey and topped the bottle up with water. Whether he ever spotted it or not they never knew. Sly? All kids are sly, Banks thought;

they have to be in their constant struggle with the inexplicable and unreasonable rules and regulations imposed on them by adults. But Banks knew how to take a compliment when he was offered one, even at the expense of his brother.

"Thanks," he said. "Roy could be a bit of a handful."

"To say the least. Anyway, I don't see much of your mum and dad anymore, except when I bump into Ida on the street," Mrs. Green went on. "That's how I knew about the golden wedding. She invited me. It's sad, though. People seem to isolate themselves when they get old. They don't get out as much, and I don't go to the Coach and Horses. How are they?"

"Same as ever," said Banks. "Mum's complaining about varicose veins and her bunions, but she doesn't seem to do too badly. Dad's still got his angina, but it doesn't seem any worse. There's a neighbor helps out. Bloke called Geoff Salisbury. Know him?"

Banks couldn't swear to it, but he thought Mrs. Green's expression darkened for a moment. Her lips certainly tightened.

"I know him," she said.

Banks leaned forward in his armchair. "You don't sound so thrilled about it."

"Can't say as I am. Oh, he's a charmer all right is Geoff Salisbury. Bit too much so for my liking."

"How did you meet him?"

"He seems to have some sort of radar for all the old folks in trouble on the estate. He turns up everywhere at one time or another. Usually when you need help."

"What do you mean?"

"More tea?"

"Please." Banks held out his cup.

"You know, you can smoke if you like." She smiled. "If I let you do it when you were fifteen, I can hardly stop you now you're . . . what would it be?"

"A lot older." Banks put his hand to his left temple. "Can't you tell by the gray?"

Mrs. Green laughed and touched her own head. "You call *that* gray?" It was true, she had an entire head of fluffy gray hair.

"Anyway," Banks said, remembering what Mr. Green had died of. "Thanks, but I've stopped."

"I won't say that's not good news. If only we'd all known all along what it was doing to us."

"You were saying? About Geoff Salisbury."

"I was, wasn't I?" She sat back in her chair, tea and saucer resting on her lap. "Oh, you know me. I tend to go off half-cocked on things."

"I'd still be interested to hear your thoughts," said Banks. "To be honest, I haven't really taken to him myself, and he seems to be spending an awful lot of time around Mum and Dad."

She waved a hand. "It's nothing, really. He started coming around when Bill was sick. It was near the end, and he was in a wheelchair, breathing from that horrible oxygen tank."

"What did he want?"

"Want? Nothing. He never asked for a thing. Only to help. Give him his due, he's a hard and willing worker, and he was certainly useful at the time. He fixed a few things around the house, ran errands."

"So what was the problem?"

"You'll think I was imagining things."

"Not necessarily."

"Well, it wasn't any one thing, really. Just little things. The wrong change, or one of Bill's tools would go missing. Nothing you could really put your finger on."

Banks remembered the short change Geoff Salisbury had handed his mother yesterday evening. "Anything else?"

"Ooh, just listen to us," said Mrs. Green, refilling her teacup. "I'm being questioned by a policeman."

Banks smiled. "I'm sorry, I didn't mean it to seem like that. Comes with the territory, I suppose."

She laughed. "It's all right, Alan. I was only teasing. But it's hard to talk about. It was only a feeling."

"What feeling?"

She clasped the collar of her frock. "That he was . . . hovering . . . like the Angel of Death or something. Listen to me now. What a fool I sound."

"You don't think Geoff Salisbury had anything to do with your husband's death, do you?"

"Of course not. No, it's nothing like that. It was a faulty valve, they said, on the oxygen tank." She gave a harsh laugh. "Someone told me if we'd been living in America I'd have got millions of dollars in compensation."

"That's probably true."

"Yes, well, if we'd been living in America we probably wouldn't have been able to afford the medical treatment in the first place, and Bill would have died a lot sooner."

"Also true," said Banks. "Can you explain a bit more clearly? About this feeling you had."

"I'm not sure. I felt as if he were, you know, waiting, waiting in the wings until Bill died."

"For what?"

"I don't know. So he could take over more, maybe, manipulate me more."

Banks smiled at her. "He obviously didn't know who he was dealing with."

She didn't smile back. "You'd be surprised how easy it is to take advantage when people are vulnerable." She looked at him. "Or maybe you wouldn't. You probably see a lot of it in your job. Anyway, I felt as if he was hovering, waiting for Bill to die so that he could be more in control."

"But what could possibly have been in it for him?"

"I don't know. Like I said, I was probably imagining things anyway."

"I don't suppose you won the lottery recently?"

"Never bought a ticket."

"And you don't have a million pounds hidden in the mattress, or anything?"

She laughed. "Wish I had. No, there's nothing, really. Bill's insurance policy. Old-age pension. I'm not complaining, mind you. It's enough to get by on."

"What happened?"

"After Bill died, I gave Geoff Salisbury his marching orders. I was nice about it. I thanked him for his help, but said I was perfectly capable of managing by myself and I'd prefer it if he didn't come around anymore. It wasn't that I couldn't still have used the sort of help he had to offer, but I just didn't feel comfortable having him around. Maybe I was being oversensitive as well as ungrateful."

"I don't know," said Banks. "As I said, I haven't taken to him myself and I'm not sure why."

"You'll be feeling guilty because he's looking after your parents while you're not there to do it."

"Perhaps. Partly, yes. But there's more. I don't trust him. I don't know what he's up to, but I don't trust him. Maybe it's copper's instinct."

"Well, I can tell you one thing for a start: you'll get no thanks around these parts for going after Geoff Salisbury."

"Popular, is he?"

"To hear some talk, you'd think the sun shone out of his . . . well, you know what."

Banks smiled. "I think I can guess. How did he take your rejection?"

Mrs. Green shrugged. "Well enough, I suppose. At least he didn't bother me after that. Oh, I see him around now and then, and he always smiles and says hello as if nothing ever happened. It's just that . . ."

"What?"

"Oh, probably me being silly again. But it feels just skin deep, as if underneath it all, if you were just to strip off the surface that, well, you'd find something else entirely under there. Something very nasty indeed."

IX

Banks decided to pay a quick visit to the city center that afternoon. He needed to pick up a couple of things from the shops for tomorrow, such as a nice anniversary card and some candles. He asked his parents if they needed anything, but they said no (implying, Banks thought, that

Geoff Salisbury was taking care of everything), so off he went. Rather than search the side streets for a vacant parking space, he parked in the short stay behind the town hall and walked through to Bridge Street.

Of course, the city center had changed quite a lot since his schooldays. Most cities *had* changed a lot in the past thirty years, but Peterborough more so than many others. Gone were the small record shop in the back alley where he used to buy a new single nearly every week and LPs whenever he could afford them—usually only Christmas and birthdays—and the musty used bookshop where he used to browse for hours among the dog-eared paperbacks, the one where the sour-faced woman behind the counter used to watch him like a hawk the entire time he was in there. The open-air market had closed; some of the pubs he used to drink in when he was sixteen and seventeen had disappeared and new ones had sprung up; an old cinema, after several years as a bingo hall, was now a nightclub; department stores had disappeared, moved or been given face-lifts; Cathedral Square was now a pedestrian precinct.

Only yards from the Queensgate Center stood the ancient cathedral itself. Throughout Banks's childhood, the majestic structure had simply *been there.* It didn't dominate the city, the way York Minster did, and like most of the other local kids, he had paid it scant attention unless school projects and organized visits demanded otherwise. After all, what kid was interested in a boring old cathedral where boring old farts had gone to pray and where even more boring ones were buried? But now he found himself admiring the west front, with its three soaring Gothic arches flanked by twin pinnacled towers, the stone cream colored in the autumn sunshine.

In the Queensgate Center, Banks bought an expensive golden anniversary card and some gold candles, then he browsed around for a while and picked up a CD he thought Kay would enjoy listening to on their way to dinner. It was one oldie he didn't have, and he had been aware of the gap in his collection for some time. Luckily, it was even on sale.

He looked at his watch. Four o'clock. He thought he just had time for a quick walk by the river before driving back to his parents' house.

As he walked down Bridge Street past the Magistrates Court and the police station, he realized that he hadn't quite been able to put Geoff Salisbury out of his thoughts completely. Something about the man was still nagging away at him. Mrs. Green had been partly right; of course he felt guilty that Geoff was doing all the things for his aging parents that a good and dutiful son ought to be doing. But also, as the astute Mrs. Green had realized, there was more to it than that. If nothing worse, he certainly got the impression that Geoff Salisbury was a petty thief.

He glanced toward the old Customs House with its light on top to guide the ships navigating the River Nene, then he made his way down to the footpath that ran along the Nene Way. There, he found a bench and, away from the crowds, took out his mobile and phoned the detectives' room back at Eastvale. Detective Inspector Annie Cabbot and Detective Constable Winsome Jackman were on weekends at Western Area HQ, and it was Annie who answered.

"DCI Banks, what a pleasant surprise. Can't leave us alone for a minute, can you, sir?"

"I take it you're not alone in the office?"

"That's right, sir. Just Winsome and I, as per the duty roster."

"Everything all right?"

"Fine. Business as usual. Couple of fights after closing time last night and a sexual assault on the East Side Estate. We've got a man in for questioning."

"Is that all?"

"Honestly, we're on top of it. Relax. Enjoy yourself."

"I'm trying, Annie, I'm trying. Actually, I wasn't calling to check up on you. I'm sure everything's under control. I need you to do a little detective work for me."

"Detective work?"

"Yes. I want you to check on a name for me. See if you come up with anything."

"I don't believe it. Even at your parents' golden wedding anniversary you're still on the job?"

"You know the rules, Annie, we can't ignore wrongdoing whether we're on or off duty."

"Oh, what a load of bollocks. Okay. Go ahead."

Banks gave her Geoff Salisbury's name and address, along with the number of his Fiesta, which he had memorized for good measure.

"What's it about?" Annie asked.

"I don't know yet," said Banks. "Probably nothing. Just a suspicious character in the neighborhood. I want to know if he's got form, first of all, then anything else you can dig up on him."

"Will do. Where can I get in touch with you?"

"Call my mobile number. I'll leave it switched on." Banks didn't want the call arriving at his parents' house. "If there's no answer, don't worry. Leave a message and I'll get back to you."

"Okay. Will do."

Feeling vaguely guilty, though he had done nothing to feel in the least bit guilty about, Banks put the phone back in his pocket and walked back toward his car.

X

Bathwater was always at a premium, even now they had a house with a real bathroom, and Banks had to be careful not to use all the hot water. After a short soak and a shave, he was ready. Not expecting to be going out on a date, he hadn't brought a great selection of clothes with him, so he had to settle for some gray, casual cotton trousers and a blue button-down Oxford shirt. He first checked the pockets of his sports jacket for car keys and wallet, then slipped in the copy of *Lady Chatterley's Lover* he had found in his bookcase before he went downstairs.

Annie hadn't rung back yet, and given that it was past seven on a Saturday evening, Banks guessed she probably wouldn't until tomorrow. He certainly didn't want his mobile ringing in the restaurant, so he turned it off for the evening. There was no real urgency about the matter, anyway; he just wanted to know if Geoff Salisbury had form.

"Here," his mother said, "you'd better take a key. You'll probably be late back."

"I shouldn't think so," said Banks.

"Take one anyway. I don't want you hammering on the door waking us up at some ungodly hour in the morning."

Banks pocketed the key. "We're only going out for dinner."

"And be quiet when you do come in," his mother went on. "You know your father's a light sleeper."

The only thing Banks knew was his *mother* had always complained of being a light sleeper, but he said nothing except good night and that he wouldn't be late.

XI

Kay came to the door in a long, dark, loose skirt, white blouse tucked in the waistband, soft suede jacket on top. Banks complimented her on her appearance, feeling for all the world like that awkward teenager taking her to the ABC to see *Here We Go Round the Mulberry Bush*, on their first date. The film had only exacerbated his teenage angst about living in a provincial town—and a "New Town," at that—but the music, mostly by Traffic and the Spencer Davis Group, was as good as it got, and what's more, a young and lovely Judy Geeson starred in it.

The main attraction of the evening, of course, was Kay Summerville.

There, on the back row with the other would-be lovers, Banks had somehow found the bottle to put his arm around Kay, and she hadn't seemed to mind. After a while, though, his arm had started to ache like hell, then he had felt it going numb, but he was damned if he was going to remove it after all the courage it had taken to put it there in the first place. Some of his school friends had told him that they had unbuttoned their girlfriends' blouses and felt their breasts in that very cinema, but Banks hadn't the nerve to try that. Not on their first time out together.

On their way home, they had held hands and necked for a while in the bus shelter, and that was as far as things had gone that night. Banks remembered it all vividly as Kay arranged herself next to him in the car: the warm, slightly hazy evening smearing the city lights; noise from a nearby pub; the fruity, chemical taste of her lipstick; the softness of her neck just below her ear; the way it made him tingle and turn hard as he touched her; the warmth of her small breasts crushed against him.

"Any ideas?" Kay asked.

"What do you mean? What ideas?"

"About where to go. I'm almost as much a stranger to these parts as you are."

"Oh, that. I thought I'd just drive out Fotheringay way. It's not too far, and we ought to be able to find somewhere decent to eat."

Kay laughed. "It'll probably be called the Mary Queen of Scots or something."

"She certainly did get around, that woman."

"Didn't have much choice, did she? What a miserable existence."

"Never wanted to be royalty?"

Kay shook her head. "Not me. I'm happy being a commoner."

Banks slipped the Blind Faith CD he had bought that afternoon in the stereo and Stevie Winwood's "Had to Cry Today" came out as crisp and heartrending as the day it was cut.

"That's not . . ." Kay began, then she put her head back. "My God, I haven't heard that in decades. You still listen to this sort of stuff?"

"A lot of old sixties and early seventies stuff, yes," said Banks. "I reckon those eight or nine years or so between "Love Me Do" and the time everyone died produced about the best rock we'll ever hear."

"That's a very sweeping statement. What about punk?"

"Too much noise and not enough talent. The Clash were all right, though."

"Roxy Music? Bowie? R.E.M.? The Pretenders?"

"There are exceptions to every rule."

Kay laughed. "And today?"

"I'm a hip-hop fan, myself. What about you?"

Kay nudged him in the ribs. "Seriously."

"Mostly jazz and classical. But I still listen to a fair bit of rock and folk: Sheryl Crow, Lucinda Williams, Beth Orton."

"I'm afraid I don't listen to much at all these days," said Kay. "Don't have the time. I have the radio on sometimes while I'm in the bath, but I hardly notice what's being played. I suppose if I had to pick something I'd choose a string quartet or some sort of chamber music. Schubert, perhaps."

"Nothing wrong with old Franz. What about this place?"

By the time the band had got to "Can't Find My Way Home," one of Banks's favorites, he had wandered off the main road a mile or so ago, and they were passing through a small village of gray stone, thatch-roofed cottages clustered around a broad green. Lights shone behind curtains, and here and there a television set flickered. The pub was not called the Mary Queen of Scots but a far more lowly Fox and Hounds. Banks parked the car out front and turned off the music.

Banks and Kay ducked as they walked under the low beam of the door. Already the place was quite busy, emanating that rosy glow of a village pub popular with the city crowd. They went up to the bar, where Banks ordered a pint of bitter and Kay a vodka and tonic, then a young girl, who looked no more than about sixteen, seated them in the dining area and pointed out that the evening's menu was written on the blackboard by the window. Just one glance told Banks they'd come to the right sort of place: a wide selection of real ale and good food beyond basic pub fare, but nothing too ambitious. The noise level was perfect, only the buzz of conversation from other tables, the thud of darts in the board at the opposite end, sometimes accompanied by a mild oath or a cheer, and the sounds of the cash register.

"Cheers," said Banks when they'd sat down and had a good look at the blackboard. "To . . . to . . ."

"To times gone by," said Kay.

"To times gone by."

They clinked glasses and each took a sip. Banks felt the need for a cigarette, partly from nerves and partly from habit—he *was* in a pub, after all—but he rode out the craving and soon forgot about it.

"Do you remember that concert?" he asked.

Kay's eyes sparkled. "Of course I do. Well, not so much the music . . . I mean, if you asked me I couldn't tell you what they played or who else was on . . . but the occasion . . . yes, how could I forget? My mother wouldn't let me out of the door for a week afterward, except to go to school."

Banks laughed. "Mine, too."

On June 7, 1969, the same day Kay had bought *Lady Chatterley's Lover* at a secondhand bookshop on Charing Cross Road, Banks and Kay had taken the train to London for the free Blind Faith concert in

Hyde Park. Through a combination of circumstances—partly to do with going off to smoke dope in a flat in Chelsea with some people they met—they had missed their train back and ended up getting home very early the following morning. Needless to say, parental recriminations were severe.

"So," said Kay, "tell me about the last thirty years. I suppose you're married? Children?"

"Two children: one girl at university, and one boy in a rock band. And don't say it serves me right."

Kay laughed. "Heaven forbid. Maybe he'll make enough money to keep you in your old age."

"That's what I'm banking on."

"What about your wife?"

The waitress came over, notepad in hand. "Have you decided yet?"

Banks glanced at Kay, who nodded and ordered the sole and salad. Banks went for venison medallions in port and mushroom sauce.

"More drinks?"

Banks looked at his half full glass and shook his head. Kay asked for a glass of white wine with her meal.

"You were saying?" Kay went on when the waitress had gone away. "About your wife."

Banks paused. "I'm divorced."

"How long?"

"Two years. She's already remarried."

Kay whistled. "That's pretty fast. Usually you'd expect some sort of . . . well . . . I don't know . . ."

"Period of mourning?"

"That's not the term I was looking for, but I suppose it'll do."

"It took me by surprise, too. I can't say I'm in any hurry to get married again."

"Is there someone?"

Banks thought of Michelle and Annie and experienced another pang of guilt as he said, "No one serious. It's too soon for that."

"Uh-huh."

"You?"

"Me? What?"

"Are you still married?"

"Not for the past five years."

"I'm sorry."

"You needn't be. He ran away with his secretary."

"That must have been tough."

"At the time, yes, I'd say it was a bit of a blow to the old self-esteem. She was much younger than me, of course. But I'm over it now."

"Someone new?"

"No one special." Kay smiled and gave a slight blush as she picked up her glass and sipped. It was the same smile and blush Banks remembered from those years ago when he first asked her out. What had happened to them? he asked himself. Why had they split up? But he knew the answer: it had been his fault.

Their meals arrived, and Kay's glass of wine soon followed. Banks stuck with his one pint, as he had to drive. "How are you coping about your mother?" he asked, after they had both eaten a couple of mouthfuls.

"Not bad. I think. I've got most of it done except the cleaning." She smiled. "Never was my strong suit, not even in my own home. I'll probably do it tomorrow. Anyway, a local dealer's coming to take away the furniture on Monday morning. Didn't offer much for it, but what the hell. . . . The rest is already packed and ready to go to my house." She shook her head. "It was difficult, you know, going through someone's life like that. Your own mother's memories. Do you know, I found letters to her from a young man—this was before she and Dad met, of course—but they were love letters. Quite spicy, too, one or two of them."

"It *is* hard to imagine your parents having lives of their own, isn't it?"

Kay nodded. "There was lots of other stuff, too. Old photos. Me when I was a kid at the seaside. Letters from me, too, when I was at university. Full of energy and ambition." Tears glistened in her eyes.

"And now?"

Kay wiped away the tears. "Oh, I suppose I'm still ambitious enough. I work practically all the hours God sends. I know I neglected Mum, especially since Dad died." Banks remembered hearing that Kay's father had been killed ten years ago in a car accident, an accident her mother survived. It had been the talk of the estate for weeks, so his mother had told him. Kay laughed and made a dismissive gesture. "I don't know, maybe there's something Freudian about it—I always was Daddy's little girl—but my career really started to take off around then, too. Life was exciting at last: lots of travel, parties, financial success. I hardly ever made time to come home and help Mum, even when she was ill. For crying out loud, I was in Zurich when she died. I barely managed to get back in time for the funeral. Some daughter. Some mother, too. Even my kids say they never see me."

"Kids?"

"Three girls. All married. I'm a grandmother, Alan. Can you believe it? A bloody grandmother."

"It is hard to believe, looking at you."

She blushed and smiled again. "Why, thank you. I'll tell you, though, it takes a lot of hard work and a lot of investment in potions and salves these days. Remember when we were kids? We thought we were immortal, that we'd be young forever."

"True enough," Banks agreed. "I'm still waiting for the wisdom that's supposed to come with age."

"Me, too."

They paused in comfortable silence for a while and ate some more food. Banks watched Kay break off flakes of moist sole with the edge of her fork. His venison was good, tender and tasty. He decided he could risk one more drink and asked the waitress to bring him a glass of red wine.

"How are your parents?" Kay asked.

"Fine. Oh, that reminds me: Mum asked me to invite you to drop by tomorrow, if you want."

Kay nodded slowly. "Yes. All right, that would be nice."

"About six, okay?"

"Fine. Just for half an hour or so." Kay frowned. "You know, there is one thing that puzzles me a bit about Mum," she said.

"Oh?"

"It's nothing, really, but I was going through her finances yesterday, and I noticed she'd withdrawn a hundred pounds from the bank machine the day she died, but I can't find it. There's only about six or seven pounds in her purse, and she wasn't the type to hide her money under the mattress."

The little scar beside Banks's right eye began to itch. "Maybe she had bills to pay, or she owed it to someone?"

"Neither a lender nor a borrower be. That was Mum's motto. And all her bills had been paid. No, it's a mystery. What do you have to say, oh great detective?"

"I still think there's probably a logical explanation."

"Probably. The other thing that puzzles me, though, is how did she get it?"

"What do you mean?"

"Well, she was bedridden for the last few days. There was a nurse on call twenty-four hours a day, of course, and Dr. Grenville dropped by quite often, but . . . I just don't see how she could even have *got* to the bank machine."

The itch got stronger. Banks scratched the side of his eye. "Have you ever heard of a fellow called Geoff Salisbury?" he asked her.

Kay frowned. "The name sounds vaguely familiar. I think he introduced himself to me at the funeral. A neighbor. Why?"

"Oh, nothing," said Banks. "Nothing important. Sweet?"

XII

"Would you like some music on?" Kay asked. They were back at her parents' house, and Banks had accepted her invitation to come in for a nightcap—a half bottle of "medicinal" brandy that Kay had found tidying up the kitchen cupboards. They drank it out of cracked teacups that she had been about to put in the dustbin.

"Sure," said Banks.

Kay walked over to the old stereo system. "Let's see," she said, flipping though a box of LPs. "I packed these last night, but I didn't really pay much attention. There's probably not a lot of choice. Dad only liked the stuff he used to listen to in the war, and Mum wasn't much interested in music at all. As you can see, they don't own a CD player. I think the last LP they bought was in 1950."

Banks went over and joined her, looking at the old-fashioned covers. At least he could read what was written on the backs of them, unlike the tiny print on CDs. "That's after 1950, he said, pointing to *Beatles for Sale.*

"That must be one of mine," Kay said. "I didn't even notice it."

Banks flipped open the cover. Written inside, in tiny blue ballpoint over the photograph, were some words. They were hard to make out, but he thought they said, "Kay Summerville loves Alan Banks." Banks passed it to Kay, who blushed and put it away. "I lent it to Susan Fish," she said. "The sneaky devil. I didn't know she'd done that." She pulled out another LP. "Ah, this will do fine."

The needle crackled as it hit the groove, a sound that gave Banks an unexpected frisson of delight and nostalgia, and then Billie Holiday started singing "Solitude."

"Couldn't do much better," he said.

"Dance?" Kay asked.

"I don't know," said Banks. "Remember the vicar wouldn't allow dancing at the youth club because he said it led to sex?"

Kay laughed. "Yes, I remember."

Then she was in his arms, Billie was singing about solitude, and they were doing what passed for dancing.

XIII

"A wise man, that vicar," said Banks about an hour later, as he lay back on the sofa, Billie Holiday long finished, a naked Kay half on top of him, her head resting on his chest, fingertips trailing languorously over his skin. It had been good—no doubt much better than their youthful fumblings, which he could scarcely remember now—though there had been something a little melancholy and desperate about it, as if both had been straining to capture something that eluded them.

"What happened to us?" Kay asked. "All those years ago."

"We were just kids. What did we know?"

"I suppose so. But have you ever wondered what would have happened? You know, if we hadn't . . ."

"Of course I have."

"And?"

"I don't know. It's hard for me to imagine a life without Sandra and the kids."

"I know that. I mean, even though it ended badly, Keith and I had some good times. And the kids are marvelous. It's just a game. Imagining. You know, sometimes I've been places or experienced things and thought I'd have liked you there to share it."

"You have?"

"Yes. Haven't you ever felt the same?"

"I can't say I have," said Banks, who had.

She nudged him in the ribs. "Bastard."

"There's something I never told you before," Banks said, stroking her silky blond hair and touching the soft skin on her neck, just below her ear.

"And you want to tell me now?"

"Yes."

"Are you sure that's a good idea?"

"The timing seems right."

"Why?"

"No particular reason."

Kay shifted position. "Okay. Go ahead."

"You know that first time when my parents were out and you came over to the house? The day we'd decided we were finally going to do it?"

"How could I forget? I was about to lose my virginity. I was scared silly."

"Me, too. On both counts. Nervous as hell."

Banks remembered that, as the months went on, he and Kay had graduated from kissing in the bus shelter to touching above the waist, first with clothing intact, then under her jumper, with only the thin bra between his hands and her bare, swollen flesh. After a few weeks of that, and much trouble fumbling with the safety pin that held the thing on, he got beyond the bra to the unimaginably firm and tender mounds beneath.

They had been going out nearly a year before the subject of moving to below the waist came up, and both were understandably a bit nervous about it. This might have been the swinging sixties, when kids were making love openly at Woodstock, but Banks and Kay were young, unsophisticated provincial kids, and the antics of drug-taking pop stars and free-loving hippies seemed as fantastic as Hollywood films.

But they had done it.

"Well," Banks went on. "I had to go and get some . . . you know . . . Durex."

"Rubber Johnnies? Yes, I suppose you did. Do you know, I never really thought about that."

"Well, I couldn't very well go to the local chemist's or the barber's, could I? They know me there. Someone would have been bound to tell my parents."

Kay propped herself on one elbow and leaned over him, her nipple hard against his chest. He could smell white wine and cheap brandy on her breath, see sparks of light dancing in her dark blue eyes. "So what did you do? Where did you go?" she asked.

"I walked miles and miles to the other side of town and found a barber's where I was certain no one would recognize me."

Kay giggled. "Oh, how sweet."

"I'm not finished yet."

"Go on."

"Do you know how the old barbershops had a sort of hallway with a counter between the outer and inner door, nice and private, where you could buy shampoo and razor blades and stuff?"

"And rubber Johnnies?"

"And rubber Johnnies."

"I remember. My dad used to take me to the barber's with him sometimes when I was a little girl."

"Right," Banks went on. "Well, as I said, I'd walked halfway to Cambridge and there I was, bold as brass, outside a barber's on a street where not a soul could possibly know who I was."

Kay smiled. "What happened?" She moved her head and her hair tickled his chest.

"Well, wouldn't you know it, but this particular establishment didn't have a discreet sales area. Oh, no. I opened the front door and I found myself standing right by the barber's chair. He was giving a bloke a shave, I remember, and the place was full of grown men. I mean, every chair in the waiting area was taken, and I swear that the minute I walked in there they all looked up from their newspapers and every eye was on me."

"My God! What did you do?"

"What could I do? I'd gone too far to turn back. I stood my ground and I said, in as deep a voice as I could manage, 'Packet of three, please.'"

Kay put her hand to her mouth to hold back the laughter. "Oh, no!" she said. "You're joking?"

"No word of a lie."

"What did he say? The barber."

"Not a word. He stopped midshave, straight-blade razor in his hand, and he went to his cabinet and got them for me. But you should have heard the other buggers laugh and cheer. You'd think Peterborough United had won a game. I went red as a beet."

Kay burst into a fit of laughter and couldn't stop. Banks started laughing with her, holding her against his chest, and after a while, laughter turned to lust.

XIV

It was after two o'clock when Banks slipped the key in the door of his parents' house and turned the lock as quietly as he could. He shut the door slowly behind him, without making much noise, and made sure the chain and bolt were on. The stairs creaked a little as he tiptoed up to bed. He couldn't very well go and brush his teeth as he would have to put the bathroom light on and the tap would make noise. He thought he could just about manage to undress and crawl into bed in the dark. The bed would make a bit of noise, but that couldn't be helped. Fortunately, he'd had the foresight to use the toilet before leaving Kay's.

The minute he got to the landing, he heard his mother muttering something to his father, who muttered something back. He couldn't catch the words but knew they were about him, how late he was. He felt himself blushing. Christ, it really didn't matter how quiet he had tried to be; she'd been lying awake until he came home, just like she used to do when he was a teenager.

XV

Despite his late night, Banks woke early on Sunday morning to the sound of rain blowing in sharp gusts against his bedroom window. The rest of the house was quiet, and he didn't think his parents were awake yet. His first thought on finding consciousness was to wonder what the hell he and Kay had thought they were up to last night, but the more he remembered, the less he regretted. Blame it on Billie Holiday, if you will, on dancing, the old estate and the romance of the past, but whatever it was, it was something special, and he refused to feel guilty.

He only hoped Kay felt the same way in the damp gray of dawn.

Two memories assailed him almost simultaneously as he got out of bed and went over to the wardrobe for his overnight bag: that he had forgotten to give Kay her old copy of *Lady Chatterley's Lover* and that he was certain he had seen a tiny, neatly folded square of silver paper in the bathroom waste bin. Perhaps Mrs. Summerville had taken to chewing gum in her final days, though he doubted it, or maybe Kay did, though he had seen no evidence of it last night, and he remembered that she had bought mints at the newsagent's, not gum. Which left him with the strongest suspicion that Geoff Salisbury had been there some time over the past few weeks, leaving Banks little doubt as to where the hundred pounds had gone.

What to do about him; that was the question.

Banks stretched as he pulled out his bag and decided to start the day dressed simply, in jeans and a polo-neck sweater. He would change for the party later. Today was his parents' big day, and Roy was due to come up from London. Banks resolved to be nice to Roy for his parents' sake. After all, the bugger could turn on the charm when he needed to.

As Banks put his bag back in the wardrobe, he noticed a cardboard box on the far side. On his previous visit he had found some old records and diaries, which were still there, but now it looked as if there was more. Curious, he opened the other door and lifted the box out. The flaps were shut, but not sealed, and written across the top, in his mother's inimitable scrawl was his name: *Alan*. More childhood stuff, then.

On top, he found yet more old school reports, from the grammar school this time, most of them urging him to try harder and assuring him he could do better if he only put his shoulder to the wheel, and so on. The reports were actually handwritten back then, in black ink, and Banks occasionally had difficulty reading the comments. He remembered some of the teachers' names—Mr. Newman, Mr. Phelps, Mr. Hawtry—but most of them were a blur.

Along with the reports was a class photograph dated 14th May, 1967. There they all were, three rows of teenage boys in their school uniforms. Banks remembered several of the faces: Steve Hill, Paul Major, Dave Grenfell, his best friends, then Tony Green, John McLeod, the school bully, and Ian Marston who, so Banks's mother had told him, committed suicide seven or eight years ago after his courier business failed. The rest of them he hardly remembered except for the odd feature here and there, such as a long, freckled face, a big nose, or prominent ears, but he couldn't put a name to them. He had met up with Dave Grenfell and Paul Major on his previous visit, and he had found out then that Steve Hill had died of lung cancer, but what had become of everyone else, he had no idea. Others would be dead, some would be dying, some would be successful, some would be failures, some would be criminals, many would be divorced. There was one angry-looking kid glaring into the camera with a cocky expression on his face, black hair just a little bit too long, tie slightly askew, top button undone, against school regulations. Himself. Even more of a mystery than all the rest.

Next came a few school exercise books full of sums and compositions. One of them contained some poems Banks had written when he went through that stage of adolescence in which poetry was an acceptable means of expression as long as you kept it to yourself. It was with excruciating embarrassment that he looked over them again now, with the autumn rain starting to spatter against his bedroom window.

There were lines about the awkwardness of being an adolescent, love poems to Julie Christie and Judy Geeson, poems about how phony the world was. None of them rhymed, of course, nor were any overly

concerned with metrics; the lines simply ended where he had decided
to end them for no other reason than that it looked like poetry on the
page. There were no capital letters, either. Still, Banks reflected, from
what he had seen that wasn't a hell of a lot different from the sort of
thing most published poets did today. Awful lines and images jumped
out at him, such as "I feel like a corpse / in the coffin of your mind."
What on earth had prompted him to write such a thing? About what?
He couldn't even remember whose mind was supposed to be the coffin.
And then there was a poem marked "For Kay," in which these immortal
lines appeared:

> i skimmed across
> your life
> like a pebble
> on the water's surface
>
> i sank
>
> quickly
> the tide went out

What had he been thinking of? There was another image about
her being "naked / on a sheepskin / by the crackling fire," but as far as
Banks could remember, they had never lain on a sheepskin rug, and
electric fires, which everyone on the estate had, didn't crackle. Poetic
license?

He remembered that first time up in this same room while his
parents were out. The event was awkward and far less momentous for
both of them than his imagination had convinced him it would be,
but it went well enough and in the end they decided they liked it and
would certainly try it again. They got better and better over the next
few months, stealing an hour or two here and there while parents were
absent. Once they almost got caught when Kay's mother came home
sooner than expected from a dental appointment. They just managed
to get their clothes on and tidy up the bed in time to tell her they'd been
listening to records, though judging by the expression on Mrs. Sum-

merville's face when she saw her daughter's disheveled hair, Banks didn't think she was convinced. Kay told him later that that very evening she had got a lecture about the dangers of teenage pregnancy and what men think of women who haven't "saved themselves" for marriage, though no overt mention was made of Banks or that afternoon's events, and nobody tried to stop them from seeing each other.

Smiling at the memory, Banks slipped the exercise book of poetry into his overnight bag, determined to remember to feed it to the fire when he got back to his Gratly cottage. As he moved it, a newspaper cutting slipped out from between some of the unfilled pages. It was a report in the local paper on the disappearance of Graham Marshall, a school friend of Banks's, and the reason for his visit home in summer. Along with the article was a photograph of Graham, his fair hair, large eyes, melancholy expression, long eyelashes and pale face like some fin de siècle poet.

A little shaken by the photograph, Banks moved on to the bottom of the box, where he found more old 45s, ones he had forgotten he had: Procol Harum's "A Whiter Shade of Pale," "Juliet," by the Four Pennies, "Hippy Hippy Shake" by the Swinging Blue Jeans, the Lovin' Spoonful's "Summer in the City," "Devil in Disguise" by Elvis Presley and "Still I'm Sad" by the Yardbirds.

Banks put the box back and tiptoed downstairs into the kitchen for a cup of tea. His heart almost stopped when he saw Geoff Salisbury sitting at the kitchen table eating buttered toast.

"Morning, Alan," Geoff said. "I've come to do some cleaning up. Already took your em and pee a cup of tea up, bless 'em. It's a big day for them, you know. Like a cuppa, yourself?"

Banks felt like saying he would make his own tea, but he remembered he hadn't been able to find the tea bags. Instead, he got himself a mug. "Thanks," he grunted.

"Not much of a morning person?" Geoff asked. "Still, I imagine after a late night like you had you must be feeling even more tired. Your poor old mum was lying awake worrying where you'd got to." Salisbury winked. "Having a good time with that Summerville girl, were you?"

So Banks's mother had already told Geoff that her son had been out with Kay Summerville and had not returned home until the early hours of the morning. He knew all this, and it wasn't even nine o'clock yet. Geoff Salisbury was starting to get *really* annoying. Even though Banks hadn't had a chance to call Annie back about criminal records, he decided that now would be as good a time as any to go on the offensive and make a couple of things clear to him.

"I'm glad you're here, actually," Banks said. "I've been wanting to have a quiet word with you."

"Oh? What about?"

"Your sticky fingers."

"Come again?"

"You know what I'm talking about. Don't come the innocent. It doesn't work with me."

"I understand that your job must make you cynical, but why are you picking on me? What have I done?"

"You know what you've done."

"Look, if it's that business about the change, I thought I'd already made it clear to you it was a genuine mistake? I thought we'd put it behind us?"

"I might have done if it hadn't been for a few other interesting tidbits I've heard since I've been down here."

"It's that Summerville girl, isn't it? If she's been saying things, she's lying. She doesn't like me."

"Well," said Banks, "that at least shows good taste on her part. It doesn't matter who's been saying what. The point is that I've been hearing from a number of independent sources about things sort of disappearing when you're in the vicinity. Money, for example."

Salisbury turned red. "I resent that."

"I should imagine you do. But is it true?"

"Of course it isn't. I don't know who's—"

"I told you, it doesn't matter who."

Salisbury stood up. "Well, it does to me. I have enemies out there. You might not believe it, but there are people who have it in for me. Not everybody appreciates what I do for the decent folk around here, you know."

"What enemies? What do you mean?"

"Never you mind. Now, if you've finished with your groundless accusations, I've got work to do. Your parents' golden wedding might not be important to you, but it is to me. Arthur and Ida mean a lot to me."

Before Banks could say another word, Salisbury had gone into the front room and started up the vacuum. Irritated both by Salisbury's reaction and his own fumbling accusation, Banks went across to the newsagent's to see if he could pick up a *Sunday Times*.

XVI

Banks went to the Bricklayer's Inn by himself for a quiet pint on Sunday lunchtime, taking the newspaper with him and promising to be back by two o'clock for lunch. It was his first real break away from everyone that weekend, and he made the best of it, even got the crossword three-quarters done, which was good for him without Annie's help. On his way home, he took cover in the rain-lashed bus shelter by the gates of the derelict factory to call Annie in Eastvale. Though the shelter hadn't been there all those years ago, Banks still couldn't help but think of Mandy, with her Julie Christie lips and that faraway look in her eyes. He wondered what had happened to her, whether she had ever found that distant thing she was looking for. Probably not; most people didn't. Though it seemed like another age, she would only be in her early fifties, after all, and that no longer sounded very old to Banks.

DC Winsome Jackman answered his ring. "Is DI Cabbot not in?" Banks asked.

"I'm afraid not, sir," said Winsome. "She's out on the East Side Estate interviewing neighbors about that sexual assault."

"Do you know when she'll be back?"

"No, sir. Sorry, but you'll just have to make do with me."

Banks could hear teasing humor in her voice, the way it tinged her lilting Jamaican speech. Did she know that Annie and he used to have a thing? He wouldn't be surprised. No matter how much you try to keep something like that a secret, there are always people who seem able to pick up on it intuitively.

"DI Cabbot did leave a message for you, though, sir," Winsome went on.

"Yes?"

"That man you were asking about, Geoffrey Salisbury."

"Right. Any form?"

"Yes, sir. One conviction. Six years ago. Served eighteen months."

"What for?"

"Fraud, sir. To put it in a nutshell, he tried to swindle a little old lady out of her life savings, but she was a lot smarter than he reckoned with."

"Did he indeed?" Banks said. "What a surprise."

"Sir?"

"Nothing. Where did this happen?"

"Loughborough, sir."

That wasn't very far away, Banks thought. "Thanks a lot," he said. "And thank DI Cabbot. That's a great help."

"There's more, sir. DI Cabbot said she's going to try to talk to the local police, the ones who handled the case. She said it looks like there might be more to it than meets the eye."

"What did she mean by that?"

"Don't know, sir. Shall I ask her to ring you when she's been in touch with Loughborough police?"

"If you would, Winsome. And thanks again."

"No problem, sir. Enjoy the party."

XVII

Roy didn't turn up in time for Sunday lunch, which was pretty much what Banks had expected. They ate without him, Ida Banks fretting and worrying the whole time, unable to enjoy her food, Arthur trying to calm her, assuring her that nothing terrible had happened and that Roy wasn't trapped in a burning car wreck somewhere on the M1. Banks said nothing. He knew his mother well enough to realize that anything he said regarding Roy would only succeed in adding fuel to the fire. Instead, he ate his roast beef and Yorkshires like a good boy—and a fine lunch it was, too, especially if you liked your meat and vegetables overcooked—and counted his blessings. In the first place, his mother was far too distracted to go on at him for being late home last night, and in the second place, Geoff bloody Salisbury had buggered off home and wasn't eating with them, though he had promised to come back early to help set up for the party.

The phone finally rang at about half past two, just as they were starting their jam roly-poly, and Banks's mother leaped up and dashed into the hall to answer it. When she came back, she was much calmer, and she informed Banks and his father that poor Roy had had a devil of a job getting away on time and the rain had caused some terrible delays. There was also a pileup on the M25, so he was stuck in traffic there at the moment and would arrive as soon as he could.

"There you are, you see," Arthur said. "All that fretting for nothing. I told you he was all right."

"But you never know, do you?" she said.

Banks offered to do the dishes and his offer was, to his surprise, accepted. His father had a nap with the open newspaper unread on his lap, and his mother went for a short lie down to calm her nerves. When Banks had finished the dishes, he sneaked a couple of fingers of his father's Johnnie Walker to calm *his* nerves. He had no sooner downed it than the explosion went off.

At least that was what it sounded like at first. Eventually, Banks's ears had adjusted enough to discern that it was music coming from next door. Heavy metal gangsta rap, music only if you used the term very loosely indeed. Banks's father stirred in his armchair. "At it again," he grumbled. "Never get a moment's peace."

Banks sat by him on the arm. "Does this happen a lot?" he asked.

His father nodded. "Too often for me. Oh, I've tried having a word, but he's an ignorant bugger. If I were twenty or thirty years younger . . ."

Banks heard his mother's footsteps on the landing. "At it again, I hear," she called down.

"It's bad for her nerves," Arthur Banks said.

"Have you talked to the council?"

"We've tried, but they say apart from issuing a warning, they can't do anything."

"What about Geoff Salisbury?"

"Geoff's got his strengths, but he's not got a lot of bottle. Proper tough guy, him next door."

"Right," said Banks, standing up. "Give me a few minutes."

"Where are you going, Alan?" his mother asked, coming down the stairs as he got to the front door.

"Just off to have a quiet word with next door, that's all."

"Don't you go causing any trouble. Do you hear? You just be careful. And remember we have to live here after you've gone, you know."

Banks patted his mother's arm. "Don't worry, Mum," he said. "I know what I'm doing. I'll make sure I don't cause you any trouble."

It was still raining outside. Banks knocked on the door but got no answer. Hardly surprising, as he supposed nobody could hear him over the music. The windows were all open and the angry heavy metal-rap spilled out into the street, someone bragging about raping a bitch and offing a pig.

Banks tried the front door. It was open. He found himself in a small hallway, where the stairs led up to the bedrooms. The wallpaper was peeling and something that looked like a sleeping bag lay on the staircase. Banks nudged it with his foot. It was empty.

He didn't like just walking in unannounced, but it seemed the only option. He called out a few times while he still stood in the hallway, but he could hardly even hear his own shouts.

Finally, he went through into the living room. Now he knew why they kept the windows open; the smell was overwhelming. It was a mixture of things—human smells definitely, such as sweat and urine, but also rotten vegetables, burned plastic and marijuana. There were also piles of old newspapers and other rubbish on the floor. It looked as though a dog had chewed up the furniture, though there wasn't one in evidence. Thankful for small mercies, Banks thought; they probably had a pit bull. Three people slumped on sofas and armchairs, and one of them stood up when Banks walked in.

"Who the fuck do you think you are?" he shouted.

"I'm not a lip-reader," Banks said, stepping over to the mound of stereo equipment and turning the volume down. "That's better."

It was the man of the house—Fred West to a tee, eyebrows and all— and the woman Banks assumed was his wife watched from one of the chairs. A girl Banks guessed to be about thirteen or fourteen sat in the other chair staring blankly at him.

The man squared up to Banks and gestured to the door with his thumb. "Right, mate," he said. "I'm done being polite. On your bike."

"I came to ask you to turn down the music," Banks said. "We can hardly hear ourselves think next door."

"What's it to you? You're not from around here."

"I was here a long time before you came on the scene. I grew up here. It's my parents' house and today's their wedding anniversary."

"Well, bully for you. Sorry we forgot to buy them a present. Now just fuck off before I do you some real damage."

"You don't understand," said Banks, slipping his warrant card out. "I'm a police officer, and I'm asking you nicely to keep the noise down."

The man actually leaned forward and scrutinized the card. "North Yorkshire!" he said. "You've got no powers down here. You're out of your jurisdiction, mate."

"Big word, that. I'm surprised you didn't choke on it."

"I'm not scared of you. Now, fuck off!"

"You should be," said Banks.

The man walked over to the stereo and cranked up the volume again. The girl and the woman hadn't moved. They were just watching. Banks guessed they were stoned on something or other. He thought he could see a crack pipe half hidden under a newspaper on the floor, but it wasn't crack they were on. These two weren't jerky or manic; they were practically comatose. Downers or smack, most likely.

With a sigh, Banks walked over to the stereo, picked up the CD player, ripped out the wires and dropped it on the floor. The music stopped. The women still didn't move, but Fred came right at him. He was a couple of inches taller than Banks, and thickset, muscular in the upper body. But Banks had his wiry and deceptive strength and speed going for him. He grabbed the man's wrist and twisted it so that he soon had him on his knees, arm up his back, foot placed solidly on his left kidney. By exerting just a little more pressure on the arm, Banks could make the pain excruciating. Even more pressure and the arm would snap or the shoulder joint would pop. The women just looked on, goggle-eyed. They'd never seen anything like this before.

"I'll do you for this!" the man yelled. "I'll see you bloody locked up, copper or no. You've got no right going around destroying a man's private property."

"Oh, give it a rest, Fred," said Banks. "It was probably nicked, anyway."

"My name's Lenny. You've got the wrong bloke."

"My mistake. Sorry, Lenny. Are you listening?"

"I'm still not scared of—"

Banks gave a little twist and Lenny screamed. Banks let him relax a moment and then repeated his question.

"All right," said Lenny. "All right, I'm listening. Let go."

Banks didn't. "I'm sorry about your CD player," he said. "I'm a music lover, myself, so it hurt me almost as much as it hurt you. I'm sure it'll be okay; it's just had rather a nasty shock, that's all. If it's not, then I'm sure you'll have no problem lifting another. But first I'd like a promise out of you."

"What promise?"

Banks gave another little twist. Lenny screamed, his face red with pain. The woman Banks assumed was his wife lit a cigarette and contemplated the scene before her with great interest, as if she were watching a television program. The girl started buffing her nails. Banks listened in the silence after the CD player's sudden demise but could hear no other sounds coming from anywhere in the house. A good sign. No ambush imminent.

"I'd like you to promise me that you won't ever, ever play your music so loud again that it disturbs my mum and dad next door. Do you think you can do that, Lenny?"

"It's my house. I'll do what I like in my own fucking house."

Twist. Scream.

"Lenny, you're not listening. If you really mean what you just said, you ought to consider moving to a detached house, you know, miles away from your nearest neighbors. Besides, it's not your house. It's the council's house. You just rent it."

"You're a bastard, you are," Lenny said, gasping. "You're worse than the fucking criminals you put away. Filth!" He spat on the floor.

"Yeah, yeah. It's all been said before. But we're not talking about me, we're talking about your promise."

"What promise. I haven't made any fucking promise."

"But you're going to, aren't you?"

Lenny said nothing. The woman frowned as she looked at him. Banks could tell the suspense was killing her. *Will he or won't he?* The young girl got up and made to leave the room.

"Where are you going?" Banks asked her.

"Bog," she said, making a squatting gesture.

Banks was a little concerned that she might reappear with a weapon. "Hold on a minute, love," he said. "Wait till I'm finished here."

"I'll piss myself."

"I said hold on. You'll live with it."

"These are me new jeans."

Banks turned back to Lenny. The girl slumped against the doorpost, legs crossed. Banks kept a close eye on her. She chewed on her lower lip and looked sulky.

"Right, Lenny, the quicker you give me your promise, the quicker your lass here will get to go to the toilet."

"She's not *my* lass. Let her piss herself. I don't care. Won't be the first time."

Banks gave a harder twist and Lenny cursed. "What I want you to promise," Banks said slowly, "is that you won't play your music so loud that it upsets my mum and dad, remember?"

"I remember."

"And if you do," Banks said, "I'll have the local drugs squad over here before you can flush a tab of E down the toilet. Is that clear?"

"It's clear."

"Is it a promise?"

"I . . ."

Banks twisted again. "Is it a promise?"

"All right, all right! Jesus Christ, yes, it's a fucking promise!"

"And if you do anything—anything at all—to harm or intimidate them in any way, I'll consider that a promise broken. And I deal with broken promises myself. North Yorkshire's not that far away. Got it?"

"Got it. Let me go."

Banks let go and Lenny squirmed on the floor for a while, rubbing his arm and his shoulder before subsiding into his armchair and lighting a cigarette with shaking hands.

"You're a nutter, you are," he said. "You ought to be locked up."

"You've got that right."

"Is it over?" the girl by the door asked. "Are you done? Are you? 'Cause I'm bleeding bursting here."

"It's over, love," said Banks. "Off you go."

"About fucking time." She dashed upstairs. The woman on the sofa looked at Lenny with contempt, but still said nothing.

"You in charge here, Lenny?" Banks asked, catching her look. "Because there's no point my talking to the monkey, if you catch my drift."

"I'm in fucking charge," he said, glaring at the woman. "They know that."

She sniffed, but Banks could see fear in her eyes, the first emotion he had noticed in her. Lenny was in charge all right, and he probably used the same tactics Banks had just used to rule his roost. That didn't make Banks feel particularly good, but needs must. He wondered what other sorts of abuse went on in this house, in addition to drugs. The young girl, for example, or the other kids, wherever they were. Nothing would have surprised him. Maybe he'd call in the drugs squad anyway, and the social. Someone ought to keep a close eye on this lot, that was for certain.

He heard the toilet flush as he left.

XVIII

Roy's arrival at about four o'clock broke the tension for Banks. Until then, he had been helping Geoff set up the bar and buffet on tables in the kitchen, keeping a tight rein on his temper for the sake of his parents, even though Geoff treated him like an employee. "Now, Alan, if you wouldn't mind just moving that over there. . . . That's a good lad. . . . If you could nip over to the shops and pick up. . . ." And so on. He had also been wanting to get Geoff alone and have another go at him in the light of Winsome's information, but his mother was always around issuing instructions, too. Wisely, his father had gone upstairs to "rest."

When the doorbell rang, Ida Banks practically ran to the front hall, and Banks heard her shouts of joy at greeting Roy. After divesting himself of his raincoat, the man himself came through to the living room, clutching a bottle-shaped bag, with a young woman in tow. She looked about twenty, Banks thought, with short, shaggy hair, black streaked with blond, a pale, pretty face, with beautiful eyes the color and gleam of chestnuts in September. She also had a silver stud just below her lower lip. She was wearing jeans and a short woolly jumper, exposing a couple of inches of bare, flat midriff and a navel with a ring in it.

"This is Corinne," said Roy. "Say hello to my brother, Alan, Corinne."

Corinne shook Banks's hand and said hello. She gave him a shy smile and averted her eyes.

Roy looked at Geoff, free hand stretched out, smiling like a salesman. "And you are . . . ?"

"Geoff. Geoff Salisbury."

"Geoff. Of course! Pleased to meet you, Geoff. I've heard a lot about you. Mum and Dad say they'd be lost without you."

Geoff beamed and shifted from foot to foot. "Well . . . that's probably a bit of an exaggeration."

Very 'umble, Banks thought.

"Not at all," said Roy. "Not at all." He gave Geoff a firm handshake and clapped him on the shoulder. "Good to meet you at last."

Geoff basked in the glow of Roy's charm like a child in his mother's embrace.

All this time, Ida Banks had stood by smiling on. Roy turned to her again and gave her a hug. Then he handed over the package he'd been carrying. Ida Banks opened it. It was a bottle of Veuve Clicquot champagne. Vintage.

She turned to her husband. "Ooh, look at this, Arthur! Champagne."

"It's the real stuff, too," Roy said, with a wink at Banks. "None of your Spanish *cava* or New World sparklers."

Arthur Banks grunted. Banks happened to know that his father hated champagne, as much as a symbol of the upper classes as for its taste.

"I'd better put it away for a special occasion," said his mother, taking it through to the kitchen and placing it into the dark depths of the larder, where it would probably remain. Banks thought to mention that today was as special an occasion as they were likely to have in a while, but he knew it was best to keep quiet when Roy was in full benevolent swing. He'd bought a few cans of beer and lager himself, and he knew that *they* would be emptied that very evening, without a doubt.

"Now, then," said Ida Banks, rubbing her hands together and reaching out to touch Corinne's shoulder. "What about a drink for everyone? Corinne, love, what'll you have?"

"Lager and lime?"

"Right you are, love. And you, Roy?"

"Just a Perrier for me, Mum," said Roy. "Driving."

"Of course." Ida Banks frowned. "What did you say? Perrier? I don't think we have any of that, do we, Alan?"

Banks shook his head. "Only tap water."

"Well, that won't do, will it?" his mother said scornfully.

"It's all right, Mrs. B," chimed in Geoff. "I'll just nip over the road. Old Ali's bound to have some. He sells everything." And before anyone could stop him, he was off.

Ida Banks turned to Roy again. "You won't be driving for ages yet, I hope, son. Won't you have a glass of something a bit stronger first?"

"Oh, go on, then," said Roy. "You've twisted my arm. I'll have a glass of white wine."

Banks's mother gave him a questioning glance. "We've got that, Mum," he said, then looked at his brother. "Screw top okay, Roy?"

"Whatever," said Roy, his lip curling.

Banks and his father both opted for beer.

"Come on, then, Corinne, love," said Ida Banks, taking Corinne by the arm. "You can keep me company and help me pour."

Banks couldn't believe it. His mother was fawning all over Roy's twentysomething bit of fluff, the sort of girl who'd have been granted no more than a sniff of distaste if Banks had brought her home. Still, he should have expected it. Roy was Banks's younger brother by five years. He had grown up watching Banks do everything wrong and getting caught for it—staying out too late as a teenager, listening to the radio under the bedsheets when he should have been asleep, smoking, leaving home to go to college in London, joining the police—and Roy had keenly observed his parents' reactions. Roy had learned well from his brother's mistakes, and he had done everything right. Now, in his mother's eyes, Roy could do no wrong, and even Arthur Banks, not given to expressions of any kind, didn't seem to disapprove of Roy as much as he did of Banks. Which was odd, indeed, Banks thought, as Roy was the consummate capitalist.

Roy sat down, first pulling at the razor-sharp crease of his black suit trousers. "So how's life at the cop shop?" he asked, looking away even before he'd got the words out, indicating to Banks that he didn't have the slightest iota of interest.

"Fine," said Banks.

"Is that your Renault out there?"

"Yes. Why?"

"Not bad. Only it looks new. Been on the take?"

"Oh, you know me, Roy. A few thousand here, a few thousand there."

Roy laughed. Corinne and Ida Banks, best friends now, came through with the drinks on a tray at the same time Geoff came back from the shop. "Sorry, they didn't have any Perrier," he said. "I got this other stuff Ali recommended. St. . . . something or other . . . I can't pronounce it. Okay?"

"It'll do," said Roy. "Be a good bloke and pop it in the fridge, would you, Geoff?"

Geoff seemed only too pleased to oblige.

"Isn't this lovely?" said Ida Banks, handing out the drinks. "We can have our own little family party before the rest of our guests arrive. Corinne tells me she's an accountant, Roy."

"That's right, Mum. Saved me a fortune in taxes."

Corinne sat on the floor near his feet and rested her head against his thigh. He stroked her hair the way one would a faithful dog. "She's very good with figures, aren't you, Corinne?"

Corinne blushed. "If you say so, Roy."

She really did seem like a "nice" girl to Banks, and that made him wonder all the more what she was doing with Roy. Not that Roy wasn't handsome or charming. In fact he possessed both of those attributes in spades. Under his suit, he wore a pale blue silk polo-neck. His hair, not quite so black as Banks's, was long, over his ears and collar, expensively cut, and he had a small shaving nick near the cleft of his chin. His energetic blue eyes resembled Banks's, except that they were predatory and calculating, whereas Banks's were curious and intense.

Banks had thought more than once that his brother Roy fit the classic definition of the psychopath; he was glib and superficial, egocentric, manipulative, shallow, and completely lacking in any feelings of remorse, empathy or guilt. Certainly all his behavior and his emotional responses were learned, assumed through close observation of others as the best way to get on in the world. Underneath it all, Banks guessed, the only thing that mattered to him were his needs and how he could meet them, his success, measured of course in money and power. Perhaps that was why he had already gone through three wives.

"Oops, mustn't forget," Roy said, putting his glass down and getting suddenly to his feet. Corinne almost fell over sideways. "Sorry, love." He patted her shoulder. "Just got to nip down to the Porsche. Forgot something. Wouldn't want to leave it out there too long. You never know on an estate like this. Give us a hand, will you, Geoff?"

Geoff, returned from the kitchen, beer in hand, expressed that he was only too willing to do anything for Roy and set his glass down on the table. Corinne smiled shyly as the two of them went out. Banks hadn't heard her speak yet and wondered what her voice was like, her accent. "Where are you from?" he asked, just to find out.

"Canterbury," she said. "Well, I grew up there. After that I went to Manchester University."

She didn't have much of a regional accent, Banks learned. She was well-spoken, clearly educated, and her voice was pleasant, soft and musical, a little reedy.

"How long have you known Roy?"

"About three months."

"They're getting engaged," Ida Banks said. "So now we've *really* got something to celebrate."

Corinne blushed.

"That true?" Banks asked.

She smiled and nodded. He felt like warning her off. Roy had been married three times, and two of his wives had ended up confiding in Banks about what an unfaithful, cruel bastard he was. He had never actually hit either of them—so they both swore—but he tyrannized them, curtailed their freedom and terrorized them psychologically. The second, a particularly bright neurosurgeon called Maria, ended up seeing a psychiatrist for years after they split up, trying to splice together the frayed strands of her self-esteem. Banks had seen her change—albeit at infrequent intervals—from a secure, confident young doctor into an apologetic, tongue-tied wreck whose hands shook so much she couldn't thread a needle. The third wife, thank God, had seen the signs before it got too late and left Roy in time.

Roy and Geoff came back carrying large cardboard boxes, which they set down on the living room floor. "Happy anniversary," Roy said. "Go on. Open them."

Banks's parents looked at each another, then his mother got some scissors from the kitchen drawer and came back and knelt by the largest box. Roy and Geoff helped, and soon between them had managed to drag out the computer monitor, processor unit and keyboard.

"It's a computer," said Ida Banks, clearly at a loss.

"Now you'll be able to go on the Internet," said Roy. "We'll be able to send each other e-mail."

"Will we?"

"Yes."

"But it's so . . . so expensive."

"Oh, it's nothing. Everyone should have a computer these days. They're the future."

Ida Banks reached out and touched it gingerly, as if it might bite. "The future . . ."

"We'd better get it out of the way for the time being," said Arthur Banks. "Our guests will be arriving soon."

"Right."

Between them, Geoff, Roy and Banks took the computer upstairs and set it up on the desk in the spare room.

"That'll be nice for them," said Geoff.

Banks thought it was the stupidest present he could think of. His parents were in their seventies; they weren't going to learn how to use a computer. His own present, a particularly moody Yorkshire landscape painting he had found in an antique shop in Richmond, had met polite praise, but he felt it was probably destined for the back of the wardrobe. The computer, he suspected, would sit at this desk, not even plugged in, just gathering dust. Unless Geoff Salisbury decided to use it.

Just as the three of them started downstairs, the front doorbell rang.

"Here come the first guests," said Geoff. "It's started."

XIX

First to arrive were Uncle Frank and Aunt Harriet, and after that Banks began to lose track. Here came relatives he hadn't seen for years, cousins he never even knew existed. It was only to be expected with both his mother and father coming from large families—six and four, respectively—but it was a shock nonetheless.

Geoff took to bartending duties like a fish to water, and Roy worked the room like a politician, all hail-fellow-well-met, as if these people he had probably never seen before meant more to him than his own life. If the truth be known, he had been home even less often than Banks and hardly ever in touch with the more distant relatives.

Arthur Banks seemed bewildered by it all, tired, sticking to his armchair, glass of beer at hand, though Ida got into the party spirit and Banks fancied she even became a little tipsy. Music played quietly in the background, mostly crooners and big bands, though pop entered the mix when someone found an old compilation album. It was pretty much the same stuff as Banks had found in his room, or at least softer stuff from the same period—Cliff Richard, Eden Kane, Frank Ifield, Billy Fury, The Bachelors and the ubiquitous Val Doonican—but it was only for background, wallpaper music.

In a lull after the first few guests had arrived, Banks managed to get Roy alone for a few minutes while a couple of young cousins, similarly bedecked, admired Corinne's body piercing.

"I've been wanting a word in your ear," Banks said. "It's about that Geoff Salisbury."

"What about him? Seems like a decent chap. Takes good care of Mum and Dad."

"That's just it. I think he steals from them."

"Oh, come on, Alan. It's that suspicious copper's mind of yours working overtime again."

"No. It's more than that." Banks told him about the short change.

"Could have been any reason for that," Roy said. "A genuine mistake. You don't always have to think the worst of people, you know."

"He's got their PIN number. They give him their Abbey card."

"He takes care of their finances. For crying out loud, *somebody*'s got to do it. I mean, it's not as if you're around much, is it?"

Banks realized he was fighting a losing battle. Roy didn't want to believe that Geoff was anything other than a godsend, and he would resist any evidence to the contrary. "He's got a criminal record," Banks went on nevertheless, pissing against the wind. "Swindling old folk out of their life savings."

Roy just laughed. "Mum and Dad haven't got anything worth swindling. You know that. And besides, don't you believe in rehabilitation? I assume he's paid his debt to society?"

"Yes, but—"

"Well, then."

"For Christ's sake, Roy. I caught him red-handed."

"Listen, big brother. So what if he is pocketing a bob or two here and there? He practically does all their shopping for them, housecleaning, too. Isn't it worth it?"

"That's not the point. If he wants paying for what he does, that's different."

"Maybe it's just his way."

"It's a funny bloody way."

Roy shrugged and laid his arm across Banks's shoulders. "Like I said, big brother. It's not as if you're around to do it, is it? Eh? I say count your blessings and let sleeping dogs lie. Look, there's Uncle Ken. See you later."

Banks muttered to himself under his breath. He should have known approaching Roy was a waste of time. Anybody suspected of swindling a penny out of *him* and he'd probably put a contract out on them, but his own parents. . . . On the other hand, was Roy right? Was Banks making too much out of all this? Being a party pooper? He looked at his parents. They seemed happy enough—his mother did, anyway—what right had he got to challenge that? What gave him the moral justification to come down here once in a blue moon and spoil what little good fortune they had going for them? His mother clearly adored Geoff—he could tell by the way she looked at him and talked about him—and having him around made life a hell of a lot easier for his father, too. Roy was right. Banks had been interfering too much, and it was about time he backed off and left people to get on with their lives.

"Penny for them?"

Banks turned. It was Kay. "I didn't hear you come in," he said. "Nice to see you."

She smiled and touched his arm. "Nice to see you, too. I was just talking to your mother. She offered her condolences."

She was wearing a lemon summer dress, which fell to just below her knees, and she had her hair tied up and held in place with a patterned leather barrette.

"You look wonderful," Banks said.

Kay blushed. "Thank you. How about a drink for the lady?"

"Of course. Vodka and tonic?"

"That'll do nicely." She took hold of his arm. "And don't go too far away. I don't know anyone else here."

"Of course you do," said Banks. "You know my parents."

"I haven't seen them for years."

"And my brother, Roy."

"He was just a little kid when we were together. Around too often, if I remember correctly."

Banks nodded. He remembered being blackmailed into giving Roy money to get lost on more than one occasion. "You know Geoff Salisbury," he said, nodding to where Geoff stood by the fireplace talking to some cousin whose name Banks couldn't remember.

Kay gave a little shudder. "Yuck. I don't know about you, but he gives me the creeps."

They got their drinks.

"Come on," Banks said to Kay. "Let's get some fresh air."

They went out to the back step. Banks could hear music next door, but only softly. The rain had stopped earlier that afternoon, and it had turned into a pleasant evening. The sky was already darkening and the stars coming out. There was even a pale quarter moon low in the sky. Banks leaned against the wall. Kay stood quietly beside him.

"Last night . . ." he began.

But Kay hushed him, putting a finger to his lips. "No. Don't say anything. That was marvelous. Special. Let's leave it at that, shall we?"

"If you like," Banks said. He'd been thinking the same thing. What had happened had been about the past, unfinished business, passing magic. It had been time out of time. Tomorrow, they would both go back to their real lives and probably would never see each other again. Banks thought about how their relationship had ended all those years ago, and how he had believed he would never see her again after he went to London. This was enough. This was more than enough. It had to be.

They went back inside. The party went on, as these things do. Banks and Kay talked to Mrs. Green for a while, and Banks promised not to be such a stranger. Aunt Florence regaled him with her cataracts, and Aunt Lynn went on about her gallbladder operation. He also heard about Cousin Patrick's prostate problems, Uncle Gerald's hemorrhoids and Cousin Louise's manic depression. It was enough to make him want to kill himself before he got old. Then there was Cousin Beth's divorce, Nick and Janet's third baby, a girl they had named Shania, Sharon's promotion, Gail's miscarriage and Ayesha's boob job. All the while Kay stood politely by, asking questions and making sympathetic comments or noises. Roy continued to work the room, energy seemingly indefatigable.

Inevitably, Uncle Ted fell asleep. Cousin Angie had too much to drink and was sick in the kitchen sink, dislodging a nose stud in the process, which she almost inhaled. Uncle Gerald and Uncle Frank almost came to blows. Aunt Ruth wet herself, and young, lovely, anorexic Cousin Sue, with all the self-esteem of a blade of grass, became tearful and made a pathetic attempt to seduce Banks.

All in all, it was just another typical family do.

Roy and Corinne left early. They sought out Banks and Kay to say their good-byes, and as usual Roy invited Banks to the South Kensington house, said they really must see more of each other and that he hoped Banks could make it to the wedding next year. Banks promised he would try, gave the blushing bride-to-be a chaste kiss on her pale, cool cheek, and they were gone.

When Banks looked around, he noticed that Geoff Salisbury had left, too. Only one or two relatives remained, and they were either very close or very drunk. Banks found his mother having a heart-to-heart with her sister, Flo, and said he'd see Kay home and be right back.

The street was quiet, the evening air cool. They only saw a few people as they walked the short distance to Kay's house.

"I'd better not come in," he said at the doorstep.

"No."

He wondered what would happen if he leaned forward and kissed her on the lips. Would their resolve melt? Somehow, he didn't think it was very strong.

"Anyway," he said, "if you're ever up Eastvale way . . ."

"Of course I will." She gave him the sort of smile that said she never would be, then after a quick kiss on the cheek, the door opened and closed and Banks was left standing there alone.

He didn't want to go back to the dregs of the party immediately, didn't want to face the drunken relatives desperately sobering up for the drive home, didn't want to face the mess of spilled drinks and food smeared on the carpets. He knew he would have to—he owed it to his parents to help clean up at least—but surely he could put it off for a little while longer.

The moon was higher now and Banks could see stars, planets, constellations even, beyond the amber glow of the streetlights. He wandered the quiet Sunday night streets of the estate feeling oddly melancholy, past the maisonettes where he used to deliver newspapers, past the house where his old, late friend Steve Hill used to live. Steve used to keep toads in a bell jar at the bottom of the garden, Banks remembered, but he was forgetful, and one summer he neglected them for so long that they shriveled up and died. They looked like dried mushrooms. That was what happened to living things you were supposed to love and care for but neglected.

His melancholy was probably something to do with Kay, he realized, though he hadn't really wanted to try to repeat last night either. Last night had had an aspect of magic about it that any attempt at repetition would fall well short of. He remembered how their relationship had fallen apart all those years ago. His fault.

It had all started to change when Kay left school at sixteen and got a job at Lloyd's Bank in the town center. She made new friends, had money to spare, started going for drinks with the office crowd regularly after work on a Friday. Banks was still at school, having stayed on for his A levels, and somehow a schoolboy had less appeal than these slightly older, better dressed, more sophisticated men of the world at the office. They had more money to flash around and, even more important, some of them had cars. One pillock called Nigel, with a plummy accent and a Triumph MG, particularly got up Banks's nose. Kay insisted there was no hanky-panky going on, but Banks became tortured with jealousy, racked by imagined infidelities, and in the end, Kay walked away. She couldn't stand his constant harping on who she was seeing and what she was doing, she said, and the way he got stroppy if she ever so much as *looked at* another man.

The irony was, given that his A-level results weren't good enough for university—the first bone of contention between him and his parents—that he might as well not have bothered staying on. He'd spent far too much time with Kay, away from his studies, listening to Hendrix, Dylan and Pink Floyd, reading books that weren't on the syllabus.

Shortly after the breakup, Banks moved to London and went to pursue business studies at the Poly. A year or two after that, and several brief, unsatisfactory, casual relationships later, he met Sandra.

A dog barked as he reached the edge of the estate, by the railway lines. A local train rattled by, one or two silhouettes visible through the windows. Banks started toward home. He had only got a few yards when the mobile in his pocket rang. He had forgotten to turn it off.

"Alan? I hope I'm not disturbing your party."

It was Annie Cabbot. Banks wondered how he would have felt if he had gone in with Kay and the phone had rung just as they were . . . it didn't bear thinking about.

"No," he said quietly. He happened to be passing the telephone boxes at the end of the street, so he decided to stand inside one and take the call. That way he didn't seem like one of those stupid wankers walking around talking to his girlfriend on his cell phone.

"I'm sorry to call so late," Annie said.

"That's all right. Aren't you off duty?"

"Yes, but I was waiting to hear from DS Ryan in Loughborough. He was out at the pictures."

"DS Ryan? So this is about Geoff Salisbury?"

"Yes. What's wrong, Alan? You sound funny. Distant."

"So would you if you were standing in the middle of a council estate talking on your mobile."

Annie laughed. "Oh, I don't know. I'm not quite as conservative as you are."

"Okay. Point taken. What did this DS Ryan come up with?"

"It's interesting, actually," said Annie. "At least, I thought you'd want to know."

"Fill me in."

"As Winsome told you, he was actually convicted of fraud. It was a neighbor, an elderly woman, and he started by helping out around the place, that sort of thing."

"Sounds familiar," said Banks. "Go on."

"Seems he managed to come between her and her children and get himself written into her will. She didn't have much. Only a few hundred quid and an insurance policy, but he copped for most of it."

"What happened?"

"The family contested it. Undue influence, that sort of thing. Hard to prove. Anyway, in the end Mr. Salisbury won out."

"Where does the conviction come in?"

"Just getting to that. During proceedings, it came out that Geoff Salisbury had persuaded the woman to invest in a nonexistent business venture of his. A garage."

"Aha."

"Again, it wasn't much. Only two hundred quid."

"Doesn't matter," said Banks. "Is a man who preys on the poor any less guilty than one who preys on the rich?"

"I'm afraid that's a bit too philosophical for me at this time on a Sunday evening, but at a guess I'd say even more so, wouldn't you?"

"I would. Thanks a lot, Annie. Above and beyond, and all that."

"Oh, that's not all."

"Really?"

"Really. While all this was going on, Mr. Salisbury's mother died. Well, she was old and—"

"Sick?"

"How did you guess? She had diabetes. Anyway, she died. Or . . ."

Banks felt a tingle go up his spine. "Or what?"

"Or he helped her on her way. Nothing was ever proven. There weren't even any charges. But DS Ryan was one of the investigating officers, and he says he was suspicious enough to ask for an autopsy. Negative. The woman was old, she went hyperglycemic, and that was that."

"What's that?"

"Hyperglycemic? It's something that happens to diabetics, apparently, caused by too much insulin or low food intake."

"He gave her an overdose of insulin?"

"No evidence of that."

"But someone could have brought it about, this hyperglycemic coma?"

"Yes. Hard to prove, though."

"What did DS Ryan say?"

"DS Ryan said that his older sister is a diabetic and she always keeps her bedside drawer full of Mars bars or chocolate of some kind for just that sort of eventuality."

"But I thought diabetics had to avoid sugar like the plague?"

"So did I. Apparently, they do. Unless they go hyperglycemic. Then they need a hit of sugar."

"Or?"

"Coma. Death. And in this case, there were other complications. Weak heart, for example."

"And DS Ryan says?"

"DS Ryan says the doctor didn't find any traces of sugar products close to Mrs. Salisbury's bed, and he found that in itself suspicious. In his opinion—DS Ryan's, that is—Geoff Salisbury was responsible, knowing it was just a matter of time before she'd need a sugar fix."

"He killed his own mother. Is that what you're saying?"

"Mercy killing, but killing all the same."

"Bloody hell," said Banks. "This changes things."

"It does?"

"I'd been thinking of leaving well alone."

"But not now?"

"Not now. Thanks a lot, Annie."

"My pleasure. See you tomorrow?"

"Okay. And thanks again."

Missing Mars bars. A faulty oxygen tank valve. Banks wondered who else Geoff Salisbury had assisted in their final moments on earth. He also wondered how long it would be before his own father suffered that fatal angina attack and was unable to find his nitroglycerine tablets in time. Putting his phone in his pocket, he headed straight for Geoff Salisbury's house.

XX

"Look, I can see you're not going to let this drop, are you," said Salisbury when Banks had told him he knew about the conviction. "So I've been to prison. It's nothing to be ashamed of. I served my time."

"As a matter of fact," said Banks, "it is something to be ashamed of. But those who've been there rarely seem to think so. Innocent, were you, like everyone else?"

"No. I did it. I was desperate and she didn't need the money, so I conned her. I'm not saying I'm proud of *that,* what I did, but like I said, I served my time, paid my debt to society."

Debt to society. Roy's words exactly, and an odd phrase when you really thought about it. "Would that it were as simple as that," Banks said. Salisbury's living room wasn't quite as clean and tidy as he had expected, but perhaps he used all his energy on other people's homes and had none left for his own. Dust gathered in the corners, the carpet was rather threadbare and lumps of mold floated on the half-empty coffee cup on the table.

"All right," said Salisbury, "suppose, just *suppose* that I was ripping people off. Some people might actually believe I'm a power for good around here."

"What do you mean?"

"An estate like this, the old folks need someone on their side, someone to look out for them. They die off, you see, and when they do it's mostly young 'uns come in off the waiting list. You know the sort. Young lasses barely out of school with three kids and no father in sight. Or that lot next door to your mum and dad's. Scum. Now, you're a copper, Alan, you tell me if he doesn't have prison written all over him. And as for the kids, well, it'll only be a matter of time. And if it's not scum like that it's foreigners. Gypos. Darkies. Pakis. Them with the turbans. All with their funny ways, slaughtering goats in the street and whatever, not giving a toss for our customs and traditions and way of life. See, the old folks, they get frightened when everything around them starts to feel threatening and *unfamiliar.* Their world's changing so fast and their bodies can't do what they used to do, so they end up feeling lost and scared. That's where someone like me comes in. I reassure them, do odd jobs, give them a friendly and familiar face to relate to. So what if I make a few bob out of it? Hypothetically."

"I'd say, hypothetically, that it makes you a thief."

"Words, Alan, just words."

"Actually, no. Legal concepts."

"Well, you would say that, wouldn't you?"

"Here's another one to try on for size. *Murder.*"

Salisbury blinked and stared at him. "What?"

"You heard me, Geoff. Oh, you might have a more fancy name for it, something high-sounding and moral, such as *mercy* killing, but in my eyes it's murder plain and simple."

Salisbury sat back in his chair. "I don't know what you're talking about."

"Oh, I think you do. There was your own mother for a start. Don't tell me a woman who's been a diabetic for a good part of her life doesn't know to keep some sugar on hand in case she goes hyperglycemic."

Salisbury banged his fist on the chair arm. "That's over and done with," he said. "I wasn't there. Nobody ever proved anything against me!"

"I'm not saying you haven't been clever, Geoff. You never were there, were you? Mr. Green's faulty valve, for example. Wouldn't be difficult for a car mechanic, would it? And what about Mrs. Summerville, Geoff, gentle pillow over the face as she slept, was it? Nobody would ask too many questions. Or perhaps a little too much morphia? She was alone. You had a key. They always give you a key, don't they? And what about the hundred quid you drew out with her bank card the day she died. Mistake, that. She couldn't get it herself, remember—she was bedridden—and her daughter could find no sign of the money."

Salisbury got to his feet. "You can't prove a damn thing. Get out of here! Go on, get out!"

Banks didn't move. "You don't get away with it that easily, Geoff, especially not when it's my parents you're playing with now. I saw the piece of silver paper you folded and dropped in the bin at Mrs. Summerville's house. I'll bet it has your prints on it."

"So I went there. I helped her. Like I helped the others. So what? That doesn't prove anything."

"I'll bet if we exhumed the body, though, we'd find some evidence of tampering, some evidence of what you did. She hasn't been dead a week, Geoff, not like the others. There'll be forensic evidence. In the house, too."

For the first time, Banks saw Salisbury falter and sit down again. He knew he had been guessing, taking a stab in the dark, but it seemed to have touched a nerve. "She had cancer and a weak heart," he went on. "All it took was a little pressure. She didn't even have the strength to fight back, did she?"

"What do you mean, *forensic* evidence?" Geoff asked. "They'd never dig her up."

"Oh, yes they would. On my say-so. And you know exactly what they'd find, don't you?"

"But the doctor signed the death certificates. There wasn't even an inquest, nothing suspicious at all."

"Why would there be, Geoff? Don't you know how it goes? All your victims were medically attended during their illnesses, they'd all been seen by their doctors within fourteen days of death, and they were all terminally ill, likely to die at any time. There were no grounds for a coroner's inquest. And remember: none of them was alone with family members when they died. Not even your mother. You made sure you were out of the house that night, didn't you?"

"This is absurd. They'll never open up her coffin."

"Yes, they will. We'd just better thank the Lord that she was buried and not cremated, don't you think? What will they find? Tell me."

Salisbury licked his lips, staring at Banks, and said nothing for a long time. "You think you're clever, don't you?" he said at last. "You don't know nothing about it."

"About what?"

"Suffering."

"Tell me about it, Geoff. I want to know."

"Why should I? You wouldn't understand."

"Believe me, I'll try. And it'll go better for you if you do. If we don't have to exhume the body. That's a lot of work. And messy. Nobody wants to do it. I think we'd be able to prove a case against you, Geoff, I really do, but if you help us, if you tell me about it, it'll go a lot easier for you."

"Why do you think they let me cheat them, take their money?"

Banks frowned. "Come again?"

"You don't think they didn't know what I was doing, do you? They knew all right, and they let it go on. Payment. That's what it was. They just couldn't come right out and say it. What they really wanted me to do. But it was their way of paying me, of letting me know what they wanted me to do."

"Hang on a minute, Geoff," said Banks. "Let me get this straight. Did you kill Mr. Green and Mrs. Summerville?"

"Yes. No. I put them to sleep. I ended their suffering."

"And your mother?"

"It was what she wanted. It was what they all wanted. It was beautiful."

"What was?"

Salisbury's eyes shone. "The transformation. From pain to peace. Suffering to grace. It was like being God."

"Did either Mrs. Green or anyone from the Summerville family suggest that you do what you did?"

"Not in so many words, no."

"But that was how you interpreted their actions in letting you get away with stealing money?"

"Like I said, they knew. It was their way of paying for what they wanted done. Close family couldn't do it, could they? They'd soon be suspects, or they didn't care enough and were never around like you and that Summerville girl. You don't see their suffering. I do. Day in, day out. I was their savior. Somebody had to be."

Banks got up.

"What are you doing?"

"I'm going to ring the local police now, and I want you to tell them what you've just told me. Tell them everything. Maybe you're sick. Maybe you need help. I don't know." *All I do know*, Banks thought as he took out his mobile, *is that I want you off this estate and as far away from my parents as possible.*

XXI

It was about an hour later when two uniformed constables and one detective sergeant, grumpy at being dragged out of the Sunday night pub darts match, arrived at Geoff Salisbury's house.

"You know, with all due respect to your rank and all, sir, we don't particularly appreciate North Yorkshire CID poking around on our patch, doing our job for us," said the surly DS, whose name was Les Kelly, and who was going prematurely bald. Luckily, Banks hadn't encountered DS Kelly on his last trip to Peterborough.

Banks smiled to himself. It would probably have been his reaction, too, had Kelly come up north. At least it would have been *if* he had been a DS and ten years younger. "Believe me, DS Kelly, it wasn't my intention," he said. "I just came for the party."

"You what?"

Banks sighed. "I was brought up around here. Down the street. I came home for my parents' golden wedding and this is what I found going on." He gestured toward Salisbury, who was giving his statement to the uniformed officers.

"How about we go outside for a minute?" said Kelly. "The uniforms can deal with his statement, and I fancy a smoke."

Banks and Kelly stood on the path. Kelly lit a cigarette and Banks craved one. A few locals had noted the arrival of the police, and a small crowd had gathered just beyond the patrol car. Not that police cars were a novelty on the estate, but it *was* nearly bedtime on a Sunday.

"I was winning, too," said Kelly.

"What?"

"The darts match."

Banks smiled. "Oh. Sorry."

"Never mind. We never sleep. Always ready to bring another wrongdoer to justice. I just transferred here from West Midlands, myself. You say you're from around these parts?"

"Uh-huh. Long time ago. Came here when I was twelve. Grew up just down the street. Used to go out with the girl whose mother that bastard killed."

"They'll put him in the nuthouse."

"Likely. As long as he's locked up."

Kelly looked around and sniffed the air, then he took a deep drag on his cigarette and blew out a long plume of smoke. "I grew up on an estate pretty much like this one," he said. "Barrow-in-Furness."

"Not a part of the world I know."

"Don't bother."

"Look, while you're here," said Banks, "there is another small matter you might be able to help with."

"Oh? And what's that?"

"The family that lives next to my parents," said Banks. "I don't know their names but the bloke looks like Fred West—"

"Ah, the Wyatts."

"Is that their name?"

"Well, it's easier that way. To be honest, though, I think he's the only true Wyatt there. She's a Fisher. Had kids with a Young and a Harrison and a Davies. Need I go on?"

"How many of them are there?"

"According to the council, only five. That's all the place is big enough for."

"I saw a sleeping bag on the staircase."

"You were in there?"

"Noise complaint."

"Ah, yes. Well, our latest estimation is about twelve, give or take a couple."

"Can you do anything?"

"About what?"

"Drugs, for a start. And I wouldn't be surprised if some of those kids are being sexually abused."

"Nor me." Kelly finished his cigarette and stamped it out on the path. "It's only a matter of time," he said. "You know how these things can drag on. But we've got an eye on them, and the social's investigating them, too, so sooner or later one of us will come up with something."

"And then?"

Kelly laughed. "And then? You know as well as I do. Then the farce just begins. They'll end up on another estate much like this one, most likely, and it'll start all over again."

The uniforms came out with Geoff Salisbury, slump shouldered, between them. "Done," one of them said. Salisbury gave Banks a look that was half pleading for understanding and forgiveness, and half pure hatred. He didn't know which half he liked least.

"Right." Kelly clapped his hands. "Let's go see what the custody sergeant has to say, shall we? And I'll say good night to you, for the moment, DCI Banks. We might need you again."

Banks smiled. "I'm only a phone call away."

XXII

By Monday morning, when Banks awoke to sunshine and the sound of birds beyond his thin curtains, news of Geoff Salisbury's arrest had spread around the entire estate. When he went down for breakfast, he found his parents sitting quietly at the table. He poured himself a cup of tea. His mother wouldn't look at him when he walked in the room.

"You've heard, then?" he asked gently.

"About Geoff?" she said, tears in her eyes. "Mrs. Wilkins came to tell me. That was your doing, wasn't it?"

"I'd no choice, Mum," said Banks, resting his hand on her arm. She jerked it away.

"How could you do that? You know what he meant to us."

"Mum, Geoff Salisbury was a murderer. He killed Mr. Green and he killed Kay's mother." *Not to mention his own mother,* Banks thought. "I don't see how you can defend him. You *knew* those people. They were your neighbors."

Mrs. Banks shook her head. "I don't believe it. Not Geoff. He wouldn't do anything like that. He's gentle as a kitten."

"He admitted it."

"You must have forced him. Interrogated him until he didn't know what he was saying."

"I don't work like that, Mum. Believe me, he did it. He might have thought he was doing good, doing the families a favor, but he did it."

Banks looked at his father, who caught his eye. He knew right away that they were thinking the same thing: who was next?

Banks stood up. "Look, Mum, I've got to go now."

"All you brought was trouble. It was supposed to be a happy occasion. Now look what you've gone and done. Spoiled it all, as usual. I wish our Roy was here."

Banks's heart felt heavy, but there was nothing more he could say. There was as much point in telling his mother that Roy didn't give a shit as there was in telling her that Geoff Salisbury was a cold-blooded murderer.

"I'm sorry, Mum," he said, then dashed upstairs to throw his few belongings in his bag. He looked at the boxes of records and exercise books again and decided to leave them. All he took was the poetry.

Let go.

He was just standing at the door of his room when he saw his father come slowly up the stairs. They stood on the landing facing each other. "She's upset," said Arthur Banks. "She doesn't know what she's saying. I'll take care of her. I'll make sure she knows what's what."

"What *is* what, Dad? I'm not even sure I know. Did I do the right thing?"

"Only you know that for certain, lad. But you did your job. You'd no choice. You're a copper and he was a bad 'un. Your mother'll get over it. She really liked him, that's all. He was useful around the house. And he could be a right charmer."

"I know," said Banks. "His type usually is."

"You know she never likes admitting she's wrong about people. But if he killed those people, you were right. You were only doing your job. I don't mind a bob or two here and there—and don't think I didn't notice, but I kept quiet for your mother's sake—but I draw the line at killing." He laughed. "Who's to say it wouldn't have been me next, eh?"

They both knew there was a lot more truth in that fear than either cared to explore. "Bye, Dad," he said. "I'll be in touch."

"Don't be a stranger, son. And don't worry. Your mother'll get over it. I'll tell her to ring you in a day or so, shall I?"

"Please do."

His father smiled. "Or send you an e-mail?"

Banks moved forward impulsively and hugged him. It was quick, and he felt only the slightest pressure of his father's hand on the back of his shoulder, but it was enough.

Banks dashed down the stairs and walked down the path to his car, tears prickling his eyes. He felt a weight in the side pocket of his jacket and realized it was Kay's copy of *Lady Chatterley's Lover.* He had forgotten to give it to her. Now he decided he might as well keep it. Maybe he would even get around to reading it, thirty years after he'd borrowed it.

When he got to the driver's side of his car, he cursed out loud. Some bastard had taken a coin or a nail and made a deep scratch along the paintwork all the way from back to front. He thought he saw someone watching out of the upstairs window of the Wyatt house.

Bugger them. Bugger the lot of them, he thought, and got into his car and drove away.

Cornelius Jubb

Most of us around these parts had never seen a colored person until Cornelius Jubb walked into the Nag's Head one fine April evening in 1943, bold as brass and black as Whitby jet.

Ernie the landlord asked him if he had a glass. Glasses being in short supply, most of us brought our own and guarded them with our lives. He shook his head. Ernie's not a bad sort, though, so he dug out a dusty jam jar from under the bar, rinsed it off and filled it with beer. The young man seemed happy enough with the result; he thanked Ernie and paid. After that, he lit a Lucky Strike and just stood there with that gentle, innocent look in his eyes, a look I came to know so well, and one that stayed with him throughout all that was to happen in the following weeks, for all the world as if he might have been waiting for a bus or something, daydreaming about some faraway sweetheart.

Now, most of us up here in Leeds are decent enough folk, and I like to think we measure a man by who he is and what he does, not by the color of his skin. But there's always an exception, isn't there? In our case it was Obediah Clough, who happened to be drinking with his cronies in his usual corner, complaining about the meager cheese ration. Obediah's too old to go to war again, and I suspect that he also sat out most of the last war at a comfortable hospital in Skegness after sustaining a blighty. Now, Obediah drills the local Home Guard and helps out with ARP, though air raids have been sporadic here since 1941, to say the least.

Obediah swaggered up to the young colored gentleman with that way he has, chest puffed out, baggy trousers held up with a length of cord, and looked him up and down, an exaggerated expression of curiosity on his blotchy red face. His pals sat in the corner sniggering at his performance. The young man ignored them all and carried on drinking and smoking.

Finally, not used to being ignored for so long, Obediah thrust his face mere inches away from the other's, which must have been terrible for the poor fellow because Obediah's breath smells worse than a pub toilet at closing time. Give him his due, though, the lad didn't flinch.

"What have we got here, then?" Obediah said, playing it up for his cronies.

Whether because he recognized the question as rhetorical, or because he simply didn't know the answer, the young man made no reply.

"What's your name, then, boy?" Obediah asked.

The man put his glass down, smiled and said, "My name's Jubb, sir. Private First Class Cornelius Jubb. I'm very pleased to meet you." He held out his hand, but Obediah ignored it.

"Jubb?" Obediah's jaw dropped. "Jubb? But that's a Yorkshire name."

"It's the name I was given by my parents," said the man.

"Tha's not a Yorkshireman," Obediah said, eyes narrowing. "Tha's having me on."

"No word of a lie," said Cornelius Jubb. "But you're right, sir. I'm not a Yorkshireman, I'm from Louisiana."

"So what're you doing with a Yorkshire name, then?"

Cornelius shrugged. "Maybe my ancestors came from Yorkshire?"

Cornelius had a twinkle in his eye, and I could tell that he was joking, but it was a dangerous thing to do with Obediah Clough. He didn't take well at all to being the butt of anyone's joke, especially after a few drinks. He glanced toward his friends and gestured for them to approach. "Look what we've got here lads, a black Yorkshireman. He must've come straight from his shift down t'pit, don't you think?"

They laughed nervously and came over.

"And what's that tha's got on thy wrist?" Obediah said, reaching toward some sort of bracelet on the GI's right wrist. He obviously tried to keep it out of sight, hidden under his sleeve, but it had slipped out. "What is tha, lad?" Obediah went on. "A bloody Nancy-boy? I've got a young lady might appreciate a present like that." The young man snatched his arm away before Obediah could grab the bracelet.

"That's mine, sir," he said, "and I'd thank you to keep your hands off it."

"Oh, would you, now? Doesn't tha know there's a price for coming and drinking our beer in here with the likes of us?" Obediah went on. "And the price is that there bracelet of thine. Give us it here, boy."

Cornelius moved a few inches along the bar. "No, sir," he said, adopting a defensive stance.

I could tell that things had gone far enough and that Obediah was about to get physical. With a sigh, I got to my feet and walked over to them, putting my hand gently on Obediah's shoulder. He didn't appreciate it, but I'm even bigger than he is, and the last time we tangled he came out with a broken rib and a bloody nose. "That's enough, Obediah," I said gently. "Let the lad enjoy his drink in peace."

Obediah glared at me, but he knew when he was beaten. "What's he think he's doing, Frank, walking into our pub, bold as you like?" he muttered, but his heart wasn't in it.

"It's a free country, Obediah," I said. "Or at least Mr. Hitler hadn't won the war last time I checked."

This drew a gentle titter from some of the drinkers, Obediah's cronies included. You could feel the tension ebb a notch. As I said, we're a tolerant lot on the whole. Muttering, Obediah went back to his corner and his pals went with him. I stayed at the bar with the newcomer.

"Sorry about that, lad," I said. "He's harmless, really."

The GI looked at me with those big brown eyes of his and nodded solemnly.

Now that I was closer, I could see that the object Obediah had referred to was some sort of gold chain with tiny trinkets suspended from it, a very unusual thing for a man to be wearing. "What exactly is that?" I asked, pointing. "Just out of curiosity."

He brought his arm up so I could see the chain. "It's called a charm bracelet," he said. "My lucky charm bracelet. I usually try to keep it out of sight."

Everything on the chain was a perfect miniature of its original: a silver locket, a gold cross, a grimacing monkey, a kneeling angel, a golden key, a tiny pair of ballet slippers, a tower, a snake, a tiger and a train engine. The craftsmanship was exquisite.

"Where did you get it?" I asked.

"Fishing," Cornelius said.

"Pardon?"

"Fishing. Caught it fishing in the Mississippi, down by the levee, when I was boy. I decided then and there it would be my lucky charm."

"It's a beautiful piece of work," I said. I held out my hand. "Frank Bascombe. Frank to my friends."

He looked at my outstretched hand with suspicion for a moment, then slowly he smiled and reached out his own, the palm as pink as coral, and shook firmly. "Pleased to meet you, Mr. Bascombe," he said. "I'm Cornelius Jubb."

I smiled. "Yes, I heard."

He glanced over at Obediah and his cronies, who had lost interest now and become absorbed in a game of dominoes. "And I don't know where the name came from," he added.

I guessed that perhaps some Yorkshire plantation owner had given it to one of Cornelius's ancestors, or perhaps it was a contraction of a French name such as Joubliet, but it didn't matter. Jubb he was, in a place where Jubbs belonged. "You don't sound southern," I said, having heard the sort of slow drawl usually associated with Louisiana on the radio once or twice.

"Grew up there," Cornelius said. "Then I went to college in Massachusetts. Boston."

"What are you doing here all by yourself?" I asked. "Most American soldiers seem to hang around with their mates, in groups."

Cornelius shrugged. "I don't know, really. That's not for me. I just don't seem to fit in. They're all . . . y'know . . . fighting, cussing, drinking and chasing girls."

"You don't want to chase girls?"

I could have sworn he blushed. "I was brought up to be a decent man, sir," he said. "I'll know when the right girl comes along." He gestured to the charm bracelet again and smiled. "And this is for her," he added.

I could have laughed at the naïveté of his statement, but I didn't. Instead, I offered to buy him another drink. He accepted and offered me a Lucky. That was the beginning of what I like to think of as an unlikely friendship, but I have found that war makes the unlikeliest of things possible.

You might be wondering by now why I wasn't at war with the rest of our fine lads. Shirker? Conchie? Not me. I saw enough carnage and breathed in enough gas at Ypres to last me a lifetime, thank you very much, but the fact of the matter is that, like Obediah, I'm too old to be a soldier again. After the first war, I drifted into the police force and finally rose to the rank of detective inspector before leaving to become a teacher. Now all the young men have gone off to fight, of course, they need us old codgers to carry the burden at home, so they called me back as a special constable. Just as I was getting ready to spend my twilight days reading all those books I never read when I was younger—Dickens, Jane Austen, the Brontës, Hardy, Trollope. Ah, well, such is life, and it's not a bad job, as jobs go. At least I thought so until events conspired to prove me wrong.

Cornelius, as it turned out, was one of about three hundred colored persons—or Negroes, as the Yanks called them—in an engineering regiment transferred up from the West Country. During our conversations, mostly in the Nag's Head, but often later at my little terraced back-to-back over carefully measured tots of whiskey, no longer readily available, I learned about hot and humid Louisiana summers; the streets, sounds and smells of New Orleans; and the nefarious ways of the color bar and segregation. I had already heard of problems between white and colored GIs in other parts of the country. Apparently, the American military command wanted to institute the same sort of color bar they had at home, but we British didn't want that. I had also heard rumors that in some towns and villages a sort of unwritten code had grown up, fostered by whispering campaigns, as regards which pubs were to be frequented by Negroes and which by whites.

I also learned very quickly that Cornelius was a shy and rather lonely young man, but that he was no less interesting or intelligent for that, once you got him talking. His father was a Baptist minister who had wanted his son to go to college and become a schoolteacher, where he might have some positive influence on young men of the future. Though Cornelius had instead followed a natural interest in and flair for the more practical and mechanical aspects of science, he was remarkably well traveled and well read, even if there were great gaps in his education. He had little geography, for example, and knew nothing beyond the rudiments of American history, yet he spoke French fluently—though not with any accent I'd heard before—and he was well versed in English literature. The latter was because of his mother, he told me. Sadly deceased now, she had read children's stories to him from a very early age and guided him toward the classics when she thought he was old enough.

Cornelius was homesick, of course, a stranger in a strange land, and he missed his daddy and the streets of his hometown. We both had a weakness for modern music, it turned out, and we often managed to find Duke Ellington or Benny Goodman broadcasts on the wireless, even Louis Armstrong if we were lucky, whenever the reception was clear enough. I like to think the music helped him feel a little closer to home.

All in all, I'd say that Cornelius and I became friends as that spring gave way to summer. Sometimes we discussed currents events—the "bouncing bombs" raid on the Eder and Möhne dams in May, for example, which he tried to explain to me in layman's terms—without much success, I might add. We even went to the pictures to see Charlie Chaplin in *The Great Dictator* with a couple of broad-minded Land Girls I knew. That raised more than a few eyebrows, though everything was aboveboard. As far as I could tell, Cornelius stayed true to his word about waiting for the right girl to come along. How he knew that he would be so sure when it happened, I don't know. But people say I'm married to my job, which is why my wife left me for a traveling salesman, so how would I know about such things?

One August night, just after the Allies had won the battle for Sicily, the local GIs all got a late pass in honor of General Patton's role in the victory. After an evening in the Nag's Head drinking watery beer, Cornelius and I stayed up late, and after he left I was trying to get to sleep, my head spinning a little from a drop too much celebratory whiskey, when there came a loud knocking at my door. It was a knocking I wish I had never answered.

Brimley Park was a thick wedge of green separating the terraces of back-to-backs on the east side and the more genteel semidetached houses on the west. There was nothing else in the place but a few wooden benches and some swings and a slide for the kiddies. Chestnut trees stood on all three sides shielding the heart of the park from view. There used to be metal railings, but the Ministry of Works appropriated them for the war effort a couple of years ago, so now you could make your way in between the trees almost anywhere.

Harry Joseph, who had been dispatched by the beat constable to fetch me, babbled most of the way there and led me through the trees to a patch of grass where PC Nash and a couple of other local men stood guard. Of course, under normal circumstances, this sort of thing would hardly be the province of a special constable, but I had one or two successes in criminal investigations under my belt, and the local force was short staffed.

It was a sultry night and the whiskey only made me sweat more than usual. I hoped the others couldn't smell it on me. It was late enough to be pitch-dark, despite double summer time, and, of course, the blackout was in force. As we approached, though, I did notice about eighteen inches of light showing through an upper window in one of the semis. They'd better be quick and get their curtains down, I thought, or Obediah Clough and his ARP men would be knocking at their door. The fines for blackout violations were quite steep.

Harry had babbled enough on the way to make me aware that we were approaching a crime scene, though I never did manage to find out exactly what had happened until I got there. PC Nash had his torch out, the light filtered by the regulation double thickness of white tissue paper, and in its diffused milky glow I could see the vague outline of a figure on the grass: a young woman with a Veronica Lake hairstyle. I crouched closer, careful not to touch anything, and saw that it was young Evelyn Fowler. She was lying so still that at first I thought she was dead, but then I noticed her head move slightly toward me and heard her make a little sound, like a sigh or a sob.

"Have you called an ambulance?" I asked PC Nash.

"Yes, sir," he said. "They said they'll be here straightaway."

"Good man."

I borrowed Nash's torch and turned back to Evelyn, whispering some words of comfort about the doctor being on his way. If she heard me, she didn't acknowledge it. Evelyn wasn't a bad sort, as I remembered. Around here, the girls were divided into those who don't and those who do. Evelyn was one who did, but only the morally rigid and the holier-than-thou crowd held that against her. It was wartime. Nobody knew which way things were going to go, how we would all end up, so many lived life for the moment. Evelyn was one of them. I remembered her laugh, which I had heard once or twice in the Nag's Head, surprisingly soft and musical. Her eyes might have been spoiled for me by that cynical, challenging look that said, "Go on, convince me, persuade me," but underneath it all, she was scared and uncertain, like the rest of us.

There was no mistaking what had happened. Evelyn's dirndl skirt had been lifted up to her waist and her drawers pulled down around her ankles, legs spread apart at the knees. She was still wearing nylons, no doubt a gift from one of our American brothers, who seemed to have unlimited supplies. Her lace-trimmed blouse was torn at the front and stained with what looked like blood. From what I could see of her face, she had taken quite a beating. I could smell gin on her breath. I looked at her fingernails and thought I saw blood on one of them. It looked as if she had tried to fight off her attacker. I would have to make sure the doctor preserved any skin he might find under her nails. There was always the possibility that it could be matched to her attacker's.

I averted my gaze and sighed, wondering what sad story Evelyn would have to tell us when, or if, she regained consciousness. Men had been fighting a deadly campaign in Sicily, and even now, as we stood around Evelyn in Brimley Park, they were still fighting the Germans and the Japanese all over the world, yet someone, some man, had taken it into his mind to attack a defenseless young woman and steal from her that which, for whatever reason, she wouldn't give him in the first place. And Evelyn was supposed to be one of those girls who did. It didn't make sense.

My knees cracked as I shifted position. I could hear the ambulance approaching through the dark, deserted streets of the city. Just as I was about to stand up, the weak light from the torch glinted on something in the grass, half hidden by Evelyn's outstretched arm. I reached forward, placed it in my palm and shone the torch on it. What I saw sent a chill down my spine. It was a tiny, perfectly crafted grimacing monkey. The very same one I had seen so many times on Cornelius Jubb's charm bracelet.

It was with a heavy heart that I approached the U.S. army base in a light drizzle early the following morning, while Evelyn Fowler fought for consciousness in the infirmary. It was a typical military base, with Nissan huts for the men, storage compounds for munitions and supplies, and the obligatory squad of soldiers marching around the parade ground. Along with all the Jeeps and lorries coming and going, it certainly gave the impression of hectic activity.

My official police standing got me in to see the CO, a genial enough colonel from Wyoming, called Hank Johnson, who agreed to let me talk to Pfc. Jubb, making it clear that he was doing me a big favor. He specified that army personnel must be present and that, should things be taken any further, the matter was under American jurisdiction, not that of the British. I was well aware of the thorny legal problems the American "occupation," as some called it, gave rise to, and had discovered in the past that there was little or nothing I could do about it. The fact of the matter was that on August 4, 1942, after a great deal of angry debate, the cabinet had put a revolutionary special bill before Parliament which exempted U.S. soldiers over here from being prosecuted in our courts, under our laws.

The colonel was being both courteous and cautious in allowing me access to Cornelius. The special USA Visiting Forces Act was still a controversial topic, and nobody wanted an outcry in the press, or on the streets. There was a good chance, Colonel Johnson no doubt reasoned, that early collaboration could head that sort of thing off at the pass. It certainly did no harm to placate the local constabulary. I will say, though, that they stopped short of stuffing my pockets with Lucky Strikes and Hershey's bars.

I agreed to the colonel's terms and accompanied him to an empty office, bare except for a wooden desk and four uncomfortable hard-backed chairs. After I had waited the length of a cigarette, the colonel came back with Cornelius and another man, whom he introduced as Lieutenant Clawson, a military lawyer. I must confess that I didn't much like the look of Clawson; he had an arrogant twist to his lips and a cold, merciless look in his eye.

Cornelius seemed surprised to see me, but he also appeared sheepish and did his best to avoid looking me directly in the eye. Maybe this was because of the scratch on his cheek, though I took his discomfort more as a reflection of his surroundings and hoped to hell it wasn't an indication of his guilt. After all, we were on his home turf now, where the colored men had separate barracks from the whites and ate in different canteens. Already I could sense the gulf and the unspoken resentment between Cornelius and the two white Americans. It felt very different from Obediah Clough's clumsy and childish attempts at bullying; it ran much deeper and was more dangerous.

"Tell me what you did last night, Cornelius?" I asked, the words out of my mouth before I realized what a mistake I had made calling him by his first name. The colonel frowned and Lieutenant Clawson smiled in a particularly nasty way. "Pfc. Jubb, that is," I corrected myself, too late.

"You know what I did," said Cornelius.

The others looked at me, curious. "Humor me," I said, feeling my mouth become dry.

"We were celebrating the victory in Sicily," Cornelius said. "We drank some beer in the Nag's Head and then we went back to your house and drank some whiskey."

The colonel looked surprised to hear Cornelius talk, and I guessed he hadn't heard his voice before. When you were expecting some sort of barely comprehensible rural Louisiana patois, what you got in fact was the more articulate and refined speech of the New Englander, a result of the time Cornelius had spent in the north.

"Were you drunk?" I asked.

"Maybe. A little. But not so much that I couldn't find my way home."

"Which way did you go?"

"The usual way."

"Through Brimley Park?"

Cornelius hesitated and caught my eye. "Yes," he said. "It's a good shortcut."

"Did you notice anything there? Anyone?"

"No," he said.

I got that sinking feeling. If I could tell that Cornelius was lying, what would the others think? He certainly wasn't a natural liar. And why was he lying? I pressed on, and never had my duty felt so much of a burden to me before.

"Did you hear anything?"

"No," said Cornelius.

"Do you know a girl by the name of Evelyn Fowler?"

"Can't say as I do."

"About five foot three, good-looking girl. Wears nice clothes, makes a lot of them herself, has a Veronica Lake hairstyle."

"Who doesn't?" said Cornelius.

It was true; there were plenty of Veronica Lake look-alikes walking around in 1943. "She's been in the Nag's Head a couple of times," I added.

"I suppose I might have seen her, then," said Cornelius. "Why?"

"She was raped and beaten last night in Brimley Park."

Now, for the first time, Cornelius really looked me in the eye. "And you think I did it?" he asked.

I shook my head. "I'm only asking if you saw anything. It was around the time you left. And," I dropped the grimacing monkey softly on the table, "I found this near the scene."

Cornelius looked at the charm, then turned up his sleeve and saw the missing spot on his bracelet. Clawson and the colonel both stared at him gravely, as if they knew they'd got him now and it was just a matter of time. I wasn't so sure. I thought I knew Cornelius, and the man I knew would no sooner rape and beat Evelyn Fowler than he would sully the memory of his own mother.

Finally, he shrugged. "Well," he said, "I did tell you I walked through the park. It must have dropped off."

"But you saw and heard nothing?"

"That's right."

"Bit of a coincidence, though, isn't it? The timing and all."

"Coincidences happen."

"Where did you get that scratch on your cheek?" I asked him.

He put his hand up to it. "Don't know," he said. "Maybe cut myself shaving."

"You didn't have it last night when you left my house."

He shrugged again. "I shave in the mornings."

"It doesn't look like a shaving cut. Are you sure you didn't get it when you were attacking Evelyn Fowler?"

He looked at me with disappointment in his eyes and shook his head. "You don't believe that."

He was right; I didn't. "Well, what did happen?" I asked. "Help me here."

"I think that's about enough for now," said Lieutenant Clawson, getting to his feet and pacing the tiny room. "We'll take it over from now on."

That was what I had been afraid of. At least with me, Cornelius would get a fair deal, but I wasn't sure how well his fellow countrymen would treat him. I was the one who had brought the trouble down on him, the one who couldn't overlook something like the little monkey charm I found at the crime scene, even though I never suspected Cornelius of rape. But these men . . . how well would he fare with them?

"This girl who was attacked," Clawson went on, "is she still alive?"

"Evelyn Fowler? Yes," I said. "She's unconscious in hospital, but she's expected to pull through."

"Then maybe she'll be able to identify her attacker."

I looked at Cornelius and saw the despair in his face.

I thought I knew why. "Yes," I said. "Perhaps she will."

Within two days, Evelyn Fowler was sitting up and talking in her hospital bed. Before the Americans arrived, I managed to persuade Dr. Harris, an old friend, to give me a few minutes alone with her.

Not surprisingly, she looked dreadful. The Veronica Lake hair hung limp and greasy, framing her heart-shaped face. She was still partially bandaged, mostly around the nose, but the dark bruises stood out in stark contrast to skin as pale as the linen on which she lay. Her eyes had lost that light, cynical, playful look and were filled instead with a new darkness. When she tried to smile at me, I could see that two of her lower front teeth were missing. It must have been a terrible beating.

"Hello, Constable Bascombe," she said, her voice oddly lisping and whistling, no doubt because of the missing teeth. "I'm sorry, it's a right mess you see me in."

I patted her hand. "That's all right, Evelyn. How are you?"

"Not so bad, I suppose, considering. Apart from my face, that is. And a bit of soreness . . . you know."

I did know.

"He must have been disturbed or something," she went on. "I suppose I was lucky he didn't kill me." She tried another smile and some of her natural sweetness and playfulness came through.

"Did you see your attacker at all?" I asked, a lump in my throat.

"Oh, yes," she said. "I mean, you can't help it, can you, when a great hulking brute's on top of you thumping you in the face? I saw him all right."

"Did you recognize him?"

Here she paused. "Well, it was dark, what with the blackout and all that. But I suppose in a way that's what made it easier."

"What do you mean?"

"The blackout. His face, it just blended right in, didn't it." She lowered her voice to a whisper and turned her head toward me. "He was a nigger."

"Evelyn, that's not a polite word to use."

"Well, it wasn't a polite thing he did to me, was it?" She pouted. "Anyway, Jim, that's my sweetheart, Jim's a GI and he says them niggers are good for nothing and they have their way with white women at the drop of a hat. Said they're hanging them over there for it all the time. They're not the same as us. Not as intelligent as us. They're just like big children, really. Or animals. They can't control themselves. I know what folks thought of me, that I'd go with anybody, but I wouldn't go with a nigger, not for a hundred pounds. No, sir."

"Was it someone you recognized?"

"I'd know him if I saw him again."

"But you'd never seen him before?"

"I didn't say that. My head still aches. I can't think clearly."

"Did you scratch him?"

"I certainly tried hard enough . . . Funny thing . . ."

"What is?"

"Well, it's just a feeling I got, I don't know, just about when I was passing out, but at one time I could have . . ."

"What?"

"Well, I could have sworn that there were two of them."

Apart from one or two brief consultations with Lieutenant Clawson and another U.S. military lawyer called William Grant, the case was taken out of my hands, and whatever investigation was done was carried out by the U.S. military. It's a sorry state of affairs indeed when a British policeman has no powers of investigation in his own country.

Naturally, the Americans were tight-lipped, and I could discover nothing from them. Evelyn came out of hospital after a week and soon got back to her old self, and her old ways, though she seemed to be avoiding me. At least she never came to the Nag's Head anymore, and I got the impression that whenever she saw me approaching in the street she crossed over to the other side. I guessed that perhaps the Americans had found out about our little chat and warned her off. Whatever the reason, they were keeping everything under wraps, and hardly a snippet of information even got out to the papers.

Of poor Cornelius, I had no news at all. I didn't see him again until the general court-martial at the base. As he sat there, flanked by a guard and his lawyer, he seemed lifeless and mechanical in his movements, and the sparkle had gone from his eyes, though the look of innocence remained. He seemed resigned to whatever fate had in store for him. When he looked at me, it seemed at first as if he didn't recognize me, then he flashed me a brief smile and turned back to examining his fingernails.

I had never been to an American GCM before, and I was surprised at how informal it all seemed. Despite the uniforms, there were no wigs in evidence, and the language seemed less weighty and less full of legal jargon than its British equivalent. There were twelve members of the court, all officers, and by law, because this was the trial of a Negro, one of them also had to be colored. This turned out to be a young first lieutenant, new to command, who seemed nervous and completely intimidated by the other eleven, all of whom had higher ranks and much greater seniority.

Cornelius pleaded not guilty, and his defense was that he had interrupted the attack and chased off the attacker, whom he had not recognized because of the blackout. When he had realized that a colored American GI standing alone in a deserted park after nightfall with a raped and beaten white girl would immediately fall under suspicion, he did what any colored man would do and hurried back to camp.

Naturally, I was called quite early in the proceedings to present my evidence, much as I would have been in an ordinary court. I described how I had been woken up and led to Brimley Park by Harry Joseph, what I had seen there and what I had found in the grass beside Evelyn Fowler. I was then asked about my relationship with the accused and about how we had spent the evening drinking previous to the attack. The problem was that whenever I tried to expand on Cornelius's good character, his virtues, and to emphasize that, drunk or sober, he was not the sort of man who could have carried out such a brutal rape, they cut me off. Even Cornelius's lawyer never really let me get very far. As a policeman, of course, I was used to giving evidence for the prosecution, not for the defense, but this time the limitations galled me.

Evelyn Fowler was a revelation. In court, she looked a lot more demure than she ever had in the Nag's Head: no dirndl skirts, bolero dresses or Veronica Lake hairstyles for Evelyn today, only a plain Utility dress and her hair tied loosely behind her neck.

Lieutenant Clawson proceeded gently at first, as if afraid to stir up her feelings and memories of the events, but I guessed that his apparent sympathy was merely an act for the court. When he got to the point, he made it brutally and efficiently.

"What were you doing in the park that night, Miss Fowler?" he asked.

"I was walking home from a dance," she said. "My friends wanted to stay, but I had to get up early for work. It's a shortcut."

"And what happened?"

"Someone grabbed me and threw me to the ground. He . . . he punched me and tore my clothing off."

"And he raped you. Is that correct?"

Evelyn looked down at the handbag clasped on her knees. "Yes," she whispered. "He raped me."

"Miss Fowler, do you see the man who raped you and beat you here in this courtroom today?"

"I do," she said.

"Can you please point him out to the court?"

"That's him," she said, pointing at Cornelius without a moment's hesitation. "The accused. That's the man who raped me."

"You have no doubt?"

"Not a shred," said Evelyn, her lips set in a determined line. "That's him."

And did Cornelius's lawyer attack her evidence? Not a bit of it. Did he challenge her character and question how she had arrived at her identification? Not at all. I knew that Evelyn hated and feared colored people, and that she had been well versed in this by her beau, GI Jim, but did the lawyer ask her about her feelings toward Negroes? No, he didn't.

I was willing to bet, for a start, that Evelyn hadn't picked Cornelius out of a lineup of similar physical types, and that as far as she was concerned one Negro looked very much like another. And Cornelius did have a scratch on his face, after all. I wouldn't even have been surprised if she had been told in advance that a charm from his bracelet had been found right beside her arm after the attack. She had told me that at one point she had sensed two men. Couldn't one of them have been Cornelius fighting off her attacker? But neither lawyer asked about that.

All in all, it was a disappointing affair, one-sided and sloppy in the extreme. I spent the entire time on the edge of my seat biting my tongue. On several occasions I almost spoke out, but knew they would only expel me from the courtroom if I did so. I could only pray for Cornelius now, and I wasn't much of a believer in prayer.

After a short recess for lunch, which I spent smoking and trying, unsuccessfully, to gain access to Cornelius's lawyer, there was little else to be done. Dr. Harris gave evidence about Evelyn's condition after the attack, not forgetting to mention that the small piece of skin found under one of her fingernails was black.

In the end, it was an easy decision. Pfc. Cornelius Jubb admitted to being in Brimley Park on the night in question, around the exact time the attack occurred. It was a particularly brutal attack, and Cornelius and Evelyn, while they might have recognized each other in passing, had no earlier acquaintance, which might have earned the court's leniency. A charm from a bracelet the accused was known to wear habitually was found at the scene. He had a scratch on his face and she had black skin under her fingernail. His defense—that he had seen a woman in trouble and come to her rescue—was too little, too late. They might as well have added that he was colored, but they didn't go that far.

But when the verdict finally came, it took the breath out of me: Pfc. Cornelius Jubb was found guilty of rape and was sentenced to be hanged by the neck until dead.

That was one little detail I had forgotten, and I cursed myself for it: Under U.S. Article of War 92, rape was a crime punishable by life imprisonment or death, which is not the case under British law. They wanted to make an example of Cornelius, so they went for the death penalty, and there wasn't a damn thing I could do about it. In a way, I had got him into this, through my bloody devotion to my job, to duty. I could have hidden the monkey charm. I knew Cornelius wasn't a rapist, no matter what happened in Brimley Park that night. But no, I had to do the right thing. And the right thing was going to get Cornelius Jubb hanged.

They let me see Cornelius the night before his execution. He seemed comfortable enough in his tiny cell, and he assured me that he had been well treated. In the dim light of a grille-covered bulb, the small windows covered by blackout curtains, we smoked Luckies and talked for the last time.

"What really happened that night, Cornelius?" I asked him. "You didn't touch that girl, did you?"

He said nothing for a moment, just sucked in some smoke and blew it out in a long plume.

"I know you didn't," I went on. "Tell me."

Finally, he looked at me, the whites of his eyes big and round. "It was a good night," he said. "One of the best. I enjoyed our talk, the whiskey. I always enjoyed our talks. You treated me like a human being."

I said nothing. I could think of nothing to say.

"It was a fine night outside. Hot and humid. It reminded me a bit of home, I suppose, of Louisiana, and I was walking along thinking about all those years ago when I was a kid fishing off the levee, hooking the bracelet. When I got to the park I heard some sounds, stifled, as if someone was being gagged. It was dark, but I could make out two figures struggling, one on top of the other. I'm not a fool. I knew what was happening. When I got closer I could see that he was . . . you know, thrusting himself in her and beating her face. I grabbed him and tried to drag him off but it took all my strength. The girl was nearly unconscious by then, but she managed to lash out and give me that scratch. Finally I pulled him loose and he ran off into the night." Cornelius shrugged. "Then I went back to the base."

"Did you recognize him?" I asked.

For a moment he didn't answer, just carried on smoking, that faraway look in his eyes.

"Yes," he said finally. "I recognized him."

"Then why the hell didn't you say so?"

"What would have been the point?"

"The truth, Cornelius, the truth."

Cornelius smiled. "Frank, my friend. You have the white man's trust in the truth. It's not quite the same for me."

"But surely they would have investigated your claim?"

"Perhaps. But the man who did it is a black man, like me. Only he's a really bad man. People are scared of him. The morning after it happened, even before you came to see me, he made it clear that he wasn't going to take the blame, that if I tried to accuse him, everyone in his hut would swear he was back on base when the attack took place."

"What about the guards on the gate?"

"They can't tell us apart. Besides, they don't even pay attention. They just sit in their gatehouse playing cards."

"So he's just going to let you die instead of him?"

Cornelius shrugged. "Well, I don't imagine he's any too keen on dying himself. Would you be? It doesn't matter anyway. What happens to him. That's between him and God."

"Or the devil."

Cornelius looked at me, a hint of the old smile in the turn of his lips. "Or the devil. But even if he hadn't managed to get it all fixed, they wouldn't have believed me anyway. They'd have simply thought it was another trick, another desperate lie, that the two of us darkies were in it together. They had all the evidence they needed, then I came up with some crazy story about trying to save the girl. What would you think?"

"I know you wouldn't do what they accused you of."

"But they don't know me. To them I'm just another no-good nigger. It's the sort of thing we do. If I'd given his name, it would have been just one more nigger trying to lie his way out of his just desserts by pointing the finger at another." Cornelius shook his head. "No, my friend, there's no way out for me."

He lifted up his sleeve. "At least I got my bracelet fixed and they let me have it back," he said. "No longer evidence, I guess." Then he unfastened the clasp and handed it to me. "I want you to have it," he said. "I know I said it was going to be for my girl, but I never did find her. Now I'd like my friend to take it."

I looked at the bracelet resting in his palm. I didn't really want it, not after everything that had happened, but I couldn't refuse. I picked it up, feeling an odd sort of tingle in my fingers as I did so, and thanked him for it.

That was the last time I saw Cornelius Jubb. The morning they hanged him, I walked and walked the length and breadth of the city, feeling as if I was the one living in a foreign country, and when I came to the biggest bomb site in the city center, I took out Cornelius's charm bracelet and threw it as far as I could into the rubble.

The Magic of Your Touch

*Above all was the sense of hearing acute. I heard all things in the heaven
and in the earth. I heard many things in hell.*
　　　　　—Edgar Allan Poe, "The Tell-Tale Heart"

*Heard melodies are sweet, but those unheard
Are sweeter.*
　　　　　—John Keats, "Ode to a Grecian Urn"

One night, many years ago, I found myself wandering in an unfamiliar part of the city. The river looked like an oil slick twisting
languidly in the cold moonlight, and on the opposite bank the
towering metal skeletons of factories and cranes gleamed silver. Steam
hissed from tubes, formed abstract shapes in the air and faded into the
night. Every now and then a gush of orange flame leaped into the sky
from a funnel-shaped chimney.

I was lost, I knew now. The bar where I had played my last gig was
miles behind me, and the path I had taken was crooked and dark. The
river lay to my right, and to the left, across the narrow, cobbled street,
tall empty warehouses loomed over me, all crumbling, soot-covered
bricks and caved-in roofs. Through the broken windows small fires
burned, and I fancied I could see ragged figures bent over the flames
for warmth. Ahead of me, just beyond the crossroads, the path continued into a monstrous junkyard, where the rusted hulks of cars and
piles of scrap metal towered over me.

Out of nowhere, it seemed, I began to hear snatches of melody: a
light, romantic, jazzy air underpinned by wondrous, heartrending
chords, some of which I could swear I had never heard before. I stopped
in my tracks and tried to discern where the music was coming from. It
was a piano, no doubt about that, and though it was slightly out of tune
that didn't diminish the power of the melody or the skill of the player. I
wanted desperately to find him, to get closer to the music.

I walked between mountains of scrap metal, sure I was getting closer, then, down a narrow side path, I saw the glow of a brazier and heard the music more clearly than I had before. If anything, it had even more magic than when I heard it from a distance. More than that, it had the potential to make my fortune. Heart pounding, I headed toward the light.

What I found there was a wizened old black man sitting at a beat-up honky-tonk piano. When he saw me, he stopped playing and looked over at me. The glow of the brazier reflected in his eyes, which seemed to flicker and dance with flames.

"That's a beautiful piece of music," I said. "Did you write it yourself?"

"I don't write nothing," he said. "The music just comes out of me."

"And this just came out of you?"

"Yessir," he said. "Just this very moment."

I might lack the creativity, the essential spark of genius, but when it comes to technical matters I'm hard to beat. I'm a classically trained musician who happened to choose to play jazz, and already this miraculous piece of music was fixed in my memory. If I closed my eyes I could even see it written and printed on a sheet. And if I let my imagination run free, I could see the sheets flying off the shelves of the music shop and records whizzing out of the racks. This was the stuff that standards were made of.

"So you're the only one who's heard it, apart from me?"

"I guess so," he said, the reflected flames dancing in his eyes.

I looked around. The piles of scrap rose on all sides, obscuring the rest of the world, and once he had stopped playing I could hear nothing but the hissing of the steam from the factories across the river. We were quite alone, me and this poor, shrunken black man. I complimented him again on his genius and went on my way. When I got behind him, he started playing again. I listened to the tune one more time, burning it into my memory so there could be no mistake. Then I picked up an iron bar from the pile of scrap and hit him hard on the back of his head.

I heard the skull crack like a nut and saw the blood splash on the ivory keys of the old piano. I made sure he was dead, then I dragged his body off the path, piled rusty metal over it, and left him there.

Now there was no one to stop me, no one to claim plagiarism, I had to get back to the hotel and write down the music before I lost it. As luck would have it, at the other side of the junkyard, past another set of crossroads, was a wide boulevard lined with a few run-down shops and low-life bars. There wasn't much traffic, and I was beginning to get nervous about the neighborhood, but after ten minutes I saw a cab with its light on coming up the road and waved it down. The cabbie stopped, and twenty minutes later I was back in my hotel room, the red neon of the strip club across the street flashing through the flimsy, moth-eaten curtains, as I furiously scribbled the notes and chords etched in my memory on to the lined music paper.

I was right about the music, and what's more, nobody even questioned that I had written it, despite the fact that I had never composed a piece of any significance in my entire life. After all, what else did Charlie Chaplin write other than "Smile," or Paul Anka besides "My Way"? Plenty, of course, but do you remember anything else? I thought not. Besides, I suppose I was well enough known as a competent jazz pianist in certain circles, so people just assumed I had suddenly been smitten by the muse one day.

I called the tune "The Magic of Your Touch," and it became a staple of the jazz repertoire, from big bands to small combos. Arrangements proliferated, and one of the band members, who fancied himself a poet, added lyrics to the melody. That was when we really struck the big time. Billie Holiday recorded it, then Frank Sinatra, Tony Bennett, Peggy Lee, Mel Tormé, Ella Fitzgerald. Suddenly it seemed that no one could get enough of "The Magic of Your Touch," and the big bucks rolled in.

I hardly need say that the sudden wealth and success brought about an immense change in my lifestyle. Instead of fleabag hotels and two-bit whores, it was penthouse suites and high-class call girls all the way. I continued to play with the sextet, of course, but we hired a vocalist and instead of sleazy bars we played halls and big-name clubs: The Blue Note, the Village Vanguard, Birdland and the rest. We even got a recording contract, and people bought our records by the thousands.

"The Magic of Your Touch" brought us all this, and more. Hollywood beckoned, a jazz film set in Paris, and off we went. Ah, those foxy little mademoiselles! Then came the world tour: Europe, Asia, Australia, South Africa, Brazil. They all wanted to hear the band named after the man who wrote "The Magic of Your Touch."

I can't say that I *never* gave another thought to the wizened old black man playing his honky-tonk piano beside the brazier. Many times, I even dreamed about that night and what I did there, on instinct, without thinking, and woke up in a cold sweat, my heart pounding. Many's the time I thought I saw the old man's flame-reflecting eyes in a crowd, or down an alley. But nobody ever found his body, or if they did, it never made the news. The years passed, and I believed that I was home and dry. Until, that is, little by little, things started to go wrong.

I have always been of a fairly nervous disposition—highly strung, my parents used to say, blaming it on my musical talent, or vice versa. Whiskey helped, and sometimes I also turned to pills, mostly tranquilizers and barbiturates or 'ludes, to take the edge off things. So imagine my horror when we were halfway through a concert at Massey Hall, in my hometown of Toronto, playing "Solitude," and I found my left hand falling into the familiar chord patterns of "The Magic of Your Touch," my right hand picking out the melody.

Of course, the audience cheered wildly at first, thinking it some form of playful acknowledgment, a cheeky little musical quotation or segue. But I couldn't stop. It was as if I was a mere puppet, and some other force was directing my movements. No matter what tune we started after that, all my hands would play was "The Magic of Your Touch." In the end I felt a panic attack coming on—I'd had them before—and, pale and shaking, numb and dizzy, I had to leave the stage. The audience clapped, but the other band members looked concerned.

Afterward, in the dressing room, Ed, our stand-up bass player, approached me. I had just downed a handful of Valium and I was waiting for the soothing effect of the pills to kick in.

"What is it, man?" he asked. "What the hell happened out there?"

I shook my head. "I don't know," I told him. "I couldn't help myself."

"Couldn't help yourself? What do you mean by that?"

"The song, Ed. It's like the song took me over. It was weird, scary. I've never experienced anything like that before."

Ed looked at me as if I were insane, the first of many such looks I got before I stopped even bothering trying to tell people what was happening to me. Because that incident at Massey Hall was, I soon discovered, only the beginning.

Playing in the band was out of the question from that night on. Whenever my hands got near a piano, they started to play "The Magic of Your Touch." The boys took it with good grace and soon found a replacement who was, in all honesty, easily as good a pianist as I was, if not better, and they carried on touring under the same name. I don't really think anyone missed me very much. My retirement from performing for "health reasons" was announced, and I imagine people assumed that life on the road just got too much for someone of my highly strung temperament. The press reported that I had had a "minor nervous breakdown," the money continued to roll in, and life went on as normal. Almost.

After the Toronto concert, I developed an annoying ringing in my ears—tinnitus, I believe it's called—and it drove me up the wall with its sheer relentlessness. But worse than that, one night when I went to bed I heard as clear as a bell, louder than the ringing, the opening chords of "The Magic of Your Touch," as if someone were playing a piano inside my head. It went on until the entire song was finished, then started again at the beginning. It was only after swallowing twice my regular nightly dose of Nembutal that I managed to drift into a comalike stupor and, more important, into something approaching blessed silence. But even then I could still hear faint strains in the distance, like ripples in still water, and when I awoke, the ringing and the music were still there, louder than ever.

No matter what I did, I couldn't get the song out of my head. Every minute of every day and every night it played, over and over again in a continuous loop tape. The pills helped up to a point, but I found my night's sleep shrinking from four hours to three to two, then one, if I was lucky. Only with great difficulty could I concentrate on anything. No amount of external noise could overcome the music in my head. I couldn't hold intelligent conversations. People shunned me, crossed the street when they saw me coming. I started muttering to myself, putting my hands over my ears, but that only served to trap the sound inside and make it louder.

One day in my wanderings, I found myself back in the part of the city where it all began, and I retraced my steps as best I could remember them. I don't know what I had in mind, only that this was where the whole thing had started, so perhaps it would end here, too. I don't know what I expected to find. I suppose I was beyond rational thought.

Soon, the landscape became a familiar one of decaying ware-houses, oily river, and factories venting steam and belching fire. I saw the junkyard looming ahead beyond the crossroads and followed the path through the towers of scrap metal, rusty cars, engine blocks, tires, axles and chrome fenders. Then I heard it again. Uncertain at first, hardly willing to believe my ears, I paused. But sure enough, there it was: "The Magic of Your Touch" played on an out-of-tune honky-tonk piano, the music outside perfectly matching the loop tape in my head.

I could see the brazier now, a patch of light at the end of the narrow path between the columns, and when I approached, the wizened old black man looked up from his keyboard with fire dancing in his eyes. Then I saw what I should have seen in the first place. The flames weren't reflections of the brazier's glow. They were *inside* his head, the way the music was inside mine.

He didn't stop playing, didn't miss a note.

"I thought I'd killed you," I said.

"Lots of folk make that mistake," he replied.

"Who are you?"

"Who do you think I am?"

"I don't know."

"You took my song."

"I'm sorry. I don't know what got into me."

"No matter. Now it's taken you."

"I can't get it out of my head. It's driving me insane. What can I do?"

"Only one thing you can do, and you know what that is. Then your soul come home to me, where it belong."

I shook my head and backed away. "No!" I cried. "I'm dreaming. I must be dreaming. This can't be real."

But I heard his laughter echoing among the towers of scrap as I ran, hands over my ears, the insufferable melody I had come to detest as much as I had once loved it now going around and around for the millionth time in my head, gaining in volume, just a fraction of a decibel each time, and I knew he was right.

When I got back to my hotel room, I took out paper and pen. You have no idea what a struggle it was to write this brief account with the music loud, relentless, precise and eternal inside my head, what an effort it cost me just to wring out these few words. But I must leave some kind of record. I can't bear the thought of everyone believing I was mad. I may be desperate. I may be beyond reason. But I am not mad. It happened exactly the way I told it.

Now, like a man who can't get rid of hiccups might contemplate slitting his throat, I have only one thought in mind. The pills are on the table and I'm drinking whiskey, waiting for the end. He said my soul would go home to him, where it belongs—a bargain I now know I made when I stole his song—and that terrifies me. But it can't be worse than this eternal repetition, driving out all human thought and feeling. It can't be. I'll have another slug of whiskey and another handful of pills, then I'm sure, soon, the blessed silence will come. *Amen.*

The Eastvale Ladies' Poker Circle

An Inspector Banks Story

The man was very dead. Even Dr. Glendenning, the Home Office pathologist, who hesitated to pronounce death even when a victim was chopped into little pieces, admitted that the man was very dead. He also speculated as to time of death—another rarity—which he placed at between 7:00 P.M. and 10:00 P.M. that same evening.

All this took place in the spacious study of the Vancalms' detached eighteenth-century manor house on the western fringe of Eastvale's chic Dale Hill area, sometime after midnight. The man lying on the carpet was Victor Vancalm, a wealthy local businessman, and a large bloodstain shaped like South America had spread from his skull and ruined the cream shag carpet.

The stain came from a massive head wound, which had been inflicted with enough force to splinter the cranium and drive several sharp shards of bone into the soft tissue of Victor Vancalm's brain. Blood spatter on the flocked wallpaper and on other areas of the carpet testified as to the power of the blow. A brass-handled poker lay on the carpet not far from the body, surrounded by a red halo, as if it were giving off heat.

The rest of the study was in just the sort of mess Detective Chief Inspector Alan Banks would have expected after someone had been pulling books from shelves and overturning furniture looking for valuables. From one wall, a gilt-framed painting of the Blessing of the Innocents had been removed and dumped on the floor, exposing a small safe, the door of which hung open. It was empty. Someone had smashed the computer monitor, which sat on a desk by the window, and emptied the contents of the drawers on the floor. The Scenes-of-Crime officers had cordoned off the study, from which they zealously repelled all comers, even Banks, who stood at the door gazing in, looking rather forlorn, a child not invited to the party.

In the living room across the hall, discreetly out of the sight line of her husband's body, Denise Vancalm sat on the sofa sniffling into a soggy tissue. Music played faintly in the background, the andante movement from Schubert's "Rosamunde" quartet, Banks noted as he returned to the room. Chandeliers blazed in the high-ceilinged hall, and outside in the night, police officers were going up and down the street waking up neighbors and questioning them.

The problem was that Hill Crest was one of those expensive streets where the houses were not exactly cheek by jowl as in the poorer neighborhoods, and some of them had high walls and gates. Hardly conducive to keeping an eye on your neighbor. Hill Crest was aptly named, Banks thought. It stood at the crest of a hill and looked out west over the river Swain, along the meandering valley where the hillsides of the dale rose steeper and steeper as far as the eye could see. On a clear day you could see the bare limestone outcrops of Crow Scar, like a skeleton's teeth grinning in the distance. The skull beneath the skin.

But this wasn't a clear day. It was a foggy night in November, not long after Bonfire Night, and the police officers outside blew plumes of mist as they came and went. Even inside the house it wasn't that warm, Banks thought, and he hadn't taken his overcoat off.

"I'm very sorry, Mrs. Vancalm," he said, sitting in an armchair opposite her, "but I do have to go over this with you again. I know you talked to the first officer on the scene, but—"

"I quite understand," said Denise Vancalm, crumpling her tissue and dropping it on top of the copy of *Card Player* that lay on the glass coffee table. The magazine looked out of place to Banks, who had been expecting something more along the lines of *Horse and Hound* or *Country Life*. But each to her own. He knew nothing about Victor and Denise Vancalm; he didn't move in those kinds of circles.

"You say you arrived home at what time?" Banks asked.

"Half past eleven. Perhaps a few minutes after."

"And you found your husband . . ."

"I found Victor dead on the study floor, just as you saw him when you arrived."

"Did you touch anything?"

"Good Lord, no."

"What did you do first?"

A V formed between her eyes. "I . . . I slumped against the wall. It was as if all the air had been forced out of me. I might have screamed, cried out, I really can't remember." She held out her hand. "I bit my knuckle. See."

Banks saw. It was a slender, pale hand with tapered fingers. The hands of an artist. She was an attractive woman in her late thirties, with tousled ash-blond hair falling over her shoulders, framing a heart-shaped face, perfect makeup ravaged by tears and grief. Her clothes were expensive casual, black trousers of some clinging, silky material, a burgundy blouse tucked in at the waist. A waft of delicate and expensive perfume emanated from her whenever she moved. "And then?"

"I called the police from the hall telephone."

"Not an ambulance?"

She shook her head impatiently. "I dialed 999. I can't remember what I said. I might have asked for all of them."

She hadn't, Banks knew. She had asked for the police, said there'd been a murder, and the emergency operator had dispatched an ambulance. Banks could see what Mrs. Vancalm meant. Even someone who has never watched *Taggart* or *Lewis* would be hard-pressed to miss a murder scene like the one in the study, a body more obviously *dead* than Victor Vancalm's. But people panic and call an ambulance anyway. Denise Vancalm hadn't.

"What did you do next?" Banks asked.

"I don't know. I suppose I just sat down to wait."

"And then?"

"Nothing. People started to arrive very quickly. The paramedics.

A police patrol car. Your assistant. Those crime scene people. You must know how long it took. I'm afraid I lost all sense of time. I was in a daze."

"That's understandable," said Banks. He also knew that it had taken seven minutes from the emergency phone call to the arrival of the first patrol car. A good response time, especially given the weather. "How many people knew about the wall safe?" he asked.

Denise Vancalm shrugged. "I don't know. Victor always kept the key in his pocket, with all his keys. I suppose Colin must have known. Anyone else who visited the house, really."

"Colin?"

"Colin Whitman. Victor's business partner."

Banks paused and made a note. "Where had you been all evening?" he asked.

"Me? Gabriella Mountjoy's house, on Castle Terrace."

Banks knew the street. Expensive, in the town center, it commanded superb views of Eastvale Castle, rumored, like so many others in the Dales, to have provided a brief home for Mary Queen of Scots. He estimated it was probably a fifteen- or twenty-minute drive from Hill Crest, depending on the traffic.

"What were you doing there? Book club or something?"

She gave Banks a cool glance. "The Eastvale Ladies' Poker Circle. It was Gabriella's *turn*."

"Poker?"

"Yes, hadn't you heard, Chief Inspector? It's become quite popular these days, especially among women. Texas Hold 'Em."

"I've heard of it," said Banks, not much of a card player himself.

"Four or five of us get together once a month for dinner, drinks and a few games. As I said, it was Gabriella's turn to host us this time."

"How many of you were there tonight?"

She raised an eyebrow at the question but said, "Five. Gabriella, me, Natasha Goldwell, Evangeline White and Heather Murchison. I'll give you their addresses if you like."

"Please," said Banks.

Denise Vancalm picked up her handbag and took out a sleek PalmPilot encased in tan leather. She read out the names and addresses. "Is that all?" she asked. "I'm tired. I . . ."

"Nearly finished," said Banks. "What time did you arrive at Ms. Mountjoy's house?"

"I went there straight from the office—well, I met Natasha in the Old Oak after work for a drink first, then I drove her over to Gabriella's. It's not far, I know, but I had the car with me for work anyway."

The Old Oak was a trendy pub off the market square. Banks knew it but never drank there. "What kind of car do you drive?" he asked.

"A Mercedes cabriolet. Red."

Hardly inconspicuous, Banks thought. "Where was your husband?"

"He'd been away on a business meeting. Berlin. He was due back from the airport about half past seven?"

"Did you see him?"

"I haven't seen him since last week. Look, Chief Inspector, I've had a terrible shock and I'm very tired. Do you think . . . ?"

"Of course," said Banks. He had wanted to get as many of the preliminaries out of the way as possible—and whether she knew it or not, the spouse was usually the first suspect in a domestic murder—but he didn't want to appear as if he were grilling Denise Vancalm. "Is there someone you can go to, or would you like me to—"

She shook her head. "There are plenty of people I could go to, but believe it or not, I just want to be by myself."

"You don't . . . I mean, are there any children?"

"No." She paused. "Thank God."

"Right. Well, you clearly can't stay here." It was true. Banks had checked out the house, and whoever had killed Victor Vancalm and ransacked the study had also been through the master bedroom, separating the expensive jewelry from the cheap—not that there was much of the latter—and even going so far as to cut up several of Denise Vancalm's most elegant dresses and strew them over the bed. It could take days to process the scene.

"I realize that," she said. "There's a small hotel just off the market square, the Jedburgh. My husband often suggests it for clients when they happen to be visiting town."

"I can take you there," said Banks.

She regarded him coolly with moist, steady blue eyes. "Yes," she said. "Thank you. I probably shouldn't be driving. May I collect a few things? My nightdress? Toothbrush?"

Banks went in to the hallway and saw Detective Constable Winsome Jackman coming through the front door. "Winsome," he said. "Mrs. Vancalm will be spending the night at the Jedburgh Hotel. Will you accompany her to her room while she gathers a few essentials?"

Winsome raised her eyes in a "Why me?" expression.

Banks whispered, certain he was out of Mrs. Vancalm's earshot, "And make sure there's someone posted outside the Jedburgh Hotel all night."

"Yes, sir," said Winsome.

A short while later, as Banks followed Denise Vancalm out into the chilly night, where his Porsche stood waiting, he again reminded himself why he was taking such precautions and feeling so many reservations in the face of the poor bereaved wife. By the looks of it, Victor Vancalm had disturbed a burglar, who might have been still in the building. Confronted with a dead husband, a wrecked den, and a big empty house, most people would have run for the hills screaming, but Denise Vancalm, after the immediate shock had worn off, had dialed 999 and sat down to wait for the police.

By late morning the next day, a weak gray sun cut through the early mist and the sky turned the color of Victor Vancalm's corpse spread out on Dr. Glendenning's postmortem table. Banks stood on the steps on Eastvale General Infirmary wishing he still smoked. No matter how many postmortems he attended, he could never get used to them, especially just after a late breakfast. It was something to do with the neatness and precision of the gleaming tools and the scientific process contrasted with the ugly slop of stomach contents and the slithery lump of liver or kidneys. As far as stomach contents were concerned, Victor Vancalm's last meal had consisted of currywurst, a German delicacy available from any number of Berlin street vendors.

There had been no surprises. Vancalm had been in general good health and the cause of death, barring any googlies from toxicology, was most certainly the head wound. The only interesting piece of news was that Vancalm's pockets had been emptied. Wallet. Keys. Pen. All gone. In Banks's experience, burglars didn't usually rob the persons of anyone they happened to bump into on a job. They didn't usually bump into people, for that matter; kids on drugs aside, burglars were generally so careful and elusive one might think them quite shy creatures. They didn't usually bump people off either.

Even after the postmortem, Dr. Glendenning stuck by his estimate of time of death: between seven and ten. If Mrs. Vancalm had gone straight from work to the Old Oak and from there to the poker evening with Natasha Goldwell, and if she had not arrived home until eleven thirty, then she couldn't have murdered her husband. Banks would still check her alibi with the rest of the poker crowd. It was a job for a detective constable, but he found he was curious about this group of wealthy and powerful women who got together once a month to play Texas Hold 'Em. Did they wear shades, smoke cigars and swear? Perhaps more to the point, could they look you straight in the eye and lie like a politician?

Banks took a deep breath of fresh air and looked at his watch. It was time to meet DI Annie Cabbot for lunch at the Queen's Arms, though whatever appetite he might have had had quite vanished down the drain of the autopsy table plug hole, along with Victor Vancalm's bodily fluids.

It was lunchtime in the Queen's Arms and the place was bustling with clerks and secretaries from the solicitors' and estate agents' offices around the market square, along with the usual retirees at the bar and terminally unemployed kids on the pool tables and slot machines. The smoke was thick and the language almost as bad. Banks found that he could hardly wait until the following July, when smoking was to be banned in all the pubs in England. He had never suspected he would feel that way, and a few years ago he wouldn't have. Now, though, the smoke was just an irritant, and the people who smoked seemed like throwbacks to another era. Banks still suffered the occasional craving, which reminded him what it had been like, but they were becoming few and far between.

Banks and Annie managed to find themselves a free table wedged between the door to the Gents and the slot machines, where Annie sipped a Britvic Orange and nibbled a cheese roll, while Banks nursed a half of Black Sheep bitter and worked on his chicken in a basket.

"So how was the redoubtable Gabriella Mountjoy?" Banks asked, when the person playing the slot machine beside them cursed and gave up.

"She seemed very nice, really," said Annie. "Not at all what I expected."

"What did you expect?"

"Oh, you know, some upper-class twit with a braying laugh and horsey teeth."

"But?"

"Well, her teeth are actually quite nice. Expensive, like her clothes. She seems every inch the thoroughly modern woman."

"What does that mean?"

"Oh, really, Alan, you're seriously out of touch."

"With the thoroughly modern woman? Tell me about her. It's not for want of trying."

"First there's the career," Annie said. "Gabriella's a book designer for a big London publisher. Works from home a lot."

"Impressive," said Banks.

"And then there's the house. Cottage, really, and only a semi at that. It's small, but the view must be worth a million quid."

"Does she live alone?"

"As far as I can gather. There's a boyfriend. A musician. He travels a lot. It suits them both perfectly."

"Maybe that's my problem with the modern woman," Banks said. "I don't travel enough. I'm always there when she needs me. Boring."

"Tell Sandra that."

Banks winced. "Touché."

"I'm sorry," said Annie. "That wasn't very nice of me."

"It's OK. Still a bit tender, that's all. That'll serve me right for being so flippant. Go on."

Annie finished her roll first. "Nothing to add, really. She swears blind that Mrs. Vancalm was there all evening. Natasha Goldwell was at the cottage, too, when I called, and she confirmed it. Said they arrived together about seven thirty after a quick drink and Mrs. Vancalm dropped her off at home—it's on her way—sometime after eleven."

"Well," said Banks, "it's not as if we expected otherwise."

"I just had a word with Winsome," Annie went on, "and she told me that the other two say exactly the same thing about the poker evening. Denise Vancalm's alibi is watertight."

"God help me, but I've never liked watertight alibis," said Banks.

"That's because you're contrary."

"Is it? I thought it was my suspicious nature, my detective's instinct, my love of a challenge."

"Pull the other one."

"Whatever it is, it seems as if we'll have to start looking elsewhere. You've checked out our list of local troublemakers?"

"Winsome has. The only possibility at all is Windows Fennester. He'd know all about wall safes."

"He's out?"

"Been out three weeks now. Living back on the East Side Estate with Shania Longbottom and her two kids. Thing is, according to Winsome, he's got a pretty good alibi, too—in the pub with his mates."

"And whatever he is, he's not a killer."

"Not as far as we know."

"The lads have also been out doing a house to house in Denise Vancalm's neighborhood," Banks said.

"And?"

"Someone heard and glimpsed a car near the house after dark. Couldn't say what make. A dark one."

"Nothing fancy like Mrs. Vancalm's red sports car, then?"

"No," said Banks. "Your standard Japanese hatchback, by the sound of it. And several witnesses have told us that Mrs. Vancalm's Cabriolet was parked outside Gabriella Mountjoy's house until after eleven."

"One woman did tell us that Denise Vancalm had a visitor the day before the murder."

Banks's ears pricked up. "A man?"

"No, a woman. During the day."

"So she wasn't at work. I wonder why?"

"From the description we got, it sounds very much like Natasha Goldwell."

"Well," said Banks, disappointed. "There's nothing odd about that. They're good friends. Must have been a coffee morning or something."

"Afternoon."

"Coffee afternoon, then. It still takes us back to square one." Banks finished his drink. Someone else came to play the slot machine and the noise started up again. "Nothing in the way of a motive."

"Not so far," said Annie. "Look, I don't want you to make too much of this, but I thought there *was* something a bit odd about Natasha Goldwell."

"Odd?"

"Well, I mean, she was convincing enough. They went to the Old Oak, where Natasha had a gin and tonic and Denise had a Campari and soda, chatted about their husbands briefly—Natasha's is a civil engineer—talked a bit about some online poker game they play regularly."

"These women are really keen, then?"

"I got the impression that Natasha was. She's the main online player. Gabriella strikes me as someone who more likes the idea of it, you know, cracking a male bastion."

"Better than cracking other male parts."

"But Natasha was more into the technical talk. It was way over my head. And the impression I got was that one of them is really involved in tournaments and all that stuff. She's even been to Las Vegas to play."

"Which one would that be?"

"Evangeline White."

"Do they play for money?"

"Of course. It's no fun if you don't have a little something riding on it, Gabriella told me. I didn't get the impression that huge fortunes changed hands, but enough to make it interesting."

"But it was nothing to do with their husbands?"

"No. The men were very much excluded."

"And what about Denise Vancalm herself?"

"I definitely got the impression that she was keen, a pretty good player, but perhaps in it more for the social aspects. You know, a chance to get together without the menfolk, have a few drinks and talk girl talk, and perhaps even do a bit of business. I mean, they're all top echelon. Almost all. Natasha runs a computer software solutions company, online security and whatnot, Evangeline White owns an upmarket travel agency—Sahara Desert holidays and roughing it in Woolawoola—and Heather Murchison . . . well, you know her."

Banks did. Heather Murchison was a familiar face and personality on the local television news, and her blond looks, buxom figure, and husky Morningside accent caused many a red-blooded male to be much more informed about local matters than previously.

"And Denise Vancalm herself is a fund-raiser and organizer of charity events," Annie went on. "She does a lot of work for hospitals and children's charities in particular."

"Five successful, attractive women," said Banks, "all in their late thirties or early forties. All, or most of them, married to or hooked up with successful, attractive men. Sounds like a recipe for disaster. Any hints of clandestine goings-on? You know, musical beds, wife swapping, that sort of thing."

"Wife swapping?" said Annie, laughing. "You really must leave the sixties behind."

"I'm sure people still do it. There was that film by Kubrick. Must have been the nineties at least."

"*Eyes Wide Shut*," said Annie. "Even Tom Cruise couldn't save that one. Yes, it was the nineties, orgies and such like. But wife swapping . . . *swinging* . . ." She shook her head and laughed again.

"Okay, I get your point," said Banks. "No need to hammer it home. I have about as much knowledge about what goes on in suburban bedrooms as I do about the thoroughly modern woman. But what I'm saying is that there might have been rivalries among these women or their husbands, liaisons—if that's not too outdated a word—affairs. Jealousy can be a powerful motive."

"Why look beyond the facts here?" said Annie. "Victor Vancalm came home and surprised a burglar, one who was somehow familiar with the layout of his house, the safe. Perhaps he decided to take the burglar on, and for his efforts he got bashed on the head with a poker. I mean, the side window had been broken from the outside."

"Yes, but what about the security system?"

"Turned off."

"So our would-be burglar would have to know how to do that, too?"

"I'm not saying it was kids, or an amateur. Any burglar worth his salt can find his way around a domestic security system."

"True enough, but when you add it all up, a little inside knowledge goes a long way. Anyway, you said there was something odd about Natasha Goldwell?"

"Yes. It was nothing, really, but there was just something a bit . . . offhand . . . about her responses. I mean, I know it was very recent, so she'd hardly have to rack her brains to remember, but it all seemed just a bit too handy, a bit too pat."

"As if she'd learned it by rote?"

"Maybe. It's something to bear in mind, at any rate." Annie reached for her glass. "You know," she said, "it's not a bad idea, this ladies' poker circle. I wouldn't mind being involved in something like that myself."

"Start one, then."

"Maybe I will. Winsome might be interested. Maybe even Superintendent Gervaise. We could get a police ladies' poker circle together."

"I can't see the chief constable approving. You know what he feels about gambling and the road to corruption."

"Still," said Annie, "I think it's sort of cool. Anyway, what next?"

"We'll have another word with Natasha Goldwell, see what she was doing at Denise Vancalm's the day before the murder, but first, I think we'll go and have a little chat with Colin Whitman, Mr. Vancalm's business partner."

The offices of the Vancalm-Whitman public relations company were above a wine shop on a side street off the main hill. Banks parked up by The Stray, and he and Annie walked down past Betty's toward the spa, the wind blowing rain against them. "If the timing's right," Banks said, "I'll take you to Betty's after the interview."

"You're on," said Annie.

A receptionist greeted them in the first office. The entire floor looked as if it had been renovated recently, the bare brick look with a few contemporary paintings stuck up here and there to liven the monotony. There was also a smell of freshly cut wood. The phone kept ringing, and between calls, the receptionist, who bore the name tag "Megan," pointed along a corridor and told them Mr. Whitman would see them. They knocked on the door and entered the spacious office, which looked over the street. It wasn't much of a view. The street was so narrow you could practically shake hands with the bloke sitting at the desk in the window of the building opposite. But if you glanced a bit to the left, you could see beyond the slate roofs to the hint of green countryside beyond.

"I wasn't sure what to do when I heard the news," said Whitman after they had all made themselves comfortable. "Open the office, close for the day. In the end I decided this is what Victor would have wanted, so we're soldiering on." He managed a grim smile. Gray-haired, perhaps in his late forties, Colin Whitman looked fit and slender, as if he put in plenty of time on the golf course, and perhaps even at the gym. He seemed relaxed at first, his movements precise, not an ounce of effort wasted. He had a red complexion, the kind that gray hair sets so much in relief.

"I understand Mr. Vancalm was away in Berlin on business until yesterday?" Banks began.

"Yes, that's right."

"Where were you yesterday evening between the hours of seven and ten?"

"Me?"

"Yes," said Annie, leaning forward. "We're just trying to eliminate all the people closest to Mr. Vancalm from our inquiry. I'm sure you understand."

"Yes, of course." Whitman scratched the side of his nose. "Well, I'm afraid I can't be much help there. I mean I was at home."

"Alone?"

"Yes. I'm not married."

"What were you doing?" Banks asked.

"Watching television, mostly. I watched *Emmerdale*, *Coronation Street*, and *A Touch of Frost* and warmed up some takeaway Chinese food for dinner. Not very exciting."

"Drink much?" Banks asked.

Whitman shifted his gaze from Annie to Banks and frowned. "Just a couple of beers, that's all."

"Good, was it, *A Touch of Frost*? I didn't see it."

Whitman laughed. "I wouldn't have thought a real policeman would have been very interested in something like that, but I enjoyed it."

"What was it about?"

"A hostage taking."

Anyone could have looked it up in the paper and come up with that vague description, Banks thought, but that was so often what constituted an alibi, and unless someone else had seen Whitman elsewhere, it would be a damned hard one to break, too. Whitman was clearly becoming unnerved by the interview. He had developed a nervous tic above his left eye and he kept tapping on the desk with a chewed yellow pencil. He clearly wanted to get this over with, wanted the box ticked, wanted Banks and Annie to get to the point and leave.

"Did you go out at all?" Annie asked.

"No. I'd no need to. It was miserable out there."

"So nobody saw you all evening?"

"I'm afraid not. But that's often the case, isn't it? How many people see you after you go home?"

"Where do you live?"

"Harewood. Look, are you almost finished? As I'm sure you can imagine, Victor's death has thrown everything into upheaval. There are a lot of clients I have to inform, and I'm not looking forward to it."

"I can understand that, sir," said Annie, "and we won't keep you much longer. Perhaps you could tell us a little bit about Mr. Vancalm?"

"Victor? Not much to tell, really. He was a good man, good at his job, loved his wife."

"Was he the kind of man who played around with other women?" Banks asked.

Whitman looked shocked. "Not that I knew of. I shouldn't think so. I mean, he seemed . . ."

"Would he have told you if he did?"

"Probably not. Our relationship was purely business. We hardly socialized unless it was with a client."

"What about Mrs. Vancalm?" Annie asked.

"Denise? What about her?"

"Did she have other men?"

"Now look here, I don't know what you're getting at, but the Vancalms' marriage was perfectly normal."

"What does that mean?" Banks asked.

"Normal?"

"Yes. You already told us you're not married yourself and that your relationship with the Vancalms was purely a business one, so how would you know?"

"I'm just going b-by what I saw, what I heard, that's all. Look, dammit, they were a happily married couple. Can't you just leave it at that?"

Banks glanced at Annie and gave her the signal to leave. "I suppose we'll have to," he said. "For now. Thanks very much for your time, Mr. Whitman."

Outside in the wet gray air, Banks looked at his watch. "Betty's? Something sinfully sweet and sticky."

"Ooh," said Annie, "you do know how to charm a woman. I can hardly wait."

It was after eight and pitch-black when Banks got back to his recently renovated Gratly cottage. After the fire had destroyed most of the place a couple of years ago, he had had the interior reconstructed, an extension added down one side and a conservatory built on at the back. He had turned the extension into an entertainment room, with a large plasma TV, comfortable cinema-style armchairs, surround sound and a drinks cabinet. Mostly he sat and watched DVDs or listened to CDs there by himself, but sometimes Annie dropped by, or one of his children, and it was good to have company.

Tonight he was alone, and that didn't make him much different from Colin Whitman, he realized. He was eating yesterday's warmed-up chicken vindaloo and drinking Tetley's bitter from a can, cruising the TV channels with the aptly-named remote, aptly named because he was finding nothing of the remotest interest.

Then Banks remembered that he had set his DVD recorder for *A Touch of Frost* last night. He always enjoyed spotting the mistakes, but perhaps even more he enjoyed David Jason's performance. Realistic or not, there was no denying the entertainment value to be got from Frost's relationship with Mullet and with his various hapless sidekicks.

He put the vindaloo containers in the rubbish bin and settled down for Frost. But it was not to be. What played instead was an old episode of *Inspector Morse* he had seen before, with Patricia Hodge guest-starring as a very upper-class Oxford wife.

At first Banks wondered if he had set up the recorder wrongly. It wouldn't have surprised him if he had; technology had never been his strong point. But his son Brian had given him a lesson, and he had been pleased that he had been able to use it a few times without messing up. He didn't have to worry about setting times or anything, just key in a number.

He played around with the remote, checked the recording date and time, and made sure that this was indeed the program he had set for last night. There was no mistake. Not that he had anything against Morse, but he had been expecting Frost. He couldn't be bothered getting up to search for something else, so he decided he might as well watch it anyway. When he started to play the DVD again, he found that it began with the end of an explanation and apology from the TV station.

From what Banks could make out, *A Touch of Frost* had been postponed and replaced by an episode of *Inspector Morse* because of its controversial subject matter: a kidnapped and murdered police officer. Over the past couple of days, the news had been full of stories of a police officer who had been abducted while trying to prevent a robbery. Only yesterday his body had been found dumped in a bin bag near Southwark. He had been shot. The TV executives clearly thought the Frost story mirrored the real one too much to be disturbing to people, so at the last minute they had pulled it.

Colin Whitman had swore blind that he had watched *A Touch of Frost*, and it hadn't been on. Banks phoned the station and asked the duty officer to see that Whitman was brought up from Harewood to Eastvale, then he rang Annie, turned off the DVD and TV and headed for the door.

"**Look, it's late,**" said Whitman. "You drag me from my home and make me sit in this disgusting room for ages. What on earth's going on? What do you think you're doing? This isn't a police state yet, you know."

"Sorry about melodrama," said Banks. "I can see why you might be a bit upset. I suppose we could have waited till morning. I don't imagine you were going to make a run for it or anything, were you? Why should you? You probably thought you'd got us all fooled."

Whitman frowned. "I'm sorry? I don't know what you're talking about."

"Suspicion of murder, Mr. Whitman," said Banks, then gave him the caution and advised him of his rights. The tape recorders made a faint whirring sound in the background, but other than that it was quiet in interview room three of Western Area Headquarters. Banks and Annie sat at the scarred wooden table opposite Whitman, and a uniformed guard stood by the door. Whitman hadn't asked for a solicitor yet, so no one else was present.

"I hope you realize this is absurd," said Whitman. "I haven't murdered anyone."

"Mr. Whitman," Annie said. "When DCI Banks and I talked to you this afternoon, you told us you spent yesterday evening at home watching *A Touch of Frost*."

"It's true. I did. What's wrong with that?"

"Nothing at all," said Annie, "except that *A Touch of Frost* was pulled from the air because of a real live hostage taking. ITV showed an old *Inspector Morse* instead."

Whitman's mouth flapped open and shut like a dying fish's. "I . . . they . . . I . . ."

"It's an easy mistake," Annie went on. "Happens sometimes, but not often. Just unlucky, this time."

"But I . . ."

"Yes, Mr. Whitman?" said Banks, leaning toward him. "You want to confess? The murder of Victor Vancalm. What were you looking for? Money? Or did he have something on you? Something incriminating? Or perhaps it was something else entirely? Mrs. Vancalm, for example. Had you been having an affair? Did the two of you plan this together?"

"No!"

"No to which question, Colin?" Annie asked.

"All of them. I told you. I was at home all evening."

"But you were lying," said Banks. "At least you were lying about *A Touch of Frost,* and if you were lying about that . . . well, there goes your alibi."

"Look, I didn't know I'd need an alibi, did I?"

"Not unless you murdered Mr. Vancalm you didn't."

"I didn't murder anybody!"

"You say you didn't, but yet when we asked you where you were around the time he died, you gave us a pack of lies. Why?"

"I . . . it just sounded so weak."

"What did?"

"That I just stopped in by myself."

"Hang on a minute," said Banks. "You're telling us that you thought it sounded weak saying you stopped in by yourself and ate some leftover Chinese takeaway, but it somehow sounded more believable that you did this while watching *A Touch of Frost*?"

"Well, I must admit, put like that it sounds rather silly, but yes."

Banks looked at Annie, who rolled her eyes.

"What?" said Whitman.

"I really think we'd better start at the beginning," said Annie. "And the truth this time."

"But it was the truth."

"Apart from *A Touch of Frost*?"

"Yes. I didn't watch television."

"What did you do?" Banks asked.

"I just sat there thinking, did a little work. I often have work to take home with me."

Banks shook his head. "I still don't get it. Why lie to us about watching television if all you were doing was work?"

"Like I said, it sounds silly now, I realize. I don't want people to think I'm a workaholic. I do have a life."

"Watching *A Touch of Frost* and eating warmed-up takeaway is a life?" Even as he spoke, Banks was aware that that was exactly what he had done, or would have done if he hadn't caught Whitman in a lie about his alibi. *Sad,* he told himself. Note to self: must get out more.

"Well, when you put it like that, as I said, it does sound rather silly."

"Not really," said Banks. "I don't think it's silly at all. Do you, Annie?"

"Not at all," Annie agreed.

"I think it was very clever of you," Banks went on. "You came home, got changed, went out and waited for Mr. Vancalm to return from Berlin, then you killed him. You knew he was away and when he'd be coming back. You also knew the layout of his study, and, I would imagine, the ins and outs of the security system and the wall safe. You didn't want too elaborate an alibi because you knew we'd be suspicious. Let's face it, most people, when questioned by the police, don't have alibis any better than yours was. It makes perfect sense to me. You were just unlucky, that's all. It only took a simple twist of fate."

Annie gave Banks a questioning look.

"Dylan," he said.

Whitman banged both fists on the table. "But I didn't do it!"

Banks folded his arms and leaned back. "Sure you weren't having an affair with Mrs. Vancalm? She's a very attractive woman."

"She's my partner's wife, for crying out loud."

"That wouldn't stop most people."

"I'm not most people."

Banks paused. "No, you're not, are you, Colin? In fact, I'm not sure what sort of person you are." He glanced at Annie and smiled back at Whitman. "I can't see that we're getting anywhere here, though, and DI Cabbot and I are both tired, so I think we'll call it a night, if that's OK with you?"

Whitman sat up straight and beamed. "OK?" he echoed. "That's the most sensible thing I've heard all evening."

Banks and Annie stood up. "Right," said Banks to the officer at the door. "Take Mr. Whitman here down to custody, make sure it's all done by the book, and find a nice cell for him for the night. A nice cell, mind you, Smithers. Not one of those vomit-filled cages you usually put people in."

PC Smithers could hardly keep back the laughter. "Yes, sir," he said, and took Whitman by the arm.

"What's this?" Whitman said. "What's going on?"

"We're detaining you until we're happy with your story," said Banks.

"But . . . but you can't do that. I've answered your questions. You have to let me go."

"Oh, dear," said Banks, looking at Annie. "You can tell this fellow doesn't watch his *Frost* and *Morse* closely enough, can't you, DI Cabbot?"

Annie smiled. "Indeed you can," she said.

Banks turned to Whitman. "As a matter of fact, Colin, you've been arrested on suspicion of murder, cautioned and advised of your rights. We can keep you for twenty-four hours without a charge—longer if we wanted to go the terrorist route, but I don't think we'll be bothering with that tonight—so that should give you plenty of time to think." And Smithers dragged Whitman, now demanding to see his solicitor, complaining and protesting all the way, along the corridor and down the stairs to the custody suite.

Thanks for agreeing to meet me, Mrs. Goldwell," said Banks. The food court of the Swainsdale Center wasn't the ideal place for an interview, but it was Wednesday morning, so things were relatively quiet. Whitman was still sulking in his cell waiting for his solicitor, who was proving very difficult to contact, saying nothing, and DCs Jackman and Wilson were trawling through his life.

"Please," she said, "call me Natasha. Is that wise?"

She was looking at Banks's Egg McMuffin with sausage. "Tastes all right," said Banks. "I reckon they're quite manageable if you only eat about five or six a year."

Natasha Goldwell smiled. It was a nice smile, pearly teeth behind the red lips. In fact, Natasha was a nice package all the way from her shaggy blond hair and winter tan to her shiny, pointed black shoes. She wrinkled her nose. "If you say so. I suppose it's hard to eat regularly when you work the hours you do."

Banks raised his eyebrows. Some hadn't seen enough cops on telly; others had seen too many. "Not really," he said. "Mostly in Major Crimes we work regular hours." He smiled. "Unless there's actually a major crime, that is. Which murder definitely is."

Natasha put her hand to her mouth. "Oh, God, yes. I'm sorry. So thoughtless of me."

"Not to worry." Banks sipped some coffee. It was hot and bitter.

"What was it you wanted to see me about?"

"It's nothing, really," said Banks. "I mean, you vouched for Mrs. Vancalm and that seems to check out OK. It's just . . . did you know Mr. Vancalm?"

"Victor? I'd met him, of course, but I wouldn't say I knew him. I got together with Denise and the others for the poker circle, of course, but outside of that we didn't live in one another's pockets."

"It's an odd hobby, poker, isn't it?"

"For a woman, you mean?"

"Well, that wasn't what I meant, but I suppose now you come to mention it, yes."

"Because you usually associate it with men in cowboy boots and six-guns on their hips?"

"Well, not these days so much, but certainly not with a group of professional women."

"And why not? If we were playing bridge or gin rummy, would it make a difference?"

"OK, I take your point."

Natasha smiled. "Anyway, we enjoy it, and it does no harm. It's not as if the stakes are beyond anyone's means."

"What about the online playing? The tournaments?"

"You've heard about those? They're not for everyone. Only Evangeline from our group goes in for them. But the online stuff . . ," She shrugged. "It's fun. Better than computer dating or chat rooms. Safer, too."

"I suppose so," said Banks, whose online experience was limited to Amazon and the occasional rock concert clip on YouTube. "What kind of person would you say Victor Vancalm was?"

"As I told you, I scarcely knew him." She chewed on her lower lip, then said, "But from what I did know, I'd say he was used to getting his own way, a bit bossy perhaps."

"Abusive?"

"Good God, no! No. Certainly not. As far as I ever knew, Denise was perfectly happy with him."

She didn't look Banks in the eye as she said this, which immediately raised his suspicions. "So she wore the trousers, then?"

Natasha Goldwell smiled. "Oh, Mr. Banks! What a quaint expression. I'm afraid you really are behind the times. It was an equal partnership."

"What were you doing at Denise Vancalm's house the day before the murder?" he asked.

A couple of women sat down at the table beside them, paper bags crinkling and crackling, chatting about some rude shopgirl they'd just had to deal with. "And did you see her hair?" one of them asked, aghast. "What sort of color would you call that? And there was enough metal in her face to start a foundry."

The interruption gave Natasha the breathing space she seemed to need after Banks's abrupt change of direction. When she answered his question, she was all poise again. "No reason in particular," she said. "We often get together for a coffee. Denise happened to be working from home that day and I had a spare hour between clients. One of the perks of running your own business is that you can play truant occasionally." She wrinkled her nose.

"What did you talk about?"

"Oh, this and that," said Natasha. "You know, girly talk."

"She didn't have any problems, any worries that she shared with you?"

"Mr. Banks, it was her husband who was murdered, not Denise."

"Just trying to find a reason for what happened."

"I would have thought that was obvious. He interrupted a burglar."

Banks scratched the scar next to his right eye. "Yes, it does rather look that way, doesn't it? Do you know if either of them had any enemies, any problems that were getting them down. Debts, for example?"

"Debts?"

"Well, there was the poker . . . and Mr. Vancalm's trips."

"Victor made business trips, it's true, and Denise plays a little online poker, but debts . . . ? I don't think so. Are you suggesting it was some sort of debt collector come to break his legs or something and it got out of hand? This is Eastvale, Mr. Banks, not Las Vegas."

Banks shrugged. "Stranger things have happened at sea. Anything else you can tell me?"

"About what?"

"About what happened that night?"

"I finished work at six thirty. Denise met me at the office. We went to the Old Oak for a drink. Just the one. We are always careful. She drove me to Gabriella's. We played poker all evening, then she dropped me off on her way home sometime after eleven. That's all there is to it."

She did sound a bit as if she were speaking by rote, Banks thought, remembering what Annie had said, but then she had already been asked to describe the evening several times. "Who won?" he asked.

"Pardon?"

"The poker circle. Who won?"

"As a matter of fact," Natasha said, "Denise did."

"It's just a minor blip on the radar, really, sir," said Winsome. She was sitting at her computer, leaning back in the chair, long legs crossed at the ankles, hands linked behind her head.

"Tell me about it, anyway," said Banks, grabbing a chair and sitting so that he could rest his arms on the back.

"Well," Winsome went on in her Jamaican-tinged Yorkshire, "you know that big operation a few years back, the one that netted Pete Townsend?"

Banks nodded. Cynical copper though he may be, he had never believed for a moment that Pete Townsend was connected with child pornography in any way other than for research, and he was certainly glad when he heard that the Who's guitarist was completely vindicated.

"That's when Colin Whitman's name came up," Winsome said. "The usual. Credit card online."

"You'd think people would know better."

"They do now, sir," said Winsome. "The online dealers have got more savvy, and some of the pros have pretty much gone back to hard copy. It's safer and less likely to be detected, especially the way the borders are throughout Europe these days."

"Everyone's too busy looking for terrorists."

"Right, sir. But there's still a lot of activity over the Internet. Anyway, as I said, it almost went under the radar, just a blip, but there it is."

"Did you check Victor Vancalm's name, too?"

"Yes. Nothing."

"Was Whitman interviewed?"

"No, sir. They just put his name in a pending file. There were hundreds of them. It was a big operation."

"I remember."

"It might not mean anything."

"But then again," said Banks, "it might. Think we can use it to get a search warrant?"

"I don't see why not, sir. Want me to get on to it?"

"Immediately." Banks looked at his watch. "We've got the pleasure of Mr. Whitman's custody until this evening."

"About bloody time," said Colin Whitman when Banks had him brought up to his office at six o'clock that evening. Banks stood with his back to the door, looking out of his window. Outside in the market square all was dark and still except for a few people heading to or from home across the cobbles. "I've spoken with my solicitor," Whitman went on, "and he advised me to cooperate, but I'd like him to be present during any further discussions we may have."

"That's your prerogative," said Banks, turning. "I suppose you'll be wanting to go home as soon as possible?"

"Naturally."

"Let's see if we can get this over with quickly then, shall we? Please, sit."

Whitman stared and stood his ground as Banks sat behind his desk. Then he slowly pulled out the hard-back chair and sat opposite. "Is this an apology?"

"Not exactly," Banks said. The radio was playing one of Beethoven's

"Razumovsky" quartets softly in the background, so softly you had to know it was there.

"What, then?"

"Our men are still at your house, but their preliminary findings have given us enough to hold you for a while longer. Superintendent Gervaise has already authorized the further detention. She takes as dim a view of what you've been up to as I do. I don't think you're going to find a lot of sympathizers here."

Whitman had turned pale, which told Banks he knew exactly what was going on. "I want my solicitor," he said.

"Thought you might. You can put another call in, of course, that's your right. And we'd be quite happy to get a duty solicitor for you if there's a problem."

Whitman reached for the phone and Banks let him call. By the sound of it, he got an answering machine. He left a message and hung up.

"Probably out at some function or other," said Banks. "As I said—"

"I'll wait for my own man, thank you very much. And I'm not saying a word until he gets here."

"Your privilege, sir," said Banks, "but remember what I said earlier: what you don't say can mean just as much in court these days as what you do say."

Whitman folded his arms. "I'm still not saying anything."

"Better let me do the talking, then," said Banks. "I'll start by saying that I'm not sure why you did it. Perhaps Victor Vancalm got on to your little game and you had to get rid of him. Or maybe there was some other reason, some business reason. But you did it. Your alibi's crap and you've lied to us through your teeth. You're also a pervert. It may be the one group that doesn't have a charter of rights yet, child molesters."

"I am not a child molester."

"Fine distinction. I know things like that are important to your lot, how you define yourselves. But let's be honest about it. Maybe you don't hang about schoolyards and playgrounds waiting for opportunities to come along, but you do diddle little kids and you do like to look at pictures of other people diddling them. In fact you had quite a collection on those DVDs we found under those loose floorboards in the spare room."

"They're not mine. I was keeping them for someone. I didn't know what was on them."

"Bollocks," said Banks. There was a tap at the door and a young uniformed officer stuck his head around. "You sent for me, sir?"

"Yes," said Banks. "Could you rustle up some tea? One as it comes and one . . . How do you take your tea, Colin? It's not a trick question."

"Milk, two sugars."

"Got that, Constable?" said Banks.

"Yes, sir."

When the constable had gone, Banks turned back to Whitman. "Are you going to tell me what happened, Colin?" he said. "Or are we just going to sit here and drink tea and listen to Beethoven until your brief gets your message and hotfoots it over? Then we can take it down to the interview room again and spend the night at it. I don't mind. I've got no plans. The result will probably be the same in the long run."

"I told you. I'm not saying anything until my solicitor gets here."

"Right. So we already know you did it. You knew when Victor Vancalm was due to arrive home from Berlin. You probably had a key to the house, but you wanted to make it look like a burglary, so you broke that side window and got in that way. Did you smash up the room before or after you killed Victor?"

Whitman said nothing. His jaw was set so tightly that Banks could see the muscles tense, the lips whitening. At this rate he'd have an aneurysm or something before his solicitor arrived.

"No matter," Banks went on. "And you've no doubt got rid of whatever you stole by now, if you've got any sense. I don't know how long you'd been planning this, but it smells of premeditation to me. At any rate, you won't be out for a long, long time. Now, correct me if I'm wrong, but I'm assuming the most obvious scenario is that Victor Vancalm found out about your odd proclivities and he didn't like them, threatened to turn you in?"

"That's rubbish."

"Is it, Colin? Then why don't you tell us where you really were on the night Victor was murdered? That would go a long way toward convincing me you didn't do it."

Whitman chewed on a fingernail, brow furrowed in thought. "Colin?"

"All right, all right! I was with a . . . a friend."

"A person of your own tastes?"

"Yes."

"Who was he? Where does he live?"

It took Whitman a few minutes, but Banks made the gravity of his situation clear again, and Whitman gave up a name and address.

"We'll check, of course," Banks said.

A curious and most unpleasant smile crept over Whitman's features. "You think you're so bloody clever, don't you?" he said.

Banks said nothing.

Whitman leaned forward. "Well, what would you think, Mr. Clever Detective, if I told you those discs your men found were Victor's?"

"I'd think you were lying to save your own neck," said Banks, who wasn't too sure. He could already hear the faint alarm bells ringing in the back of his mind, sense the disparate observations and inchoate imaginings suddenly taking shape and forming recognizable images.

Whitman laughed. "All right, you've got me. Or you think you've got me. We'll see about that when my solicitor gets here. But don't assume Victor Vancalm was the innocent in all this. How do you think we met in the first place?"

"Do you mean what I think you mean?"

"Even PC Plod could figure that one out," Whitman went on. He was clearly enjoying his newfound sense of superiority, and Banks was not going to disabuse him of the notion.

"You'll have to be a bit clearer than that," he said.

"I don't think I'd be incriminating myself if I told you that Victor Vancalm was an aficionado of the kind of thing you mentioned earlier."

"You mean Vancalm was into child pornography?"

Whitman sighed. "It looks as if I do have to spell it out for you. Yes. That's what I'm saying. That was how we met in the first place. A shared interest in a special kind of love." He folded his arms again. "And you won't get another word out of me until my solicitor arrives. This time I mean it."

Banks nodded. He didn't really need another word from Colin Whitman. Not just yet, at any rate

"Have you found anything out yet, Mr. Banks?" asked Denise Vancalm. They were sitting in the same room as they had sat in two days ago, at Banks's request, though the police hadn't quite finished with the house yet, and Mrs. Vancalm was still staying at the Jedburgh Hotel. When Banks suggested the house as a venue, she had readily agreed as she said she had some more clothes she wanted to pick up. DI Annie Cabbot was there too, notebook open, pen in hand.

"Quite a bit," said Banks. "Mr. Whitman is under arrest."

"Colin? My God. Did Colin . . . ? I mean, I can't believe it. Why?"

"Don't worry, Mrs. Vancalm. Colin Whitman didn't kill your husband."

"Then I don't understand." She clutched at the gold pendant around her neck. "Why? Who?"

"You killed your husband," Banks said.

"Me . . . ?" She pointed at her own chest. "But that's absurd. I was at the poker circle. You know I was."

"You told me that was where you were."

"But Natasha, Gabriella, Evangeline, Heather . . . they all corroborated my story."

"Indeed they did," said Banks. "And that caused me no end of problems."

"What do you mean?"

"I just couldn't think at first what would make four law-abiding professional women alibi a friend for the murder of her husband. It didn't make sense. In almost every scenario I could think of, someone would have spoken out against it, suggested another course of action, refused to be involved."

"Of course," said Denise Vancalm. "That's why it's *true*."

Banks shook his head. "No, it's not. I said I couldn't think of anything, and at first I couldn't. Perhaps spousal abuse came close, but even then there was certain to be a voice of reason, a dissenting voice. And there were no hints that your husband abused *you*. Maybe if he were a serial killer . . . but that clearly wasn't the case either. Only when Mr. Whitman told me the truth did I understand it."

"I don't know what you're talking about."

"Of course you do. Your husband was a child pornographer. All these trips. Amsterdam. Berlin. Brussels. Oh, he did business, of course, but then there was the *other* business, wasn't there? The secret meetings, the swaps, the children, often smuggled in from eastern Europe, bought and paid for."

"This is absurd. I want my solicitor."

"All in good time," said Banks, who was getting sick and tired of hearing that request. "Somehow," he went on, "you found out about it. Perhaps he let something slip on the computer, or maybe it was something else, but you found out. You were shocked, horrified, of course. You didn't know what to do. Horror turned to disgust. It sickened you. You had to do something about it, but you didn't know what. All you knew was that you couldn't go on living with a man like that, and that he couldn't be allowed to keep on doing what he was doing. Am I right so far?"

Denise Vancalm said nothing, but her expression spoke volumes. "Do go on, Chief Inspector," she said softly. "It's a fascinating story."

"No doubt your first thought, as an honest citizen, was to report him to the authorities. But you couldn't do that, could you?"

"Why not?" she asked.

"I think there were two reasons. First, you couldn't live with it, with the shame of knowing who, or what, you had been married to for fifteen years. It would have been an admission of weakness, of defeat."

"Very good," said Denise. "And the other reason?"

"Professional. Your business is important to you. You couldn't afford for your husband to go on trial for what he did. You're a fundraiser and event organizer for charities, predominantly *children's* charities. Imagine how it would go down with your colleagues that you were married to a child pornographer and you didn't even know it. Oh, there would be sympathy enough at first. Poor Denise, they'd say. But there'd always be those important little questions at the backs of their minds. *Did* she know? How could she *not* have known? Why did it take her so long to turn him in? It would have meant the end for you. You couldn't have lived with both that *and* with your own personal shame. But the widow of a murder victim? A burglary gone wrong. There you get all the sympathy without the vexing questions. *As long as you have a watertight alibi.* And with Gabriella Mountjoy, Natasha Goldwell, Evangeline White and Heather Murchison all swearing you were with them all evening, the old surprising-a-burglar routine should have worked very well."

"But how could I have done it?"

"Very easily. After you got to Gabriella's, you left your car there. There's nothing much more distinctive than a red sports car, and you didn't want anyone to see that around your home that evening. You borrowed one of the others' cars, probably Evangeline White's. She wasn't particularly a *Top Gear* type. All she wanted was a nice little runner that would get her from a to b. Nondescript. You drove back home shortly before your husband was due to arrive and parked out of the way. You broke in through the side window to make it look as if a burglar had gained entry, and then you waited for him. I don't know if there was any discussion when he arrived, any questioning, any chance to offer an explanation, or whether you simply executed the sentence the moment he walked into his study."

"All this is very clever," Denise said, "but it assumes you have evidence that my husband was what you say he was, and that I knew about it."

"Friends can only be relied on up to a point," said Banks. "Natasha Goldwell values her freedom, and when she found it under threat she decided that it might be best to make a clean breast of things. It doesn't get her off without punishment completely, of course, but I think we can be confident that a judge will view her with a certain amount of lenience. And, of course, once Natasha decided to tell the truth, it didn't take the others long to follow."

Pale and trembling, Denise Vancalm reached in her handbag for a tissue and blew her nose. "And what did Natasha have to say?" she asked, trying to sound casual.

"That not only did she and the others provide you with an alibi because they were as horrified as you were about your husband's activities, but that she went over to your house the day before and cleaned off your husband's computer. She's good at it. It's her job. Computer software design, specializing in security. Our experts found traces when she told them where to look. Not a lot, but enough to show what was there and to give us a few more leads to chase down. And they're still working on it. You also cleaned out the safe. No doubt there were discs and photographs there, too."

"It was the computer," Denise said, her voice no more than a whisper.

"What?" said Banks.

"The computer. Victor was away in Berlin and my Web service was on the blink. We have different services. Sounds silly, I know, but there it is. Different businesses, different providers. He wasn't aware of it, but I'd known his password for ages. I saw him type it in once, the keys he used. I have a good visual memory. Anyway, I wasn't prying. Not at first. I just wanted to look up a company online. When I started Internet Explorer, I accidentally caused a list of the last few sites he'd visited to drop down. Some of them sounded odd. I visited them out of curiosity. I'm sure you know what it's like. Well, let's say I tried. I couldn't get beyond the security, the passwords and what have you. Then I checked his e-mail browser and found a few dodgy messages. Oh, there were no photographs of naked children or anything like that, and they were clearly using some sort of code, but it was pretty obvious what the sender was referring to. At first I thought it might have been some sick sort of spam, but I checked his other folders. There were more. Some were from people we'd socialized with. Business colleagues. It sickened me. There were . . . pictures, too. I didn't find those until Natasha came. They were well hidden, secured."

"Is that why you smashed the computer screen?"

"Yes. I wasn't thinking. I just lashed out."

"He took a tremendous risk in keeping them."

"Don't they all? But he needed them. Obviously the compulsion overcomes all the risks. Maybe it's even a part of the excitement, the possibility of being caught. I don't know. I really don't know."

"So you decided to kill him?"

She nodded and sighed. "You're right. What's the point in lying anymore? I don't blame Natasha. She was never really comfortable with the plan from the start. She was appalled by what she saw on the screen, of course, and she went along with it, but of all of them she had the most reservations. As I say, I don't blame her. If I could only have come up with some other way . . ."

"You could have reported him."

"No. You were right about that. And there would have been a trial. Victor wouldn't have given up without a fight. I couldn't have stood that. Everyone knowing."

The irony, Banks thought, was that even now it had come out and Denise Vancalm would certainly go to trial, she would probably get more public sympathy as the murderess of a child pornographer than she would have got as the wife of a live one. As for her alibi, the Eastvale ladies' poker circle, Banks didn't know what would happen. Their fate lay in the hands of the Crown Prosecution Service and the courts, not in his, thank God. As he and Annie walked Denise Vancalm out to the waiting police car, Banks found himself thinking that she would probably not have to look very far to find a poker game in prison.

The Ferryman's Beautiful Daughter

The strangers came to live on the island at the beginning of summer, 1969, and by the end of August my best friend, Mary Jane, was dead. The townsfolk blamed the Newcomers and their heathen ways, but I was certain it was something else. Not something new, but something old and powerful that had festered in these parts for years, or perhaps had always been here.

I remember the morning the Newcomers arrived. We were all in chapel. It was stifling hot because the windows were closed, and there was no air-conditioning. "Stop fidgeting and listen to the preacher," hissed Mother. I tried my best, but his words made no sense to me. Flecks of spittle flew from his mouth like when water touches hot oil in a griddle. Something about Judgment Day, when the dead would rise incorruptible.

Next to me, Mary Jane was looking down at her shoes trying to hold back her laughter. I could see the muscles tightening around her lips and jaw. If we started giggling now we were done for. The preacher didn't like laughter. It made him angry. He finally gave her one of his laserlike looks, and that seemed to settle her down. He'd never liked Mary Jane ever since she refused to attend his special instruction evening classes. She told me that when he had asked her, he had put his face so close to hers that she had been able to smell the bourbon on his breath, and she was sure she had seen the outline of his thing pushing hard against his pants. She also said she had seen him touching

Betsy Goodall where he shouldn't have been touching her, but when we asked Betsy, she blushed and denied everything. What else could she have done? Who would have believed her? In those days, as perhaps even now, small, isolated communities like ours kept their nasty little secrets to themselves.

Across the aisle, Riley McCorkindale kept glancing sideways at Mary Jane when he thought she couldn't see him. Riley was sweet on her, but she gave him a terrible runaround. I thought he was quite nice, but he *was* very shy, and he seemed far too young for us, no matter how tall and strong he was. Besides, he was always chewing gum, and we thought that looked common. We were very sophisticated young ladies. And you have to understand that Mary Jane was very beautiful, not gawky and plain like me, with lustrous dark hair hanging over her shoulders and the biggest, bluest eyes you have ever seen.

At last the service ended and we ran out into the summer sunshine. Our parents lingered to shake hands with neighbors and talk to the preacher, of course. They were old enough to know that you weren't supposed to seem in too much of a hurry to leave God's house. But Mary Jane and I were only fifteen, sophisticated as we were, and everybody knew that meant trouble. Especially when they said we were too old for our own good or too big for our boots. "Precocious" was the word they used most often to describe us. I looked it up and felt quite flattered. I didn't like it when I heard Mrs. Hammond in the general store call us "brazen hussies" when she thought I couldn't hear her. That wasn't fair.

It was that day after chapel when we noticed the Newcomers. I think Mary Jane saw them first, because I remember seeing her expression change from laughter to wonder as I followed her gaze to the old school bus pulling into the parking lot. It wasn't yellow, but was painted all colors, great swirls and blobs and sunbursts of green, red, purple, orange, black and blue, like nothing we'd ever seen before. And the people! We didn't own a television set in our house—the preacher was against them and Mother was devout—but I'd seen pictures in magazines that tourists left on the ferry sometimes, and I'd even read in Father's newspaper about how they took drugs, listened to strange, distorted loud music and held large gatherings outside the cities, where they indulged in unspeakable practices. But I had never seen any of them in the flesh before.

They certainly did look strange, the girls in long loose dresses of pretty colorful patterns of silk and cotton, denim jackets embroidered with flowers, the men with their long hair over their shoulders or tied back in ponytails, wearing Mexican-style ponchos and bell-bottom jeans and cowboy boots, the children scruffy, dirty and long-haired, running wild. They looked at us and smiled without much curiosity as they boarded the ferryboat carrying their few belongings. I suppose they'd seen plenty of people who looked like us before, and who looked at them the way we must have done. Even Riley, who had clearly been plucking up the courage to come over and say hello to Mary Jane before his ferry left, had stopped dead in his tracks, mouth gaping open. I could see the piece of gum lying there on his tongue like a rotten tooth.

Once the Newcomers had all boarded the ferry, the regulars got on. There was no chapel on the island. Only about thirty people lived there, and not all of them were religious. The preacher said that was because most of them were intellectuals and thought they knew better than the Scriptures. Anyway, the ones who weren't businessmen like Riley's father taught at the university in the city, about forty miles away, and commuted. They left their cars in the big parking lot next to the harbor because there were no roads on the island.

Just because we had the ferry, it didn't make our little town an important place; it was simply the best natural harbor closest to Pine Island. We had a general store, a run-down hotel with a Chinese restaurant attached, the chapel, and an old one-room schoolhouse for the children. The high school was fifteen miles away in Logan, the nearest large town, and Mary Jane and I had to take the bus. The sign on the road in read JASMINE COVE, POP. 2,321 and I'd guess that was close enough to the truth, though I don't think they could have counted Sally Jessop's new baby because she only gave birth the day before the Newcomers arrived.

Over the next few days, we found out a little more about the Newcomers. They were from San Francisco, over a thousand miles away, in California, according to Lenny Hammond, who ran the general store with his nasty wife. There were about nine of them in all, including the children, and they'd bought the land fair and square from the government and had all the right papers and permissions. They kept to themselves and didn't like outsiders. They shunned the rest of society—that's the word Lenny used, "shunned," I looked it up—and planned to live off the land, growing vegetables. They didn't eat meat or fish, but they did have a generator for electricity.

According to Lenny, they didn't go to chapel, or even to church. He said they worshipped the devil and danced naked and sacrificed children and animals, but Mary Jane and I didn't believe him. Lenny had a habit of getting carried away with himself when it came to new ideas. Like the preacher, he thought the world was going to hell in a handbasket, and almost everything he saw and heard proved him right, especially if it had anything to do with young people.

That day, as we wandered out of the general store on to Main Street, Mary Jane turned to me, smiled sweetly and said, "Grace, why don't we take a little ferry ride tomorrow and find out about the Newcomers for ourselves?"

Mary Jane's father, Mr. Kiernan, was the ferryman and in summer, when we were on holiday from school, he let us ride for free whenever we wanted. Sometimes I even went by myself. Pine Island wasn't very big—about two miles long and maybe half a mile wide—but it had some very beautiful areas. I loved the western beach most of all, a lonely stretch of golden sand at the bottom of steep, forbidding cliffs. Mary Jane and I knew a secret path down, and we spent many hours exploring the caves and rock pools, or lounging about on the beach just talking about life and things. Sometimes I went there alone when I felt blue, and it always made me feel better.

Most of the inhabitants of Pine Island lived in a small community of wood-structure houses nestled around the harbor on the east coast, but the Newcomers had bought property at the wooded southern tip, where two abandoned log cabins had been falling to ruin there as long as anyone could remember. Someone said they'd once been used by hunters, but there was nothing left to hunt on Pine Island anymore.

We saw the Newcomers in town from time to time, when they came to buy provisions at Lenny's store. Sometimes one or two of them would drive the school bus to Logan for things they couldn't find here. They were buying drugs there, and seeds to grow marijuana, which made folk crazy, so Lenny said. Perhaps they were.

Certainly the preacher found many new subjects for his long sermons after the arrival of the Newcomers—including, to the dismay of some members of his congregation, the evils of tobacco and alcohol—but whether word of his rantings ever got back to them, and whether they cared if it did, we never knew.

The preacher was in his element. He told us that the Newcomers were nothing other than demons escaped from hell. He even told Mr. Kiernan that he should have nothing to do with them and that he shouldn't use God's ferryboat for the transporting of demons. Mr. Kiernan explained that he worked for the ferry company, which was based in the city, not for the preacher, and that it was his job to take anyone who paid the fare to or from Pine Island. The preacher argued that the money didn't matter, it was the devil's currency, that there was a "higher authority," and the ferry company was as bad as the Newcomers; they were all servants of Beelzebub and Mammon and any other horrible demon names he could think of and they would be damned for all eternity. In the end, Mr. Kiernan gave up arguing and simply carried on doing his job.

One bright and beautiful day in July around the time when men first set foot on the moon, Mary Jane and I set off on our own exploratory mission. Mr. Kiernan stood at the wheel, for all the world looking as proud and stiff as if he were piloting *Apollo 11* itself. We weren't going to the moon, of course, but we might as well have been. It was only later, in university, that I read *The Tempest,* but had I known it then, Miranda's words would surely have echoed in my mind's ear: "O brave new world that has such people in't!"

The little ferry didn't have any fancy restaurants or shops or anything, just a canvas-covered area with hard wooden benches and dirty plastic windows, where you could shelter from the rain—which we got a lot of in our part of the world—and get a cup of hot coffee from the machine, if it was working. Through fair and foul, Mr. Kiernan stood at the wheel, his cap at a jaunty angle, pipe clamped in his mouth. Some of the locals made fun of him behind his back and called him Popeye. They thought we hadn't heard them, but we had. I thought it was cruel, but Mary Jane didn't seem to care. Our town was full of little cruelties, like the way the Youlden kids made fun of Gary Mapplin because there was something wrong with his spine and he had to go around in a wheelchair, his head lolling on his shoulders as if it were on a spring. Sometimes it seemed to me that everywhere Mary Jane and I went in Jasmine Cove, people gave us dirty looks, and we knew that if we spoke back or anything, they'd report us to our parents. Mr. Kiernan was all right—he went very easy on Mary Jane—but my father was very strict, and I had to watch what I said and did around him.

Riley McCorkindale was hanging around the ferry dock, as usual, fishing off the small rickety pier with some friends. I don't think they ever caught anything. He blushed when Mary Jane and I walked by giggling, and said hello. I could feel his eyes following us as we headed for the path south through the woods. He must have known where we were going; it didn't lead anywhere else.

Soon we'd left the harbor and its small community behind us and were deep in the woods. It was cooler there, and the sunlight filtered pale green through the shimmering leaves. Little animals skittered through the dry underbrush, and once a large bird exploded out of a tree and startled us both so much our hearts began to pound. We could hear the waves crashing on the shore in the distance, to the west, but all around us it was peaceful and quiet.

Finally, from a short distance ahead, we heard music. It was like nothing I'd ever heard before, and there was an ethereal beauty about it, drifting on the sweet summer air as if it belonged there, like the scent of rosemary or thyme.

Then we reached a clearing and could see the log cabins. Three children were playing horseshoes, and someone was taking a shower in a ramshackle wooden box rigged up with some sort of overhead sieve. The music was coming from inside one of the cabins. You can imagine the absolute shock and surprise on our faces when the shower door opened and out walked a young man naked as the day he was born.

We gawped, I'm sure. I had certainly never seen a naked man before, not even a photograph of one, but Mary Jane said she once saw her brother playing with himself when he thought she was out. We looked at each other and swallowed. "Let's wait," Mary Jane whispered. "We don't want them to think we've been spying."

So we waited. Five, ten minutes went by. Nothing much happened. The children continued their game and no one else entered the shower. Finally, Mary Jane and I took deep breaths, left the cover of the woods and walked into the clearing.

"Hello," I called, aware of the tremor in my voice. "Hello. Is anybody home?"

The children stopped their game and stared at us. One of them, a little girl, I think, with long dark curls, ran inside the nearest cabin. A few moments later a young man stepped out. Probably only three or four years older than us, he had a slight, wispy blond beard and beautiful silky long hair, still damp, falling over his shoulders. It was the same man we had seen getting out of the shower, and I'm sure we both blushed. He looked a little puzzled and suspicious. And why not? After all, I don't think anyone else from Jasmine Cove had been out to welcome them.

Mary Jane seemed suddenly struck dumb, whether by the man's good looks or the memory of his nakedness I don't know, and it was left to me to speak. "Hello," I said. "I'm Grace Vincent, and this is my friend Mary Jane Kiernan. We're from the town, from Jasmine Cove. We've come to say hello."

He stared for a moment, then smiled and looked at Mary Jane. His eyes were bright green, like the sea just beyond the sands. "Mary Jane," he said. "Well, how strange. This must be a song about you. The Mad Hatters."

"What?" I said.

"The name of the band. The Mad Hatters. They're English."

We listened to the music for a moment, and I thought I caught the words, "Mary Jane is dreaming of an ocean dark and gleaming." I didn't recognize the song, or the name of the group, but that didn't mean much. My parents didn't let me listen to pop music. Mary Jane seemed to find her voice and said something about that being nice.

"Look, would you like to come in?" the young man said. "Have a cold drink or something. It's a hot day."

I looked at Mary Jane. I could tell from her expression that she was as uncertain as I was. Now that we were here, the reality was starting to dawn on us. These were the people the preacher had called the spawn of Satan. As far as the townsfolk were concerned, they drugged young girls and had their evil way. But the young man looked harmless and it *was* a hot day. We were thirsty. Finally, we sort of nodded and followed him inside the cabin.

The shade was pleasant and a gentle cross-breeze blew through the open shutters. Sunlight picked out shining strands of silver and gold in the materials that draped the furnishings. The Newcomers didn't have much, and most of it was makeshift, but we made ourselves comfortable on cushions on the floor and the young man brought us some lemonade. "Homemade," he said. "I'm sorry it's not as cold as you're probably used to, but we don't have a refrigerator yet." He laughed. "As a matter of fact, we've only just got that old generator working, or we wouldn't even have any music." He nodded toward the drinks. "We keep some lemonade chilled in the stream out back."

By this time the others had wandered in to get a look at us, most of them older than the young man, and several of them lovely women in bright dresses with flowers twined in their long hair.

"I'm Jared," said the young man, then he introduced the others—Star, Leo, Gandalf, Dylan—names we were unfamiliar with. They sat cross-legged on the floor and smiled. Jared asked us some questions about the town, and we explained how the people there were suspicious of strangers but were decent folks underneath it all. I wasn't certain that was true, but we weren't there to say bad things about our neighbors and kin. We didn't tell them what lies the preacher had been spreading.

Jared told us they had come here to get away from the suspicion, corruption and greed they had found in the city, and they were going to live close to nature and meditate. Some of them were artists and musicians—they had guitars and flutes—but they didn't want to be famous or anything. They didn't even want money from anyone. One of them—Rigel, I think his name was—said mysteriously that the world was going to end soon and that this was the best place to be when it happened. In an odd way, his words and his tone reminded me of the preacher.

Someone rolled a funny-smelling cigarette, lit it and offered it to us, but I said no. I'd never smoked any kind of cigarette, and the thought of marijuana, which I assumed it was, terrified me. To my horror, Mary Jane took it and inhaled. She told me later that it made her feel a bit light-headed, but that was all. I must admit, she didn't act any differently from normal. At least not that day. We left shortly after, promising to drop by again, and it was only over the next few weeks that I noticed Mary Jane's behavior and appearance gradually start to change.

It was just little things at first, like a string of beads she bought at a junk shop in Logan. It was nothing much, really, just cheap colored glass, but it was something she would have turned her nose up at just a short while ago. Now, it replaced the lovely gold chain and heart pendant that her parents had given her for her fifteenth birthday. Next came the red cheesecloth top with the silver sequins and fancy Indian embroidery, and the first Mad Hatters LP, the one with "her song" on it.

We went often to Pine Island to see Jared and the others, and I soon began to sense something, some deeper connection, between Mary Jane and Jared and, quite frankly, it worried me. They started wandering off together for hours, and sometimes she told me to go back home without her, that she'd catch a later ferry. It wasn't that Mary Jane was naïve or anything, or that I didn't trust Jared. I also knew that Mary Jane's father was liberal, and she said he trusted her, but I still worried. The townsfolk were already getting more than a bit suspicious because of the odd way she was dressing and behaving. Even Riley McCorkindale gave her strange looks in chapel. It didn't take a genius to put two and two together. At the very least, if she wasn't careful, she could end up grounded for the rest of the summer.

Things came to a head after chapel one Sunday in August. The preacher had delivered one of his most blistering sermons yet about what happens to those who turn away from the path of righteousness and embrace evil, complete with a graphic description of the torments of hell. Afterward, people were standing talking, as they do, all a little nervous, and Mary Jane actually said to the preacher that she didn't believe there was a hell, that if God was good, he wouldn't do such horrible things to people. The preacher turned scarlet, and it was only the fact that Mary Jane ran off and jumped on the ferry that stopped him taking her by the ear and dragging her back inside the chapel for special instruction whether she liked it or not. But he wouldn't forget. You didn't cross the preacher and get away with it. No, sirree. One way or another, there'd be hell to pay.

Or there would have been, except that was the evening they found Mary Jane's body on the western beach of Pine Island.

The fisherman who found her body said he first thought it was a bundle of clothes on the sand. Then, when he went to investigate, he realized that it was a young girl and sailed back to Jasmine Cove as fast as he could. Soon, the police launch was heading out there, the parking lot was full of police cars and the sheriff had commandeered the ferry. Mr. Kiernan was beside himself, blaming himself for not keeping a closer eye on her. But it wasn't his fault. He wasn't as mean-spirited as the rest, and how could he know what would happen, anyway?

By the time it started to get dark, word was spreading around town that a girl's body had been found, that it was the body of Mary Jane Kiernan, and that she had been strangled.

I can't really describe the shock I felt when I first heard the news. It was as if my whole being went numb. I didn't believe it at first, of course, but in a way I did. So many people said it had happened that in the end I just had to believe it. Mary Jane was gone.

The next few days passed as in a dream. I remember only that the newspapers were full of stories about some huge gathering out east for folks like the Newcomers, at a place called Woodstock, where it rained cats and dogs and everyone took bad drugs and rolled in the mud. The police came around and questioned everybody, and I was among the first, being Mary Jane's closest friend. The young detective, Donovan was his name, seemed nice enough, and Mother offered him a glass of iced tea, which he accepted. His forehead and upper lip were covered by a thin film of sweat.

"Now then, little lady," he began.

"My name's Grace," I corrected him. "I am not a little lady."

I'll give him his due, he took it in his stride. "Very well, Grace," he said. "Mary Jane was your best friend. Is that right?"

"Yes," I answered.

"Were you with her when she went to Pine Island last Sunday?"

"No," I said.

"Didn't you usually go there together?"

"Sometimes. Not always."

"Why did she go there? There's not exactly a lot to see or do."

I shrugged. "It's peaceful. There's a nice beach . . ." I couldn't help myself, but as soon as I thought of the beach—it had been *our* beach—the tears started to flow. Donovan paused while I reached for a tissue, dried my eyes and composed myself. "I'm sorry," I went on. "It's just a very beautiful place. And there are all kinds of interesting sea birds."

"Yes, but that's not why Mary Jane went there, is it, for the sea birds?"

"Isn't it? I don't know."

"Come on, Grace," said Donovan, "we already know she was seeing a young man called David Garwell."

David Garwell. So that was Jared's real name. "Why ask me, then?"

"Do you know if she had arranged to meet him that day? Last Sunday?"

"I'm sure I don't know," I said. "Mary Jane didn't confide in me about everything." Maybe he did know that Mary Jane was "seeing" Jared, but I wasn't going to tell him that she had told me just two days before she died that she was in love with him, and that as soon as she turned sixteen she planned to go and live with him and the others on Pine Island. That wouldn't have gone down at all well with Detective Donovan. Besides, it was our secret.

Donovan looked uncomfortable and shuffled in his seat, then he dropped his bombshell. "Maybe she didn't tell you that she was having a baby, Grace, huh? And we think it was his. Did Mary Jane tell you she was having David Garwell's baby?"

———

In the end, it didn't matter what I thought or said. While the bedraggled crowds were heading home from Woodstock in the east, the police arrested Jared—David Garwell—for the murder of Mary Jane Kiernan. They weren't giving out a whole lot of details, but rumor had it that they had found Mary Jane's gold pendant in a drawer in his room.

"He did it, Grace, you know he did," said Cathy Baker outside the drugstore a few days later. "People like that . . . they're . . . ugh!" She pulled a face and made a gesture with her hands as if to sweep spiders off her chest. "They're not like us."

"But why would he hurt her?" I asked. "He loved her."

"*Love?*" echoed Cathy. "They don't know the meaning of the word."

"They call it *free* love, you know," Lynne Everett chirped in. "And that means they do it with anyone."

"And everyone," added Cathy, with a sly glance at me. "Maybe they even did it with you. You were over there often enough. Did they, Grace? Did they do it with you, too?"

"Oh, shut up!" I said. Then I gave up. What was the point? They weren't going to listen. I walked down Main Street with my head hung low and the sun beating on the back of my neck. I'd lost my best friend, and the boy I thought was in love with her had been arrested for her murder. Things couldn't get much worse. It just didn't make sense. Mary Jane had stopped wearing the pendant when she bought the cheap colored beads. Jared couldn't have stolen it from her, even if he was capable of such a thing, unless he had broken into her house on the mainland, which seemed very unlikely to me. And she hadn't been wearing it on the day she died, I was certain of that. It made far more sense to assume that she had given it to him as a token of her love.

The problem was that I hadn't seen Jared or any of the others since the arrest, so I hadn't been able to ask them what happened. The police had searched the cabins, of course, and they said they found drugs, so they hauled everybody into the county jail and put the children in care.

I was so lost in thought that I didn't even notice Detective Donovan walking beside me until he spoke my name and asked me if I wanted to go into Slater's with him for a coffee.

"I'm not allowed to drink coffee," I told him, "but I'll have a soda, if that's all right."

He said that was fine and we went inside and took a table. He waited awhile before speaking, then he said, "Look, Grace, I know that this is all a terrible shock to you, that Mary Jane was your best friend. I respect that, but if you know anything else that will help us in court against the man who killed her, I'd really be grateful if you'd tell me."

"Why do you need me?" I asked. "I thought you knew everything. You've already put him in jail."

"I know," Donovan agreed. "And we've probably got enough to convict him, but every little bit helps. Did she say anything? Did you see anything?"

I told him why I thought Jared couldn't possibly have stolen the locket unless he went to the mainland.

Donovan smiled. "I don't know how you know about that," he said. "I suppose I shouldn't underestimate small-town gossip. We know she wasn't wearing the locket on the day she died, but we don't know when he stole it."

"He didn't steal it! Jared's not a thief."

Donovan coughed. "I beg to differ, Grace," he said. "David Garwell has a record that includes petty larceny and possession of dangerous drugs. He should have been in jail to start with, but he skipped bail."

"I don't believe you."

"That's up to you. I could show you the evidence if you want to come to headquarters."

"No, thank you."

"It's your choice."

"But *why* would he hurt Mary Jane? He told her he loved her."

Donovan's ears pricked up. "He did?" He toyed with his coffee cup on the saucer. It still had an old lipstick stain around the rim. "We think they had an argument," he said. "Maybe Mary Jane discovered the theft of the pendant. Or perhaps she told Garwell that she was pregnant, and he wanted nothing further to do with her. Either way, she ran off down to that cozy little beach the two of you liked so much. He followed her, maybe worried that she'd tell her parents, or the police. They fought, and he strangled her."

"But then he'd *know* for certain that the police would suspect him!"

"People aren't always thinking straight when they're mad, Grace."

I shook my head. I know what he said made sense, but it *didn't* make sense, if you see what I mean. I didn't know what else to say.

"You're going to have to accept it sooner or later, Grace," Donovan said. "This Jared, as you call him, murdered your friend, and you're probably the only one who can help us make sure he pays for his crime."

"But I can't help you. Don't you see? I still don't believe Jared did it."

Donovan sighed. "They had an argument. She walked off. He admits that much. He won't tell us what it was about, but like I said, I think she confronted him over the gold pendant or the pregnancy. He followed her."

I squirmed in my seat, took a long sip of soda and asked, "Who else was on the island that day? Have you checked?"

"What do you mean?"

"You must have asked Mr. Kiernan, Mary Jane's father, who he took over and brought back that day. Was there anyone else who shouldn't have been there? Have you questioned them all, asked them for alibis?"

"No, but . . ."

"Don't you think you ought to? Why can't it be one of those people?"

"Like who?"

"The preacher!" I blurted it out.

Donovan shook his head, looking puzzled. "The preacher? Why?"

"Was he there? Was he on the ferry?"

"You know I can't tell you that."

"Well, you just ask him," I said, standing up, "because Mary Jane told me she saw him touching Betsy Goodall somewhere he shouldn't have been touching her."

The preacher was waiting for me after chapel the following Sunday. "Grace, a word in your ear," he said, leading me by the arm. He was smiling and looked friendly enough, in that well-scrubbed way of his, to fool anyone watching, including my parents, but his grip hurt and his clawlike fingers dug deep into my flesh. He took me back inside the dark chapel and sat me down in a corner, crowding me, his face close to mine. I couldn't smell bourbon on his breath, but I could smell peppermint. "I had a visit from the police the other day," he said. "A most unwelcome visit. And I've been trying to figure out ever since who's been telling tales out of school. I think it was you, Grace. You were her friend. Thick as thieves, the two of you, always unnaturally close."

"There was nothing unnatural about it," I said, my heart beating fast. "And yes, we were friends. So what?"

His upper lip curled. "Don't you give me any of your smart talk, young lady. You caused me a lot of trouble, you did, a lot of grief."

"You've got nothing to worry about if you're pure in heart and true in the eyes of the Lord. Isn't that what you're always telling us?"

"Don't take the Lord's word in vain. I swear, one day . . ." He shook his head. "Grace, I do believe you're headed for a life of sin, and you know what the wages of sin are, don't you?"

"Did you go to Pine Island that day, Preacher? The day Mary Jane died. Were you on the ferry? You were, weren't you?"

The preacher looked away. "As a matter of fact, I had some important business there," he said. "Real estate business." We all knew about the preacher and his real estate. He seemed to think the best way of carrying out God's plan on earth was to take ownership of as much of it as he could afford.

"Why haven't they arrested you?" I asked.

"Because I haven't done anything wrong. I am a man of God. The police believe me. So should you. There's no evidence against me. I didn't strangle that girl."

"Mary Jane told me about Betsy Goodall, about what she saw."

"And just what did she see? I'll tell you what she saw. Nothing. Ask Betsy Goodall. The police did. Your friend Mary Jane was a wayward child," the preacher said, his voice a sort of drone. "An abomination in the face of the Lord. She had a vile imagination. Evil. She made up stories. The police know that now. They talked to me and they talked to Betsy. I just want to warn you, Grace. Don't you go around making any more grief for me, or you'll have more trouble than you can imagine. Do you understand me?"

"Betsy was too scared to say anything, wasn't she? She was frightened of what you might do to her. What did you do to Mary Jane?"

There. It was out before I realized it. That's the problem with me sometimes: I speak before thinking. I felt his fingers squeeze even deeper into my arm and I cried out. "Do you understand me?" he asked again, his voice a reptilian whisper.

"Yes!" I said. "You're hurting me! Yes, I understand. Leave me alone. Let go of me!" And I wrenched my arm free and ran out of the chapel over to the ferry dock. I wanted to be by myself, and I wanted to walk where Mary Jane and I had walked. There was really only one place I could go, and I was lucky, I had only ten minutes to wait.

The day had turned hazy, warm and sticky. There'd be a storm after dark, everyone said. Mr. Kiernan seemed worried about me and told me if I wasn't on the next ferry home he'd send someone looking for me. I said that was sweet but I would be all right. Then he said he'd keep an eye on the weather to make sure I didn't get stuck out there when the storm came.

I walked past the houses and through the woods to the southern tip of the island, where the Newcomers used to live. They had been taken away so fast they hadn't even had time to grab what few belongings they had. Nobody seemed to know what would happen to their things now, whether anyone would come for them. I stood behind the cover of the trees looking into the clearing, the way Mary Jane and I had done that first time, when we saw Jared come out of the shower. And there it was again, faint, drifting, as if it belonged to the air it traveled on: Mary Jane's song. "And Mary Jane is dreaming / Of oceans dark and gleaming."

But who was playing it?

Heart in my mouth, I ducked low and waited. I wanted to know, but I didn't want to go in there, the way people went into basements and rooms in movies when they knew evil lurked there. So I hid.

As it turned out, I didn't have long to wait. As soon as the song ended, a head peeped out of the doorway and, gauging that all was clear, the young man stepped out into the open. My jaw dropped. It was Riley McCorkindale.

Some instinct still held me back from announcing my presence, so I stayed where I was. Riley stood, ears pricked, glancing around furtively, then he headed away from the cabins—not back toward his parents' house, but west, toward the cliffs. Now I was really puzzled.

When I calculated that Riley had got a safe distance ahead of me, I followed through the trees. I couldn't see him, but there weren't many paths on the island, and not many places to go if you were heading in that direction. Once in a while I would stop and listen, and I could hear him way ahead, snapping a twig, rustling a bush as he walked. I hoped he didn't stop and listen the same way and hear me following him.

As I walked, I wondered what on earth Riley had been doing at the Newcomers' cabin. Playing the record with the Mary Jane song on it, obviously. But why? And how did he know about it? He must have been eavesdropping. I knew he had been sweet on her, of course, but he had always been too shy to say hello. Had he made friends with the Newcomers? After all, they were practically neighbors. But Riley went to chapel, and he seemed the type to take notice of the preacher. His father was a property developer in Logan, so they were a wealthy and respected family in the community, too, which made it even more unlikely that Riley would have anything to do with Jared and the others.

When I reached the cliffs, there was no one in sight. I glanced over the edge, down toward the beach, but saw no one there, either. I wasn't sure whether Riley knew about the hidden path Mary Jane and I used to take. He lived on the island, so perhaps he did. I stood still for a moment and felt the wind whipping my hair in my eyes and tugging at my clothes, bringing the dark clouds from far out at sea. I heard the raucous cries of gulls over a shoal of fish just off the coast and smelled the salt air. Then, just as I started to move toward the path, I heard a voice behind me.

"Hello, Grace."

I turned. Riley stepped out from the edge of the woods.

"Riley," I said, smiling, trying to sound relaxed, and holding my hair from my eyes. "You startled me. What are you doing here?"

"You were following me."

"Me? No. Why would I do that?" I felt vulnerable at the edge of the cliff, aware of the golden sand so far below, and as I spoke I tried edging slowly forward. But Riley stood his ground, and right now he didn't seem shy at all.

"I don't know," he said. "But I saw you. Maybe it's something to do with Mary Jane?"

"Mary Jane?"

"You know I loved her. Until that . . . that freak came and took her away from me. Still, he's got what he deserves. Let him rot in jail."

"Now, listen, Riley. You don't have to say anything to me." The last thing I wanted was to be Riley's confessor with a hundred-foot drop behind me. "Let's just go back, huh? I don't want to miss my ferry."

"I used to watch them, you know," Riley said. "Watch them doing it."

I didn't know what to say to that. I swallowed.

"They'd do it anywhere. They didn't care who was watching."

"That's not true, Riley," I said. "You know that can't be true. You were spying on them. You said so."

"Maybe so. But they did it down there." He pointed. "On the beach."

"It's a very secluded spot." I don't know what I meant by that, whether I was defending Mary Jane's honor, deflecting the shock I felt, or what. I just wanted to keep Riley talking until I could get around him and . . . well, getting back to the ferry was my main thought. But if Riley had other ideas, there wasn't much I could do. He was bigger and stronger than me. Drops of rain dampened my cheek. The sky was becoming darker. "Look, Riley," I said. "There's going to be a storm. Move out of the way and let me go back to the ferry dock. I'll miss my ferry. Mr. Kiernan will come looking for me."

"I didn't mean to do it, you know," Riley said.

I had been trying to skirt around him, but I froze. "Didn't mean to do what?" There I was again, speaking without thinking. I didn't want to know what he had done, but it was too late now.

"Kill her. It just happened. One minute she was . . ."

Now he'd told me I just had to know the full story. Unless I could make a break into the woods when he wasn't expecting it, I was done for anyway. I didn't think I could outrun him, but with the cover of the trees, and the coming dark, perhaps I had a chance of staying ahead of him as far as the ferry dock. By far my best option was to keep him talking. "How did it happen?" I asked, still moving slowly.

"They had a fight. I was watching the cabin and they had a fight and Mary Jane ran out crying."

The baby, I thought. *She told him about the baby.* But why would that matter? The Newcomers loved children. They would have welcomed Mary Jane and her child. It must have been something else. Perhaps she wanted to get married? That would have been far too conventional for Jared but just like Mary Jane. Whatever it was, they had argued. Couples do argue. I'd even heard my parents do it. "What happened?" I asked.

"I followed her like you followed me. She went down to the beach. Down that path you both thought was your little secret. I went after her. I thought I could comfort her. You know, I thought she'd dumped him and maybe she would turn to me if I was nice to her."

"How did it go wrong?"

"She did it with him, didn't she?" Riley said, his voice rising to a shout against the coming storm. "Why wouldn't she do it with me? Why did she have to laugh?"

"She laughed at you?"

He nodded. "That's when I grabbed her. The next thing I . . . I guess I don't know my own strength. She was like a rag doll."

There was a slim chance that I could slip into the woods to the left of him and make a run for it. That was when he said, "I'm glad I told you. I've been wanting to tell somebody, just to get it off my chest. I feel better now."

I paused before speaking. "But Riley, you have to go to the authorities. You have to tell them there's an innocent man in jail."

"No! I ain't going to jail. I won't. Only you and me know the truth."

"Riley, if you hurt me they'll know," I said, my voice shaking as I judged the distance between his reach and the gap in the trees. "They'll know it was you. I told Mr. Kiernan I came here to talk to you." It was a lie, of course, but I hoped it was an inspired one.

"Why would you do that?" Riley seemed genuinely puzzled. "You didn't know anything about it until just now. You didn't even know I existed. You didn't want to know. None of you did."

"I mean it, Riley. If you hurt me, they'll find out. You can't get away with murder twice. You'll go to jail then for sure."

"They say killing's easier the second time. I read that in a book."

"Riley, don't."

"It's all right, Grace," he said, leaning back against the tree. "I ain't going to hurt you. Don't think I don't regret what I did. Don't think I enjoyed it. I'm just not going to jail for it. Go. Catch your ferry. See if I care."

"B-but . . ."

"Who'd believe you? The police have got the man they want. There sure as hell's no evidence against me. My daddy doesn't know where I was, but he already told them I was home all day. Last thing he wants to know is that his son killed some girl. That would surely upset the applecart. Nobody saw me. The preacher's with us, too. He was at the house talking real estate with Daddy. I don't know if he knows I did it or not, but he don't care. He was the one told me about Mary Jane and that freak, what they were doing and how it was a sin. That's why I went to spy on them. He told me he knew she was really my girl, but she'd been seduced by the devil. He told me what that long-haired pervert was doing to her and asked me what I was going to do about it. Said I ought to act like a real man. The preacher won't be saying nothing to no police. So go on. Go."

"But why did you tell me?"

Riley thought for a moment. "Like I said, I knew I'd feel better if I told someone. I'm truly sorry for what I did, but going to jail ain't going to bring Mary Jane back."

"But what about Jared? He's innocent."

"He's the spawn of Satan. Now go ahead, Grace. Catch the ferry before the storm comes. It's going to be a bad one."

"You won't . . . ?"

He shook his head. "Nope. Don't matter what you say. Go ahead. See if I'm not right."

And I did. I caught the ferry. Mr. Kiernan smiled and said I was lucky I just made it. The storm broke that night, flooded a few roads, broke a few windows. The next day I took the bus into the city to see Detective Donovan and told him about what Riley had said to me on the beach. He laughed, said the boy was having me on, giving me a scare. I told him it was true, that Riley was in love with Mary Jane and that he tried to . . . I couldn't get the words out in front of him, but even so he was shaking his head before I'd finished.

So Riley McCorkindale turned out to be right. The police didn't believe me. I didn't see any point running all over town telling Mr. Kiernan, Father, the preacher, or anyone else, so that was the end of it. Riley McCorkindale strangled Mary Jane Kiernan and got away with it. Jared—David Garwell—went to jail for a crime he didn't commit. He didn't stay there long, though. Word made it back to town about a year or two later that he got stabbed in a prison brawl, and even then everyone said he had it coming, that it was divine justice.

None of the Newcomers ever returned to Jasmine Cove. The cabins fell into disrepair again, and their property reverted to the township in one of those roundabout ways that these things often happen in small communities like ours. I thought of Mary Jane often over the years, remembered her smile, her childlike enthusiasm. The Mad Hatters became famous and once in a while I heard "her" song on the radio. It always made me cry.

After I had finished college and started teaching high school in Logan, the property boom began. The downtown areas of many major cities became uninhabitable, people moved out to the suburbs and the rich wanted country, or island, retreats. One day I heard that McCorkindale Developments had knocked down the cabins on Pine Island and cleared the land for a strip of low-rise, ocean-front luxury condominiums.

I suppose it's what you might call ironic, depending on the way you look at it, but by that time the preacher and Riley's father had managed to buy up most of the island for themselves.

Walking the Dog

The dog days came to the Beaches in August and the boardwalk was crowded. Even the dog owners began to complain about the heat. Laura Francis felt as if she had been locked in the bathroom after a hot shower as she walked Big Ears down to the fenced-off compound on Kew Beach, where he could run free. She said hello to the few people she had seen there before while Big Ears sniffed the shrubbery and moved on to play with a Labrador retriever.

"They seem to like each other," said a voice beside her.

Laura turned and saw a man she thought she recognized, but not from the Beaches. She couldn't say where. He was handsome in a chis-eled, matinee-idol sort of way, and the tight jeans and white T-shirt did justice to his well-toned muscles and tapered waist. Where did she know him from?

"You must excuse Big Ears," she said. "He's such a womanizer."

"It's nothing Rain can't handle."

"Rain? That's an unusual name for a dog."

He shrugged. "Is it? It was raining the day I picked her up from the Humane Society. Raining cats and dogs. Anyway, you're one to talk, naming dogs after English children's book characters."

Laura felt herself flush. "My mother used to read them to me when I was little. I grew up in England."

"I can tell by the accent. I'm Ray, by the way. Ray Lanagan."

"Laura Francis. Pleased to meet you."

"Laura? After the movie?"

"After my grandmother."

"Pity. You do look a bit like Gene Tierney, you know."

Laura tried to remember whether Gene Tierney was the one with overbite or the large breasts. As she had both herself, she supposed it didn't really matter. She blushed again. "Thank you."

They stood in an awkward, edgy silence while the dogs played on around them. Then, all of a sudden, Laura remembered where she had seen Ray before. Jesus, of course, it was *him,* the guy from the TV commercial, the one for some sort of male aftershave or deodorant where he was stripped to the waist, wearing tight jeans like today. She'd seen the ad in a magazine, too. She had even fantasized about him, imagined it was him there in bed with her instead of Lloyd grunting away on top as if he were running a marathon.

"What is it?" Ray asked.

She brushed a strand of hair from her hot cheek. "Nothing. I just remembered where I've seen you before. You're an actor, aren't you?"

"For my sins."

"Are you here to make a movie?" It wasn't as stupid a question as it might have sounded. The studios were just down the road, and Toronto had almost as big a reputation for being Hollywood North as Vancouver. Laura ought to know; Lloyd ran a postproduction company, and he was always telling her so.

"No," Ray said. "I'm resting, as we say in the business."

"Oh."

"I've got a couple of things lined up," he went on. "Commercials, a small part in a new CBC legal drama. That sort of thing. And whatever comes my way by chance."

"It sounds exciting."

"Not really. It's a living. To be honest, it's mostly a matter of hanging around while the techies get the sound and light right. But what about you? What do you do?"

"Me?" She pointed her thumb at her chest. "Nothing. I mean, I'm just a housewife." It was true, she supposed: "housewife" was about the only way she could describe herself. But she wasn't even that. Phaedra did all of the housework, and Paula handled the garden. Laura had even hired a company to come in and clear the snow from the steps and the driveway in winter. So what did she do with her time, apart from shop and walk Big Ears? Sometimes she made dinner, but more often than not she made reservations. There were so many good restaurants on her stretch of Queen Street East—anything you wanted, Japanese, Greek, Indian, Chinese, Italian—that it seemed a shame to waste them.

The hazy bright sun beat down mercilessly and the water looked like a ruffled blue bedsheet beyond the wire fence. Laura was feeling embarrassed now that she had openly declared her uselessness.

"Would you like to go for a drink?" Ray asked. "I'm not coming on to you or anything, but it *is* a real scorcher."

Laura felt her heart give a little flutter, and, if she were honest with herself, a pleasurable warmth spread through her lower belly.

"Okay. Yes, I mean, sure," she said. "Look, it's a bit of a hassle going to a café or a pub with the dogs, right? Why don't you come up to the house? It's not far. Silver Birch. There's cold beer in the fridge and I left the air-conditioning on."

Ray looked at her. He certainly had beautiful eyes, she thought, and they seemed especially steely blue in this kind of light. Blue eyes and black hair, a devastating combination. "Sure," he said. "If it's okay. Lead on."

They put Big Ears and Rain on leashes and walked up to Queen Street, which was crowded with tourists and locals pulling kids in bright-colored carts, all OshKosh B'Gosh and Birkenstocks. People browsed in shop windows, sat outdoors at Starbucks in shorts drinking their Frappuccinos and reading the *Globe and Mail,* and there was a queue outside the ice cream shop. The traffic was moving at a crawl, but you could smell the coconut sunblock over the gas fumes.

Laura's large detached house stood at the top of a long flight of steps sheltered by overhanging shrubbery, and once they were off the street, nobody could see them. Not that it mattered, Laura told herself. It was all innocent enough.

It was a relief to get inside, and even the dogs seemed to collapse in a panting heap and enjoy the cool air.

"Nice place," said Ray, looking around the modern kitchen, with its central island and pots and pans hanging from hooks overhead.

Laura opened the fridge. "Beer? Coke? Juice?"

"I'll have a beer, if that's okay," said Ray.

"Beck's all right?"

"Perfect."

She opened Ray a Beck's and poured herself a glass of orange juice, the kind with the extra pulp. Her heart was beating fast. Perhaps it was the heat, the walk home? She watched Ray drink his beer from the bottle, his Adam's apple bobbing. When she took a sip of juice, a little dribbled out of her mouth and down her chin. Before she could get a napkin and wipe it off, Ray had leaned forward just as far as it took, touched his tongue on the curve under her lower lip, and licked it off.

She felt his heat and shivered. "Ray, I'm not sure . . . I mean, I don't think we should . . . I . . ."

The first kiss nearly drew blood. The second one did. Laura fell back against the fridge and felt the Mickey Mouse fridge-magnet that held the weekly to-do list digging into her shoulder. She experienced a moment of panic as Ray ripped open her Holt Renfrew blouse. What did she think she was doing, inviting a strange man into her home like this? He could be a serial killer or something. But fear quickly turned to pleasure when his mouth found her nipple. She moaned and pulled him against her and spread her legs apart. His hand moved up under her long, loose skirt, caressing the bare flesh of her thighs and rubbing between her legs.

Laura had never been so wet in her life, had never wanted it so much, and she didn't want to wait. Somehow, she maneuvered them toward the dining room table and tugged at his belt and zipper as they stumbled backward. She felt the edge of the table bump against the backs of her thighs and eased herself up on it, sweeping a couple of Waterford crystal glasses to the floor as she did so. The dogs barked. Ray was good and hard, and he pulled her panties aside as she guided him smoothly inside her.

"Fuck me, Ray," she breathed. "Fuck me."

And he fucked her. He fucked her until she hammered with her fists on the table and a Royal Doulton cup and saucer joined the broken crystal on the floor. The dogs howled. Laura howled. When she sensed that Ray was about to come she pulled him closer and said, "Bite me."

And he bit her.

"I really think we should have that dog put down," said Lloyd after dinner that evening. "For God's sake, biting you like that. It could have given you rabies or something."

"Don't be silly. Big Ears isn't in the least bit rabid. It was an accident, that's all. I was just a bit too rough with him."

"It's the thin end of the wedge. Next time it'll be the postman, or some kid in the street. Think what'll happen then."

"We are not having Big Ears put down, and that's final. I'll be more careful in future."

"You just make sure you are." Lloyd paused, then asked, "Have you thought any more about that other matter I mentioned?"

Oh God, Laura thought, *not again.* Lloyd hated their house, hated the Beaches, hated Toronto. He wanted to sell up and move to Vancouver, live in Kitsilano or out on Point Grey. No matter that it rained there 364 days out of every year and all you could get to eat was sushi and alfalfa sprouts. Laura didn't want to live in Lotus Land. She was happy where she was. Even happier since that afternoon.

As Lloyd droned on and on, she drifted into pleasant reminiscences of Ray's body on hers, the hard, sharp edges of his white teeth as they closed on the soft part of her neck. They had done it again, up in the bed this time, her and Lloyd's bed. It was slower, less urgent, more gentle, but if anything, it was even better. He was a good kisser, and the tip of his tongue found a sensitive spot at the front between her upper lip and gum that connected directly with her loins. She could still remember the warm ripples and floods of pleasure, like breaking waves running up through her loins and her belly, and she could feel a pleasant soreness between her legs even now, as she sat listening to Lloyd outline the advantages of moving the postproduction company to Vancouver. Plenty of work there, he said. Hollywood connections. But if they moved, she would never see Ray again. It seemed more imperative than ever now to put a stop to it. She had to do *something.*

"I really don't want to talk about it right now, darling," she said.

"You never do."

"You know what I think of Vancouver."

"It doesn't rain that much."

"It's not just that. It's . . . Oh, can't we just leave it be?"

Lloyd put his hand up. "All right," he said. "All right. Subject closed for tonight." He got up and walked over to the drinks cabinet. "I feel like a cognac," he said.

Laura had that sinking feeling. She knew what was coming.

"Where is it?" Lloyd asked.

"Where is what, darling?"

"My snifter, my favorite brandy snifter. The one my father bought me."

"Oh, that," said Laura, remembering the shattered glass she had swept up from the hardwood floor. "I meant to tell you. I'm sorry, but there was an accident. The dishwasher."

Lloyd turned to look at her in disbelief. "You put my favorite crystal snifter in the *dishwasher*?"

"I know. I'm sorry. I was in a hurry."

Lloyd frowned. "A hurry? You? What do you ever have to be in a hurry about? Walking the bloody dog?"

Laura tried to laugh it off. "If only you knew half the things I had to do around the place, darling."

Lloyd continued to look at her. His eyes narrowed. "Had quite a day, haven't you?" he said.

Laura sighed. "I suppose so. It's just been one of those days."

"This'll have to do then," he said, pouring a generous helping of Rémy into a different crystal snifter.

It was just as good as the one she had broken, Laura thought. In fact, it was probably more expensive. But it wasn't *his*. It wasn't the one his bloody miserable old bastard of a father, God rot his soul, had bought him.

Lloyd sat down and sipped his cognac thoughtfully. The next time he spoke, Laura could see the way he was looking at her over the top of his glass. *That* look. "How about an early night?" he said.

Laura's stomach lurched. She put her hand to her forehead. "Oh, not tonight, darling," she said. "I'm sorry, but I have a terrible head-ache."

She didn't see Ray for nearly a week, and she was going crazy with fear that he'd left town, maybe gone to Hollywood to be a star, that he'd just used her and discarded her the way men did. After all, they had only been together the once, and he hadn't told her he loved her or anything. All they had done was fuck. They didn't really *know* each other at all. They hadn't even exchanged phone numbers. She just had this absurd feeling that they were meant for each other, that it was *destiny*. A fool-ish fantasy, no doubt, but one that hurt like a knife jabbing into her heart every day she didn't see him.

Then one day, there he was at the beach again, as if he'd never been away. The dogs greeted each other like long-lost friends while Laura tried to play it cool as lust burned through her like a forest fire.

"Hello, stranger," she said.

"I'm sorry," Ray said. "A job came up. Shampoo commercial. On the spot decision. Yes or no. I had to work on location in Niagara Falls. You're not mad at me, are you? It's not as if I could phone you and let you know or anything."

"Niagara Falls? How romantic."

"The bride's second great disappointment."

"What?"

"Oscar Wilde. What he said."

Laura giggled and put her hand to her mouth. "Oh, I see."

"I'd love to have taken you with me. I know it wouldn't have been a disappointment for us. I missed you."

Laura blushed. "I missed you, too. Want a cold beer?"

"Look," said Ray, "why don't we go to my place. It's only a top-floor flat, but it's air-conditioned, and . . ."

"And what?"

"Well, you know, the neighbors . . ."

Laura couldn't tell him this, but she had got such an incredible rush out of doing it with Ray in *her own bed* that she couldn't stand the thought of going to his flat, no matter how nice and cool it was. Though she had changed and washed the sheets, she had fancied she could still smell him when she laid her head down for the night, and now she wanted her bed to absorb even more of him.

"Don't worry about the neighbors," she said. "They're all out during the day, anyway, and the nannies have to know how to be discreet if they want to stay in this country."

"Are you sure?"

"Perfectly."

And so it went on. Once, twice, sometimes three times a week, they went back to Laura's big house on Silver Birch. Sometimes they couldn't wait to get upstairs, so they did it on the dining room table like the first time, but mostly they did it in the king-size bed, becoming more and more adventurous and experimental as they got to know each other's bodies and pleasure zones. Laura found a little pain quite stimulating sometimes, and Ray didn't mind obliging. They sampled all the positions and all the orifices, and when they had exhausted them, they started all over again. They talked, too, a lot, between bouts. Laura told Ray how unhappy she was with her marriage, and Ray told her how his ex-wife had ditched him for his accountant because his career wasn't exactly going in the same direction as Russell Crowe's, as his bank account made abundantly clear.

Then, one day when they had caught their breath after a particularly challenging position that wasn't even in the *Kama Sutra*, Laura said, "Lloyd wants to sell up and move to Vancouver. He won't stop going on about it. And he never gives up until he gets his way."

Ray turned over and leaned on his elbow. "You can't leave," he said.

It was as simple as that. *You can't leave.* She looked at him and beamed. "I know," she said. "You're right. I can't."

"Divorce him. Live with me. I want us to have a normal life, go places together like everyone else, go out for dinner, go to the movies, take vacations to Florida every winter."

It was everything she wanted, too. "Do you mean it, Ray?"

"Of course I mean it." He paused. "I love you, Laura."

Tears came to her eyes. "Oh my God." She kissed him and told him she loved him, too, and a few minutes later they resumed the conversation. "I can't divorce him," Laura said.

"Why on earth not?"

"For one thing, he's a Catholic. He's not practicing or anything, but he doesn't believe in divorce." Or more important, Laura thought, his poor dead father, who *was* devout in a bugger-the-choirboys sort of way, didn't believe in it.

"And . . . ?"

"Well, there's the money."

"What money?"

"It's mine. I mean, I inherited it from my father. He was an inventor and he came up with one of those simple little additives that keep things fresh for years. Anyway, he made a lot of money, and I was his only child, so I got it all. I've been financing Lloyd's postproduction career from the beginning, before it started doing as well as it is now. If we divorced, with these no-fault laws we've got today, he'd get half of everything. That's not fair. It should be all mine by rights."

"I don't care about the money. It's you I want."

She touched his cheek. "That's sweet, Ray, and I wouldn't care if we didn't have two cents between us as long as we were together, honest I wouldn't. But it doesn't have to be that way. The money's there. And everything I have is yours."

"So what's the alternative?"

She put her hand on his chest and ran it over the soft hair down to his flat stomach and beyond, kissed the eagle tattoo on his arm. She remembered it from the TV commercial and the magazine, had thought it was sexy even then. The dogs stirred for a moment at the side of the bed, then went back to sleep. They'd had a lot of exercise that morning. "There's the house, too," Laura went on, "and Lloyd's life insurance. Double indemnity, or something like that. I don't really understand these things, but it's really quite a lot of money. Enough to live on for a long time, maybe somewhere in the Caribbean? Or Europe. I've always wanted to live in Paris."

"What are you saying?"

Laura paused. "What if Lloyd had an accident? No, hear me out. Just suppose he had an accident. We'd have everything then. The house, the insurance, the business, my inheritance. It would all be ours. And we could be together for always."

"An accident? You're talking about—"

She put her finger to his lips. "No, darling, don't say it. Don't say the word."

But whether he said it or not, she knew, as she knew he did, what the word was, and it sent a delightful shiver up her spine. The word was *murder. Murder* was what they were talking about. After a while, Ray said, "I might know someone. I did an unusual job once, impersonated a police officer in Montreal, a favor for someone who knew someone whose son was in trouble. You don't need to know who he is, but he's connected. He was very pleased with the way things worked out and he said if ever I needed anything . . ."

"Well, there you are, then," said Laura, sitting up. "Do you know how to find this man? Do you think he could arrange something?"

Ray took her left nipple between his thumb and forefinger and squeezed. "I think so," he said. "But it won't be easy. I'd have to go to Montreal. Make contact. Right at the moment, though, something a bit more urgent has come up."

Laura saw what he meant. She slid down and took him in her mouth.

Time moved on, as it does. The days cooled, but Ray and Laura's passion didn't. Just after Thanksgiving, the weather forecasters predicted a big drop in temperature and encouraged Torontonians to wrap up warm.

Laura and Ray didn't need any warm wrapping. The rose-patterned duvet lay on the floor at the bottom of the bed, and they were bathed in sweat, panting, as Laura straddled Ray and worked them both to a shuddering climax. Instead of rolling off him when they had finished, this time Laura stayed on top and leaned forward, her hard nipples brushing his chest. They hadn't seen each other for a week because Ray had finally met his contact in Montreal.

"Did you talk to that man you know?" she asked after she had caught her breath.

Ray linked his hands behind his head. "Yes," he said.

"Does he know what . . . I mean, what we want him to do?"

"He knows."

"To take his time and wait for absolutely the right opportunity?"

"He won't do it himself. The man he'll put on it is a professional, honey. He knows."

"And will he do it when the right time comes? It *must* seem like an accident."

"He'll do it. Don't worry."

"You know," Laura said, "you can stay all night if you want. Lloyd's away in Vancouver. Probably looking for property."

"Are you sure?"

"He won't be back till Thursday. We could just stay in bed the whole week." Laura shivered.

"Cold, honey?"

"A little. Winter's coming. Can't you feel it?"

Ray smiled. "I can definitely feel something," he said.

Laura gave him a playful tap on the chest, then gasped as he thrust himself inside her again. So much energy. This time he didn't let her stay in control. He grabbed her shoulders and pushed her over on her back, in the good old missionary position, and pounded away so hard Laura thought the bed was going to break. This time, as Laura reached the edges of her orgasm, she thought that if she died at this moment, in this state of bliss, she would be happy forever. Then the furnace came on, the house exploded, and Laura got her wish.

"**Two Dogs Perish** in Beaches Gas Explosion," Lloyd Francis read in the *Toronto Star* the following morning. "House-Owners Also Die in Tragic Accident." *Well, they got that wrong on two counts,* thought Lloyd. He was sitting over a cappuccino in his shirtsleeves at an outdoor café on Robson Street, in Vancouver. While the cold snap had descended on the east with a vengeance, the west coast was enjoying record temperatures for the time of year. And no rain.

Lloyd happened to know that only one of the house's owners had died in the explosion, and that it hadn't been an accident. Far from it. Lloyd had planned the whole thing very carefully from the moment he had found out that his wife was enjoying a *grand passion* with an out-of-work actor. That hadn't been difficult to do. For a start, she had begun washing the bedsheets and pillowcases almost every day, though she usually left the laundry to Phaedra. Despite her caution, he had once seen blood on one of the sheets. Laura had also been unusually reluctant to have sex with him, and on the few occasions he had persuaded her to comply, it had been obvious to him that her thoughts were elsewhere and that, in the crude vernacular, he had been getting sloppy seconds.

Not that Laura hadn't been careful and cleaned herself up well. Lord only knew, she had probably stood under the shower for hours. But he could still tell. There was another man's smell about her. And then, of course, he had simply lain in wait one day when she thought he was at the studio and seen them returning together from the beach. After that, it hadn't been hard to find out where the man, Ray Lanagan, lived, and what he did, or didn't do. Lloyd was quite pleased with his detective abilities. Maybe he was in the wrong profession. He had shown himself to be pretty good at murder, too, and he was certain that no one would be able to prove that the explosion in which his wife and her lover had died had been anything but a tragic accident. Things like that happened every year in Toronto when the heat came on. A slow leak, building over time, a furnace not serviced for years, a stray spark or a naked flame, and *BANG!*

Lloyd sipped his cappuccino and took a bite of his croissant.

"You seem preoccupied, darling," said Anne-Marie, looking lovely in a low-cut white top and a short denim skirt opposite him, her dark hair framing the delicate oval face, those tantalizing ruby lips. "What is it?"

"Nothing," said Lloyd. "Nothing at all. But I think I might have to fly back to Toronto today. Just for a short while."

Anne-Marie's face dropped. She was so expressive, showing joy or disappointment, pleasure or pain, without guile. This time it was clearly disappointment. "Oh, must you?"

"I'm afraid I must," he said, taking her hand and caressing it. "I have some important business to take care of. But I promise you I'll be back as soon as I can."

"And we'll live in that house we saw near Spanish Beach?"

"I'll put in an offer before I leave," Lloyd said. "It'll have to be in your name, though."

She wrinkled her nose. "I know. Tax reasons."

"Exactly. Good girl." It was only a little white lie, Lloyd told himself. But it wouldn't look good if he bought a new house in a faraway city the day after his wife died in a tragic explosion. This called for careful planning and pacing. Anne-Marie would understand. Marital separations were complicated and difficult, as complex as the tax laws, and all that really mattered was that she knew he loved her. After the funeral, of course, he might feel the need to "get away for a while," and then perhaps Toronto would remind him too much of Laura, so it would be understandable if he moved the business somewhere else, say Vancouver. After a decent period of mourning, it would also be quite acceptable to "meet someone," Anne-Marie, for example, and start anew, which was exactly what Lloyd Francis had in mind.

Detective Bobby Aiken didn't like the look of the report that had landed on his desk, didn't like the look of it at all. He worked out of police headquarters at 40 College Street, downtown, and under normal circumstances, he would never have heard of Laura Francis and Ray Lanagan. The Beaches was 55 Division's territory. But these weren't normal circumstances, and one of Aiken's jobs was to have a close look at borderline cases, where everything *looked* kosher but someone thought it wasn't. This time it was a young, ambitious beat cop who desperately wanted to work Homicide. There was just something about it, he'd said, something that didn't ring true, and the more Bobby Aiken looked at the files, the more he knew what the kid was talking about.

The forensics were clean, of course. The fire department and the Centre for Forensic Sciences had done sterling work there, as usual. These gas explosions were unfortunately commonplace in some of the older houses, where the owners might not have had their furnaces serviced or replaced for a long time, as had happened at the house on Silver Birch. An accident waiting to happen.

But police work, thank God, wasn't only a matter of forensics. There were other considerations here. Three of them.

Again, Aiken went through the files and jotted down his thoughts. Outside on College Street it was raining, and if he looked out of his window, all he could see were the tops of umbrellas. A streetcar rumbled by, sparks flashing from the overhead wire. Cars splashed up water from the gutters.

First of all, Aiken noted, the victims hadn't been husband and wife, as the investigators and media had first thought. The husband, Lloyd Francis, had flown back from a business trip to Vancouver—giving himself a nice alibi, by the way—as soon as he had heard the news the following day, and he was doubly distraught to find out that not only was his wife dead, but that she had died in bed with another man.

No, Lloyd had said, he had no idea who the man was, but it hadn't taken a Sherlock Holmes to discover that his name was Ray Lanagan, and that he was a sometime actor and sometime petty crook, with a record of minor fraud and con jobs. Lanagan had been clean for the past three years, relying mostly on TV commercials and bit parts in series like *Da Vinci's Inquest*, before the CBC canned it, and *The Murdoch Mysteries*. But Aiken knew that didn't necessarily mean he hadn't been up to something. He just hadn't got caught. Well, he had definitely been up to one thing—screwing Lloyd Francis's wife—and the penalty for that had been far more severe than for any other offense he had ever committed. He might have been after the broad's money, too, Aiken speculated, but he sure as hell wasn't going to get that now.

The second thing that bothered Aiken was the insurance and the money angle in general. Not only were the house and Laura Francis's life insured for hefty sums, but there was the postproduction company, which was just starting to turn a good profit, and Laura's inheritance, which was still a considerable sum, tied up in stocks and bonds and other investments. Whoever got his hands on all of that would be very rich indeed.

And then there was Lloyd Francis himself. The young beat cop who rang the alarm bell had thought there was something odd about him when he had accompanied Lloyd to the ruins of the house. Nothing obvious, nothing he could put his finger on, of course, but just that indefinable policeman's itch, the feeling you get when it doesn't all add up, like when the sound track doesn't synchronize with the picture in a movie. Aiken hadn't talked to Lloyd Francis yet, but he was beginning to think it was about time.

Because finally there was the one clear and indisputable fact that linked everything else, like the magnet that makes a pattern out of iron filings: Lloyd Francis had spent five years working as a heating and air-conditioning serviceman from just after he left school until his early twenties. And if you knew that much about gas furnaces, Aiken surmised, then you didn't have to bloody well be there when one blew up. You could be in Vancouver, for example.

Lloyd felt a little shaken after the policeman's visit, but he still believed he'd held his own. One thing was clear, and that was that they had done a lot of checking, not only into his background, but also into the dead man's, Ray Lanagan. What on earth had Laura seen in such a loser? The man had petty criminal stamped all over him.

But what had worried Lloyd most of all was the knowledge that the man, Aiken, seemed to have about his own past, especially his heating and air-conditioning work. Not only did the police know he had done that for five years, but they seemed to know every job he had been on, every problem he had solved, the brand name of every furnace he had ever serviced. It was all rather overwhelming. Lloyd hadn't lied about it, hadn't tried to deny any of it—that would have been a sure way of sharpening their suspicions even more—but the truth painted the picture of a man easily capable of rigging the type of furnace in the Silver Birch house until it blew up on the first cold snap of the year.

Luckily, Lloyd knew they had absolutely no forensic evidence. If there had been any, which he doubted, it would have been obliterated by the fire. All he had to do was stick to his story, and they would never be able to prove a thing. Suspicion was all very well, but it wasn't sufficient grounds for a murder charge.

After the funeral, he had lain low in a sublet condominium at Victoria Park and Danforth, opposite Shopper's World. At night the streets were noisy and a little edgy, Lloyd felt, the kind of area where you might easily get mugged if you weren't careful. More than once he had had the disconcerting feeling that he was being followed, but he told himself not to be paranoid. He wouldn't be here for long. After a suitable period of mourning he would go to Vancouver and decide he couldn't face returning to the city where his poor wife met such a terrible death. He still had a few colleagues who would regret his decision to leave, perhaps, but there wasn't really anybody left in Toronto to care that much about Lloyd Francis and what happened to him. At the moment, they all thought he was a bit depressed, "getting over his loss." Soon he would be free to "meet" Anne-Marie and start a new life. The money should be all his by then, too, once the lawyers and accountants had finished with it. Never again would he have to listen to his wife reminding him where his wealth and success came from.

The Silver Birch explosion had not only destroyed Lloyd's house and wife, it had also destroyed his car, a silver Toyota SUV, and he wasn't going to bother replacing it until he moved to Vancouver, where he'd probably buy a nice little red sports car. He still popped into the studios occasionally, mostly to see how things were going, and luckily his temporary accommodation was close to the Victoria Park subway. He soon found he didn't mind taking the TTC to work and back. In fact, he rather enjoyed it. They played classical music at the station to keep away the hooligans. If he got a seat on the train, he would read a book, and if he didn't, he would drift off into thoughts of his sweet Anne-Marie.

And so life went on, waiting, waiting, for the time when he could decently and without arousing suspicion, make his move. The policeman didn't return, obviously realizing that he had absolutely no chance of making a case against Lloyd without a confession, which he knew he wouldn't get. It was late November now, arguably one of the grimmest months in Toronto, but at least the snow hadn't come yet, just one dreary cold gray day after another.

On one such day Lloyd stood on the crowded eastbound platform at the St. George subway station wondering if he dare make his move as early as next week. At least, he thought, he could "go away for a while," maybe even until after Christmas. Surely that would be acceptable by now? People would understand that he couldn't bear to spend his first Christmas without Laura in Toronto.

He had just decided that he would do it when he saw the train come tearing into the station. In his excitement at the thought of seeing Anne-Marie again so soon, a sort of unconscious sense of urgency had carried him a little closer to the edge of the platform than he should have been, and the crowds jostled behind him. He felt something hard jab into the small of his back, and the next thing he knew, his legs buckled and he pitched forward. He couldn't stop himself. He toppled in front of the oncoming train before the driver could do a thing. His last thought was of Anne-Marie waving good-bye to him at Vancouver International Airport, then the subway train smashed into him and its wheels shredded him to pieces.

Someone in the crowd screamed and people started running back toward the exits. The frail-looking old man with the walking stick who had been standing directly behind Lloyd turned to walk away calmly through the chaos, but before he could get very far, two scruffy-looking young men emerged from the throng and one took him by each arm. "No, you don't," one of them said. "This way." And they led him up to the street.

Detective Bobby Aiken played with the worry beads one of his colleagues had brought him back from a trip to Istanbul. Not that he was worried about anything. It was just a habit, and he found it very calming. It had, in fact, been a very good day.

Not because of Lloyd Francis. Aiken didn't really care one way or another about Francis's death. In his eyes, Francis had been a cold-blooded murderer, and he had got no less than he deserved. No, the thing that pleased Aiken was that the undercover detectives he had detailed to keep an eye on Francis had picked up Mickey the Croaker disguised as an old man at the St. George subway station, having seen him push Francis with the sharp end of his walking stick.

Organized Crime had been after Mickey for many years now but had never managed to get anything on him. They knew that he usu-ally worked for one of the big crime families in Montreal, and the way things were looking, he was just about ready to cut a deal: amnesty and the witness relocation plan for everything he knew about the Montreal operation, from the hits he had made to where the bodies were buried. Organized Crime were creaming their jeans over their good luck. It would mean a promotion for Bobby Aiken.

The only thing that puzzled Aiken was why? What had Lloyd Francis done to upset the mob? There was something missing, and it irked him that he might never uncover it now the main players were dead. Mickey the Croaker knew nothing, of course. He had simply been obeying orders, and killing Lloyd Francis meant nothing more to him than swatting a fly. Francis's murder was more than likely connected with the postproduction company, Aiken decided. It was well known that the mob had its fingers in the movie business, often for the purpose of money laundering. A bit of digging around might uncover something more specific, but Aiken didn't have the time. Besides, what did it matter now? Even if he didn't understand how all the pieces fit together, things had worked out the right way. Lanagan and Francis were dead and Mickey the Croaker was about to sing. It was a shame about the wife, Laura. She had been a good-looking woman, from what Aiken had been able to tell from the family photographs, and it was a pity she had died so young. But those were the breaks. If she hadn't being playing the beast with two backs with Lanagan in her own bed, for Christ's sake, then she might still be alive today.

It was definitely a good day, Aiken decided, pushing the papers aside. Even the weather had improved. He looked out of the window. Indian summer had come to Toronto in November. The sun glinted on the apartment windows at College and Yonge, and the office workers were out on the streets, men without jackets and women in sleeveless summer dresses. A streetcar rumbled by, heading for Main station. Main. Out near the Beaches. The boardwalk and the Queen Street cafés would be crowded and the dog walkers would be out in force. Aiken thought maybe he'd take Jasper out there for a run later. You never knew who you might meet when you were walking your dog on the beach.

Blue Christmas

An Inspector Banks Story

A *three-day holiday.* Banks sat down at the breakfast table and made some notes on a lined pad. If he was doomed to spend Christmas alone this year, he was going to do it in style. For Christmas Eve, Alastair Sim's *Scrooge,* the black-and-white version, of course. For Christmas Day, *Love, Actually.* Mostly it was a load of crap, no doubt about that, but it was worth the silliness for Bill Nighy's Billy Mack, and Keira Knightley was always worth watching. For Boxing Day, *David Copperfield,* the one with the Harry Potter actor in it, because it had helped him through a nasty hangover one Boxing Day a few years ago, and thus are traditions born.

Music was more problematic. Bach's *Christmas Oratorio* and Handel's *Messiah,* naturally. Both were on his iPod and could be played through his main sound system. But some years ago, he had made a Christmas compilation tape of all his favorite songs, from Bing's "White Christmas" to Elvis's "Santa Claus Is Back in Town" and "Blue Christmas," The Pretenders' "2000 Miles" and Roland Kirk's "We Free Kings." Unfortunately, that had gone up in flames along with the rest of his music collection. Which meant a quick trip to HMV in Eastvale that afternoon to pick up a few seasonal CDs so he could make a playlist. He had to go to Marks and Spencer's, anyway, for his turkey dinner, so he might as well drop in at HMV while he was in the Swainsdale Center. As for wine, he still had a more than decent selection from his brother's cellar—including some fine amarone, chianti classico, clarets and burgundies—which would certainly get him through the next three days without any pain. Luckily, he had bought and given out all his Christmas presents earlier—what few there were: money for Tracy, a Fairport Convention box-set for Brian, chocolates and magazine subscriptions for his parents, and a silver and jet bracelet for Annie Cabbot.

Banks put his writing pad aside and reached for his coffee mug. Beside it sat a pristine copy of Kate Atkinson's *Behind the Scenes at the Museum,* which he fully intended to read over the holidays. There should be plenty of peace and quiet. Brian was with his band in Europe and wouldn't be able to get up to Gratly until late on Boxing Day. Tracy was spending Christmas with her mother, Sandra; stepdad, Sean; and baby Sinead, and Annie was heading home to the artists' colony in St. Ives, where they would all no doubt be having a good weep over *The Junky's Christmas,* which, Annie had told him, was a Christmas staple among her father's crowd. He had seen it once himself, and he had to admit that it wasn't bad, but it hadn't become a tradition with him.

All in all, then, this Christmas was beginning to feel like something to be got through with liberal doses of wine and music. Even the weather was refusing to cooperate. The white Christmas that everyone had been hoping for since a tentative sprinkle of snow in late November had not materialized, though the optimists at the meteorological center were keeping their options open. At the moment, though, it was uniformly gray and wet in Yorkshire. The only good thing that could be said for it was that it wasn't cold. Far from it. Down south people were sitting outside at Soho cafés and playing golf in the suburbs. Banks wondered if he should have gone away, taken a holiday. Paris. Rome. Madrid. A stranger in a strange city. Even London would have been better than this. Maybe he could still catch a last-minute flight.

But he knew he wasn't going anywhere. He sipped some strong coffee and told himself not to be so maudlin. Christmas was a notoriously dangerous time of year. It was when people got depressed and gave in to their deepest fears, when all their failures, regrets and disappointments came back to haunt them. Was he going to let himself give in to that, become a statistic?

He decided to go into town now and get his last-minute shopping over with before it got really busy. Just before he left, though, his phone rang. Banks picked up the receiver.

"Sir? It's DC Jackman."

"Yes, Winsome. What's the problem?"

"I'm really sorry to disturb you at home, sir, but we've got a bit of a problem."

"What is it?" Banks asked. Despite having to spend Christmas alone, he had been looking forward to a few days away from the Western Area Headquarters, if only to relax and unwind after a particularly difficult year. But perhaps that wasn't to be.

"Missing person, sir."

"Can't someone else handle it?"

"It needs someone senior, sir, and DI Cabbot's already on her way to Cornwall."

"Who's missing?"

"A woman by the name of Brenda Mercer. Forty-two years old."

"How long?"

"Overnight."

"Any reason to think there's been foul play?"

"Not really."

"Who reported her missing?"

"The husband."

"Why did he leave it until this morning?"

"He didn't. He reported it at 6:00 P.M. yesterday evening. We've been looking into it. But you know how it is with missing persons, sir, unless it's a kid. It was very early days. Usually they turn up, or you find a simple explanation quickly enough."

"But not in this case?"

"No, sir. Not a sign. The husband's getting frantic. Difficult. Demanding to see someone higher up. And he's got the daughter and her husband in tow now. They're not making life any easier. I've only just managed to get rid of them by promising I'd get someone in authority to come and talk to them."

"All right," Banks said with a sigh. "Hang on. I'll be right in."

Major Crimes and CID personnel were thin on the ground at Western Area Headquarters that Christmas Eve, and DC Winsome Jackman was the one who had drawn the short straw. She didn't mind, though. She couldn't afford to visit her parents in Jamaica, and she had politely passed up a Christmas dinner invitation from a fellow member of the potholing club, who had been pursuing her for some time now, so she had no real plans for the holidays. She hadn't expected it to be particularly busy in Major Crimes. Most Christmas incidents were domestic and, as such, they were dealt with by the officers on patrol. Even criminals, it seemed, took a bit of time off for turkey and Christmas pud. But a missing person case could turn nasty very quickly, especially if it was a woman.

While she was waiting for Banks, Winsome went through the paperwork again. There wasn't much other than the husband's report and statement, but that gave her the basics.

When David Mercer got home from work on December 23 at around 6:00 P.M., he was surprised to find his wife not home. Surprised because she was always home and always had his dinner waiting for him. He worked in the administration offices of the Swainsdale Shopping Centre, and his hours were regular. A neighbor had seen Mrs. Mercer walking down the street where she lived on the Leaview Estate at about a quarter past four that afternoon. She was alone and was wearing a beige overcoat and carrying a scuffed brown leather bag, the kind with a shoulder strap. She was heading in the direction of the main road, and the neighbor assumed she was going to catch a bus. She knew that Mrs. Mercer didn't drive. She said hello, but said that Mrs. Mercer hadn't seemed to hear her, had seemed a bit "lost in her own world."

Police had questioned the bus drivers on the route, but none of them recalled seeing anyone matching the description. Uniformed officers also questioned taxi drivers and got the same response. All Mrs. Mercer's relatives had been contacted, and none had any idea where she was. Winsome was beginning to think it was possible, then, that someone had picked Mrs. Mercer up on the main road, possibly by arrangement, and that she didn't want to be found. The alternative, that she had been somehow abducted, didn't bear thinking about, at least not until all other possible avenues had been exhausted.

Winsome had not been especially impressed by David Mercer—he was the sort of pushy, aggressive alpha white male she had seen far too much of over the past few years, puffed up with self-importance, acting as if everyone else were a mere lackey to meet his demands, especially if she happened to be black and female. But she tried not to let personal impressions interfere with her reasoning. Even so, there was something about Mercer's tone, something that didn't quite ring true. She made a note to mention it to Banks.

The house was a modern Georgian-style semi with a bay window, stone cladding and neatly kept garden, and when Banks rang the doorbell, Winsome beside him, David Mercer opened it so quickly he might have been standing right behind it. He led Banks and Winsome into a cluttered but clean front room, where a young woman sat on the sofa wringing her hands, and a whippet-thin man in an expensive, out-of-date suit paced the floor. A tall Christmas tree stood in one corner, covered with ornaments and lights. On the floor were a number of brightly wrapped presents and one ornament, a tiny pair of ice skates, which seemed to have fallen off the tree. The radio was playing Christmas music faintly in the background. Fa-la-la-la-lah.

"Have you heard anything?" David Mercer asked.

"Nothing yet," Banks answered. "But, if I may, I'd like to ask you a few more questions."

"We've already told everything to her," he said, gesturing in Winsome's direction.

"I know," said Banks. "And DC Jackman has discussed it with me. But I still have a few questions."

"Don't you think you should be out there on the streets searching for her?" said the whippet-thin man, who was also turning prematurely bald.

Banks turned to face him slowly. "And you are?"

He puffed out what little chest he had. "Claude Mainwaring, solicitor." He pronounced it "Mannering," like the Arthur Lowe character on *Dad's Army*. "I'm David's son-in-law."

"Well, Mr. Mainwaring," said Banks, "it's not normally my job, as a detective chief inspector, to get out on the streets looking for people. In fact, it's not even my job to pay house calls asking questions, but as it's nearly Christmas, and as Mr. Mercer here is worried about his wife, I thought I might bend the rules just a little. And believe me, there are already more than enough people out there trying to find Mrs. Mercer."

Mainwaring grunted as if he were unsatisfied with the answer, then he sat down next to his wife. Banks turned to David Mercer, who finally bade him and Winsome to sit, too. "Mr. Mercer," Banks asked, thinking of the doubts that Winsome had voiced on their way over, "can you think of anywhere your wife might have gone?"

"Nowhere," said Mercer. "That's why I called you lot."

"Was there any reason why your wife might have gone away?"

"None at all," said Mercer, just a beat too quickly for Banks's liking.

"She wasn't unhappy about anything?"

"Not that I know of, no."

"Everything was fine between the two of you?"

"Now, look here!" Mainwaring got to his feet.

"Sit down and be quiet, Mr. Mainwaring," Banks said as gently as he could. "You're not in court now, and you're not helping. I'll get to you later." He turned back to Mercer and ignored the slighted solicitor. "Had you noticed any difference in her behavior before she left, any changes of mood or anything?"

"No," said Mercer. "Like I said, everything was quite normal. May I ask what you're getting at?"

"I'm not getting at anything," Banks said. "These are all questions that have to be asked in cases such as these."

"Cases such as these?"

"Missing persons."

"Oh God," cried the daughter. "I can't believe it. Mother a missing person."

She used the same tone as she might have used to say "homeless person," Banks thought, as if she were somehow embarrassed by her mother's going missing. He quickly chided himself for being so uncharitable. It was Christmas, after all, and no matter how self-important and self-obsessed these people seemed to be, they *were* worried about Brenda Mercer. He could only do his best to help them. He just wished they would stop getting in his way.

"Has she ever done anything like this before?" Banks asked.

"Never," said David Mercer. "Brenda is one of the most stable and reliable people you could ever wish to meet."

"Does she have any close friends?"

"The family means everything to her."

"Might she have met someone? Someone she could confide in?"

Mercer seemed puzzled. "I don't know what you mean. Met? Confide? What would Brenda have to confide? And if she did, why would she confide in someone else rather than in me? No. it doesn't make sense."

"People do, you know, sometimes. A girlfriend, perhaps?"

"Not Brenda."

This was going nowhere fast, Banks thought, seeing what Winsome had meant. "Do you have any theories about where she might have gone?"

"Something's happened to her. Someone's abducted her, obviously. I can't see any other explanation."

"Why do you say that?"

"It stands to reason, doesn't it? She'd never do anything so irresponsible and selfish as to mess up all our Christmas plans and cause us so much fuss and worry."

"But these things, abductions and the like, are much rarer than you imagine," said Banks. "In most cases, missing persons are found healthy and safe."

Mainwaring snorted in the background. "And the longer you take to find her, the less likely she is to be healthy and safe," he said.

Banks ignored him and carried on talking to David Mercer. "Did you and your wife have any arguments recently?" he asked.

"Arguments? No, not really."

"Not really?"

"I mean nothing significant, nothing that would cause her to do something like this. We had our minor disagreements from time to time, of course, just like any married couple."

"But nothing that might upset her, make her want to disappear?"

"No, of course not."

"Do you know if she has any male friends?" Banks knew he was treading on dangerous ground now, but he had to ask.

"If you're insinuating that she's run off with someone," Mercer said, "then you're barking up the wrong tree. Brenda would never do that to me. Or to Janet," he added, glancing over at the daughter. "Besides, she's . . ."

"She's what?"

"I was simply going to say that Brenda's not exactly a *Playboy* centerfold, if you catch my drift. Not the sort of woman men would chase after or fantasize about."

Nice one, Banks thought. He had never expected his wife, Sandra, to run off with another man, either—and not because he didn't think she was attractive to men—but she had done. No sense in laboring the point, though. If anything like that had happened, the Mercers would be the last people to admit it, assuming that they even knew themselves. But if Brenda had no close friends or relatives, then there was no one else he could question who might be able to tell him more about her. All in all, it was beginning to seem like a tougher job than he had imagined.

"We'll keep you posted," he said, then he and Winsome headed back to the station.

Unfortunately, most people were far too absorbed in their Christmas plans—meals, family visits, last-minute shopping, church events and what have you—to pay as much attention to local news stories as they did the rest of the year, and even that wasn't much. As Banks and Winsome whiled away the afternoon at Western Area Headquarters, uniformed police officers went from house to house asking questions and searched the wintry Dales landscape in an ever-widening circle, but nothing came to light.

Banks remembered, just before the shops closed, that he had things to buy, so he dashed over to the Swainsdale Centre. Of course, by closing time on Christmas Eve it was bedlam, and everyone was impatient and bad tempered. He queued fifteen minutes to pay for his turkey dinner because he would have had nothing else to eat otherwise, but just one glance at the crowds in HMV made him decide to forgo the Christmas music for this year, relying on what he had already, and what he could catch on the radio.

By six o'clock he was back at home, and the men and women on duty at the police station had strict instructions to ring him if anything concerning Brenda Mercer came up.

But nothing did.

Banks warmed his leftover lamb curry and washed it down with a bottle of Black Sheep. After he'd finished the dishes, he made a start on *Behind the Scenes at the Museum,* then he opened a bottle of decent claret and took it with him into the TV room. There, he slid the shiny DVD of *Scrooge* into the player, poured himself a healthy glass and settled back. He always enjoyed spotting the bit where you could see the cameraman reflected in the mirror when Scrooge examines himself on Christmas morning, and he found Alastair Sim's over-the-top excitement at seeing the world anew as infectious and uplifting as ever. Even so, as he took himself up to bed around midnight, he still had a thought to spare for Brenda Mercer, and it kept him awake far longer than he would have liked.

The first possible lead came early on Christmas morning, when Banks was eating a soft-boiled egg for breakfast and listening to a King's College Choir concert on the radio. Winsome rang to tell him that someone had seen a woman resembling Mrs. Mercer in a rather dazed state wandering through the village of Swainshead shortly after dawn. The description matched, down to the coat and shoulder bag, so Banks finished his breakfast and headed out.

The sky was still like iron, but the temperature had dropped overnight, and Banks thought he sniffed a hint of snow in the air. As he drove down the dale, he glanced at the hillsides, all in shades of gray, their peaks obscured by low-lying cloud. Here and there a silver stream meandered down the slope, glittering in the weak light. Whatever was wrong with Brenda Mercer, Banks thought, she must be freezing if she had been sleeping rough for two nights now.

Before he got to Swainshead, he received another call on his mobile, again from Winsome. This time she told him that a local train driver had seen a woman walking aimlessly along the tracks over the Swainshead Viaduct. When Banks arrived there, Winsome was already waiting on the western side along with a couple of uniformed officers in their patrol cars, engines running so they could stay warm. The huge viaduct stretched for about a quarter of a mile across the broad valley, carrying the main line up to Carlisle and beyond, into Scotland, and its twenty or more great arches framed picture-postcard views of the hills beyond.

"She's up there, sir," said Winsome, pointing as Banks got out of the car. Way above him, more than a hundred feet up, a tiny figure in brown perched on the edge of the viaduct wall.

"Jesus Christ," said Banks. "Has anyone called to stop the trains? Anything roaring by her right now could give her the fright of her life, and it's a long way down."

"It's been done," said Winsome.

"Right," said Banks. "At the risk of stating the obvious, I think we'd better get someone who knows about these things to go up there and talk to her."

"It'll be difficult to get a professional, sir, on Christmas Day."

"Well, what do you . . . ? No. I can read your expression, Winsome. Don't look at me like that. The answer's no. I'm not a trained psychologist or a counselor. We need someone like Jenny Fuller."

"But she's away, and you know you're the best person for the job, sir. You're good with people. You listen to them. They trust you."

"But I wouldn't know where to begin."

"I don't think there are any set rules."

"I'm hardly the sort to convince someone that life is full of the joys of spring."

"I don't really think that's what's called for."

"But what if she jumps?"

Winsome shrugged. "She'll either jump or fall if someone doesn't go up there soon and find out what's going on."

Banks glanced up again and swallowed. He thought he felt the soft, chill touch of a snowflake melt on his eyeball. Winsome was right. He couldn't send up one of the uniformed lads—they were far too inexperienced for this sort of thing—and time was of the essence.

"Look," he said, turning to Winsome, "see if you can raise some sort of counselor or negotiator, will you? In the meantime, I'll go up and see what I can do. Just temporary, you understand?"

"Right you are, sir." Winsome smiled. Banks got back in his car. The quickest way to reach the woman was to drive up to Swainshead station, just before the viaduct, and walk along the tracks. At least that way he wouldn't have to climb any hills. The thought didn't comfort him much, though, when he looked up again and saw the woman's legs dangling over the side of the wall.

"Stop right there," she said. "Who are you?"

Banks stopped. He was about four or five yards away from her. The wind was howling more than he had expected, whistling around his ears, making it difficult to hear properly, and it seemed much colder up there, too. He wished he were wearing something warmer than his leather jacket. The hills stretched away to the west, some still streaked with November's snow. In the distance, Banks thought he could make out the huge rounded mountains of the Lake District.

"My name's Banks," he said. "I'm a policeman."

"I thought you'd find me eventually," she said. "It's too late, though."

From where Banks was standing, he could only see her in profile. The ground was a long way below. Banks had no particular fear of heights, but even so, her precarious position on the wall unnerved him. "Are you sure you don't want to come back from the edge and talk?" he said.

"I'm sure. Do you think it was easy getting here in the first place?"

"It's a long walk from Eastvale."

She cast him a sidelong glance. "I didn't mean that."

"Sorry. It just looks a bit dangerous there. You could slip and fall off."

"What makes you think that wouldn't be a blessing?"

"Whatever it is," said Banks, "it can't be worth this. Come on, Brenda, you've got a husband who loves you, a daughter who needs—"

"My husband doesn't love me, and my daughter doesn't need me. Do you think I don't know? David's been shagging his secretary for two years. Can you imagine such a cliché? He thinks I don't know. And as for my daughter, I'm just an embarrassment to her and that awful husband of hers. I'm the shopgirl who married up, and now I'm just a skivvy for the lot of them. That's all I've been for years."

"But things can change."

She stared at him with pity and shook her head. "No, they can't," she said, and gazed off into the distance. "Do you know why I'm here? I mean, do you know what set me off? I've put up with it all for years, the coldness, the infidelity, just for the sake of order, not rocking the boat, not causing a scene. But do you know what it was, the straw that finally broke the camel's back?"

"No," said Banks, anxious to keep her talking. "I don't know. Tell me." He edged a little closer so he could hear her voice above the wind. She didn't tell him to stop. Snowflakes started to swirl around them.

"People say it's smell that sparks memory the most, but it wasn't, not this time. It was a Christmas ornament. I was putting a few last-minute decorations on the tree before Janet and Claude arrived, and I found myself holding these tiny, perfect ice skates I hadn't seen for years. They sent me right back to a particular day, when I was a child. It's funny because it didn't seem like just a memory. I felt as if I was *really* there. My father took me skating on a pond somewhere in the country. I don't remember where. But it was just getting dark and there were red and green and white Christmas lights and music playing—carols like "Silent Night" and "Away in a Manger"—and someone was roasting chestnuts on a brazier. The air was full of the smell. I'll never forget that smell. I was . . . My father died last year." She paused and brushed tears and melted snowflakes from her eyes with the back of her hand. "I kept falling down. It must have been my first time on ice. But my father would just pick me up, tell me I was doing fine, and set me going again. I don't know what it was about that day, but I was so happy, the happiest I can ever remember. Everything seemed perfect and I felt I could do anything. I wished it would never end. I didn't even feel the cold. I was just all warm inside and full of love. Did you ever feel like that?"

Banks couldn't remember, but he was sure he must have. Best to agree, anyway. Stay on her wavelength. "Yes," he said. "I know just what you mean." It wasn't exactly a lie.

"And it made me feel worthless," she said. "The memory made me feel that my whole life was a sham, a complete waste of time, of any potential I once might have had. And it just seemed that there was no point in carrying on." She shifted on the wall.

"Don't!" Banks cried, moving forward.

She looked at him. He thought he could make out a faint smile. She appeared tired and drawn, but her face was a pretty one, he noticed. A slightly pointed chin and small mouth, but beautiful hazel eyes. Obviously this was something her husband didn't notice. "It's all right," she said. "I was just changing position. My bum's gone numb. The wall's hard and cold. I just wanted to get more comfortable."

She was concerned about comfort. Banks took that as a good sign. He was within two yards of her now, but he still wasn't close enough to make a grab. At least she didn't tell him to move back. "Just be careful," he said. "It's dangerous. You might slip."

"You seem to be forgetting that's what I'm here for."

"The memory," said Banks. "That day at the pond. It's something to cherish, surely, to live for?"

"No. It just suddenly made me feel that my life's all wrong. Worthless. Has been for years. I don't feel like *me* anymore. I don't feel anything. Do you know what I mean?"

"I know," said Banks. "But this isn't the answer."

"I don't know," Brenda said, shaking her head then looking down into the swirling white of the chasm below. "I just feel so sad and so lost."

"So do I sometimes," said Banks, edging a little closer. "Every Christmas since my wife left me for someone else and the kids grew up and moved away from home. But it doesn't mean that you don't feel anything. You said before that you felt nothing, but you do, even if it is only sadness."

"So how do you cope?"

"Me? With what?"

"Being alone. Being abandoned and betrayed."

"I don't know," said Banks. He was desperate for a cigarette, but remembered that he had stopped smoking ages ago. He put his hands in his pockets. The snow was really falling now, obscuring the view. He couldn't even see the ground.

"Did you love her?" Brenda asked.

The question surprised Banks. He had been quizzing her, but all of a sudden she was asking about him. He took that as another good sign. "Yes."

"What happened?"

"I suppose I neglected her," said Banks. "My job . . . the hours . . . I don't know. She's a pretty independent person. I thought things were OK, but they weren't. It took me by surprise."

"I'm sure David thinks everything is fine as long as no one ruffles the surface of his comfortable little world. And I know he doesn't think I'm attractive. Were you unfaithful?"

"Once. A long time ago. I always felt guilty about it. And many years later, my wife left me for another man. Had a baby with him."

"She had a baby with another man?"

"Yes. I mean, we were divorced and they got married and everything. My daughter's spending Christmas with them."

"And you?"

Was she starting to feel sorry for him? If she did, then perhaps it would help to make her see that she wasn't the only one suffering, that suffering was a part of life and you just had to put up with it and get on with things. "By myself," he said. "My son's abroad. He's in a rock group. The Blue Lamps. They're doing really well. You might even have heard of them."

"David doesn't like pop music."

"Well . . . they're really good."

"The proud father. My daughter's a stuck-up, social-climbing bitch who's ashamed of her mother."

Banks remembered Janet Mainwaring's reaction to the description of her mother as missing: an embarrassment. "People can be cruel," he said. "They don't always mean what they say."

"But how do you cope?"

Banks found that he had edged closer to her now, within a yard or so. It was almost grabbing range. That was a last resort, though. If he wasn't quick enough, she might flinch and fall off as he reached for her. Or she might simply slip out of his hands. "I don't know," he said. "Christmas is a difficult time for all sorts of people. On the surface, it's all peace and happiness and giving and family and love, but underneath . . . You see it a lot in my job. People reach a breaking point. There's so much stress."

"But how do *you* cope with it alone? Surely it must all come back and make you feel terrible?"

"It does, sometimes. I suppose I seek distractions. Music. *Scrooge. Love, Actually*—for Bill Nighy and Keira Knightley—and *David Copperfield*, the one with the Harry Potter actor. I probably drink too much as well."

"Daniel Radcliffe. That's his name. The Harry Potter actor."

"Yes."

"And I'd watch *Love, Actually* for Colin Firth." She shook her head. "But I don't know if it would work for me."

"I suppose it's all just a pointless sort of ritual," said Banks, "but I'd still recommend it. The perfect antidote to spending Christmas alone and miserable."

"But I wouldn't be alone and miserable, would I? That's the problem. I'd be with my family and I'd still be bloody miserable."

"You don't have to be."

"What are you suggesting?"

"I told you. Things can change. You can change things." Banks leaned his hip against the wall. He was so close to her now that he could have put his arms around her and pulled her back, but he didn't think he was going to need to. "Do it for yourself," he said. "Not for them. If you think your husband doesn't love you, leave him and live for yourself."

"Leave David? But where would I go? How would I manage? David has been my life. David and Janet."

"There's always a choice," Banks went on. "There are people who can help you. People who know about these things. Counselors, social services. Other people have been where you are now. You can get a job, a flat. A new life. I did."

"But where would I go?"

"You'd find somewhere. There are plenty of flats available in Eastvale, for a start."

"I don't know if I can do that. I'm not as strong as you." Banks noticed that she managed a tight smile. "And I think if I did, I would have to go far away."

"That's possible, too." Banks reached out his hand. "For crying out loud, you can come and have Christmas dinner with *me* if you want. Just let me help you." The snow was coming down heavily now, and the area had become very slippery. She looked at his hand, shaking her head and biting her lip.

"*Scrooge?*" she said.

"Yes. Alastair Sim."

"I always preferred James Stewart in *It's a Wonderful Life*."

Banks laughed. "That'll do nicely, too. I've got the DVD."

"I couldn't . . . you know . . . If I . . . well, I'd have to go home and face the music."

"I know that. But after, there's help. There are choices."

She hesitated for a moment, then she took hold of his hand, and he felt her grip tightening as she climbed off the wall and stood up. "Be careful now," he said. "The ground's quite treacherous."

"Isn't it just," she said, and moved toward him.

Shadows on the Water

We were meant to be getting some sleep, but how you're supposed to sleep in a cold, muddy, rat-infested trench, when the uppermost thought in your mind is that you're going to be shot first thing in the morning, is quite beyond me.

Albert Parkinson handed around the Black Cats to the four of us who clustered together for warmth, mugs of weak Camp coffee clutched to our chests, almost invisible to one another in the darkness. "Here you go, Frank," he said, cupping the match in his hands for safety, even though we were well below ground level. I thanked him and inhaled the harsh tobacco, little realizing that soon I would be inhaling something far more deadly. Still, we needed the tobacco to mask the smell. The trench stank to high heaven of unwashed men, excrement, cordite, black powder and rotting flesh.

Now and then, distant shots broke the silence, someone shouted a warning or an order, and an exploding shell lit the sky. But we were waiting for dawn. We talked in hushed voices, and eventually the talk got around to what makes heroes of men. We all put in our twopenn'orth, of course, mostly a lot of cant about courage, patriotism and honor, with the occasional, begrudging nod in the direction of folly and luck, but instead of settling for a simple definition, Joe Fairweather started to tell us a story.

Joe was a strange one. Nobody quite knew what to make of him. A bit older than the rest of us, he already had a reputation as one of the most fearless lads in our regiment. It never seemed to worry him that he was running across no-man's-land in a hail of bullets; he seemed either blessed or indifferent to his fate. Joe had survived Ypres one and two, and now here he was, ready to go again. Some of us thought he was more than a little a bit mad.

"When I was a kid," Joe began, "about eleven or twelve, we used to play by the canal. It was down at the bottom of the park, through the woods, and not many people went there because it was a hell of a steep slope to climb back up. But we were young, full of energy. We could climb anything. There were metal railings all along the canal side, but we had found a loose one that you could lift out easily, like a spear. We always put it back when we went home so nobody would know we had found a way in.

"There wasn't much beyond the canal in those days, only fields full of cows and sheep, stretching away to distant hills. Very few barges used the route. It was a lonely, isolated spot, and perhaps that was why we liked it. We used to forge sick notes from our mothers and play truant from school, and nobody was ever likely to spot us down by the canal.

"Not that we got up to any real mischief, mind you. We just talked the way kids do, skimmed stones off the water. Sometimes we'd sneak out our fishing nets and catch sticklebacks and minnows. Sometimes we played games. Just make-believe. We'd act out stories from *Boy's Own*, cut wooden sticks from the bushes and pretend we were soldiers on patrol." Joe paused and looked around at the vague outlines of our faces in the trench and laughed. "Can you believe it?" he said. "We actually *played* at being soldiers. Little did we know . . .

"One day, I think it was June or July, just before the summer holidays, at any rate, a beautiful sunny, still day, the kind that makes you believe that only good things are going to happen, my friend Adrian and I were sitting on the stone bank dipping our nets in the murky water when we saw someone on the other side. I say *saw*, but at first it was more like sensing a presence, a shadow on the water, perhaps, and we looked up and noticed a strange man standing on the opposite bank, watching us with a funny sort of expression on his face. I remember feeling annoyed at first because this was our secret place, and nobody else was supposed to be there. Now this grown-up had to come and spoil everything.

"'Shouldn't you boys be at school?' he asked us.

"There wasn't much we could say to that, and I daresay we just fidgeted and looked shifty.

"'Well,' he said. 'Don't worry, I won't tell anyone. What are you doing?'

"'Just fishing,' I said.

"'Just fishing? What are you fishing for? There can't be much alive down there in that filthy water.'

"'Minnows and sticklebacks,' I said.

"'How old are you?'

"We told him.

"'Do your parents know where you are?'

"'No,' I said, though I remember feeling an odd sensation of having spoken foolishly as soon as the word was out of my mouth, but it was too late to take it back.

"'Why do you want to know?' Adrian asked him.

"'It doesn't matter. Want to play a game with me?'

"'No, thanks.' We started to move away. Who did he think he was? We didn't play with grown-ups; they were no fun. Besides, we'd been warned to stay away from strangers.

"'Oh, I think you do,' he said, and there was something about his voice that made the hackles on the back of my neck stand up. I glanced at Adrian, and we turned to look across the canal to where the man stood. When we saw the gun in his hand, both of us froze.

"He smiled, but it wasn't a nice smile. 'Told you so,' he said.

"Now I looked at him closely for the first time. I was just a kid, remember, so I couldn't say how old he was, but he was definitely a grown-up. A man. And he was wearing a sort of uniform, like a soldier's, but it looked shabby and rumpled, as if it had been slept in. I couldn't see the revolver very clearly, not that I'd have had any idea what make it was, as if that even mattered. All that mattered was that it was a gun and that he was pointing it at us.

"Then, out of sheer nerves I suppose, we laughed, hoping maybe it was all a joke and it was just a cap gun he was holding. 'All right,' Adrian said. 'If you really want to play . . .'

" 'Oh, I do,' the man said. Then he pulled the trigger.

"It wasn't as loud as I had expected, more of a dull popping sound, but something whizzed through the bushes beside me and dinged on the metal railing as it passed by. I felt deeply ashamed as the warm piss dribbled down my bare legs. Thankfully, nobody seemed to notice it but me.

" 'That's just to show you that it's a real gun,' the man said, 'and that I mean what I say. Do you believe me now?'

"We both nodded. 'What do you want?' Adrian asked.

" 'I told you. I want to play.'

" 'Look,' I said, 'you're frightening us. Why don't you put the gun away? Then we'll play with you, won't we, Adrian?'

"Adrian nodded. 'Yes.'

" 'This?' The man looked at his revolver as if seeing it for the first time. 'But why should I want to put it away?'

"He fired again, closer this time, and a clod of earth flew up and stung my cheek. I was damned if I was going to cry, but I was getting close. I felt as if we were the only people for hundreds of miles, maybe the only people in the whole world. There was nobody to save us, and this lunatic was going to kill us after he'd had his fun. I didn't know why, what made him act like that, or anything, but I just knew he was going to do it.

" 'Don't you like this game?' he asked me.

" 'No," I said, trying to keep my voice from shaking. 'I want to go home.'

" 'Go on, then,' he said.

" 'What?'

" 'I said go on.'

" 'You don't mean it.'

" 'Yes, I do. Go.'

"Slowly, without taking my eyes off him, I backed up the grassy bank toward the hole in the railings. Only when I got there, and I had to turn sideways to squeeze through the gap, did I take my eyes off him.

As soon as I did, I heard another shot and felt the air move as some-thing zipped by my ear. 'I've changed my mind,' he said. 'Come back.'

"Knowing, deep down, that it had been too good to be true, I slunk back to the canal bank. The man was muttering to himself now, and neither Adrian nor I could make out what he was saying. In a way, that was even more frightening than hearing his words. He was pacing up and down, too, staring at the ground, his gun hanging at his side, but we knew that if either of us made the slightest movement, he would start shooting at us again.

"This went on for some time. I could feel myself sweating, and the wetness down my legs was uncomfortable. Apart from the incompre-hensible muttering across the water, everything was still and silent. No birds sang, almost as if they knew this was death's domain and had got out when they could. Even the cows and sheep were silent and looked more like a landscape painting than real, living creatures. Maybe a barge would come, I prayed. Then he would have to hide his gun, and we would have time to run up to the woods. But no barge came.

"Finally, he paused in his conversation with himself, at least for the time being. 'You,' he said to Adrian, gesturing with his gun. 'You can go now.'

" 'I don't believe you mean it,' Adrian said.

"The man pointed the gun right at him. 'Go. Before I change my mind and shoot you.'

"Adrian scrambled up the grassy bank. I could hear him crying. I had never felt so alone in my life. Inside, I was praying for the man to tell Adrian to come back, the way he had with me. I didn't want to die alone by the dirty canal. I wanted to go home and see my mum and dad again.

"This time my prayers were answered.

" 'Come back,' he said. 'I've changed my mind.'

" 'Are you going to shoot us?' I asked, when Adrian once again stood at my side, wiping his eyes on his sleeve.

" 'I don't know,' he said. 'It depends on what they tell me to do. Just shut up and let me think. Don't talk unless I ask you to.'

"*They?* What on earth was he talking about? Adrian and I looked at each other, puzzled. There was nobody else around. Who was going to tell him what to do? You have to remember, we were only kids, and we didn't know anything about insane people hearing voices and all that.

" 'But *why*?' I asked. 'Why are you doing this? We haven't done you any harm.'

"He didn't say anything, just fired a shot—*pop*—into the bushes right beside me. It was enough. Then he started talking again, and I think both Adrian and I now had an inkling that he was hearing the voices in his head, and that maybe he was having a conversation with the mysterious 'they' he had mentioned.

" 'All right,' he said, the next time he calmed down. He pointed the gun at me. 'What's your name?' he asked.

" 'Joe,' I said.

" 'Joe. All right, Joe. You can go. What's your friend's name?'

" 'Adrian.'

" 'Adrian stays.'

"I stood my ground. 'You're not going to let me go,' I told him. 'You'll only do the same as you did before.'

"That made him angry, and he started waving the gun around again. 'Go!' he yelled at me. 'Now! Before I shoot you right here.'

"I went.

"Sure enough, when I got to the hole in the fence, I heard him laugh, a mad, eerie sound that sent a chill through me despite the heat of the day. 'You didn't think I meant it, did you? Come back here, Joe.'

"Somehow, the use of my name, the sound of it from *his* lips, on *his* breath, was worse than anything else. For a moment, I hesitated, then I slipped through the hole in the railings and started running for my life.

"I knew that there was a hollow about thirty feet up the grassy slope, and if I reached it I would be safe. It was only a quick dash from there to the woods.

"I heard him shout again. 'Joe, come back here right now!'

"I ran and ran. I heard the dull *pop* of his revolver and sensed something buzz by my right side and thud into the earth. My heart was pumping for all it was worth, and the muscles on my legs felt fit to burst.

" 'Joe, come back or I'll shoot Adrian!' he yelled after me.

"But still I didn't stop.

"I made it. I made it to the hollow and dived into the dip in the ground that would protect me from any more bullets. I heard just one more popping sound before I made my dash for the woods, and that was it. I was certain it was Adrian."

Here, Joe paused, as if recounting the narrative had left him as out of breath as outrunning the lunatic's bullets. From our trench, we could hear more shots in the distance now, and a shell exploded about two hundred yards to the west, lighting up the sky. Farther away, somewhere behind our lines, a piper played. I handed around my cigarettes and noticed Jack Armstrong in the subdued glow of the match. Face ashen, eyes glazed, lips trembling, the kid was terrified, and it was my guess that he'd freeze when the command to go over came. I'd seen it happen before. Not that I blamed him. I sometimes wondered why we didn't all react that way. There but for the grace of God. . . . I remembered Harry Parker, who had tried for a blighty in the foot and ended up losing the entire lower half of his left leg. Then there was Ben Castle, poor, sad Ben, who swore he'd do it himself before the Germans did it to him, and calmly put his gun in his mouth and pulled the trigger. So who were the heroes? And why?

"What happened next?" asked Arthur. "Did you run and fetch the police?"

"The police? No," said Joe. "I don't really remember what I did. I think I just wandered around in a daze. I couldn't believe it had happened, you see, that I had been so close to death and escaped."

"But what about your friend? What about Adrian?" Arthur persisted.

Joe looked right through him, as if he hadn't even heard the question. "I waited until it was time to return home from school," he went on, "and that's exactly what I did. Went home. The piss stains on my trousers and underwear had dried by then, and if my mother noticed the next time she did the washing, then she didn't say anything to me about it. We went on holiday the next day to stay for a week with my aunt Betty on the coast near Scarborough. Every day I scoured my dad's newspaper when he'd put it aside after breakfast, but I could find no reference to the lunatic with the gun or to a boy being found shot beside the canal. I even started to believe that it had all been a figment of my imagination, that it hadn't happened at all."

"But what about Adrian?" Arthur asked.

"Adrian? I had no idea. That whole week we were with Aunt Betty I wondered about him. Of course I did. Had the lunatic *really* shot him? But surely if anything had happened it would have been in the papers. Still, I knew I had deserted Adrian. I had dashed off to freedom and hadn't given him a second thought once I was in the woods."

"But you must have seen him again?" I said.

"That's the funny thing," Joe said. "I did. It was about two days after we got back from our holiday. I saw him in the street. He started walking toward me. I was frightened because he was a year older than me, and bigger. I thought he was going to beat me up for leaving him behind."

"What did he do?" Arthur asked.

Joe laughed. "He walked up to me. I braced myself for an assault, and he said, 'Thank you.'

"I wasn't certain I'd heard him correctly, so I asked him to repeat what he'd said.

" 'Thank you,' he said again. 'That was a very brave thing you did, dodging the bullets like that, risking death.'

"I was stunned. I didn't know what to say. I must have stood there looking like a complete idiot, with my mouth hanging open.

" 'Had he gone?' he asked me next.

" 'Who?' I replied.

" 'You know. The lunatic with the gun. I'll bet he'd gone when you came back with the police, hadn't he?'

"Now I understood what Adrian was thinking. 'Yes,' I said. 'Yes, he'd gone.'

"Adrian nodded. 'I thought so. Look, I'm sorry,' he went on, 'sorry I didn't hang around till you got back with them, to help you explain and all, but I was so scared.'

" 'What happened?' I asked.

" 'Well,' Adrian said, 'as soon as you made it to the woods, he ran off down the canal bank. He must have known you'd soon be back with help, and he didn't want to hang around and get caught. I probably stood there for a few moments to pull myself together, then I headed off in the same direction you did. I just went home as if I'd been to school and didn't say a word to anyone. I'm sorry,' he said again. 'I should have stuck around when you came back with the police.'

" 'It's all right,' I said. 'They didn't believe me. They thought I was just a troublemaker. One of them gave me a clip around the ear and they sent me home. Said if anything like that ever happened again they'd tell my mum and dad.'

"Adrian managed to laugh at that. I was feeling so relieved I could have gone on all day making things up. How I went back to try and rescue Adrian by myself and found the man a little farther down the bank. How I carried the loose railing like a spear and threw it at him across the canal, piercing him right through the heart. Then how I weighted his body with stones and dropped it in the water. But I didn't. It was enough that I was exonerated in Adrian's eyes. Good enough that I was a *hero*."

Joe began to laugh, and it sounded so eerie, so *mad*, that it sent shivers up our spines. Jack Armstrong started crying. He wasn't going anywhere. And Joe was still laughing when the black night inched toward another gray dawn and the orders came down for us to go over the top and take a godforsaken blemish on the map called Passchendaele.

The Cherub Affair

PART ONE

Dazzling sunlight spun off the glass door of Angelo's when I pulled it open and walked in at eleven that morning, as usual.

"Morning, Mr. Lang," said Angelo. "What'll it be?"

"I'll have a cup of your finest java and one of those iffy-looking crullers, please."

"Iffy-looking! All our doughnuts are fresh this morning."

"Sure, Angelo. I'll take one anyway. How's business?"

"Can't complain."

"Watch the game last night?"

"Uh-huh."

"Don't tell me, they lost again, right?"

"Uh-huh."

Angelo is a die-hard Blue Jays fan. He gets depressed when they lose. He's been depressed a lot this summer.

Angelo looked over my shoulder, out to the street. "Hey, wonders never cease," he said. "Looks like you've got a customer."

"Client, Angelo, client. You get customers. I get clients."

"Whatever. Anyways, this one you'll want to see." He whistled lasciviously and sculpted an impossibly voluptuous shape in the air with his hands.

Curious, I took a plastic lid for my coffee and, juggling the cruller in my other hand, tried to make a dignified exit. Could this be it, after all this time? The legendary beautiful blonde of private eye fiction come to life at last. In *my* office?

I took the stairs two at a time and saw her standing there in the hallway, about to knock on my door. She turned, and I could see an expression of distaste on her face. I couldn't blame her. She was Holt Renfrew from head to toe, and the place doesn't get cleaned often. Under the dim glow of a bare sixty-watt bulb, the old linoleum was cracked and veined with years of ground-in dirt.

Angelo's mimed shape hadn't been far wrong, if a tad overgenerous. She was certainly beautiful, but there was something else. I knew her. Damned if I could remember from where, but I knew her.

She smiled and held out her hand. "Mr. Lang. It's nice to see you again."

I gestured her into the office, where she brushed crumbs off the chair with her white-gloved hand before sitting down, crossing her legs and turning her nose up at the view. It's not great, I know, but it's cheap. We're in a strip mall on the Scarborough side of Kingston Road, opposite one of those clapboard hotels where the government houses refugee claimants. I parked my coffee and cruller on the cluttered desk and sat down. Now I knew where I recognized her from, but the name still wouldn't come.

She peeled off her gloves and gave me another smile. "Susan," she said, as if sensing my embarrassment. "Susan Caldwell."

"Of course," I said. "Nice to see you again, Susan."

Susan Caldwell. She had been one of my students ten years ago, in another life, when I was a teaching assistant at the University of Toronto. Now I remembered. Susan had been notable mostly for her long blond hair and a rather ill-advised essay on Darwin's influence on Wordsworth's *Lyrical Ballads.* The blond hair was still there, along with the dark blue eyes, button nose, long, shapely legs and a nice curve at the hips. Impure thoughts passed through my mind. After all, she was only about five years younger than me, and she wasn't my student anymore.

"What can I do for you?" I asked.

"I need help."

"Why choose me?" Nobody else ever does, I might have added, but didn't.

"I remembered that article about you in the paper a while back."

Ah, yes, the famous article. When I couldn't find an academic position after getting my PhD in English, I followed my adolescent fantasy, fueled by years of Hammett and Chandler, and enrolled in a private investigator's course. I got the qualification, served my apprenticeship with a large firm, and now I was out on my own. LANG INVESTIGATIONS. It had a ring to it. Anyway, the newspaper had done a feature on me, labeled me "The PhD P.I.," and it sort of stuck. Embarrassing, but it brought in a curious client or two, and now here was the lovely Susan Caldwell sitting opposite me.

"People who need me are usually in trouble," I said.

"It's not me. It's my brother."

"What's the problem?"

"He's been arrested."

"What for?"

"Murder." She leaned forward and rested her hands on the desk, so bound up in her plea for her brother that she didn't even notice the dust. "But he didn't do it, Mr. Lang. I *know* my brother. He wouldn't harm a fly."

Now that she mentioned it, I did remember hearing something about the case. I don't usually pay a lot of attention to true crime stories, especially when they involve celebrities, but sometimes you can't avoid picking up a few details, especially if it's close to home. "Tony Caldwell, right?" I said. "The famous fashion photographer. He's accused of murdering his wife."

"Yes. But he didn't do it."

"Ms. Caldwell, Susan," I said, "I don't usually investigate murders. The police don't like it, for a start, and I try to stay on good terms with them."

"The police." She spat out the word as if it were a cockroach. "Don't talk to me about the police! They've just decided Tony's guilty and that's that. They're not even looking for the real killer."

"They must have a good reason," I said.

"Well, maybe they *think* they have a good reason, but they don't know Tony like I do."

"What could I do that the police can't?"

She looked me in the eye. "You could believe me for a start," she said. "Then maybe you could talk to him. At least you could keep an open mind."

She had a point. There's nothing the police like more than an open-and-shut case; it's neat, like balancing the books, and it makes the statistics look good. And most cases *are* open and shut. Why should Tony Caldwell's be so different? Because his sister said so? If I killed someone, I'd hope that *my* sister would refuse to believe it, too, and defend me just the way Susan was defending Tony. Still, I was tempted to give it a try.

"Where is he?" I asked.

"He's staying with me. He just came out on bail. Our parents live in Sarnia and Tony's not supposed to leave Toronto."

"Give me the details," I said.

Susan sat back in her chair and spoke softly. "It was about one o'clock in the morning. Tony and Val—that's Valerie Pascale, his wife—had been out, and they just got home."

"Where do they live?"

"The Beaches. Or Beach. I never know which."

"Either's fine with me. Go on."

"The neighbors said they heard them arguing loudly. Then, after it had been quiet for a while, Tony called the police and said his wife was dead."

"Is that exactly what he said?"

"On the phone, yes, but when they came, before they warned him, or whatever they do, they say he said, 'I didn't mean it. I'm sorry, Val.'"

That didn't sound good. "Did they argue often?"

"They loved each other very much, but it was a pretty volatile relationship. Valerie grew up in Vancouver, but she was half French," Susan added, as if that explained it all.

"Did Tony explain what he meant by the comment?"

"He said that he was apologizing for the argument, that he was sorry the last words they'd had together were angry, and that he'd never have a chance to make up."

"Did he say anything else?"

"He admitted they'd had a quarrel, and said he stormed upstairs. I know this might sound odd, Mr. Lang, but he had a shower. If you knew Tony, you'd know he's a compulsive showerer, and he always does it when he gets upset. Ever since he was a kid. When he went downstairs about twenty minutes later, he found Valerie dead in the living room, stabbed. He says he doesn't remember much after that."

"You say she was stabbed. What about the knife? Did the police find it? Were Tony's fingerprints on it?"

"It was just a kitchen knife, I think. He said he'd been using it earlier to cut the string on a parcel."

"So his prints *were* on it?"

"Only because he'd been using it to cut the string."

Again, it wasn't looking good. "Did he confess?"

"No. Of course not."

"Was there any other reason the police charged him so quickly, then?" I asked, almost dreading the answer.

"Well," said Susan, shifting uneasily in her chair. "I suppose so . . . I mean, you know, when they got there . . . it *might* have looked bad."

"Yes?"

"Well, when the police arrived, Tony was kneeling beside her body holding the knife, and he was covered in blood. Valerie's blood."

PART TWO

"Look, the kid did it. Period. It's a cut-and-dried domestic. And the only reason I'm talking to you is because my boss told me to. Money swears almost as loudly as public relations." He stabbed a finger at my chest. "But I don't like private eyes, and I want you to know that. You should get back to the gutter where you belong."

The speaker was Detective Nick Enamoretto, chief investigator on the Caldwell investigation. If you could call it an investigation, that is.

We were talking in the divisional canteen, a few stained and cracked Formica-topped tables and an alcove full of vending machines—coffee, soup, sandwiches, chocolate, you name it. Ignoring me, Enamoretto put his money in a slot and picked up a cup of black coffee. I followed suit and ended up with scalding, bitter tea. We sat down at the nearest table, where Enamoretto lit a cigarette so quickly I hardly saw the flame. He was a slim, dark, hatchet-faced man with darting hazel eyes and a droopy moustache.

"I thought there was no smoking in the workplace," I said.

"So arrest me."

"Look, there's no need to be so hostile," I went on. "All I want to know is could it have happened any other way?"

He scrutinized me, blew out a mouthful of smoke, and stubbed out his cigarette. "I can't see how."

"Was the back door open?"

"Yes. But the screen door was locked."

"Windows?"

"Closed."

"And there were no signs of forced entry?"

"Of course there weren't," Enamoretto snapped. "Do you think we didn't bother to look?"

I shrugged. "I don't know what you did and didn't do. Did you look out back, down the ravine?"

"Listen, wise guy, if you're asking did we go over the area with a fine-tooth comb, the answer's no, we didn't. We didn't need to. Have you any idea how expensive an investigation like that is? It was a routine case, and it still is as far as I'm concerned."

I took a sip of tea. It tasted as bad as it looked. "What if she let somebody in while Caldwell was taking his shower? Someone she knew."

"Give me a break, Lang. A friend doesn't climb a ravine at one o'clock in the morning and knock at your screen door."

"Some people have weird friends. Maybe it was someone who didn't want to be seen, especially if he had murder on his mind."

"If she let someone in, how did he get out again? The screen was locked when we got there. That type of door locks from the inside."

"How about the front?"

Enamoretto shook his head. "Locked, chained and bolted. Besides, the neighbors would've noticed. They were still worried after overhearing the argument. They didn't see anybody except the Caldwells come or go."

"His sister said he was covered in blood."

Enamoretto scowled. "On his hands. Down the front of his dressing gown. But there wasn't that much. Most of the bleeding was internal."

I was getting nowhere fast. Enamoretto kept tapping on the table. I felt my time running out as quickly as the level in his coffee cup dropped. Finally, he moderated his harsh tone just a little. "Look, Lang, why don't you drop it? You're wasting the family's money and giving them false hopes. Caldwell's guilty and he'll go away for it. Oh, not for very long, maybe, but he'll go away. In a few years he'll be out and about again. Maybe get another wife and knife her, too."

"Don't you think it's odd that he hasn't confessed? Isn't that what most domestics do?"

Enamoretto said nothing, and I could see that it bothered him, too. All the evidence was stacked against Tony Caldwell. His crime matched a common domestic pattern, but all along he maintained that he was innocent. That didn't fit the profile. I found myself thinking that perhaps Enamoretto wished he had time to get to the bottom of it himself. Cops are under so much pressure that they can't afford long and expensive investigations. They take things at face value unless something very obvious points them in another direction. To Enamoretto, this was just another boring domestic crime, with only one negligible difference, and perhaps he was resentful because I had all the time in the world to devote to that one case, and I might just find out something he had missed.

"I know what you're thinking, but you're wasting your time, Lang. The fight was between Caldwell and his wife, and the wife lost. Save the family a lot of heartbreak and get back to hanging around sleazy motels."

"I think I'll just dig around a bit first," I said, "and see if I come up with anything. Give it a couple of days."

Enamoretto shrugged and stretched out his hands. "What more can I say?"

I smiled. "Thanks for your time, anyway. You've been very helpful." Enamoretto scowled. "Let's just hope we don't meet again."

PART THREE

Susan Caldwell lived in a two-bedroom apartment in the Yonge and Eglinton area, or "Young and Eligible," as it was known locally because of the hordes of singles who filled the apartment buildings and frequented the restaurants, bars and clubs every night. Susan was waiting when I arrived, and without further ado she showed me into her brother's room.

Tony Caldwell lay sprawled on his bed reading a photographic magazine. He looked more Queen Street West than East in a white T-shirt with Japanese characters scrawled in red across the front, black jeans, hollow cheeks and gelled, spiky blond hair. Handsome if you liked that sort of look, effeminate if you didn't. I didn't care either way. I just wanted to know if he was a murderer.

I introduced myself, and he gestured me to a hard-backed chair by the window. We were on the twelfth floor, and below I could see lunchtime swarms of office workers hitting the trendy Yonge Street bistros and trattorias.

"I really didn't do it, you know," Tony said. "It happened exactly the way I told the police."

"Tell me about that evening. Who was there? What were you doing?"

Tony propped himself up on a cushion. "Val and me, Jacqui Prior, my business partner Ray Dasgupta, and Scott Schneider and his wife, Ginny. We were supposed to be celebrating. Jacqui had just been chosen as the new *Cherub* girl. It's a whole range of soaps, bath oils, shampoos and stuff due to be launched next year. Major, multinational campaign. Anyway, Jacqui was the face, the look, and our studio got the contract for the still photography, so we all had a lot to celebrate. Scott is Jacqui's agent, so he and Ginny were over the moon, too. You've no idea what a boost that will give Jacqui's career—not that she's done badly so far, but it's a whole new ball game for her. For all of us, in fact. It's like we've all suddenly moved into the big time."

"When did things start to go wrong?"

"Just before the cappuccino. We'd had quite a bit to drink, and Val had been moody all evening. Finally, she hit us with the news. When everyone got around to toasting Jacqui for the fiftieth time, Val said something about her face not being so photogenic if she didn't keep her hands off me. You can imagine how that heated things up."

"Was it true? About the affair?"

"I'm not proud of it, but I won't deny it."

"How did Valerie find out?"

"I don't know. I thought we were discreet."

"Could someone have told her?"

"I suppose so, but I can't imagine who. I didn't think anyone else knew."

"What happened next?"

"Well, there was a very embarrassing scene in the restaurant, and Jacqui had to take Val to the washroom to quiet her down."

"Didn't that surprise you, Jacqui and Val going off together after what had just happened?"

"I never looked at it that way. They'd been best friends for an awful long time. But Val was a lot calmer when she came back, and Jacqui left almost immediately with Scott and Ginny. Val and I stayed a bit longer with Ray, drank some more champagne, but it was obvious the party was over. We started arguing again in the cab on the way home. When we got there, the fight went on. I tried to calm things down, but Val was really wild. She's always been extremely jealous. Anyway, I was looking for a distraction, and I remember there was a package of books I wanted to open. Modern first editions. I hadn't had time in the morning. I got a kitchen knife to cut the string, then Val started on at me again for being more interested in the books than in what she had to say, which, to be honest, was nothing really but a string of insults aimed at me. That was when I threw the knife down and went for a shower—they always seem to calm me down—and when I came back she was dead. That's all there is to it."

"You didn't hear anything?"

"Nothing at all. The shower's pretty loud."

"Could someone have got in the house while you were showering?"

"I don't see how. The front door was locked and bolted, with the chain on."

"And the back?"

"The door was open because it was a warm evening, and we get a nice breeze from the lake, up the ravine, but the screen door was locked. I know because the police kept going on about it when they were trying to get me to confess. They kept telling me how it couldn't have been anyone else, that there were no signs of a break-in."

It was exactly as Enamoretto had said it was. "How long had you been seeing Jacqui?" I asked.

"Only a couple of months."

"Was it serious?"

"I don't know." Tony sighed, running long, bony fingers through his hair. "She's a hard one to fathom. I thought I was serious, but maybe I was just infatuated. Jacqui's a fascinating woman, complicated, very difficult to get to know."

"You say she and Val were old friends?"

"Yes. Had been since high school. They both got into modeling together out in Vancouver first, then they came to Toronto about five years ago. That was what hurt Val most—that it was her closest friend. It wasn't so much that I'd been with another woman, though that would have been bad enough, but that I'd been with Jacqui. We'd always flirted a bit in public, you know, just in fun. But one time we were alone and things just got out of hand."

"Can you think of anyone else who might have had a reason to hurt Valerie?"

"So you *do* believe me?"

I remembered Susan's plea. "I'm keeping an open mind."

Tony thought for a moment. "No," he said. "Since Val gave up modeling, she's been doing a bit of teaching at the agency. Deportment, public speaking, that sort of thing. She gets along well with everyone."

"Did she have any lovers?"

"Not that I knew of, and I'm pretty sure I would have known."

"Okay," I said, getting up to leave. "Thanks a lot, Tony. If anything comes up, I'll be in touch right away."

Tony seemed surprised and alarmed that I was leaving so soon. He sat up abruptly and crossed his long legs. "You *are* going to help me, aren't you? You do believe me?"

"What I believe doesn't really matter," I said. "It's what I can get the police to believe that counts. But don't worry, I'll do my best. One more thing: do you think I could have the house keys? It would help if you'd write down the address, too. I'd like to have a look around."

"Sure. You can take Valerie's set," he said. "I picked them up last time I was over there, after the police let me out. I couldn't stand to stay in the house, not after what happened, but I didn't like the idea of them just lying around like that."

I took the ring of keys. A Mickey Mouse key chain. Cute. "Do you know what all these are for?" I asked.

Tony started counting them off. "Front door, back door, studio, agency. That one I don't know."

There was one key left, but it didn't look like a door key to me. Too small. I thought I had a pretty good idea what it was.

"Did Valerie keep a safety-deposit box?" I asked Tony.

He seemed surprised by the question. "Not that I know of. Why?"

I held up the key. "That's why," I said.

PART FOUR

I wanted to find out where the safety-deposit box was located and what its contents were, but I didn't know whether I'd be able to get into it even if I found it. Technically, Tony would inherit everything of Valerie's, unless her will specified otherwise, but criminals aren't permitted to gain financially from their crimes. On the other hand, Tony hadn't been convicted of anything yet, so nothing would happen. In the meantime, I had asked Tony to check with Valerie's bank, and there was plenty of digging around for me to do while I waited for a result.

The Caldwell house looked like a cozy English vicarage right out of *Masterpiece Theater.* I parked my 1998 Neon across the street among the BMWs and Audis, and, feeling vaguely ashamed of its unwashed state and the dent in the front right wheel arch, I walked up to the door.

Outside the house stood a huge old oak tree, and I wondered if it would provide an intruder enough cover from the nosy neighbors. Even so, anyone who wanted to get in would have to get past the heavy door, which Tony told me had been locked, bolted and chained. There was no porch, just the dark, paneled door set in the sandy stonework. The key let me into a small hallway, and a second door led into the living room. The police had taken the carpet, leaving the polished wood floor bare.

Three of Tony's photographs hung on the wall. They were very good, as far as I could tell. I'd expected modernistic effects and cut-up contact sheets, but two of the three were landscapes. One looked like a Beach sunset, showing the Leuty lifeguard station in effective, high-contrast black and white, and the other was a view of a rocky coastline, probably in Nova Scotia, where the cliff edges cut the land from the sea like a deformed spine. Again, Tony had used high contrast.

The third was a portrait signed by Valerie, along with what I took to be her lip prints, dated two years ago. She was posing against a wall, just head and shoulders, but there was such sensuality about her Bardot-like pout and the way her raven's-wing hair spilled over her bare, white shoulders. There was something about the angle of her head that seemed to challenge and invite at the same time, and the look in her dark eyes was intelligent, humorous and questioning. For the first time in the case, I had a real sense of the victim, and I felt the tragedy and waste of her death.

Upstairs, I rummaged through her bedside drawers and checked out the walk-in closet, but found nothing I didn't expect to. I assumed the police had already been through the place before me and taken anything they thought might be related to the crime. On the other hand, if they believed they had caught the criminal and had enough evidence against him, then they wouldn't go to the expense of an all-out, lengthy crime scene investigation. Not exactly *CSI*; they'd leave their lasers and luminal at home. Valerie's clothes were high-quality designer brands, her underwear black and silky. I felt like a voyeur so I went back downstairs.

Next I moved into the kitchen, where the parcel of books still lay on the table, brown paper and string loose around it. The books, first editions of early Mavis Gallant and Alice Munro, were from an antiquarian dealer in Halifax, I noticed, and the string was a quaint, old-fashioned touch. The only thing missing was the knife itself, which the police had taken as evidence.

The door opened onto a back stoop, and my intrusion scared off a flock of red-throated house finches from the bird feeder. Judging by the untidy lawn surrounded by its flagstone path, neither Tony nor Valerie had been very interested in gardening. At the far end, the lawn petered off into bracken and roots where the ravine threatened to encroach, and finally the land dropped away. I walked to the end of the garden and noticed that the ravine was neither too steep nor too overgrown to be accessible. There was even a path, narrow and overgrown, but a path nonetheless. You certainly wouldn't have had to be a mountain lion to gain easy access from the back.

The ground had been hard and dry at the time of the murder, I remembered, and we'd had a couple of heavy storms in the last week, so there was no point in getting down on my hands and knees with a magnifying glass, even if I had had one. I stood at the end of the lawn for a while enjoying the smell of the trees and wild flowers, listening to the cardinal's repetitive whistling and the *chip-chip* sounds of warblers, then I went back inside.

Fine. Now I knew that it was possible for someone to get up and down the ravine easily enough. But how about getting into the house? I sat at the kitchen table toying with the string. I could think of no way of getting through a locked screen door without leaving a trace, unless it were either open in the first place, or somebody had opened it for me. Valerie might have opened it to someone she knew, someone she felt she had no reason to fear. If she were distracted by her anger at Tony, her surprise at seeing a friend appear at the back door would surely have overruled any caution or suspicion she might otherwise have felt. On the other hand, if the door was locked when the police arrived, that was a problem.

As I sat twirling the string around my fingers and idly glancing at the two first editions in their nest of brown paper, I became aware of a niggling discrepancy. It was unconscious at first, nothing I could put my finger on, but as it turned out, it was *on* my finger. I unraveled the string and tried to fasten it around the books. It didn't fit. Much too short. I looked around on the floor but saw no more, and I could think of no reason why either Tony or the police would secrete a length of string.

I went over to the screen door and examined the catch, which looked like an upside-down earlobe, and surely enough, when I looked closely, I noticed faint scuff marks around the narrow neck. Making sure I had the house keys in my pocket, as an experiment I opened the door, hooked a length of string over the catch, then shut the door, standing outside, holding the string. When I tugged gently, the catch engaged and the screen door locked. I let go of one end and pulled the string toward me. It slid free. Like many old screen doors, it wasn't a tight fit.

I still had nothing concrete, no real evidence, but I did have the solution to a very important problem. If Valerie *had* let someone in through the back, then whoever it was could easily have killed her, left the same way, and locked the screen door from outside. Now I knew that it *could* be done.

PART FIVE

Jacqui Prior, my next port of call, lived in an apartment off the Esplanade, close to the St. Lawrence Market, the Sony Centre for the Performing Arts, and all the wine bars and restaurants that had sprung up around there. I found her in torn jeans and a dirty T-shirt, lustrous dark hair tied back in a ponytail, busily packing her belongings into boxes she had clearly picked up from the local LCBO store. While she seemed surprised to see me, she was also curious. She said she was just about to take a break anyway and offered me a cup of Earl Grey, which I gladly accepted.

There was a superficial resemblance to the photograph of Valerie Pascale I had seen at Tony Caldwell's house, but Jacqui seemed somehow unformed, incomplete. She had the kind of face that was beautiful but lacked the stamp of a personality. I imagined that was probably what made her a good model. She must be the kind of person who would shine and sparkle in front of the camera, given a role to play. Her olive skin was smooth as silk, perfect for beauty soap, shampoo and bath oil commercials, and I could imagine her looking wholesome in a way that Valerie Pascale didn't.

"Where are you moving to?" I asked.

"I've found the perfect little house in Leaside."

"Leaside? Won't that be a bit quiet for you after all this?"

She smiled, showing perfect dimples. "I like things quiet. I need my beauty sleep."

There wasn't much I could say to that, so I sipped some Earl Grey.

Jacqui frowned. It could have been real, or it could have been a model's frown. I didn't know. "It's awful about Valerie and Tony," she said. "I feel terribly responsible in a way, but I don't see how I can help you."

"It's not your fault," I said. "People do what they do. I'm just not convinced that Tony Caldwell did what he's been accused of."

"Oh? What makes you think that?"

"Just a few inconsistencies, that's all. You and Valerie were old friends. How did you meet?"

"We were at high school together, then we both went to UBC. We shared an apartment in Kitsilano."

"So you knew her pretty well?"

"As well as one could know Valerie."

"What do you mean by that?"

"She wasn't exactly an open book, you know."

"She had secrets?"

"We all have secrets. Valerie could make the most innocent thing into a secret. It was her nature to be mysterious, enigmatic. And she liked to be in control, liked to have the upper hand. She needed to feel that, ultimately, if the walls came tumbling down, she'd be safe, she'd have an escape route."

"Didn't work this time," I said.

Jacqui wiped away a tear. "No."

"Who told her about your affair with her husband?"

Jacqui looked shocked, and I was beginning to feel more and more that I was being treated to her repertoire of faces. She was good. "Do we have to talk about that?"

"I'm trying to help Tony."

"Yes. Yes, of course. I'm sorry. I don't know how she found out. I was sure nobody knew about us."

"What happened when the two of you went to the washroom?"

"Nothing. We just talked it out, that's all. Sort of made up."

"Sort of?"

"I told her I'd end it with Tony. She was still upset, but she accepted my word."

"Would finishing with Tony have been difficult for you?"

"A little, perhaps. But it's not as if we were in love or anything."

"So it was just an affair? A fling?"

"Yes. Oh, don't sound so disapproving. We're both adults. And it's not as if I was the first."

"Tony had other affairs?"

"Of course."

"Did Valerie know?"

"She never said anything to me."

"Are you sure you don't plan to go on seeing Tony now that Valerie is conveniently out of the way?"

"I don't like what you're implying. I've just lost a very dear old friend. There's nothing 'convenient' about that."

"A dear friend whose husband you stole."

"I didn't steal him. Don't be so melodramatic. These things happen all the time."

"Where did you go after you left the restaurant that night, Jacqui?"

"I came here. Scott and Ginny dropped me off. They'll tell you."

"Did you visit Tony and Valerie's house often?"

"Sometimes."

"When was the last time?"

"About a month ago. They had a barbecue. We were all there. Me, Ray, Ginny, Scott."

"So you knew the ravine well enough?"

"We all went for a walk there, yes, but, look—"

"And you had plenty of time to get back out to the Beach the night Valerie was killed, if you wanted to."

"I don't drive."

"There are taxis."

"They'd have records."

"Maybe. But Valerie would have let you in the back door, no problem, wouldn't she?"

"What are you talking about? Why should I go to the back door?"

"So you wouldn't be seen from the street. Because you went with the intent of killing Valerie. You just didn't know that Tony would get the blame. When you found out he was in the shower and Valerie was all alone, you seized the opportunity and killed her."

Jacqui stood up, hands on hips. "This is ridiculous. On the one hand you're saying I went there with the intention of killing Valerie, which is absurd, and on the other hand you accuse me of seizing the moment. Which is it? It can't be both. Look, I don't want to talk to you anymore. You're not a real policeman. You can't make me."

She was right. I had no special powers. Standing, I reached in my pocket for the key. "Recognize this?" I asked.

She looked at it, pouting. "No."

"It's a safety-deposit key," I told her. "Were you ever aware of Valerie having a safety-deposit box?"

"No. But I told you she could be very secretive."

"Any idea what she might have kept in it if she had one?"

"I don't know. Money? Jewelry? Now, if you don't mind, I've got more packing to do."

Jacqui's response to the whole safety-deposit box issue was just a bit too rushed and casual for my liking. I followed her to the door trying to decide whether I believed her or not. I wasn't sure. The problem was that Jacqui Prior wasn't a WYSIWYG sort of woman. Tony Caldwell had called her complicated, but in a way she struck me as shallow, empty without the role to assume, the correct expression to wear or gesture to make. As I rode the elevator down to my car, I found myself wondering if I was being manipulated. Just how much did Jacqui and Tony's affair have to do with what happened to Valerie? In my mind's eye, I saw myself as Charles Laughton riding his stair lift in *Witness for the Prosecution*. Had they planned it between the two of them, I wondered, and was my getting Tony off part of their plan? Was I being used in their game?

If Tony Caldwell or Jacqui Prior hadn't murdered Valerie, then who else might have done it? Discounting the passing tramp theory, my money was still on one of the dinner guests: Jacqui, Ray Dasgupta, Scott and Ginny Schneider. Valerie would have let any one of those four in the back door. But which one? And why? And what part did the safety-deposit box play? Maybe I would find out something from the others who'd been at dinner that night.

PART SIX

I found both Scott and Ginny Schneider in the office of their modeling agency just off Spadina, in the garment district. On the surface, Scott seemed very much the outgoing, charming type, while Ginny was more reserved. They were both in their late thirties, and I'd guess from her cheekbones that Ginny had probably been a model herself in the not-too-distant past. Her husband looked more like a trendy stockbroker in casual business attire.

"I thought the police had settled the matter of Valerie's death," Scott said.

"They've arrested Tony Caldwell, if that's what you mean," I said. "But that doesn't settle anything."

"How so?"

"I'm just not convinced. I understand Valerie worked for you?"

"She helped out sometimes, yes. She'd been a model herself, and quite a good one, too, so she was able to work with some of the girls and with the clients, help us with our selections. It's an important part of the business, and it can be very tricky, matching the model to the product."

"Was anything bothering her around the time of her death?"

"Her husband's affair with Jacqui Prior, I should imagine."

"Did she talk to you about that?"

"No. We only found out at the dinner, along with everyone else."

"You, too?" I asked Ginny.

"Yes."

"And were you surprised?"

"Naturally," said Scott, looking over at his wife. "We both were."

"Do you have any idea how Valerie knew?"

"I'm afraid not. We certainly didn't tell her."

"Well, you couldn't tell her if you yourselves didn't know, could you? You must have worked closely with Jacqui, though. Did she ever let anything slip?"

"Nothing. Look, Mr. Lang, I'm very sorry about Tony and everything. I've known him for a number of years and count him as a good friend as well as a business colleague, but don't you think the police know what they're about? He and Valerie did have a terrific row—we all witnessed that—and not long afterward, she was dead. It makes sense. Any one of us could snap under pressure like that."

"Indeed we could," I said. "Any one of us. Where did you go after you left the restaurant?"

"We dropped Jacqui off at her apartment, then we went home," Ginny answered.

"Did anything unusual happen on the way?"

"No. Scott had had too much to drink, so I drove."

"Where's home?"

Scott answered this time. "Scarborough, down near the bluffs."

"So you weren't too far away from Tony and Valerie's place?"

Scott's bonhomie vanished in an instant, and he stuck his chin out. Ginny watched on coolly. "What are you getting at?" Scott said. "You come around here asking damn fool questions, and then you start accusing me of murdering Valerie."

"I haven't accused you of anything," I said.

"You know what I mean. You certainly implied it."

"I merely implied that someone other than Tony could have done it." I looked at Ginny. "Did either of you go out after you got home?"

Ginny looked down at her hands folded on her lap before answering, "No."

"Of course we didn't," Scott snapped. But something was wrong. Ginny didn't want to look me in the eye, and Scott was blustering. Was she protecting him? I took the safety-deposit box key from my pocket. "Have either of you seen this before?"

They both looked genuinely puzzled. "No," said Scott.

"Never," said Ginny.

"Okay. Thanks for you time." I pocketed the key and headed back to my car.

Tony Caldwell's photographic studio was located in that urban wasteland of movie studios and soundstages between Eastern Avenue and the Gardiner, where Toronto pretends to be New York, London, and even a distant galaxy. At least parking in one of the vast, empty lots was easier than around Spadina, which had cost me a small fortune. The studio had an empty feel to it, but Ray Dasgupta was in the office working at the computer. He stopped and looked up when I knocked and entered. I told him who I was and what I was doing.

"You probably think it's odd, me working here while all this is going on?" he said.

"I suppose it takes your mind off other things," I said. "And no doubt there's work to be done."

"Mostly bookkeeping."

"What's going to happen to the studio now?"

"I don't know. Tony was the real creative energy behind us. I'm not much more than a glorified administrator. Oh, I know a shutter speed from an f-stop, but that's about as far as it goes. Tony has a flair for striking up relationships with his models . . ." He paused. "That wasn't meant to come out the way it did," he said. "I mean behind the camera."

"I know what you mean," I said. "But seeing as you mention it, how much do you know about these other relationships?"

Ray sucked on his lower lip, frowning.

"It's not that tough a question, Ray," I said. "Jacqui wasn't the first, was she?"

"How do you know?"

"Never mind. But if anyone ought to know, it's you, his partner. How many? How long?"

Ray squirmed in his chair. "Always," he said. "As long as I've known him Tony's been chasing women. He couldn't seem to help himself."

"And Valerie didn't know?"

"I don't know whether she suspected or not, but she never acted as if she did. Not in public."

"And you think she would have done something if she'd known?"

"Yes. Valerie is a proud woman, and jealous, too, not someone to take an affair lightly. She might not have divorced Tony. After all, she'd given up her own career, and she liked the lifestyle, but . . ."

"Maybe she'd have killed him?"

"But he's not the one who's dead, is he?"

Still, it was another possible scenario. Maybe Jacqui was the last straw. Perhaps there'd been a struggle, Valerie with the knife, trying to kill Tony, and things had turned around. That didn't help me much, though, as he hadn't even tried to claim self-defense. "What do you think of Jacqui?" I asked.

Ray's lip curled. "Jumped-up little slut. It's not as if she can't have any man she wants. Why Tony? Why steal her best friend's husband?"

"And Valerie?"

Ray looked away, clearly disturbed by the question.

"Ray? Something you want to tell me?"

"Look, I . . . I would never have . . . I mean . . ."

"Were you in love with her, Ray?"

His silence told me all I needed to know.

"Was it you who told Valerie about Tony and Jacqui?"

Ray jerked his head in an abrupt nod, then turned damp brown eyes on me. "How could he? How could he treat her like that. Oh, she never looked at me twice. It's not that I thought . . . or even hoped . . . but I couldn't bear to see it anymore, them carrying on the way they did, and Valerie not knowing."

"So you told her."

"Yes."

"When?"

"Just before dinner."

"Did you kill her, Ray?"

"Why would I kill her? I loved her."

"Maybe you went round to the house later and found her alone, Tony in the shower. You thought you were in with a chance now, but she turned you down, laughed at you, and you lost it. Is that how it happened, Ray?"

For a moment, I thought he was going to confess, then he said, "No. I didn't do it. But I'd have a closer look at Jacqui Prior if I were you."

"Why's that?"

"Because of something Valerie said when I told her about the affair."

"What did she say?"

"She said, 'I'll ruin her. The little bitch. You see if I don't. And don't think I can't do it, either.' "

PART SEVEN

"You'd better not have come around with more of those ridiculous accusations," Jacqui Prior said, flopping on the sofa and crossing her long legs.

I took out the safety-deposit box key and held it in front of her. "I've been talking to Tony," I said, "and we've been through some of Valerie's papers. According to her Visa bills, there's an annual fee of $40 at a BC credit union. The people there were not forthcoming, but they did admit that Valerie rented a safety-deposit box. I asked myself why she kept a box in Vancouver when she lived in Toronto."

"And?"

"It's my guess she got it while she was still living there, and she doesn't need frequent access."

"So it's probably empty."

"But why keep paying? She can't have forgotten about it. The annual bill would remind her."

"So what's your explanation, great detective?"

"That there's something in it she wants to keep."

"And how does that relate to me?"

"The two of you grew up together in Vancouver."

"So?"

"What's in the box, Jacqui?"

"I've no idea."

"You're lying."

"How dare you!"

"What's in it? Was it worth killing her over?"

"I didn't kill her."

"So you say. But the way it looks to me is that you had the best motive. You were having an affair with her husband. She threatened you. And she was keeping something in a safety-deposit box in Vancouver that may be related to you."

"That's just conjecture."

"But it's a pretty reasonable conjecture, you must admit."

"I'm admitting nothing."

"Well," I said, standing to leave, "the police will probably be less polite than me, and there'll no doubt be media interest. Your choice, Jacqui. If you're innocent, you'd be far better off telling me the truth. I don't have to tell anyone."

I could see her thinking over her options: Whether to tell me anything. How much to tell. How many lies she might get away with. What she might use to bribe me to keep silent. In the end, she came to a decision. "I need a drink first," she said, and went over to the cocktail cabinet and poured herself a Pernod. It turned cloudy when she added a few drops of water. As an afterthought, she asked me if I wanted anything. I said no.

"Strictly between you and me?"

"Of course."

"When Valerie dropped her little bombshell and all hell broke loose, I took her to the washroom."

"I've always wondered what went on in there."

"She told me she'd ruin me."

"How?"

"When Val and I were students," Jacqui said, "we were . . . well, to put it mildly, we were a bit wild. We got into coke and stuff in a fairly big way and it can skewer your judgment. There was a man. We were so high we thought it would be fun to make a video. He didn't know. No copies. Only the original. Need I say more?"

"The three of you?"

"Yes."

"And Valerie kept this?"

"I told you she liked control."

"Why would she want to have control over you?"

"Not me, you fool. Him. He was a politician. Still is, and climbing the ranks."

"So Valerie used it to blackmail him?"

"She never used it for anything as far as I know."

"But that gave him a motive for killing her. Who is he?"

"He didn't even know about it. I'm sure of that."

"But Valerie threatened to use it against you?"

"Yes. This *Cherub* contract is a really big deal, and I need to be squeaky-clean. It's a family line, so if it got around that their cherub wasn't quite as cherubic as they thought, I think you can see where that might lead."

"The unemployment line?"

"Exactly."

"You do realize, don't you, that you've just given me another motive for killing Valerie? If she made the video public, you'd have been ruined."

"No. You don't understand. There was no video."

Now it was my turn to look puzzled. "What do you mean?"

"You don't think I wanted that thing lying around, do you? I can make myself look enough like Valerie to fool people, especially strangers behind the counter in a bank, and her signature is easy enough to forge. One day, while she was at the dentist's, I borrowed her key and her ID."

"So you're saying—"

"Valerie didn't know, because she never checked from one year to the next, but the video was gone. I destroyed it. That safety-deposit box was empty."

"Then who . . . ?"

Jacqui put her hand to her mouth. "Oh, no," she said, turning pale. "Oh, God, no!"

PART EIGHT

"You again," said Scott, when I called at their Scarborough home early that evening. I had spent the rest of the afternoon doing the sort of digging I usually do when I'm not investigating murders. Ginny walked through from the kitchen and nodded a curt greeting.

"What can I help you with this time?" Scott asked.

"When you were driving Jacqui home from the restaurant the night Valerie was murdered, you asked her about what went on in the washroom, didn't you?"

"So what? I was curious."

"And she told you that Valerie had threatened her with something that could ruin the whole *Cherub* deal."

"She did? I don't remember."

"Oh. Come off it, Scott! You mean to tell me you were so curious you can't even remember what she told you?"

"What does it matter?"

I leaned forward. "It matters because it gave you a motive to kill Valerie."

"That's absurd."

"No, it's not. I've been doing a bit of research this afternoon, and I've discovered that your precious agency is in serious financial trouble. You're in debt up to your eyeballs, second mortgages, the lot, and you can't afford to lose the *Cherub* contract. When you thought that was in jeopardy, you knew you had to get rid of Valerie. Maybe you planned on killing them both and making it look as if there'd been an intruder, but when you saw Tony wasn't there, you changed your plan."

"It's an interesting theory," said Scott, "but that's all it is."

I knew he was right. What I'd discovered, and what Jacqui had told me, might point the police in Scott's direction, but they'd need much more if Tony were to be exonerated.

"You know what the sad thing is ?" I said. "You did it all for nothing."

"What do you mean?"

"Jacqui was upset. All she said was that Valerie had threatened to ruin her. What she didn't tell you was that Valerie no longer had the means to do it. You killed Valerie Pascale for nothing, Scott."

Ginny turned pale. "What did you say?" she asked.

"Don't, Ginny!" Scott warned her.

But it was too late. Ginny glanced at her husband, turned back to me and said, "Do you think for a moment I would let her destroy everything we'd worked for?" She looked over tenderly at Scott, who was gnawing on a fingernail. All his deepest fears had now come true. If he wasn't an accomplice and had, say, passed out after drinking too much, he must at least have suspected and worried that the truth would come out. "She deserved to die," Ginny went on. "She was going to ruin all of us just because of a stupid adolescent affair. And now you tell us it was all for nothing." Her laugh sounded like a harsh bark.

"You still have no evidence," Scott said. "Ginny will deny everything. I'll say she was with me the whole time. Do you realize what you're doing? You could ruin all of us, Jacqui, Tony, Ray included."

I stood up to leave. "Jacqui will survive. And so will Tony and Ray. The one thing neither of you seem to have given a moment's thought to," I said, as I headed for the door, "is that Tony Caldwell is awaiting trial on a murder charge. A murder he didn't commit. Think about that when you lament your business losses."

After I'd shut the door behind me, I slid my hand in my inside pocket and turned off the tiny digital recorder that had been on the whole time I'd been with Scott and Ginny. Maybe it wouldn't stand up in court, but it would be enough to convince Enamoretto, get Tony off the hook and reopen the case. And, who knows, perhaps Susan Caldwell would be grateful enough to have dinner with me. We could talk about Darwin's influence on Wordsworth.

The Price of Love

Tommy found the badge on the third day of his summer holiday at Blackpool, the first holiday without his father. The sun had come out that morning, and he was playing on the crowded beach with his mother, who sat in her striped deck chair smoking Consulate, reading her *Nova* magazine and keeping an eye on him. Not that he needed. an eye kept on him. Tommy was thirteen now and quite capable of amusing himself. But his mother had a thing about water, so she never let him near the sea alone. Uncle Arthur had gone to the amusements on the Central Pier, where he liked to play the one-armed bandits.

The breeze from the gray Irish Sea was chilly, but Tommy bravely wore his new swimming trunks. He even dipped his toes in the water before running back to warm them in the sand. It was then when he felt something sharp prick his big toe. Treasure? He scooped away the sand carefully while no one was looking. Slowly he pulled out the object by its edge and dusted it off with his free hand. It was shaped like a silver shield. At its center was a circle with "METROPOLITAN POLICE" curved around the top and bottom of the initials "ER." Above this was a crown and a tiny cross. The silver glinted in the sunlight.

Tommy's breath caught in his throat. This was exactly the sign he had been waiting for since ever his father died. It was the same type of badge he had worn on his uniform. Tommy remembered how proud his dad had sounded when he spoke of it. He had even let Tommy touch it and told him what "ER" meant: *Elizabeth Regina*. It was Latin, his father had explained, for Queen Elizabeth. "That's our Queen,

Tommy," he had said proudly. And the cross on top, he went on, symbolized the Church of England. When Tommy held the warm badge there on the beach, he could feel his father's presence in it.

Tommy decided not to tell anyone. They might make him hand it in somewhere, or just take it off him. Uncle Arthur was always doing that. When Tommy found an old tennis ball in the street, Uncle Arthur said it might have been chewed by a dog and got germs on it, so he threw it in the fire. Then there was the toy cap gun with the broken hammer he found on the recreation ground—"It's no good if it's broken, is it?"—Uncle Arthur said, and out it went. But this time Uncle Arthur wasn't going to get his hands on Tommy's treasure. While his mother was reading her magazine, Tommy went over to his small pile of clothes and slipped the badge in his trouser pocket.

"What are you doing, Tommy?"

He started. It was his mother. "Just looking for my handkerchief," he said, the first thing he could think of.

"What do you want a handkerchief for?"

"The water was cold," Tommy said. "I'm sniffling." He managed to fake a sniffle to prove it.

But his mother's attention had already wandered back to her magazine. She never did talk to him for very long these days, didn't seem much interested in how he was doing at school (badly), or how he was feeling in general (awful). Sometimes it was a blessing because it made it easier for Tommy to live undisturbed in his own elaborate secret world, but sometimes he felt he would like it if she just smiled at him, touched his arm and asked him how he was doing. He'd say he was fine. He wouldn't even tell her the truth because she would get bored if she had to listen to his catalog of woes. His mother had always gotten bored easily.

This time her lack of interest was a blessing. He managed to get the badge in his pocket without her or anyone else seeing it. He felt official now. No longer was he just playing at being a special agent. Now that he had his badge, he had serious standards to uphold, like his father had always said. And he would start his new role by keeping a close eye on Uncle Arthur.

———

Uncle Arthur wasn't his real uncle. Tommy's mother was an only child, like Tommy himself. It was three months after his father's funeral when she had first introduced them. She said that Uncle Arthur was an old friend she had known many years ago, and they had just met again by chance in Kensington High Street. Wasn't that a wonderful coincidence? She had been so lonely since his father had died. Uncle Arthur was fun and made her laugh again. She was sure that Tommy would like him. But Tommy didn't. And he was certain he had seen Uncle Arthur before, while his father was still alive, but he didn't say anything.

It was also because of Uncle Arthur that they moved from London to Leeds, although Tommy's mother said it was because London was becoming too expensive. Tommy had never found it easy to make friends, and up north it was even worse. People made fun of his accent, picked fights with him in the schoolyard, and a lot of the time he couldn't even understand what they were saying. He couldn't understand the teachers, either, which was why the standard of his schoolwork slipped.

Once they had moved, Uncle Arthur, who traveled a lot for his job but lived in Leeds, became a fixture at their new house whenever he was in town, and some evenings he and Tommy's mother would go off dancing, to the pictures or to the pub and leave Tommy home alone. He liked that because he could play his records and smoke a cigarette in the back garden. Once he had even drunk some of Uncle Arthur's vodka and replaced it with water. He didn't know if Uncle Arthur ever guessed, but he never said anything. Uncle Arthur had just bought his mother a brand-new television, too, so Tommy sometimes just sat eating cheese and onion crisps, drinking pop and watching *Danger Man* or *The Saint*.

What he didn't like was when they stopped in. Then they were always whispering or going up to his mother's room to talk so he couldn't hear what they were saying. But they were still in the house, and even though they were ignoring him, he couldn't do whatever he wanted, or even watch what he wanted on television. Uncle Arthur never hit him or anything—his mother wouldn't stand for that—but Tommy could tell sometimes that he wanted to. Mostly he took no interest whatsoever. For all Uncle Arthur cared, Tommy might as well not have existed. But he did.

Everyone said that Tommy's mother was pretty. Tommy couldn't really see it himself because she was his mother, after all. He thought that Denise Clark at school was pretty. He wanted to go out with her. And Marianne Faithfull, who he'd seen on *Top of the Pops.* But she was too old for him, and she was famous. People said he was young for his years and knew nothing about girls. All he knew was that he definitely *liked* girls. He felt something funny happen to him when he saw Denise Clark walking down the street in her little gray school skirt, white blouse and maroon V-neck jumper, but he didn't know what it was, and apart from kissing, which he knew about, and touching breasts, which someone had told him about at school, he didn't really know what you were supposed to do with a girl when she was charitable enough to let you go out with her.

Tommy's mother didn't look at all like Denise Clark or Marianne Faithfull, but she wore more modern and more fashionable clothes than the other women on the street. She had beautiful long blond hair over her shoulders and pale flawless skin, and she put on her pink lipstick, black mascara and blue eye shadow every day, even if she was only stopping in or going to the shops. Tommy thought some of the women in the street were jealous because she was so pretty and nicely dressed.

Not long after they had moved, he overheard two of their neighbors saying that his mother was full of "London airs and graces" and "no better than she ought to be." He didn't know what that meant, but he could tell by the way they said it that it wasn't meant as a compliment. Then they said something else he didn't understand about a dress she had worn when his father was only four months in his grave, and made tut-tutting sounds. That made Tommy angry. He came out of his hiding place and stood in front of them red faced and told them they shouldn't talk like that about his mother and father. That took the wind out of their sails.

Every night before he went to sleep, Tommy prayed that Uncle Arthur would go away and never come back again. But he always did. He seemed to stop at the house late every night, and sometimes Tommy didn't hear him leave until it was almost time to get up for school. What they found to talk about all night, he had no idea, though he knew that Uncle Arthur had a bed made up in the spare room, so he could sleep there if he wanted. Even when Uncle Arthur wasn't around, Tommy's mother seemed distant and distracted, and she lost her patience with him very quickly.

One thing Tommy noticed within a few weeks of Uncle Arthur's visits to the new house was that his father's photograph—the one in full uniform his father was so proud of—went mysteriously missing from the mantelpiece. He asked his mother about it, but all she said was that it was time to move on and leave her widow's weeds behind. Sometimes he thought he would never understand the things grown-ups said.

When Tommy got back to his room at the boardinghouse, he took the badge out of his pocket and held it in his palm. Yes, he could feel his father's power in it. Then he took out the creased newspaper cutting he always carried with him and read it for the hundredth time:

POLICE CONSTABLE SHOT DEAD:
BIGGEST HAUL SINCE THE GREAT TRAIN ROBBERY AUTHORITIES SAY

A police constable accompanying a van carrying more than one million pounds was shot dead yesterday in a daring broad daylight raid on the A226 outside Swanscombe. PC Brian Burford was on special assignment at the time. The robbers fled the scene and police are interested in talking to anyone who might have seen a blue Vauxhall Victor in the general area that day. Since the Great Train Robbery on 8th August, 1963, police officers have routinely accompanied large amounts of cash. . . .

Tommy knew the whole thing off by heart, of course, about the police looking for five men and thinking it must have been an inside job, but he always read the end over and over again: "PC Burford leaves behind a wife and a young son." *Leaves behind.* They made it sound as if it was his father's fault, when he had just been doing his job. " 'It is one of the saddest burdens of the badge of office to break the news that a police officer has been killed in the line of duty,' said

Deputy Chief Constable Graham Brown. 'Thank God this burden remains such a rarity in our country.' "

Tommy fingered his badge again. *Burden of the badge of office.* Well, he knew what that felt like now. He made sure no one was around and went to the toilet. There, he took some toilet paper, wet it under the tap and used it to clean off his badge, drying it carefully with a towel. There were still a few grains of sand caught in the pattern of lines that radiated outward, and it looked as if it was tarnished a bit around the edges. He decided that he needed some sort of wallet to keep it in, and he had enough pocket money to buy one. Uncle Arthur was still at the pier, and his mother was having a lie down, having "caught too much sun," so he told her he was going for a walk and headed for the shops.

Tommy went into first the gift shop he saw and found a plastic wallet just the right size. He could keep his badge safe in there, and when he opened it, people would be able to see it. That would be important if he had to make an arrest or take someone in for questioning. He counted out the coins and paid the shopkeeper, then he put the wallet in his back pocket and walked outside. The shop next door had racks of used paperback books outside. Uncle Arthur didn't approve of used books— "Never know where they've been"—but Tommy didn't care about that. He had become good at hiding things. He bought *The Saint in New York,* which he hadn't read yet and had been looking for for ages.

The sun was still shining, so Tommy crossed over to the broad promenade that ran beside the sands and the sea. There was a lot of traffic on the front, and he had to be careful. His mother would have gone spare if she had known he hadn't looked for a zebra crossing but had dodged between the cars. Someone honked a horn at him. He thought of flashing his badge but decided against it. He would only use it when he really had to.

He walked along the prom, letting his hand trail on the warm metal railing. He liked to watch the waves roll in and listen to them as they broke on the shore. There were still hundreds of people on the beach, some of them braving the sea, most just sitting in deck chairs, the men in shirtsleeves and braces reading newspapers, knotted hankies covering their heads, the women sleeping, wearing floppy hats with the brims shading their faces. Children screamed and jumped, made elaborate sandcastles. A humpbacked man led the donkeys slowly along their marked track, excited riders whooping as they rode, pretending to be cowboys.

Then Tommy saw Uncle Arthur on the prom and froze.

He was wearing his dark blue trousers and matching blazer with the gold buttons, a small straw hat perched on his head. He needed a haircut, Tommy thought, looking at where the strands of dark hair curled out from under the straw. It wasn't as if he was young enough to wear his hair long like the Beatles. He was probably at least as old as Tommy's mother. As Uncle Arthur walked along with the crowds, he looked around furtively, licking his lips from time to time, and Tommy hardly even needed the magic of his badge to know that he was up to something. Tommy leaned over the railings and looked out to sea, where a distant tanker trailed smoke, and waited until Uncle Arthur had passed by. As he did so, he slipped his hand into his pocket and fingered the wallet that held his badge, feeling its power.

He could see Uncle Arthur's straw hat easily enough as he followed him through the crowds along the prom away from the Central Pier. Luckily, there were plenty of people walking in both directions, and there was no way Uncle Arthur could spot Tommy, even if he turned around suddenly. It was as if the badge had given him even extra power to be invisible.

Shortly before Chapel Street, Uncle Arthur checked the traffic and dashed across the road. Tommy was near some lights, and luckily they turned red, so he was able to keep up. There were just as many people on the other side because of all the shops and bingo halls and amusement arcades, so it was easy to slip unseen into the crowds again.

The problems started when Uncle Arthur got into the backstreets, where there weren't as many people. He didn't look behind him, so Tommy thought he would probably be OK following, but he kept his distance and stopped every now and then to look in a shop window. Soon, though, there were no shops except for the occasional newsagent's and bookie's, with maybe a café or a run-down pub on a street corner. Tommy started to get increasingly worried that he would be seen. What would Uncle Arthur do then? It didn't bear thinking about. He put his hand in his pocket and fingered the badge. It gave him courage. Occasionally, he crossed the street and followed from the other side. There were still a few people, including families with children carrying buckets and spades heading for the beach, so he didn't stick out like a sore thumb.

Finally, just when Tommy thought he would have to give up because the streets were getting too narrow and empty, Uncle Arthur disappeared into a pub called the Golden Trumpet. That was an unforeseen development. Tommy was too young to enter a pub, and even if he did, he would certainly be noticed. He looked at the James Bond wristwatch he had got for his thirteenth birthday. It was a quarter to three. The pubs closed for the afternoon at three. That wasn't too long to wait. He walked up to the front and tried to glance in the windows, but they were covered with smoked glass, so he couldn't see a thing.

There was a small café about twenty yards down the street, from which he could easily keep an eye on the pub door. Tommy went in and ordered a glass of milk and a sticky bun, which he took over to the table near the window, and watched the pub as he drank and ate. A few seedy-looking people came and went, but there was no sign of Uncle Arthur. Finally, at about ten past three, out he came with two other men. They stood in the street talking, faces close together, standing back and laughing as if they were telling a joke when anyone else walked past. Then, as if at a prearranged signal, they all walked off in different directions. Tommy didn't think he needed to follow Uncle Arthur anymore, as he was clearly heading back in the direction of the boardinghouse. And he was carrying a small holdall that he hadn't had with him before he went into the pub.

"Where do you think you've been?"

Tommy's mother was sitting in the lounge when he got back to the boardinghouse. Uncle Arthur was with her, reading the afternoon paper. He didn't look up.

"Just walking," said Tommy.

"Where?"

"Along the front." Tommy was terrified that Uncle Arthur might have seen him and told his mother, and that she was trying to catch him out in a lie.

"I've told you not to go near the sea when I'm not with you," she said.

"I didn't go near the sea," Tommy said, relieved. "All the time I was on the prom I was behind the railings."

"Are you certain?"

"Yes, Mummy. Honest. Cross my heart." At least he could swear to that without fear of hellfire and damnation. When he had been on the prom, he *had* been behind the railings at the top of the high sea wall, far away from the sea.

"All right, then," she said. "Mrs. Newbiggin will be serving dinner soon, so go up and wash your hands like a good boy. Your uncle Arthur had a nice win on the horses this afternoon, so we'll be going out to the Tower Ballroom to celebrate after. You'll be all right here on your own reading or watching television, won't you?"

Tommy said he would be all right alone. But it wasn't watching television that he had in mind, or reading *The Saint in New York*.

The boardinghouse was quiet after dinner. When they had cleared the table, Mrs. Newbiggin and her husband disappeared into their own living quarters, most of the younger guests went out, and only the two old women who were always there sat in the lounge knitting and watching television. Tommy went up to his room and lay on his bed reading until he was certain his mother and Uncle Arthur hadn't forgotten something, then he snapped into action.

Ever since he had been little, he had had a knack for opening locks, and the one on Uncle Arthur's door gave little resistance. In fact, the same key that opened his own door opened Uncle Arthur's. He wondered if the other guests knew it was that easy. Once he stood on the threshold, he had a moment's panic, but he touched the badge in his trouser pocket for luck and went inside, closing the door softly behind him.

Uncle Arthur's room was a mirror image of his own, with a tall wardrobe, single bed, chair, chest of drawers and a small washstand and towel. The flower-patterned wallpaper was peeling off at a damp patch where it met the ceiling, and Tommy could see the silhouettes of dead flies in the inverted lampshade. The wooden bed frame was scratched, and the pink candlewick bedspread had a dark stain near the bottom, as if someone had spilled tea on it. The ashtray on the bedside table was overflowing with crushed-out filter-tipped cigarettes. The narrow window, which looked out on the Newbiggins' backyard, where the dustbins and the outhouse were, was covered in grime and cobwebs. It was open about an inch, and the net curtains fluttered in the breeze.

First, Tommy looked under the bed. He found nothing there but dust and an old sock. Next, he went through the chest of drawers, which contained only Uncle Arthur's clean underwear, a shaving kit, aspirin and some items he didn't recognize. He assumed they were grown-ups' things. The top of the wardrobe, for which Tommy had to enlist the aid of the rickety chair, proved to be a waste of time, too. The only place remaining was inside the wardrobe itself. The key was missing, but it was even easier to open a wardrobe than a door. Uncle Arthur's shirts, trousers and jackets hung from the rail, and below them was his open suitcase containing a few pairs of dirty socks and underpants. No holdall.

Just before he closed the wardrobe door, Tommy had an idea and lifted up the suitcase. Underneath it lay the holdall.

He reached in, pulled it out and put it on the bed. It was a little heavy, but it didn't make any noise when he moved it. There was no lock, and the zip slid open smoothly when he pulled the tab. At first, he couldn't see what was inside, then he noticed something wrapped in brown paper. He lifted it out and opened it carefully. Inside was a gun. Tommy didn't know what kind of gun, but it was heavier than any cap gun he had ever owned, so he assumed that it was a real one. He was careful not to touch it. He knew all about fingerprints. He wrapped it up and put it back. Then he noticed it was lying on a bed of what he had thought was paper, but when he reached in and pulled out a wad, he saw it was money. Five-pound notes, crumpled and dirty. He didn't know how much there was, and he wasn't going to count it. He had discovered enough for one evening. Carefully, he put everything back as it was. What he had to work out next was what he was going to do about it.

That night as Tommy lay in bed unable to sleep, he heard hushed voices in his mother's room. He didn't like to eavesdrop on her, but given what he had just found in Uncle Arthur's room, he felt he had to.

It was almost impossible to hear what they were saying, and he only managed to catch a few fragments.

"Can't . . . money here . . . wait," he heard Uncle Arthur say, and missed the next bit. Then he heard what sounded like, "Year . . . Jigger says Brazil," and after a pause, ". . . the kid?" Next his mother's voice said, ". . . grandparents." He missed what Uncle Arthur said next, but distinctly heard his mother say, "have to, won't they? . . ."

Tommy wondered what they meant. Was Uncle Arthur planning a robbery, or had he already committed one? He certainly had a lot of money. Tommy remembered the three men talking outside the pub. One of them must have given Uncle Arthur the holdall. What for? Did it represent the proceeds or the means? Were Uncle Arthur and his mother going to run away to Brazil and leave him with his grandparents? He didn't believe she would do that.

The bedsprings creaked, and he thought he heard a muffled cry from the next room. His mother obviously couldn't sleep. Was she crying about his father? Then, much later, when he was finally falling asleep himself, he heard her door close and footsteps pass by his room as if someone were walking on tiptoe.

The next day at breakfast his mother and Uncle Arthur didn't have very much to say. Both of them looked tired, and his mother had applied an extra bit of makeup to try to hide the dark pouches under her eyes. Uncle Arthur's hair stuck up in places, and he needed a shave. The two old ladies looked at them sternly and clucked.

"Stupid old bags," muttered Uncle Arthur.

"Now, now," said Tommy's mother. "Be nice, Arthur. Don't draw attention to yourself."

The conversation he had overheard last night still worried Tommy as he ate his bacon and eggs. They had definitely mentioned the money. Was his mother about to get involved in something criminal? Was it Uncle Arthur who was going to involve her? If that was so, he had to stop it before it happened, or she would go to jail. The money and the gun were in Uncle Arthur's room, after all, and his mother could deny that she knew anything about them. Tommy had heard his mother insisting before they came away that they would have a room each. Uncle Arthur hadn't liked the idea because it would cost more money, but he had no choice. Tommy knew what it was like when his mother made her mind up.

The bag and gun would have Uncle Arthur's fingerprints all over them. Tommy was certain that Uncle Arthur must have handled the bag and the items in it since he had picked them up at the pub, if only to check that everything was there and to take out enough money for their trip to the Tower Ballroom last night. But his mother would have had no reason to touch them, or even see them, and Tommy himself had been careful when he lifted and opened the bag.

"Pass the sauce," said Uncle Arthur. "What we doing today?"

Tommy passed him the HP sauce. "Why don't we go up the Tower?" he suggested.

"I don't like heights," said Uncle Arthur.

"I'll go by myself, then."

"No, you won't," said his mother, who seemed as concerned about heights as she was about water.

"Well, what *can* we do, then?" Tommy asked. "I don't mind just looking at the shops by myself."

"Like a bloody woman, you are, with your shops," said Uncle Arthur.

Tommy had meant bookshops and record shops. He was still look-ing for a used copy of *Dr. No* and hoping that the new Beatles single "Help" would be released any day now, even though he would have to wait until he got home to listen to it. But he wasn't planning on going to the shops, anyway, so there was no sense in making an issue of it. "I might go to the Pleasure Beach as well," he said, looking at Uncle Arthur. "Can you give me some money to go on the rides?"

Uncle Arthur looked as if he was going to say no, then he sighed, swore and dug his hand in his pocket. He gave Tommy two ten-shilling notes, which was a lot of money. He could buy *Dr. No* and "Help" *and* go on rides with that much, and still have change for a Mivvi and five Park Drive tipped. But he wasn't sure that he should spend it because he didn't know where it had come from. "Cor," he said. "Thanks, Arthur."

"It's Uncle Arthur to you," said his mother.

"Yeah, remember that," said Uncle Arthur. "Show a bit of respect for your elders and betters. And don't spend it all on candy floss and toffee apples."

"What about you?" Tommy asked. "Where are you going?"

"Dunno," said Uncle Arthur. "You, Maddy?"

"You know I hate being called that," Tommy's mother said. Her name, Tommy knew, was Madeleine, and she didn't like it being shortened.

"Sorry," said Uncle Arthur with a cheeky grin.

"Do you know, I wouldn't mind taking the tram all the way along the seafront to Fleetwood and back," she said, then giggled. "Isn't that silly?"

"Not at all," said Uncle Arthur. "That sounds like a lot of fun. It looks like a warm day. We can sit upstairs in the open. Give me a few minutes. I've just got to get a shave first."

"And comb your hair," said Tommy's mother.

"Now, don't be a nag," said Uncle Arthur, wagging his finger. "Maybe we'll see if we can call in at one of them there travel agents, too, while we're out."

"Arthur!" Tommy's mother looked alarmed.

"What? Oh, don't worry." He got up and tousled Tommy's hair. "I'm off for a shave, then. You'll have to do that yourself one day, you know," he said, rubbing his dark stubble against Tommy's cheek.

Tommy pulled away. "I know," he said. "Can I go now? I've finished my breakfast."

"We'll all go," said his mother. And they went up to their rooms.

Tommy took a handkerchief from his little suitcase and put it in his pocket, because he really was starting to sniffle a bit now, made sure he had his badge and the money Uncle Arthur had given him, then went back into the corridor. Uncle Arthur was standing there, waiting and whistling, freshly shaven, hair still sticking up. For a moment, Tommy felt a shiver of fear ripple up his spine. Had Uncle Arthur realized that someone had been in his room and rummaged through his stuff, found the money and the gun?

Uncle Arthur grinned. "Women," he said, gesturing with his thumb toward Tommy's mother's door. "One day you'll know all about them."

"Sure. One day I'll know everything," muttered Tommy. He pulled his handkerchief from his pocket to blow his nose, and it snagged on the plastic wallet, sending his badge flying to the floor.

"What have we got here, then?" said Uncle Arthur, bending down to pick it up.

"Give me it back!" said Tommy, panicking, reaching out for the wallet.

But Uncle Arthur raised his arm high, out of Tommy's reach. "I said what have we got here?" he repeated.

"It's nothing," Tommy said. "It's mine. Give it to me."

"Mind your manners."

"Please."

Uncle Arthur opened the wallet, looked at the badge and looked at Tommy. "A police badge," he said. "Like father, like son, eh? Is that it?"

"I told you it was mine," Tommy said, desperately snatching. "You leave it alone."

But Uncle Arthur had pulled the badge out of its transparent plastic covering. "It's not real, you know," he said.

"Yes, it is," Tommy said. "Give us it back."

"It's made of plastic," said Uncle Arthur. "Where did you get it?"

"I found it. On the beach. Give it to me."

"I told you, it's just plastic," said Uncle Arthur. And to prove his point he dropped the badge on the floor and stepped on it. The badge splintered under his foot. "See?"

At that moment, Tommy's mother came out of her room, ready to go. "What's happening?" she said, seeing Tommy practically in tears.

"Nothing," said Uncle Arthur, stepping toward the stairs. He gave Tommy a warning look. "Is there, lad? Let's go, love. Our carriage awaits." He laughed.

Tommy's mother gave a nervous giggle, then bent and pecked Tommy on the cheek. He felt her soft hair touch his face and smelled her perfume. It made him feel dizzy. He held back his tears. "You'll be all right, son?" She hadn't seen the splintered badge, and he didn't want her to. It might bring back too many painful memories for her.

He nodded. "You go," he said. "Have a good time."

"See you later." His mother gave a little wave and tripped down the stairs after Uncle Arthur. Tommy looked down at the floor. The badge was in four pieces on the lino. He bent and carefully picked them up. Maybe he could mend it, stick it together somehow, but it would never be the same. This was a bad sign. With tears in his eyes, he put the pieces back in the plastic wallet, returned it to his pocket and followed his mother and Uncle Arthur outside to make sure they got on the tram before he went to do what he had to do.

"You ready yet, Tom?"

"Just a minute, Phil," Detective Chief Inspector Thomas Burford shouted over his shoulder at DI Craven. He was walking on the beach, the hard wet sand where the waves licked in and almost washed over his shoes, and DI Craven, his designated driver, was waiting patiently on the prom. Tom's stomach was churning, the way it always did before a big event, and today, July 13, 2006, he was about to receive a Police Bravery Award.

If it had been one of his men, he would have called it folly, not bravery. He had thrown himself at a man holding a hostage at gunpoint, convinced in his bones, in his every instinct, that he could disarm the man before he hurt the hostage. He had succeeded, receiving for his troubles only a flesh wound on his shoulder and a ringing in his ears that lasted for three days. And the bravery award. At his rank, he shouldn't even have been at the hostage-taking scene—he should have been in his cubicle catching up on paperwork or giving orders over the police radio—but paperwork had always bored him, and he had sought out excitement whenever he had the chance. Now he walked with the salt spray blowing through his hair trying to control his churning bowels just because he had to stand up in front of a crowd and say a few words.

Tom did what he usually did on such occasions and took the old plastic wallet out of his pocket as he stood and faced the gray waves. The wallet was cracked and faded with time, and there was a tear reaching almost halfway up the central crease. Inside, behind the transparent cover, was a police badge made out of plastic. It had been broken once and was stuck together with glue and Sellotape. Most of the silver paint had worn off over the years, and it was now black in places. The crown and cross had broken off the top, but the words were still clearly visible in the central circle: "METROPOLITAN POLICE" curved around "ER." *Elizabeth Regina.* "Our Queen," as his father had once said so proudly.

In the opposite side of the wallet was a yellowed newspaper clipping from July 1965, forty-one years ago. It flapped in the breeze, and Tommy made sure he held on to it tightly as he read the familiar words:

SCHOOLBOY FOILS ROBBERS.

A thirteen-year-old schoolboy's sense of honor and duty led to the arrest of Arthur Leslie Marsden in the murder of PC Brian Burford during the course of a payroll robbery last August. Five other men and one woman were also arrested and charged in the swoop, based on evidence and information given by the boy at a Blackpool police station. Also arrested were Madeleine Burford, widow of the deceased constable, named as Marsden's lover and source of inside information, Len Fraser, driver of the getaway car, John Jarrow. . . .

Tommy knew it by heart, all the names, all the details. He also remembered the day he had walked into the police station, showed his badge to the officer on the front desk and told him all about the contents of Uncle Arthur's holdall. It had taken a while, a bit of explaining, but in the end the desk sergeant had let him in, and the plainclothes detectives had shown a great deal of interest in what he had to say. They accompanied him to the boardinghouse and found the holdall in its hiding place. After that, they soon established that the gun was the same one used to shoot his father. The gang had been lying low, waiting for the heat to die down before daring to use any large quantities of the money—a year, they had agreed—and they had been too stupid to get rid of the gun. The only fingerprints on it were Uncle Arthur's, and the five hundred pounds it was resting on was just a little spending money to be going on with.

The one thing the newspaper article didn't report was that the "boy" was Tommy Burford, only son of Brian and Madeleine Burford. That came out later, of course, at the trial, but at the time, the authorities had done everything within their power to keep his name out of it. Every time he read the story over again, Tom's heart broke just a little more. Throwing himself at gunmen, tackling gangs armed with hammers and chains and challenging rich and powerful criminals never came close to making the pain go away; it only took the edge off for a short while, until the adrenaline wore off.

His *mother*. Christ, he had never known. Never even suspected. She had only been twenty-nine at the time, for crying out loud, not much more than a girl herself, married too young to a man she didn't love, for the sake of their imminent child, and bored with her life. She wanted romance and glamour and all the nice things that his father couldn't give her on a policeman's wage, the life she saw portrayed on posters, in magazines, at the pictures and on television, and Arthur Marsden had walked into her life and offered them all, for a price.

Of course Tom's father had talked about his job. He had been excited about being chosen for the special assignment and had told both his wife and son all about it. How was Tommy to know that his mother had passed on the information to Marsden, who was already her lover, and that he and his gang had done the rest? Tommy knew he had seen her with Uncle Arthur before his father's death, and he wished he had said something. Too late now.

Whether the murder of Tom's father had ever been a part of the master plan, or simply an unforeseen necessity, nobody ever found out. Uncle Arthur and Tom's mother never admitted anything at the trial. But Tom remembered the look his mother gave him that day when he came back to the Newbiggins' boardinghouse with the two plain-clothes policemen. She came out of the lounge as they entered the hall, and it was as if she knew immediately what had happened, that it was all over. She gave Tommy a look of such deep and infinite sadness, loss and defeat that he knew he would take it with him to his grave.

"Hurry up, Tom, we'd better hurry up or we'll be late!" called DI Craven from the prom.

"Coming," said Tom. He folded up the newspaper clipping and put it away. A wave rolled in and touched the very tips of his polished black shoes. He stepped back. How upset his mother would have been if she had known he had stood so close to the water. Brushing his hands across his eyes, which had started watering in the salt wind, he turned away from the sea and walked toward the waiting car, thinking how right they had all been back then, when they said he was young for his age and knew nothing about girls.

Birthday Dance

My very first memory is of Mother putting makeup on me when I was a little girl. The greasy red lipstick tasted like candle wax, and when I cried the mascara ran down my cheeks like black teardrops. I had lost two of my front baby teeth, and Mother got the dentist to fit some false ones for me. They felt like cold pebbles in my mouth, and I couldn't stop probing them with my tongue. Later, Mother held my hand and we stood on a glittering stage in a huge ballroom with crystal chandeliers spinning in the light and rows and rows of people watching. I was wearing my powder blue satin dress and matching bows in my hair. I was nervous, but I knew it was an important night for Mother. She told me pageants and talent contests would give me poise and confidence and help me to make friends, and soon I began to feel excited about them. I smiled and danced and sang, and people clapped for me. I felt warm all over.

Perhaps the terrible thing that happened on Father's birthday happened because I was always a well-behaved little girl. I did what Mother told me to do. Father, too, of course—well, he's my stepfather, really—but I see less of him, so it's not often that he tells me to do anything. He's an important businessman with an empire to rule, so Mother says, and I am under strict instructions not to bother him unless he asks to see me. Not that he doesn't love me. I know for a fact that he does. He asks to see me every day and tells me I am the apple of his eye. Sometimes he gives me expensive presents, or if he's really pleased with me, he tells me I can have anything I want in the world. *Anything.*

Father protects me, too. Mother told me once, after one of my friends started crying at a pageant and no one would tell me why, that I was to report to her immediately if anyone ever bothered me or touched me, and Father would have them taken care of. Those were her words: "Have them taken care of." I didn't know what she meant, but I thought it must be something to do with doctors and nurses and hospitals. Nobody ever did bother me, though. I suppose they must have known they would have to go to the hospital if they did. Father can be frightening, I know because I've heard him shouting at people, but he's always very gentle and silly when I'm with him, laughing and tickling me and playing games.

We live in a huge mansion surrounded by woods and trimmed green lawns as big as playing fields. We have two swimming pools, one indoors and one outside, garages for the cars, and stables where I keep my pony Arabella. I love it when the wind is blowing through my hair and Arabella is galloping over the fields. There is one point where you get to the top of a short hill and you can see the sea in the distance all blue and green and white. Sometimes we stop there and rest, and I watch the waves roll in and out. Times like that I feel happiest, riding Arabella or swimming in one of the pools. They are the only times when I can do what I really want.

Of course, I have to go to school like everyone else, though it is a very good school. Bennett drives me there and back again every day in the Rolls. I like drawing and music most, but my teacher says I'm really good at writing, and I do like to write. I also love to read. My favorite book of all time is *Alice in Wonderland,* but I like *A Woman of Substance,* too.

Even when I'm not in at school, it seems that I am forever going to dancing classes, singing lessons, piano lessons, acting classes and all kinds of other lessons and classes, like flower arranging and tennis. And then there are the auditions. I hate auditions. That's when you have to sing and dance, sometimes in a small room with only one person watching you. It's no fun, not like pageants. You don't get to be with your friends and nobody claps. They just put on a face so you can't see what they're thinking and then they phone Mother later to say whether they want you or not. I've done some television commercials, and I even had my photo on an advert for lotion in a woman's magazine once, when I was seven. I haven't been in any movies or plays or TV shows yet, but I know that's what Mother really wants me to do.

You see, Mother is very beautiful, and she used to be a model, but she told me once that she regretted she never quite managed to get the successful stage career she wanted. I think she wants me to do that for her. I tell her she's still beautiful and there's still lots of time for her to be a big film star, but she just says I'm sweet and I don't really understand. I don't suppose I do. There are so many things I don't understand.

Take Uncle John, for example.

I think the trouble all started because of Uncle John.

He wasn't really my uncle, he was a business colleague of Father's, but we called him uncle anyway. That was before we started seeing less and less of him because he was getting really strange. Not in a nasty way, of course, or we wouldn't have had anything to do with him at all. Mother wouldn't have him in the house, like she won't have Ruth's father. Uncle John just has some silly ideas about a big change coming that's going to affect us all, and he's not always happy about the way Father conducts his business, or about him marrying Mother. Father says he ought to keep his mouth shut, but Uncle John can't seem to help himself, and we all get embarrassed when that distant look comes into his eyes and he starts his rambling. And Mother leaves the room.

I suppose we're not exactly the most normal family in the world. Most of my friends come from normal families, but not us. Mother was married to my real father for many years, and I am their only child. Then, though my father was still alive and she wasn't a widow or anything, like Carly's mother, she went to live with Father. I never see my real father anymore, and sometimes that makes me feel sad. I think about him and the way he used to sit me on his knee and wipe away the tears when I was unhappy, and that makes me unhappy all over again.

But to get back to Uncle John. Things had been uncomfortable for a long time. I had heard him arguing with Father, though I never really understood what they were talking about. Mother tried to be nice to him at first after his fights with Father, even sometimes reaching out to stroke him the way she does Tabby, our cat, but he always flinched from her and treated her even worse than he treated Father. I'd like to say that he was always nice to me, but most of the time he just ignored me. I didn't really care because, to tell the truth, I was a little bit frightened of him, especially when he got that faraway look in his eyes and began talking about things I couldn't understand. I don't think anyone else understood, either, because I'd even overheard people saying they thought he was mad. Father always defended him and said that he had his uses, but sometimes you could see it was really an effort, especially when Uncle John called his business immoral and told him it was all going wrong because he had married Mother and that judgment day would soon come for us all.

I suppose, in a way, it did, but not exactly the way Uncle John imagined it.

The day it happened was a Saturday, Father's birthday, and I saw Uncle John with Mother talking by the outside pool that morning when they didn't know I was watching them. There was nobody else at home except Bennett, who was up in his flat over the garage, and Mother had just been swimming. She was still wet, the water dripping from her hair and legs, relaxing with a martini and a Danielle Steel in one of the loungers beside the pool, still wearing her pretty, flowered bikini. Uncle John was in a dark suit and a tie, though it was a hot day. His face was tanned dark brown and oily with sweat, and he had curly black hairs on the backs of his hands.

I couldn't hear very much because they were far away and the window was closed, but he was shouting at her, and I heard him say the words *whore* and *bitch* and *adulteress* before he finally turned and left. I remember the words because I didn't know what they meant and had to look them up in the dictionary. I didn't understand what the definitions in the dictionary meant, either, so that didn't do me any good. I wanted to ask Mother, but I thought that if I did, she would know I had been eavesdropping on her and Uncle John, and she would be angry. Father is not the sort of person you can ask things like that. He's far too busy to be disturbed with such trivia.

Anyway, after Uncle John left, Mother was upset and didn't seem able to relax with her martini and her Danielle Steel. She put the book down—some of the pages were wet from her hands—finished the drink quickly, then came into the house. The next time I saw her, maybe two hours later, she was dry and dressed in the kitchen, preparing some canapés at the island. It was Father's birthday—an important one, Mother said, with a "0" in it—and that evening there was going to be a special birthday party with all his family and friends and tons of food and presents. Most of the food was being catered, of course, but Mother always like to make "a little something special" for us all.

"Sal," she said. "I wondered where you'd got to. Is everything all right?"

"Yes, Mother," I answered. I could tell by the way she was looking at me that she was trying to figure out if I'd seen her and Uncle John arguing earlier. I tried to give nothing away.

"You'd better get ready," she said. "It's nearly time for your ballet lesson."

"I'm ready," I told her. And I was. I had my tutu and my ballet shoes packed in my backpack.

"Bennett will drive you," she said.

"Where's Father?" I asked.

"Your father's playing golf," she said. "He went with Uncle Tony."

"OK." I knew that Uncle Tony sometimes came by and picked Father up. He had a brand-new Mercedes-Benz and he liked to show it off. Uncle Tony's all right, though. He always gives me chocolates or comics when he visits.

Mother paused and wiped her hands on a towel. "Sal," she said, "you know what tonight is?"

"Father's birthday. Of course. I'm going to get him a present after ballet. A box of his favorite cigars."

"That's nice, sweetheart. But, you know, I was just thinking how nice it would be if you did something special for him, too."

"Like what?"

"Dance for him. You know how much he loves to see you dance."

It was true. Father did love to see me dance, and he would always offer me any present I wanted in the whole world when I danced especially well for him. "What sort of dance?" I asked.

"Oh, I don't know. Maybe something new, something he hasn't seen before. How are you doing in those belly-dancing classes?"

"Not bad," I said. "It's fun. I don't have much of a belly, though."

Mother smiled. We both knew that I was a bit on the skinny side, but she always told me it was a fine balance, and the last thing a pageant judge wanted to see was folds of puppy fat. Maybe with belly dancing, though, it's different. I just don't feel I have anything to roll around, if you know what I mean. No belly to dance with.

"Well, what about some ballet?" she said. "What are you learning at the moment?"

I told Mother about *Swan Lake,* which is my all-time favorite ballet, even though we were just doing boring exercises in class.

"Maybe you can dance something from *Swan Lake,* then?" Mother said. "If you'd like. I'm sure your Father will just love it."

"Okay," I said. "I'll do something from *Swan Lake.* I have to go now."

She pointed to her cheek, and I walked over and kissed her, then I went outside and found Bennett in front of the garage, waiting, already in his uniform, the engine of the Rolls purring.

Ballet class was boring, as I expected, just doing the same movements over and over again. I have to admit that I spent most of the time daydreaming of the coming evening's performance from *Swan Lake.* It would have to be a short and fairly easy piece, I knew—nothing complicated like the dying swan—because I'm not *that* good, but I also knew I could do such a fragment justice. I pictured myself dancing really well, hearing the music, imagining Father's pleasure. Sometimes when I do this, it helps me when the time comes for the real thing.

I could hardly wait to get home, but I hung around for a soda with Veronica and Lisa for half an hour, as usual, then I remembered the present and got Bennett to go into Father's favorite cigar shop and buy a box of Coronas and have them wrapped. All the way home I was almost jumping up and down in the seat with excitement.

Even though it was still only late afternoon, the house was starting to fill up. I knew most of the people and said hello as I went up to my room to change. There were marquees on the grounds and people already swimming in the pool. There must have been a hundred barbecues grilling hamburgers, steaks, chicken and hot dogs. It was going to be a great party.

When I had put on my party dress and was heading out to get something to eat at one of the barbecue stands, Mother pulled me into her room and asked me about ballet class. I told her it was fine.

"I suppose you're excited about tonight?" she said.

"Yes."

She turned her eyes away from me. "Look, Sal," she said, "do you think you could do your mother a favor? A big favor?"

"Of course!" I said, anxious to please her after I'd seen her upset with Uncle John that morning.

"You know when you dance well and your father promises you anything you want?"

"Yes."

"Well, when that happens, will you ask him for Uncle John's head?"

"Uncle John's head?"

"Yes."

"Yuk."

"For me."

"Is it a game? Like in *Alice*? 'Off with his head!' "

"Yes, that's right," said Mother. "A game. Like the Red Queen. Will you ask him?"

"Uncle John's head! Uncle John's head! Yes, I'll ask him. I can't wait to hear what he says."

"He probably won't say very much," said Mother very quietly, "but he's a man of his word, your father."

And with that she let me skip down the stairs to join the party. My cousins Janet and Maria were both there, and their creepy brother Marlon, so we found some earwigs in the garden and put them in his hot dog. That was fun, but all the time I was excited about dancing. I looked around for Uncle John, but I couldn't see him anywhere. When the time came, I went upstairs and changed quickly while Father gathered with his closest family and business colleagues in his den. Uncle

John wasn't with them, but Godfather was there, an old man with dry, wrinkled skin and a voice like a rasp file on stone. He made me a bit nervous, but he had a kind smile.

And how well did I dance?

It's hard for me to judge my own performance, but I did feel that my movements seemed to go with the music. There was no hesitation, the dance flowed from me, and there were no wrong moves or trips. I didn't stumble or fall once. On the whole, I think I danced rather well, if I say so myself. Father certainly enjoyed it, for he started clapping the moment I finished, and it took the others a couple of seconds to join in with him. Mother sat on the other side of the room with the womenfolk, smiling and clapping along. When I'd finished, I curtsied for Father and he beckoned me to come closer. I stood in front of him and he gave me a little kiss on my cheek.

"Bravo!" he said. "That was marvelous. What a talented girl you are. And because you've made me so happy you can have anything you want in the world. All you have to do is ask."

I paused for a moment and looked over at Mother. Father saw me do this, and he also looked her way. She didn't turn to face him or say anything, but I could tell by her eyes that she was telling me to go ahead and ask him. Then I said, "I want Uncle John's head."

Father's face changed, and he suddenly seemed older and sadder. Everyone else was completely silent. You could hear a pin drop.

"Are you sure that's what you want, sweetheart?" he asked.

I nodded. "Yes," I said. "Off with his head!"

Father looked at me in silence for a long time before answering, then he looked over at Mother, who kept her eyes on me. Finally, he looked at Godfather, who gave him such a brief, tiny nod it could have been a twitch.

"Very well," Father said sternly. "You shall have what you want." Then he clapped his hands. "Now away with you, before I change my mind."

But I knew Father never changed his mind, and Mother said he was a man of his word.

The party was still going on, so I changed into jeans and a T-shirt and rejoined my cousins and friends, who were now playing hide-and-seek in the shrubbery. There were lots of bushes shaped like animals, and sometimes you could even work your way inside them and find a clear space to hide. As I hid in the peacock, holding my breath for fear that Janet would find me first, I thought about the dance and the strange request Mother had asked me to make.

I know that Father still liked Uncle John, despite the problems he was causing, but Uncle John was getting more difficult to keep in line. I had actually heard Father saying this to some of his colleagues not long ago, the same time I overheard him telling Bruno, who I don't like at all—he's got no neck and has shoulders like a bull—to "clip" someone, which sounds like something they do at the hairdresser's, and to "take care of" Mr. Delasanto. I never saw Mr. Delasanto again, and I guessed he must have been taken to the hospital. But they didn't want to clip or take care of Uncle John, and now I had asked for his head. I began to feel just a little uneasy and nervous about what would happen. They had all seemed very serious about it, for a game. At that moment, Janet peered through the branches, shouted my name and ran back to the tree where she had counted to a hundred. By the time I got through the branches I hadn't a hope of beating her.

The party wound down later in the evening—at least for me it did. Janet and Maria went home, taking with them the horrible Marlon, who hadn't said much since he bit into his hot dog earlier in the day. I was still too excited to go to bed and there were plenty of adults around. Nobody paid any attention to me. The pool lights were on and some people were even swimming, others sipping drinks and talking at the poolside. There was music coming out of a pair of big speakers outside the pool house, but it was grown-up music, all violins and smoochy singing. Frank Sinatra, probably. Father loves Frank Sinatra.

I was feeling hot and I thought a swim might be nice, so I went to my room to change into my bathing costume. On my way I passed Mother's room and heard raised voices. I paused by the door, unsure what to do. I had been brought up not to spy on people or listen in on their conversations—Father was very particular about his privacy—but sometimes I just couldn't help it.

"It was your idea," Father was saying. "You put her up to it. How could you?"

Mother said nothing.

"It'll have a bad effect all around. There'll be trouble," Father went on. "He still has his uses. And he's got a lot of followers."

"Rubbish," said Mother. "He's a madman and everyone knows it. An embarrassment. He's losing it, baby. You'll be doing us all a favor. Next thing you know he'll be talking to the feds."

"That's crazy. Johnny would never do that."

"You haven't been paying attention, sweetie. You're blinded by loyalty. I had to do *something* to bring it to your attention. God knows, you wouldn't listen to *me*. I tell you, if you don't do something soon, we're all down the creek without a paddle."

At that moment, I heard one of them walking toward the door, so I made off quickly and hurried to my room. It was odd, finding Mother and Father together like that, I thought, because they don't talk much anymore. I haven't seen them laugh and hold hands for ages. Still, I don't suppose they have much time together: Father has his empire to keep him busy, and Mother has me and all my contests and lessons and pageants.

Nobody seemed to mind me swimming with the grown-ups, and I even had a cool splashing fight with Uncle Mario, who's so fat it's a wonder all the water doesn't go out of the pool when he jumps in. After that I ate more food—cakes and ice cream and Jell-O—until I was too full to eat another bite. I was feeling tired by then, and even some of the grown-up guests were starting to say their good-byes and drift away.

When most of them had gone, Bennett came along the driveway in the Rolls and parked in front of the garage. One of Father's colleagues got out, a man I didn't like, and leaned back in to pick something off the seat. It was a large metal plate with a domed cover, the kind they use to keep food warm, but bigger. He saw me just about to go back inside, walked over and said. "I think this is for you, little lady." I hate it when people call me little lady. After all, I *am* eleven. Then he offered me the plate. It was heavier than I expected.

"Or maybe you should take it to your mother," he said, with a nasty grin.

I turned away and heard him laugh as I walked into the house. I was going to take his advice but I didn't want him to know that. Outside

Mother's room, I put the plate on a small polished table under the hall mirror and knocked. Mother answered. She was quite alone.

"Someone brought me this plate," I said. "But I think it's for you."

She looked at the covered plate, then at me. I couldn't tell what she was thinking from her expression, but she seemed a bit glazed and didn't really look very well. I thought perhaps she might have had one of her "attacks" and taken her pills. Anyway, she seemed eager enough to take the plate. Without so much as a thank you, she picked it up, turned and kicked the door shut with her heel. By then I was beginning to realize that it wasn't just a game, that when I asked Father for Uncle John's head, that was *exactly* what he had given me. I had to know. Trembling, I sank to my knees and looked through the keyhole.

What I saw then I will remember for the rest of my days.

Mother set the plate down on her dressing table beside the potions and creams and combs and brushes, then she lifted off the cover. She stepped back and gasped, putting her hand to her mouth and let the cover drop to the floor where it clanged on the hard wooden surface. Then, slowly, she moved toward the plate from which Uncle John stared at her with unseeing eyes. She stared back for the longest time, then she picked up the head in both hands and kissed him on the lips. Something dark and shiny dangled from his neck and dripped like black teardrops down the front of Mother's white blouse. I jumped up feeling sick and dizzy and I ran up to my room, pulled the covers over my head and didn't come out until my singing lesson on Sunday morning.

Like a Virgin

An Inspector Banks Novella

Banks held the letter between his thumb and forefinger and tapped its edge against the palm of his hand. He knew who had sent it and what it was about, but not exactly what it would reveal, what it might change. A phone call would have been quicker and easier, perhaps, but there was something more solid and satisfying about the formal sheets of paper Banks knew were neatly folded inside the white envelope. And the post only took a day. After this long, there was no hurry, no hurry at all.

As he gazed out over Eastvale's cobbled market square—the ancient cross, the squat church, the castle on its hill in the background, children dashing to school, socks around their ankles, delivery vans making their rounds, shops opening—he realized that he had been there for over twenty years and that when he had first arrived his life had been in every bit as much of a mess as it was now.

That was a sobering thought for a man in his midfifties. In those twenty plus years, he had lost his wife to another man, his children had grown up and moved away, lovers had come and gone, and he had lost much of his faith in his fellow man. He had suffered betrayal more than once, by those closest to him and by strangers in secret, shady offices in Westminster. He had failed many and perhaps given some slight solace to others. But all in all, he felt that the tally sheet was woefully weighted down on the side of his failures and shortcomings, and it was hard to believe in the job anymore.

Now here he stood contemplating a temporary flight, as if he might perhaps leave himself behind and start again. He knew that couldn't happen. It hadn't happened the last time he had tried it, but some things had changed after his move up north, and many of them for the better. It was years since he had thought about those final days in London, and when he did, they had the quality of a dream, or a nightmare. His conversation with an old colleague the previous week had brought it all back with a vengeance.

Banks leaned his forehead against the cool glass. His hair had been a bit longer then, touching his collar, without the streaks of gray, and he had believed he could make a difference. He had been full of romantic idealism and knightly vigor, ready to tilt at windmills and take on the world without even noticing at first that he was breaking apart under the weight of it. If he closed his eyes, he could see it all as it had been: Soho nights, the late summer of 1985 . . .

In the soft light of the red-shaded bulb that hung over the center of the room, the girl's body looked serene. She could easily have been sleeping, Banks thought, as he moved forward to get a better view of her. She lay on her back on the pink candlewick bedspread, covered from neck to toe by a white sheet, hands clasped together above the swell of her breasts in an attitude of prayer or supplication, her long dark hair spread out on the pillow. Her pale features were delicate and finely etched, and Banks imagined she had been quite a beauty in life. He wondered what she had looked like when she smiled or frowned. Her hazel eyes were devoid of life now, her face free of makeup, and at first glance there wasn't a mark on her. But when Banks peered closer he could see the petechial hemorrhages, the tiny telltale dots of blood in her conjunctiva, a sign of death by asphyxia. There was no bruising on her neck, so he guessed suffocation rather than strangulation, but Dr. O'Grady, the Home Office pathologist who knelt beside her at his silent ministrations would be able to tell him more after his in situ examination.

The room was small and stuffy, but the Persian-style carpet and striped wallpaper gave it a homely touch. It seemed well maintained,

despite its location on the fringes of Soho. No sleazy backstreet hovel
for this girl. The window hadn't been open when Banks arrived, and
he knew better than to tamper with the scene in any way, so he left it
closed. There wasn't much space for furniture—a small dressing table
with mirror, washstand in the corner, next to the cubicle WC, and a
bedside table, on which stood a chipped enamel bowl where a facecloth
floated in discolored water. In the drawer were condoms, tissues and
an assortment of sex aids. Did she live here? Banks doubted it. There
were no clothes and no cooking facilities.

The victim could have been anywhere between fifteen and twenty-
five, Banks thought, and her youth certainly added to the aura of innocence that surrounded her in death. Whether she had appeared that
way in life, he didn't know, but he didn't think so.

Someone had clearly gone to great pains to make her *look* innocent.
Her legs were stretched out straight together, and even under the sheet
she was fully dressed. Her clothes—a short skirt, patent-leather high
heels, dark tights and a green scallop-neck top—were provocative, but
not too tarty. Much more tasteful than that. So what was it all about?

Her handbag contained the usual: cigarettes, a yellow disposable
lighter, keys on a fluffy rabbit's foot ring, makeup, tampons, a cheap
ballpoint pen and a purse with a few pounds and some loose change.
There was no address book or diary and no credit cards or identification of any kind. The only item Banks found of any interest was a
creased photograph of a proud, handsome young man in what looked
like his best suit, bouncing a little girl on his knee. There was a resemblance, and Banks guessed it was the victim and her father. According to the girlfriend who had found her, Jackie Simmons, the victim's
name was Pamela Morrison.

Banks went back to stand in the doorway. He had soon learned
that the fewer people who had entered the room before the SOCOs got
to work, the better. He was on detachment from Soho Division to the
West Central Murder Squad. Everything was squads and specialists
these days, and if you didn't find your niche somewhere pretty quickly,
you soon became a general dogsbody. Nobody wanted that, especially
Banks. He seemed to have a knack for ferreting out murderers, and
luckily for him the powers that be in the Metropolitan Police Force

agreed. So here he was. His immediate boss, Detective Superintendent Bernard Hatchard, was officially in charge of the investigation, of course, but he was so burdened by paperwork and public relations duties that he rarely left the station and was more than happy to leave the legwork to his DI and his oppo DS Ozzy Albright—as long as he got regular updates so he didn't sound like a wanker in front of the media.

Banks liked the way things were, but lately he had started to feel the pressure. It wasn't that there were more murders to deal with, simply that each one seemed to get to him more and take more out of him. But there was no going back. That way lay a desk piled with papers or, worse, traffic duty. He would just have to push on through whatever it was that was dragging him down, keeping him awake at nights, making him neglect his family, drink and smoke too much . . . the litany went on.

Harry Beckett, the police photographer, was next to arrive, and he went about his business with the usual professional detachment, as if he were photographing a wedding. Dr. O'Grady, who had been called from a formal dinner at the Soho Club, not far away, finally finished his examination, stood up and gave a weary sigh. His knees cracked as he moved.

"I'm getting too old for this, Banks," he said. And he *was* looking old, Banks thought. Neat but thinning gray hair, the veins around his nose red and purple, perhaps due to his known fondness for fine claret.

"Any idea when she might have been killed?" Banks asked.

"Somehow, I knew you'd ask me that first," the doctor said. "None of this is written in stone, mind you, especially given the temperature in the room, but judging by the rigor I'd say she's been dead since last night, say between ten and one in the morning."

"Know how she was killed?"

"I'll have to get her on the table to make sure, of course," said O'Grady, "but barring any hidden stab wounds or bullet holes, not to mention poison, it appears very much like suffocation. You can see that the pillow next to her had been scrunched up and creased, as if someone had been holding it, pressing it down. No doubt your SOCOs will be collecting the trace evidence, but there seems to me to be a drop of blood on it. There will certainly be saliva if it was used on her."

"Her blood, or her killer's?"

"There's no way of knowing yet. Her nose might have bled, or she could have bitten her lip. Perhaps she scratched him as she struggled? I'll know more later. You might also have noticed," he went on, "that one side of the pillow was smeared with a number of colored substances."

"I noticed," said Banks. "Any theories?"

"Again, it's impossible to say accurately at this point—you'll have to carry out forensic tests—but at a guess I'd say it's makeup. Mascara, red lipstick, blue eyeliner or eye shadow."

"But she isn't wearing any makeup," Banks said.

"Ah, I know," said O'Grady. "Interesting, isn't it? I think I need a bit of fresh air. Seen enough?"

Banks nodded. He had seen enough; every inch of the scene was imprinted on his memory. It was like that with all of them, and they came back to haunt him every night, even the ones he had solved.

Before Banks and O'Grady could leave the room, DS Ozzy Albright appeared at the top of the stairs outside. "The SOCOs are here, sir."

"OK, send them up," said Banks. "Where's the girl? I asked you to stay with her."

"I left her with WPC Brown, sir. They're in that Italian café just around the corner, on Old Compton Street. She's in a bit of a state, sir. We thought she needed a cup of tea or something."

"OK."

"Er . . . there's someone else."

"Oh?"

A dark, bulky figure mounted the stairs slowly and appeared behind Albright, gasping and wheezing from the climb, a sheen of sweat on his brow. Detective Chief Inspector Roland Verity. With his round face and ruddy complexion, and the shock of ginger hair, he had always reminded Banks of a farmer, but there was a coldness and a calculating glint in his eyes that were bred of the back alley and the boardroom, not the meadows and pastures.

Verity patted his chest and grinned. "I'll have to give up smoking," he said. "Or climbing stairs."

"Roly, what brings you here?" said Banks, as if he didn't know. Though Verity technically outranked Banks, a DI didn't have to call a

DCI sir, and they knew each other well enough to be on first name terms.

"Word gets around," said Verity. "Suspicious death in a knocking shop on my turf."

To say this was his turf was no more true than to describe the building they were in as a knocking shop, but Banks knew there was no point challenging him. Roly Verity worked Vice, and they also had their headquarters at West End Central, in Savile Row. The proximity to Soho, for many years London's red-light district, was certainly no coincidence, and it couldn't be denied that Verity might have a legitimate interest in the investigation. Banks only hoped he wasn't going to throw his considerable weight around too much and get in the way. From what Banks knew, though, Verity was more interested in power and politics than in the mechanics and techniques of a murder investigation. He also had a reputation as an honest copper, but Banks had never fully trusted him.

Verity stood in the doorway, practically filling it with his bulk, and took a cursory glance at the victim, then he gave a world-weary nod toward Dr. O'Grady and turned back to Banks. "On your way out, were you?" he asked.

"The doctor would like a little air," said Banks.

"And I'd like a pint," said Verity. "There's a decent enough boozer just around the corner. It's warm enough to stand outside, so we can all get what we want. What say?"

Banks and O'Grady followed Verity down the creaky stairs.

"Stay here and deal with the SOCOs," Banks said to Albright. "I'll be back."

"Sir," said Albright, managing to put as much disbelief into the simple word as he put disappointment at being denied a pint himself.

It was a relief to get outside. Even though the evening was warm and close, the air was fresh and not tainted with the smell of stale sex and death, only with cigarette smoke and the occasional whiff of cigar or marijuana. The building was on a side street, a little off the beaten track, but even so a small crowd had gathered, and the PCs on duty had their work cut out moving people on. It was just an ordinary black door with a brass knocker, stuck between a sex shop and a sixties-style boutique, that led up to a number of rooms on the first, second and third floors, but there was already so much police activity, cars parked at odd angles, or in no-parking areas, and uniformed officers milling around, that people couldn't fail to know something was amiss.

Banks turned the corner and walked a few yards up Old Compton Street, one of the busiest streets in Soho, where he saw WPC Brown and Jackie Simmons sitting outside at the Italian coffee shop over the street. "I'll catch up with you," he said to Roly and O'Grady, then dashed over, dodging the traffic, to join the women.

"Sir," said WPC Brown, standing up to leave when Banks sat at the table.

"No, it's all right," he said. "Sit down. Finish your coffee. I want you to stay."

"All right, sir." She sat down again and sipped from a cup of frothy liquid. It left a little white moustache on her upper lip, which she licked off and blushed when she saw that Banks was watching her. Banks just smiled.

Jackie Simmons wasn't drinking anything, though a full cup of tea stood just beside her.

"I'd have some of that if I were you," Banks said. "Hot sweet tea. Nothing like it when you've had a shock."

She sniffed and shook her head, then wiped her eyes with a tissue. It was already damp and falling apart and Banks wished he had a fresh handkerchief to give her. He handed her a paper serviette instead. She took it and thanked him, then she blew her nose. "Sorry," she said. "It just hit me, really. We were flatmates, Pam and me."

"Okay," said Banks. "I'm going to need to ask you a few questions, and then WPC Brown here will take you home. I'll send DS Albright with her, and they'll need to have a look at Pamela's room, at her things, if that's all right?"

"She doesn't have much, but it doesn't matter now, does it?"

"It could be important, that's all. Do you know of anyone who would want to hurt Pamela?"

"No. No one."

"Ex-boyfriend, prospective boyfriend, or someone like that?"

"She had a boyfriend back home in West Yorkshire. Castleford. But she hasn't seen him since she came here."

"Is that why she came? To get away from him?"

"I don't think so. She just said he was a lazy sod and they were going nowhere fast."

"How old are you, Jackie?"

"Me? Twenty-one."

"And Pamela?"

"She was nineteen."

"When did she come here?"

"Early in the new year. I can't remember the exact date, but it was when it was really cold, like minus twenty or something. Poor thing didn't even have a proper winter coat."

"Where do you share a flat?"

"Shoreditch."

"What did Pamela do for a living?"

Jackie seemed embarrassed. There was nobody sitting next to them and the people at the other tables were deep in their own conversations. "I think you probably know that already, if you saw her," she said finally. "She did what she had to do to make a living."

"I want you to tell me. Exotic dancing? Prostitution?"

"It sounds so ugly when you put it like that."

"How else should I put it?"

Jackie looked down at her clasped hands. She was playing with a ring on her thumb. "No, I don't mean it's wrong to call it what it is." She gave him a brief smile, and he saw in the split second it took what a sweet beauty she was, and what intelligence there was in her eyes. She wasn't wearing much makeup, and her silky long hair had covered most of her features, her slightly upturned nose and almond-shaped eyes a little red from sniffling and crying, but she was certainly an attractive young woman. "It's just that we none of us like to admit the truth if we don't have to," she said. "We talk about dancing and dates as if taking your clothes off and sleeping with strange men for money were a perfectly normal thing to do."

"Well, it *is* the oldest profession," said Banks, "so I imagine there must be something in it."

"You know what I mean."

"I suppose I do. But that doesn't concern me right now. It's Pamela and what happened to her that interests me."

"God, I saw her," said Jackie. "What could he . . . I mean, why . . . ?" Her eyes filled with tears again.

"She was posed in an unusual way," said Banks. "Any idea why?"

"No. How could I? It was like one of those carved figures you see on old stone coffins in churches. It was spooky."

"We don't know why she was posed that way, either, yet. And we don't want anyone else to know that she was. This is very important, Jackie. These are the sort of details we like to keep out of the papers. I'm sure you wouldn't want what you've just seen to be splashed all over the front pages in a lurid way."

"God, no. I won't say anything."

"What can you tell me about Pamela?"

"She was a good person. I liked her. Not terribly bright, perhaps, but good-natured, good-hearted. She'd do anything for you."

"Where did she dance?"

"Different places. Mostly Naughty Nites. Other places, too, but that was the main one."

"And you?"

"I helped get her the dancing job."

"And the other work?"

Jackie buried her face in her hands. "Yes," she whispered. "God forgive me."

Banks touched her lightly on the arm. "It wasn't your fault, Jackie. There's nothing to forgive. I need to know about the room, then you can go home. How did you know about it? How did you know where to find her? What happened there?"

"I think you can guess what happened there," Jackie said. "It was a room she used for . . . for entertaining men friends."

"How did she find these men friends?"

"Well, she didn't walk the streets. Just people she met, I suppose, at the clubs . . . you know. She danced at some of them, and in others she . . . you know, she was a hostess. She chatted with the customers, drank with them, made them feel good."

"She rented the room?"

Jackie shrugged.

"Who did she rent it from?"

"Dunno."

"Who takes care of her, Jackie?"

"I don't know. Really, I don't."

Banks could tell she was lying by her slight hesitation and the way she averted her eyes, but he decided to leave it for the moment. It shouldn't be too hard to find out. "OK," he said. "How did you know she would be in the room? Did she have a date?"

"Last night. Yes. She didn't come home all night or all day, which wasn't too unusual, but when she didn't turn up at the club tonight, I got worried. You get fined by the owner for being late, you see, and Pam couldn't afford that. The room was the only place I could think to look, really. The door wasn't locked, nobody answered, so I went in and found her there."

"Do you know who the date was with?"

"No. She didn't tell me."

"You didn't touch anything?"

"Nothing. I ran straight out and rang the police."

"Thanks for doing that," said Banks.

She glared at him. "I might be a whore, but I'm not a fool," she said.

Banks stood up and glanced at WPC Brown. "I'll send Ozzy round," he said. "Can one of you also get in touch with the local police in West Yorkshire and have someone tell her parents? We'll need them to identify the body as soon as possible."

Whether the boozer was a decent one or not didn't really matter as O'Grady and Verity were standing outside on the pavement when Banks joined them. O'Grady was sipping a double brandy instead of his customary glass of wine. He told Banks that he'd asked the barman about the wine selection and was told that he could have red or white, sweet or dry, so he'd chosen brandy instead. Verity had a pint of lager and Banks stuck with bitter.

"So who is she?" Verity asked.

"Her name's Pamela Morrison," Banks told him. "Ring any bells?"

"They come and go. How and when was she found?"

Banks told Verity what Jackie Simmons had just told him.

Verity grunted. "This girlfriend a tom, too?"

"So it seems."

"Most of them are. Any particular club connection?"

"Naughty Nites Club, mostly."

"I know it," said Verity. "As such places go, it's not bad."

O'Grady put his empty glass down on the window ledge. "Unless there's anything else," he said, "I'm off. Busy day tomorrow. I'll give you a call when I'm ready to start. Oh, what about the parents?"

"They'll be told tonight," Banks said, "and we'll get a driver to bring them down from Castleford first thing in the morning."

"Right-ho." O'Grady wandered off toward the Tottenham Court Road tube.

"He's looking old," said Verity, staring after the doctor. "Another pint?"

"Better not," Banks said. "I should get back and see how the SOCOs are doing."

"They won't thank you for it."

Banks laughed. "Don't I know it? Maybe some other time." He turned to leave. Before he had moved away he felt Verity's hand tighten around his upper arm, almost circling it completely. "I might be able to help you on this," Verity said. "The bloke you want to talk to is called Matthew Micallef. Maltese."

"And he does what?"

"He's a pimp." Verity gestured toward the house. "If this Pamela Morrison was connected to Naughty Nites and she was on the game, it's likely she was one of his. He does the rounds, takes the pick of the crop. Just trying to save you a bit of legwork."

"Thanks, Roly," said Banks. "I appreciate it."

"And this Micallef . . ."

"Yes?"

"Tread carefully. He's a nasty piece of work."

"Aren't they all?"

"Just one more thing."

"Yes?"

"Keep me informed."

The Naughty Nites Club was just getting into its swing when Banks arrived there close to midnight. A doorman built like a brick shithouse tried to block his way, but Banks flashed his warrant card and was reluctantly waved in. A well-endowed young black girl in white bra and panties was going through the motions onstage to an old Stones number while punters watched from tables or bar stools. Booths around the walls offered some privacy, and Banks noticed a couple of groups of businessmen—or gangsters, perhaps—involved in intense discussions. In most booths, though, a girl or two would be having drinks with customers and maybe negotiating terms for a little extra entertainment later. The lighting was such that everything white glowed like an advert for Daz. The black girl slipped out of her bra, and some audience members cheered. You wouldn't get cheering like that in a real top-of-the-line club, Banks thought. Probably a bunch of northern oiks down for a football match.

After taking in the lie of the land, Banks ventured over to the bar. Mirrors reflected the rows of bottles, and the bar staff consisted entirely of attractive young women in low-cut tops, fishnet tights and skimpy red satin shorts. Banks caught the attention of the nearest girl and asked for the manager. He had to speak loudly to make himself heard over the music. Finally, she understood and pointed to a burly, bald man in a tight-fitting black suit near the door. Banks knew he wasn't the manager; he was more of a bouncer or a minder, but he would do for a start. He went over, flashed his card and said, "Take me to your leader."

The bouncer pulled a face, then gestured for Banks to follow him. They went through a door marked private and along a narrow corridor before arriving at another door at the end. It was unmarked. "This it?" Banks asked.

"This is it," said the bouncer, and turned to leave. He seemed to be smiling to himself.

Banks tapped quickly on the door and opened it. The man he took to be the manager was slouching at his desk, chair pushed back a few feet, head tilted, breathing fast and muttering words of obscene encouragement to the woman on her knees before him. When he saw Banks, he sat up and the woman almost fell on her face. She pulled herself to her feet, fussed with the few clothes she was wearing and left the room with as much dignity as she could muster.

"Didn't Jock tell you I wasn't to be disturbed?" the man said.

"I'm afraid not," said Banks.

"Bastard. Don't think I don't know he's got his beady little eyes on Melissa. Well, he'll get his bloody marching orders now." He rubbed his crotch. "Bloody hell, that was close. Could do a man serious damage, that sort of thing. What if she'd snapped her jaw shut in panic?"

Banks smiled. "Then you'd be singing soprano, wouldn't you, Mr. . . . ?"

"Police, I assume, by the looks of you. At least you'd better be after an entrance like that."

Banks showed his warrant card.

"Cornell. Gerry Cornell." The man stood up, slicked his greasy hair back and offered his hand.

"Better not," said Banks. "I don't know where it's been. And maybe you should zip up your fly before anyone gets the wrong idea."

"Oh, right," said Cornell. "Put Percy away, eh?" He zipped up his fly, grinned and sat down again. "What can I do you for?"

"You new here? I don't remember you."

"Six months."

It had been more than that long since Banks had last been called to the Naughty Nites, and then it had to do with fencing stolen jewelry, he remembered. "Just a friendly chat, for starters, Gerry. Pamela Morrison. Name ring a bell?"

"Pamela? Sure. She works here sometimes. Little bitch didn't turn up tonight, mind you. Some of them seem to think I run a charity here. You'd be—"

"She's dead, Mr. Cornell. Murdered. Anything you can tell me about her would be much appreciated."

Cornell's mouth flapped like a dying fish's. "B-b-b-but . . . dead . . . ?"

"Yes."

"Pamela? How?"

"Maybe we could start with where you were last night?"

"Me? I was here."

"All night?"

"Eight till three, same as always. You ask anyone. Surely you can't think I had anything to do with it. Why would I want—"

"I don't think anything yet," said Banks. "It's too early for that. I don't have many facts, and I don't like to speculate too much in advance of the facts."

Cornell blinked twice and reached for a cigarette. "Right," he said. "Drink?"

"No, thanks." Banks wasn't being particularly moral. He had no qualms against taking drinks from people like Cornell when they were offered. It was just that he thought he might have time to nip over to Linda's for an hour or so to unwind before going home, and he didn't want to spoil it by having too much to drink beforehand. He could have one there. Linda always kept a bottle of good Scotch handy. He sat down.

"Okay, Mr. Cornell," said Banks, "even if you didn't kill her, you might be able to tell us something about her."

"Pamela? Not much to tell, really. She was usually reliable. Pretty. Good dancer. Not like some of them. Not a lot up there." He paused and tapped his head. "But she really knew her stuff, like she'd had lessons, you know, ballet school or something."

"Yeah," said Banks. "I can imagine ballet lessons would come in really useful in a place like this."

"No need to be insulting. You know what I mean. Not that she was cultured or anything. Had one of those northern accents you could scale a fish with."

"When did you last see her?"

Cornell sucked on his cigarette and furrowed his brow. "Yesterday, I suppose," he said. "She was working the lunch shift. She didn't like it. None of them do. Lousy tips at lunchtime. But you've got to please the punters, and we get quite a lot of respectable businessmen in at that time of day. City gents and the like, relaxing after a tough morning wheeling and dealing. People who wouldn't be caught dead here after dark."

"I'll bet you do," said Banks. "So Pamela would have been free to pursue her other activities yesterday evening?"

"What other activities?"

"Don't be coy with me, Mr. Cornell. We know that most of your dancers are on the game. Who runs them? You?"

"What they do in their own time is nothing to do with me. I run a respectable business here catering to—"

"Never mind the bollocks, Gerry. I know how it works. The girls make dates in the booths. They—"

Cornell stubbed out his cigarette and licked his lips. "All right," he said. "I'm not saying it doesn't go on. Of course it does. This is Soho. But what can you do? I turn a blind eye. Maybe some of them are on the game. But I mean it when I say that's got nothing to do with me. I'm not a pimp. I'm a club manager. I have no desire to be a pimp. It's an ugly business. I—"

"Matthew Micallef."

Banks could swear that Cornell turned a shade paler. "Come again?"

"Don't tell me you've never heard of him," Banks went on. "How does it work? Do you get a piece of the action? You let him use your club to prey on the dancers, see if they maybe want to supplement their measly incomes with a bit of freelance work, and in return he gives you—"

"Micallef gives nobody nothing," said Cornell. "If you're lucky he leaves you alone. And alive. If you're lucky, he doesn't slit your throat or torch your club."

"Sounds like a nice bloke."

"You think you're funny He's a big man around here, and he's big because people are scared of him. And people are scared of him because he doesn't make empty threats. He goes where he wants, he does what he wants and nobody—not even your lot—even thinks about trying to stop him. And you didn't hear any of that from me."

"Is he here tonight?"

"I haven't seen him."

"Was he here last night?"

"I didn't see him. He doesn't come in here, not often. He's not interested in the clubs."

"Only as a hunting ground?"

"Yeah, well . . . they're hardly the only places these days, or even the best, especially after the cleanup campaign. But I'm telling you the truth. I haven't seen him in . . . must be three or four weeks. And if I never see him again it'll be fine with me."

"Did you notice Pamela with anyone yesterday lunchtime while she was here?"

"No. I wasn't really paying attention. I just had to drop by the office to pick something up, and she happened to be dancing at the time."

"Who should I talk to?"

"Cathy Carson. Day manager."

"A woman?"

Cornell shrugged. "It's an equal opportunities business."

Banks stood up. "OK, Gerry," he said, "I'm going to rustle up a couple of DCs and they'll have a chat with as many of your customers and dancers as they can get through tonight. Then they'll come back and continue tomorrow."

"Do you have any idea what that—"

"I don't care what it will do to your business, Gerry. There's been a murder here and somebody has to know something."

"Fine, fine," said Cornell, holding his palms up in mock surrender. "Do what you have to do. I'm just a poor bloke trying to make an honest living."

"You wouldn't know an honest living if one bit you on the arse," said Banks.

"Can you do me a favor?" Cornell asked as Banks opened the door.

Banks turned. "What?"

Cornell scratched his car. "Can you ask Melissa to come back in? We've got a bit of unfinished business."

"Christ," said Linda when Banks finally rolled off her. "You were a real animal tonight. Is that what hanging around the Soho clubs does to you?"

"Must be." Banks reached for a cigarette, lit two and passed one to Linda. She pulled up the sheet around her throat. Why did women do that? Banks wondered. It wasn't only in movies, but in real life, too. It wasn't cold, and he'd seen it all before. Recently, in fact. He reached for his tumbler of Scotch on the bedside table and took a sip. The amber liquid burned his throat going down. Linda kissed him briefly, then jumped out of bed and wrapped her black and red kimono-style dressing gown around her, fastening the sash. She was a long-legged, willowy brunette in her midtwenties, and the kimono looked good on her. "I fancy a cup of chamomile tea," she said. "Want some?"

"No, ta," said Banks, waving the tumbler. "I'll stick with this."

Linda went into the kitchen and Banks sat up and worked on his whiskey. What the hell was he doing here, he asked himself, when he had a wife and two children at home? He liked Linda well enough, and the sex was good—terrific, in fact—but he had always thought of himself as the faithful, monogamous type, hardly a philanderer.

He had met her on a course at Hendon, and there had been something about her natural self-possession and air of solitariness that drew him to her. It had still taken him a long time to ring the phone number she had given him, and even longer to make the leap into her bed, but he had done it. There was no justification, no excuse; it was an unpleasant truth that he had to accept about himself. He was being unfaithful for the first time in his life. He felt guilty most of the time, but he had learned to live with it.

It had worked well enough so far. And because she was a copper, too, they understood each other. They could talk about things he would never even think of mentioning to Sandra. In fact, they could talk about anything with a level of understanding that amazed him. Sometimes they didn't even need to talk. Each knew, or sensed, the mood of the other, the kind of day they'd had. Sometimes he even carried on conversations with her in his mind when they were apart.

But they weren't *in love*. That wasn't what it was about. If the arrangement ended tomorrow, Banks knew he would miss his stolen hours with Linda—the lovemaking, the talks, the smell of chamomile tea, the swishing sound her kimono made when she walked, the untidiness of her flat—but nothing more. And she gave no signs of feeling any differently.

Linda came back in with her tea and nestled beside him on the large bed. "You'll be leaving here soon, won't you?" she said.

"I'll have to go home before long, yes."

Linda blew on her tea and watched the steam rise. "No, I don't mean that. Here. London. You are thinking of leaving, aren't you?"

"How did you know that?" Banks was astonished. He hadn't told anyone of his tentative forays into North Yorkshire—only by telephone and letter so far, but even so . . .

"Call it woman's intuition," she said. "On second thoughts, you'd better not, or I'll bash you. I can say it but you can't."

"No, seriously."

"I don't know. Just something about you these past few weeks. Something's changed. I can't put my finger on it. I know it sounds weird, but I feel you sort of slipping away. Not from me, so much. I mean, this isn't personal, I'm not coming on all possessive or anything, but it's like you're slowly withdrawing, fading away. Soon there'll be nothing left but your smile, like the Cheshire cat."

Banks supposed it was a fairly accurate summary of how he was feeling, though from his perspective, perhaps Alice falling down the rabbit hole was a better image. She was a smart one, that Linda, no doubt about it. "You should be a psychiatrist, or a psychic," he said.

"So it's true?"

"There's an opening coming up in North Yorkshire later this year. Retirement. It's a DCI position, but it's not so much the promotion I'm after. I've made a few inquiries, and I've been invited up there for an informal chat with the super."

"You're serious about it?"

"Yes." Banks turned to face her. "It's not you, nothing like that. My life is . . . I don't know. It feels like it's sort of spiraling out of control.

Things are getting too weird. Maybe you're part of it, too, my being here. I don't know."

She rested her hand on his bare chest. "Alan, there never were any strings or expectations. Remember that. I'll miss you if you go away, but I'm a big girl. I can take care of myself. I'll survive."

"I know you will. I didn't mean that. It's just me. I don't feel grounded at all. I'm all over the map."

"And you think moving up north will help?"

"I don't know. It'll be different, that's for sure. All I know is that I feel the need to get away. From London, not you. I can still come down and see—"

Linda laughed. "Let's not fool ourselves," she said. "It's been fun. Will be for a bit longer, I hope. But when you're gone, you're gone. Let go with both hands."

Banks looked at her, the dark eyes, smooth pale skin, the tiny rose-patterned teacup with its gold rim pressing against her lower lip. She was beguiling, and in another life . . . "Maybe nothing will come of it," he said.

"And what will you do then?"

"I don't know."

Linda put her cup down, and as she leaned over to do so, the top of her kimono slid off her shoulder. "Look at me," she said, blushing, moving to rearrange it.

But Banks grasped her hand and pulled her gently toward him. "Leave it," he said.

They kissed, then she nestled her head against his chest. "Hold me, Alan," she said. "Just hold me for a while."

While Banks was waiting for Pamela's parents to arrive and make the formal identification the following morning, he read over the statements taken at the Naughty Nites Club, and finding nothing of interest there, he decided to pay Jackie Simmons a visit in Shoreditch. She knew more than she had told him, and perhaps a night's sleep had altered her perspective. Albright could go to the Naughty Nites and question Cathy Carson. Not that she was likely to know anything, either.

Things had been cool at home, perhaps because he hadn't got in until past two. Of course, everyone was asleep by then. He had glanced in on the children first, and when he got into bed, Sandra had stirred and murmured something, but he hadn't caught it. He had turned over, wrapped himself up in his mantle of guilt and drifted off into what passed for sleep these days. Sandra had caught him at the door the next morning trying to sneak out before anyone else woke up and asked him in a frosty tone when he thought they might be able to eat dinner again as a family. He had muttered something about a new murder investigation and left in a hurry.

Now it was close to lunchtime and, as he'd had no breakfast, he was starving. He thought he might take Jackie to the local pub for a drink and a bite to eat. She might relax a bit more in that sort of environment than in the flat she had shared with her murdered friend. He had had a word with Albright at the station and the search of Pamela's room had turned up nothing of interest.

Jackie answered the door dressed in jeans and a Eurythmics T-shirt. Banks didn't reckon much to the Eurythmics. In fact, he didn't reckon much to any of the pop music he'd heard in the past ten years apart from some of the punk and new wave bands—The Clash, Talking Heads, Television. As far as he was concerned you could keep your Phil Collins, Tears for Fears and Fine Young Cannibals. Even his old sixties favorites, like Van Morrison, the Stones and Dylan, seemed to have fallen into a rut. Mostly, he'd been exploring jazz and had recently become interested in opera—a whole new world to explore. But he didn't have the free time he needed to devote to long operatic works lately, and he certainly had neither the time nor the money to go to Covent Garden.

"It's you again," Jackie said when she opened the door.

"Did you manage to get any rest?"

"A bit. Your lot were here until the small hours, then I took a Valium. It's all right. I've got a prescription."

"I didn't doubt it for a moment."

"I suppose you want to come in? I was just vacuuming the living room. Takes my mind off things."

"Well, I'm afraid I'm going to put it back on them. What if we go out for a spot of lunch? I'm starving."

"As long as you're paying."

"I'm paying."

"Hang on a minute; I'll get my jacket."

She came back a moment later in a denim jacket with a suede bag hung over her shoulder. Her hair was tied back in a ponytail and along with the freckles it made her appear even younger than she was. For the first time, Banks noticed her shapely figure. He wondered if she was a good dancer, as she had told him Pamela had been.

"This one's not bad," she said, leading him to Punch Bowl just a hundred yards or so down the street. "Quiet, at any rate."

And on a weekday lunchtime, away from the office crowds, it really was quiet. Banks and Jackie attracted a few glances when they went in, some disapproving, others envious. They settled at a table by the window. Someone had scratched their initials inside a heart, Banks noticed: JK = AM. He wondered who JK and AM were and what had become of them, whether they still felt the same way about each other. "What do you recommend?" he asked.

"It's all pretty much bog-standard pub grub," she said. "Take your pick."

Banks picked bangers and mash and Jackie went for the chicken and chips. He lit a cigarette to go with his pint while he waited for the food. Jackie drank lager from the bottle.

"Not worried about your figure?" Banks asked.

"Should I be?" She did a little model's wiggle in her chair.

"No," he said.

"I seem to be able to eat what I want without putting on weight, and it's not as if I don't get plenty of exercise dancing."

"I suppose so," said Banks. "But it must get to you."

"What?"

"You know. Dancing like that. In front of all those blokes ogling you."

"You get used to it."

"I can't imagine how."

"Well, you wouldn't know, would you? You're a bloke. Probably one of those blokes who goes to the clubs, for all I know. You're all the same. All bloody hypocrites."

"I'm not judging you," said Banks.

"Of course you're judging me. Everybody does. They can't help it. All right, I'm a stripper and I turn the occasional trick. Does that make you happy?"

"I can't say as it does, no."

"There you are, then. Tough."

Banks stared at her.

She shifted in the chair. "What?"

"Nothing," he said.

She blew out a lungful of smoke and took another swig of lager. "If you must know," she said, "things were crap at home, then my dad got made redundant and . . . well, I was going to go to university, but that went down the tubes, didn't it, so it was a part-time job at a funeral home, for fuck's sake, and evenings working at the local boozer to help out Mum and Dad. There are five of us altogether, but my brothers are too young to go to work. I got groped often enough by the pub manager and the funeral director that I thought I might as well make a living at it. All right? I did a bit of exotic dancing locally, like, but my mum and dad got wind of it and threw me out. In the end, what with the strike and all, and everybody at each other's throats, calling people scabs and blacklegs, I'd had about as much as I could take up there, so I came to London to make my fortune. The trains from the north are full of us, didn't you know? 'Thatcher's Children,' they call us."

It was the first time Banks had heard the term, but it seemed apt. It struck him what a dubious legacy it would be for a politician.

"I'm saving up," Jackie went on, "and when I've got enough I'm going to live in Canada, way out on the Pacific coast, and become a marine biologist. This country's fucked."

"Was your father a miner?"

"Fuck, no. You wouldn't catch him down the pit. His father was, though. Died when he was fifty-five. Lungs. No, my dad was a steelworker. We lived near Sheffield."

"Mine, too," said Banks. "Well, a sheet-metal worker at any rate. In Peterborough. He also got made redundant not long ago."

"He did? Really?"

"Yeah."

She held him with her level gaze, then held her hand out. They shook. "Life's a bummer, sometimes, isn't it?" she said.

"It has its moments."

"Tell me something. Why do you do what *you* do? What's in it for you?"

"I don't know. I suppose there's some satisfaction in putting villains away, making the world—or a little part of it—a bit safer, a better place," Banks said. "Then there's finding out the truth about something, trying to get justice done."

"So you're a romantic, really?"

"I don't know."

"You are. You think you can save the world. The rest of us aren't like that. We just want to take what we can from it. You're out of step. A throwback."

"And you're far too sharp to be doing what you're doing."

"Don't be patronizing. Are you married?"

"Yes."

"Kids?"

"Two. A boy and a girl."

She fixed him with her disconcerting gaze. "I'll bet you have a bit on the side, don't you? And I'll bet you feel guilty about it. You're just that kind of bloke."

Banks felt himself redden. "I really do need to ask you a few more questions," he said.

She tapped out a cigarette. "Good deflection. Back to business. I know. I know. Go on. It's all right. Oh, here it comes." She set the unlit cigarette down on the table beside her.

Their food arrived. Banks went to the bar and got a couple more drinks, and when he returned, Jackie was well into the chicken and chips. He started on his sausage and gave up trying to find any traces of meat pretty quickly. At least it tasted all right. Someone put Madonna's "Into the Groove" on the jukebox. Banks groaned.

"What's wrong?" Jackie asked. "Don't you like Madonna?"

"I could live without her."

"I'll bet you like Bob Dylan and the Beatles and all that crap, don't you? You're just an old fogey."

"Less of the old. When were you born?"

"Nineteen sixty-four."

"I'm not that much older than you, then. I just have better taste in music. But enough about me. What do you know about a man called Matthew Micallef?"

Jackie paused with her fork halfway to her mouth, "You don't mess about when you get going, do you?"

"You didn't tell me about him last night when I asked."

"Someone else obviously did."

"I've got my sources. I must say, he's a bit of a mystery to us, though." Banks had also spent part of the morning trying to find out what he could about Micallef, and it wasn't much. "He doesn't appear to have a criminal record, though one of my colleagues thinks he's into all kinds of nasty business."

"He's clever, that's all," said Jackie. "That's why you haven't caught him for anything. Or maybe he's paying you off?"

Banks ignored her comment. "So he's a pimp?"

"Among other things."

"He calls himself a property developer. It took us a while to work our way through the nominees, but we finally discovered that his company owns the building where we found Pamela's body."

"I didn't know that."

"I suppose it explains why she was there. He must have set her up with the place to entertain clients."

"I suppose."

"You didn't use it yourself?"

"Not that place, no. Somewhere else. I thought this was about Pamela, not me?"

Banks put his knife and fork down. "Come on, Jackie. I'm trying to find out who killed your friend and you're not giving me much help. You could be in danger yourself, you know. Have you thought about that?"

Jackie looked at him with her serious eyes again and sighed. She pushed her plate away as if she had suddenly lost her appetite, took another swig of lager and lit a cigarette.

"Another drink?" Banks said.

"Might as well if you're paying."

Banks went to the bar and bought two more drinks. When he came back, Jackie was smoking, staring out of the window and playing with her ponytail with her free hand.

"Micallef," said Banks. "What do you know?"

Jackie paused, then said, "I'm sorry if I don't seem to be very cooperative, but he's not the sort of person who likes people talking about him."

"How would he find out?"

"He has his methods."

"I'm not asking you to finger him for the murder or anything. I doubt that he did that. But he might know something. I'm going to be talking to him soon, anyway. I'd just like to be forearmed."

She shot him a nervous glance. "You're going to question him?"

"Of course."

"You won't mention me, will you?"

"Of course not. Why should I? All I want is a bit of background on him."

"I don't know much about him. Most of us . . . well, we stay as far away as we can. Sometimes he takes a shine to a girl and . . . well, he's very possessive. You wouldn't want him to fix his eye on you, that's all. He's the kind who never gives up until he's got what he wants."

"Has he bothered you?"

"Me? No, I've managed to stay below his radar."

"Pamela?"

"Her, too. The way it works is that Matthew befriends young runaway girls. He usually has a kindred spirit hanging around King's Cross station to offer a bed for the night to a pretty young girl just off the train. Someone nonthreatening. Another girl with a similar story. Then Matthew comes round in a day or two and introduces himself as a friend and ends up seducing the newcomer. He's a very attractive bloke, really. And quite young. About thirty. I know he's Maltese, but he doesn't look it. I mean, he's very fair-haired and all. His mother was English, apparently. He doesn't even have an accent. Anyway, he's authoritative and seems to be in control. The sort of person you want on your side, someone who'll take care of you.

"He showers her with presents, sets her up in a nice flat, takes her to the best restaurants. But there's a price, of course. There always is. When it comes to the nitty-gritty, he doesn't lie. He plays straight. He tells the girls he's got some work lined up for them if they want to continue their new lifestyle—and who wouldn't if they come from Rotherham or Cleckheaton?—and it involves exotic dancing, hostessing, escort services, massages, and maybe even photos and movies. That could lead to the big time, of course. They all want to be film stars.

"He plays down the sex angle. He says he'll leave the choice up to the girls, however far they want to go, but by then they don't have a lot of choice. If someone approaches him and wants one of them, he puts on the pressure. They don't walk the streets, none of them. They work through the clubs, escort agencies and massage parlors. That's where the johns come from. They're usually businessmen in town for a few days. Some are regulars, live here. And the girls usually go along with what Matthew says once he's got them started. If nothing else, he's persuasive. Some of the girls even fall in love with him."

"Not you, though?"

"I like to think I saw through him the first time we met."

"But you still work for him. He's still your pimp."

"You're a real bastard, you know," Jackie said, reaching for another cigarette. "You know that? Besides, if it wasn't him it'd be someone else. There's worse. I had no illusions."

"We all have illusions at some time or other."

"Well, I lost mine a long time ago."

Banks paused and took a sip of beer. "Have you ever seen him behave violently toward any of the girls?" he asked.

"Only once."

"And?"

"It wasn't pretty. One of his girlfriends two-timed him and he found out about it. He smashed a bottle in her face. Just like that." Jackie swung the lager bottle with a speed that surprised Banks and stopped a couple of inches from his nose. "She needed fourteen stitches. Her nose was flat against her cheek. Ruined her looks. I never saw her again after that. And he said that was someone he loved."

Banks sipped some beer and lit another cigarette while he digested what Jackie had just told him. "Why don't you leave?" he asked.

"Because I'm almost there. It's good money. And I manage to stay out of his way most of the time. He doesn't like me. He knows I can see through him. But he tolerates me because I'm a good earner."

"What about Pamela? What was his relationship with her?"

"Purely business. There was something about Pam—maybe a touch of innocence, that northern naïveté, the ingénue in her, whatever—but it drove some men crazy. She was good business for him. Better than me. And she was a terrific dancer, too. She did have classical training, though her parents couldn't afford to keep it up to the point where she might have made something of it." She gave a harsh laugh.

"What?"

"She was going to have her breasts enhanced. Pam. She thought her breasts were too small. That was the sort of thing she dreamed about."

"Did she sleep with him?"

"Pam and Micallef?" Jackie thought for a moment and shook her head. "No, I don't think so. She would have told me. She wasn't his type."

"What about Gerry Cornell?"

Jackie blew out some smoke and laughed. "Blow-job Gerry? Give me a break. He's strictly lightweight."

"So Pamela wasn't involved with either Micallef or Cornell, and you don't know of any boyfriends she had down here?"

"That's right. Only the one she dumped back up in Yorkshire. Nick, or something like that. She said he was about as much use as a spare prick at a wedding."

"Has he been around pestering her or anything?"

"Not that I've ever seen."

"Do you know if Pamela had any regular clients?"

"I'm sure she did. We all do. After all, if you like something, you go back for more, don't you?"

"But do you know any names?"

"No. It's a very private thing. We don't keep lists, you know."

"Any clients she talked about as being troublesome, violent, weird in any way?"

"They're all pretty weird," Jackie said "But the most trouble any of them have is getting it up. Sometimes they needed a lot of coaxing, if you know what I mean. Pam never mentioned anyone in particular."

"What about you? Anyone who stands out as being odd in any way. Maybe someone who wants to save you? Reform you?"

Jackie gave a harsh laugh. "Christ Almighty, there's plenty want to save me. Even you want to save me. There's nothing weird about that."

"Think about it, will you? Try to remember. Anything, however insignificant."

"I can't think clearly right now, but I'll try. There might be a couple of possibilities."

Banks finished his pint, contemplated another, then decided against it. There was more to be done, including the postmortem and a little visit to Matthew Micallef. "What about drugs?" he asked.

"What about them?"

"Was Pamela a user?"

"No. But some of the girls are. And before you ask, I'm not one of them." She held her bottle up. "I like a drink or two, and I drop a Valium from time to time for my nerves, but that's as far as it goes. I smoked pot once and got so frightened I thought I'd never be right in the head again, so I've stayed away from that sort of thing. And needles scare me."

"But some of the girls use, you say. Heroin? Coke?"

"Sure."

"Who's their supplier? Does Micallef get them the drugs, too?"

"I really don't know. I don't think so. I mean, like I said, I stay away from him, but I've never heard anything about him dealing. I suppose he could do, but I think he's got enough other stuff going on, stuff he can make seem legal. It's probably not worth the risk to him. He's got quite a thing going with the Chinese, so maybe he gets stuff from them. I just don't know. Are you sure there's no way any of this will get back to him?"

Banks glanced around the pub. "There's only you and me talking here," he said, "and I'm not telling." He took out a card from his wallet and gave it to her. "If you see or hear anything," he said, "give me a ring. And if you're ever in the least bit worried about something happening to you, about your safety, no matter how wildly unbelievable you think it is, call me."

"You're asking me to spy for you?"

"No," said Banks. "Quite the opposite. I'm asking you to be careful and lie low until we get this sorted out. If you want my advice, you'll pack up and leave. Take what you've got, cut your losses and get out now."

She clapped her hands together. "You see? You *do* want to save me."

"I'm not joking."

"I can't do that. Not just yet." She held her thumb and forefinger in a circle that wasn't quite complete. "I'm *that* close."

"Then stay as far away as you can from Micallef, and don't take any dodgy clients. At the first hint of anything wrong, get out. Don't stop to argue. Just go. You can keep your eyes and ears open, if you insist on staying around, but don't take any risks. Don't go asking questions, drawing attention to yourself. From what you've told me, this Micallef is dangerous."

"Do I get paid if I find out anything? Like a real police informant?"

Banks laughed and stood up. "Sure," he said. "Next time I see you, I'll buy you another drink. Chicken and chips again, too, if you're lucky."

"The last of the big spenders," she said. "Bye." And she waved at him as he walked away, her other hand shaking a cigarette out of the packet.

It was after two o'clock by the time Pamela's parents had made the official identification, and Dr. O'Grady hadn't even begun the preliminary task of removing Pamela's outer clothing before Banks arrived at the autopsy suite. Banks wanted to talk to the parents, too, but they could wait till later.

He stood by and watched as Dr. O'Grady began, reciting his findings into the microphone that hung over the table, occasionally asking his assistant for some instrument or other. Banks was glad he'd had a couple of drinks at lunchtime, as he always found postmortems disturbing.

The clothes were bagged and sealed for forensic examination as they were removed, along with the pillows, bedsheets, facecloth and water from the scene. There didn't appear to be any blood apart from a tiny spot on the pillowcase, but if there was, it would show up in the lab.

Underneath, Pamela wore silky black underwear, which Dr. O'Grady also removed. Naked, she looked even younger, though both Jackie Simmons and Pamela's parents swore blind that she was nineteen.

Dr. O'Grady began his external examination, noting the petechial hemorrhages, first, then removing the plastic bags from her hands and pointing out the traces of blood and skin under her fingernails, some of which were broken.

"She clearly struggled for her life," O'Grady said as he took samples.

"Lucky for us," said Banks. "If we can identify his blood group, it should help."

"Shouldn't be a problem."

He finished with the hands and moved on, using a large magnifier suspended beside the microphone to zoom in on the details of her skin.

But he didn't need the magnifier when he got to her thighs.

"Jesus Christ," he muttered, stepping back, "will you come and have a look at this?"

Banks moved in close and leaned over the body. "She's been shaved," he said. "That's not so unusual with exotic dancers. It doesn't mean the killer did it. And I think I might be able to find out."

"Not only that." O'Grady pointed. "This, too."

Banks could see a strip of transparent tape between her legs. "What is it? Surely it's not . . ."

"If I'm not mistaken," said O'Grady, removing the tape carefully with a pair of surgical tweezers, "it most certainly is." He held up a broad strip of Sellotape in the tweezers and looked at Banks. "Would you believe it?" he said. "The bastard Sellotaped her labia together."

"Are there any signs of sexual activity?"

O'Grady bent over the body again and Banks backed away. He had no desire to watch the doctor probing Pamela Morrison's private parts. *Sellotape.* He'd never seen anything like that before. Mutilation, yes. But not this. Why?

"Possibly," said O'Grady. "I think we have traces of semen here, if I'm not mistaken."

"She'd had sex recently?"

"Seems that way. It doesn't have to be the killer, of course. You don't need me to tell you. A woman in her line of work . . ."

"I know," said Banks. "But I don't think she worked the streets. I mean, I don't think she took punter after punter back to that room. It's possible she had only the one date that night."

"A bit exclusive?"

"The impression I got, yes. By arrangement."

"Should make finding him a bit easier, then."

"Except nobody's talking," said Banks.

O'Grady put the strip of Sellotape into a bag and sealed it.

"Better send that over to fingerprints right away," said Banks. "According to the SOCOs, the bastard was clever enough to wipe down the surfaces in the room, but you never know."

"Will do." O'Grady turned back to the body. "So what do you make of it?"

"I really don't know," said Banks. "But the way I'm seeing things now, our killer comes up to the room with her, or she's already waiting there for him. They undress and have sex, then he suffocates her with the pillow, either while they're doing it or after. Then he shaves her, or she's shaved already, places a strip of Sellotape over her vagina, dresses her, poses her under the sheet with her hands and legs together."

"Washes all the makeup off her face."

"That, too."

"Pure. Like a virgin."

"Like a virgin," Banks agreed.

"But what kind of nutter does that?"

"I don't know," said Banks. "But I'd hazard a guess that it's the kind of nutter who doesn't stop at one."

"He Sellotaped her cunt shut?" said DCI Roly Verity. "I don't fucking believe it."

Banks was no prude, but he found Verity's language deeply offensive on this occasion. Verity hadn't been there. He hadn't watched Pamela Morrison's postmortem, hadn't seen her cut open, smelled her insides, like raw lamb.

A couple of fresh-faced DCs lounging with their feet on the table giggled at the comment. Detective Superintendent Hatchard, nominally in charge of the meeting, puffed on his pipe and muttered something about bad taste. Banks said nothing. He still felt sick.

They were in the incident room, about ten of them in all. A coffee urn stood on a table near the door, wadded paper towel under its spout to catch the drips, and a stack of Styrofoam cups leaning like the Tower of Pisa beside it. One wall was dotted with crime scene photos, maps, floor plans and scribbled time lines. The ashtrays were already overflowing.

"The way it seems," Banks went on, ignoring Verity, who was only present at Hatchard's invitation anyway, a public relations exercise in interdepartmental cooperation, "and Dr. O'Grady and the lab have verified all this now, is that Pamela took her killer to the room with her, or was already waiting for him there. It was a place she used frequently for such assignations."

Verity laughed. *"Assignations?* That's a good one, that is, for what *she* did."

"DCI Verity," said Hatchard. "If you wish to remain present at this meeting, please refrain from interrupting Detective Inspector Banks in his explanation."

Verity feigned the look of a chastised schoolboy. "Sorry, sir," he said, turning to share a smirk with one of the DCs.

Hatchard stuck his pipe back in his mouth.

The whole exchange reminded Banks of how all Hatchard's meetings were like a class at school with a dull teacher whose grip on discipline was tenuous, to say the least. He went on, "According to my information, she wasn't a common prostitute, more of a middle-class call girl," he explained. "She didn't walk the streets trolling for johns. They came to her. Or they were sent."

"Did they have references and all?" said Verity, to much laughter from the DCs.

Hatchard tut-tutted.

"Something like that," said Banks. "Anyway, on the surface of it, this occasion was no different. There were no traces of forced entry, and the door was unlocked when her flatmate Jackie Simmons went there to look for her. She found the body. It says a great deal for her that she called us. A lot of girls in her position wouldn't, as I'm sure you all know."

Even Verity nodded knowingly at this remark.

"So it might indicate that she has nothing to hide," Banks added.

"Or it might mean she's guilty, sir," said Ozzy Albright.

Banks gave him an appreciative glance. "Yes," he conceded. "It might, at that. Except we're pretty sure the killer was a man. Reconstructing from the evidence and what I've got from the doc and the lab so far, they had sex—or she had sex with someone that night. It doesn't appear as if they used any protection, because the doctor found traces of semen in the vagina."

"The johns pay extra for bareback," said Verity.

"Thanks for that little gem, Roly," said Banks, flashing him a smile. "I'm sure we're all that much the wiser for it. Anyway, whatever he paid her, if anything, he took it away with him, because all we found in her purse was a few measly quid and some loose change. At this point, we're assuming she had her clothes off, or most of them, at any rate. We don't know how or why it happened, what changed things, but then he suffocated her with the pillow. When she was dead, he applied the Sellotape, put her clothes back on and washed all the makeup off her face. The lab confirms traces of lipstick and mascara on the pillowcase, so she was wearing it when he suffocated her, and the bowl on the bedside table also contained traces of the same substances, as did the facecloth. After this, we assume he arranged the body in the way we found it, covering her with a sheet from the bed. We thought he might also have shaved her pubic hair, but I checked with her flatmate, Jackie Simmons, and it turns out she shaved it herself for the dancing job."

"Those costumes they wear are a little skimpy," said Verity. "I can see you wouldn't want a couple of short and curlies peeking out the sides. Spoil the effect."

Hatchard ignored him and scratched the side of his nose. "That's very . . . er . . . interesting, Alan," he said "but do we have any idea why he'd go to all this trouble?"

"I think you'd need a shrink to work that one out, sir," said Banks.

"Hmm. Might be worthwhile getting in touch with one of those specialist psychologists we hear about from time to time."

"It might be," Banks agreed. Like most police, he didn't really trust the psychologists they sometimes used to work on possible profiles of criminals. It was too much like hocus-pocus to him. They might as well use a psychic. But he was willing to keep an open mind.

"What about prints?" Hatchard asked.

"I was just getting to that. It looks very much as if our killer didn't wear gloves, but he did wipe the place. From what the SOCOs can gather, the surfaces—door, table, drawers, what have you—have all been wiped clean. One of our techs found tiny linen fibers caught on a rough wooden surface, so he probably used a handkerchief. You'd expect prints in a room like . . . a room used for sexual encounters, but we found none, so he did a pretty good job of obliterating everything."

"A linen handkerchief, too," muttered Albright. "Posh."

"But where he did slip up," Banks went on, "was the Sellotape. We've got a partial from it, and it's not hers."

"So if we can find a match . . ." Hatchard said.

"Then we may have our killer. But it's not on file, so we've still got a lot to do."

"Even so," said Hatchard. "I'd say our SOCOs and lab did an excellent job. A partial print and traces of semen. I trust he's a secretor?"

"Yes," said Banks, "so we'll be able to identify his blood group."

"Good, good." Hatchard puffed on his pipe. It had gone out, so he lit it again. Clouds of blue smoke poured out of the bowl and he disappeared in the fog. "I've already got the press sniffing around," he said. "What should I do about them?"

"I think we should keep the evidence of the print and semen, along with the unusual details, to ourselves, sir," Banks said. "I mean the odd posing of the body and the Sellotape. That gives us something up our sleeves when the false confessions come in. And something we can use to nail the real killer when we find him."

"I agree," said Hatchard. "Let's make sure there are no leaks, everyone."

"Right now," Banks went on, "all we can do is the usual. We've found nobody who admits to seeing Pamela and her killer enter the building, or her killer leave. Someone must have seen something, though. Even though it's a fairly quiet side street, there are cafés, pubs and lots of street traffic around the corner. We can put an appeal out in the media. We can also follow up on any known perverts in the area, ask around the girls and the clubs and massage parlors about anyone who's been behaving oddly."

"But he wouldn't necessarily have been behaving oddly, would he?" said Albright. "From what I've read, people like him often appear normal on the surface."

Some of the others laughed, but Banks said, "That's true enough, Ozzy, but he might have let something slip to someone. Maybe one of the girls will remember a bloke who worried her, someone who talked crazy or tried some weird stunt. And there are a couple of points to remember. First, he must have gone prepared. We found no Sellotape at the scene, so he must have brought it with him. Which probably means he knew what he was going to do with it."

"Or he found some there and took it with him," said Albright.

"Possibly," Banks agreed.

"And the second point?" Hatchard asked.

"Well, if she didn't just pick up a bloke from the street, then this meeting was probably arranged, and if that's the case, there's a damn good chance someone arranged it for her, or at least *knew* about it. Anyway, I've got actions for all of you, and enough interviews to keep you going for a while."

The DCs groaned in chorus.

"And you, Alan?" said Hatchard.

"After we've had a quick word with the parents, I think Ozzy and I should pay a visit to Matthew Micallef," said Banks. "He was Pamela's pimp and he owns the building where she died. Maybe he knows who she was meeting there."

———————

Banks had discovered from Verity that Micallef liked to hold court most afternoons in a Chinese restaurant on Gerrard Street, so he and Albright headed over there after speaking briefly with Pamela's parents. Banks learned little from them. Her mother sniffled the whole time, and her father maintained a monosyllabic stoicism. The only time he showed any emotion at all was when Banks handed him the photograph he had found in Pamela's handbag, upon which Mr. Morrison uttered a gruff, hasty thank-you and made a quick exit.

Chinatown used to be in Limehouse, close to the docks, and to Banks it evoked images from his adolescent reading: pea-soup fogs, Sherlock Holmes, inscrutable orientals, and the ne'er-do-well sons of the gentry idling away their lives in opium dens. But the modern-day reality wasn't like that at all, if it ever had been. Most of the Chinese immigrants had moved after the blitz destroyed much of the East End. They settled in Soho in the 1950s and spilled over into an area between Shaftesbury Avenue and Leicester Square in the 1970s. It wasn't a very large Chinatown, but the streets were ornamented with pagodas and arches, and the place was full of Chinese restaurants, supermarkets and shops overflowing with exotic and often unfamiliar Asian produce, little white delivery vans all over the place.

Albright glanced around keenly at the activity and sniffed the exotic air. "I always liked this place," he said to Banks. "Do you know where the biggest Chinatown in the world is? Outside China itself, that is, sir."

"You've got me there, Ozzy." Banks sidestepped a few leaves of decaying bok choy.

"San Francisco."

"Is it, indeed?" said Banks. "Now, that's a city I've always wanted to visit."

"It's not the one in the film. That was Los Angeles. Talking about films, sir, did you see *A View to a Kill*? I must say, I think Roger Moore is getting a bit long in the tooth to play James Bond. And that Grace Jones . . . I'm not sure I'd want her in *my* bed. Some very nasty habits she's got, sir."

"You should be so lucky," said Banks. "Here we are, I think."

The façade of the restaurant was painted black and red, and the signage was lettered in gold. The windows were smoked, the glass etched and covered with net curtains, so it was impossible to see inside.

Banks hadn't really formed a plan, but he had told Albright just to play it by ear, see how Micallef reacted to the questions they asked him, note down any uncertainties and obvious lies to return to later, perhaps in the more formal surroundings of the station, if they felt he warranted bringing in.

Albright was a good head taller than Banks and had to stoop slightly as they went in. A doorbell pinged. When their eyes adjusted to the darkness, Banks noticed it was a relatively large room, and several tables were occupied. He scanned the diners, thinking Micallef would probably be sitting with a couple of bruisers. But there were no bruisers. Most of the clientele looked like businessmen. The maître d' approached them, and Banks asked for Mr. Micallef. The maître d' gave a slight bow and walked over to one of the tables. He spoke to a fair-haired man who glanced at Banks and Albright, still standing in the foyer. The maître d' came back and led them over to the table. There were no plates of food, just an almost empty bottle of white burgundy.

Banks and Albright introduced themselves.

"Please, sit down," said Micallef. "My meeting's over, anyway." He gave a signal to the two men and a woman who were sitting with him, and they left.

Banks could have sworn that Micallef had been expecting their visit, and perhaps he had. He would know about the murder and, whether he was guilty or not, he would also know that the police would quickly make the connection between him and the dead girl.

"Can I tempt either of you to a drink?" Micallef offered. "Or is it a duty call?"

"Duty," said Banks as he and Albright sat down.

Micallef smiled in a slightly lopsided way, head tilted in amusement. "Pity." He emptied the burgundy into his glass. "It's a very fine vintage."

"Then it would probably be wasted on a dull plod like me," said Banks. He lit a cigarette.

"Oh, come, come. I'm sure you do yourself an injustice. What do you say, Sergeant?"

"It's true that 1983 was a very good year for white burgundy, but I still think it could benefit from another couple of years in the cellar."

Micallef laughed, then stopped as abruptly as he had started. "Perhaps," he said. "But I happen to be a very impatient man. And busy." He looked at his watch, a chunky Rolex. "Shall we get down to business, or do I need my solicitor present?"

"No need for that," said Banks. "Just a friendly chat." Since the Police and Criminal Evidence Act had been passed the previous year, criminals had more rights than ever before. The police, Banks included, hadn't quite got used to the shift of power yet, so they were nervous and usually erred on the side of caution. Even so, unless Micallef was going to confess to murder, he hardly had need for a lawyer, and he was probably too shrewd to give anything away. What else would they charge him with? Living off immoral earnings?

Micallef spread his hands. "So what can I do for you?"

Banks had to admit that the man had taken him by surprise. Despite what he had already heard from Verity and from Jackie Simmons, he had still expected a swarthy, barrel-chested man surrounded by gorillas. But what he got could well have been, to all intents and purposes, an ex–public schoolboy, a lock of blond hair hanging over his left eye, fair complexion, an air of natural superiority, a haughty demeanor and easy exercise of power. His mother was English, Banks knew, so he had obviously inherited his looks from her, slightly effeminate, but of a kind that is attractive to women. His accent was pure Eton and Oxford. But Banks also knew that behind this veneer of civilized urbanity was a vicious streak and the morals of a common criminal, a pimp, no less, and that was the image he tried to keep in his mind as he spoke with Micallef.

"It's about the murder of Pamela Morrison," Banks began.

"Yes, I heard. Tragic business."

"Word has it that you knew the girl."

"I wouldn't say I *knew* her. Certainly not in the carnal sense. I've seen her around the clubs, that's all."

"You frequent many clubs in Soho?"

"*Many?* There aren't many left," said Micallef. "Not since the City of Westminster started its clean up Soho campaign. But I think vice will always flourish in such an environment, don't you, Inspector?" Micallef shrugged in a man-of-the-world sort of way. "Anyway, I frequent one or two of the handful that remain. I'm a red-blooded male. What can I say? You have some very beautiful women here in London."

"Where are you from?"

"Valletta. Malta. Though I was educated here. My mother insisted. Harrow and King's College, Cambridge. I read mathematics, if you're interested."

"I see you put your education to good use," Banks said.

"I'm a property developer," Micallef announced proudly, "and I like to play the stock market. I find a little background in arithmetic doesn't go amiss."

"What about your other business?" Banks asked.

"What would that be? I have a number of side interests."

"The girls. Pimping."

Micallef wagged his finger. "You should know better than that, Inspector. That's illegal, and I don't do anything illegal."

"You own the building where Pamela Morrison's body was found."

Micallef swirled the wine in his glass. "My company owns it, as you are obviously aware. Are you saying that makes me responsible?"

"No. I'm saying she was found dead in a room you let her use—or rented for her use—to entertain men for money. Who had Pamela arranged to meet in that room, or take there, two nights ago?"

"How should I know? As I said, what she did in the room was her business. I have nothing to do with such things. Even if I did let this woman use the room, as you suggest, or rented it to her, I had no idea what she did in it. How could I? I don't spy on my tenants, Inspector."

"What about the other rooms in the building? What are they used for?"

"I don't know."

"Perhaps it could be called a brothel?"

"I wouldn't know."

"Don't you think you should take a closer interest in your business affairs."

"I employ others to do that for me. That's why I have nominees."

"Who are they? Will you give me some names?"

Micallef smiled. It was a reptile's smile. "Help the police with their inquiries? Of course. No doubt you already have some, or you wouldn't be here making these wild accusations. Talk to Benny on your way out." Micallef gestured toward the entrance, and Banks noticed one of the men who had been sitting at the table earlier was now chatting and laughing with the maître d' near the front desk. Perhaps he wasn't a gorilla, but "Benny" certainly had the appearance of a minder—broad chest, arm muscles bulging none too discreetly under his tight-fitting Armani suit. Micallef glanced at his watch again. "I have to leave. Why don't you stay here and enjoy Yuan's excellent hospitality? I assume I'm free to terminate this interview at any time?"

"Of course," said Banks.

"Then I'm sure you understand that I really have nothing more to say on the matter."

Micallef stood up to move away, but Banks grabbed his wrist. He noticed Benny stiffen over by the door, and he also noticed the subtle shift in position and sudden alertness that meant Albright was ready for action. Nobody else moved as Banks slowly pulled Micallef toward him. Though the Maltese was tall, he was not especially strong. "Mr. Micallef," said Banks. "Do you have any idea who Pamela Morrison met in that room two nights ago? Or do you know the name of anyone who might know?"

"No, I don't," said Micallef, gently freeing himself from Banks's grip and dusting off his cuff with his hand. "Now if you'll excuse me, I have a business to run."

And with that, he was gone.

"Well, that went well, sir, didn't it?" said Albright.

"About as well as can be expected," said Banks, smiling. "At least we've rattled his cage. Come on, let's go. There should still be somewhere open around here where we can get a decent pint."

It was shortly after closing time when Banks got back to the Kennington flat that evening, and Sandra was waiting up for him. He poured a large Scotch, then flopped next to her on the living room sofa and lit a cigarette.

"Do you really need that?" she said, meaning the whiskey.

"It's been a rough day."

"It's always a rough day. But by the smell of you, you've been in the pub most of the evening already."

"What if I have?"

"Oh, Alan, come on. You know what I'm saying. Stop acting like a spoiled child. You're never home anymore. You never spend any time with *us*."

"What do you mean?"

"*Us*. When was the last time you saw Tracy or Brian? Remember them, your children? *Our* children. *Us*."

"Last night. I looked in—"

"I mean *really* saw them. Talked to them. Found out what they're doing at school, what they're interested in, what's happening in their lives. When's the last time we ever did anything together as a family?"

"Like what?"

"Oh, I don't bloody know. A day at the zoo or something. That's not the point."

"Then what is?"

"That you just don't seem like you want to be a member of this family anymore. You just don't care. You'd rather hang out boozing with your cop cronies or visit the Soho clubs watching strippers and talking to pimps and prostitutes. What kind of life is that?"

"It's my life, Sandra. It's a copper's life. It's—"

"Oh, don't give me that crap, Alan. I've heard it all before. You should know better than that. It's worse now than when you worked undercover. At least then we never saw you at all. Now you just pop up whenever you feel like it, whenever you need a place to sleep or eat, like some eccentric down-and-out uncle. And *sleep* is the right word. I can't remember the last time we made love. God knows where you've been till all hours. You could have another woman for all I know."

"Oh, come on, Sandra—"

"No. I mean it. I don't know what's going on in your life—you don't talk to me—and you don't know what's going on in ours. And what's more, you don't care."

Banks sat up straight. "I do bloody care, if you'd just give me a chance!"

"How? Show me how you care. How much you care. What have you done lately to let us know you care? When did we last have sex?"

"I told you, things have been a bit tough, lately, I'm tired when I get home, or you're out down at the arts center. . . . I—"

"Oh, bollocks, Alan. Bollocks. It's just excuse after excuse with you."

"I'm thinking of transferring up north," Banks blurted out.

Sandra's jaw dropped. "You're what?"

Now he'd said it, there was no going back. "Well, all of us, of course. Not just me. But if I can get a transfer—"

Sandra put her palm to the side of her head and tapped gently. "Hang on a minute. Am I hearing you right? Am I missing something here? Did you ever hear me say I wanted to move up north?"

"Well, not in so many words, but you've complained often enough about the size of the flat here, and we'd be able to afford somewhere bigger up there. Maybe in the country. We—"

"I complain about the flat because it *is* too small for the four of us. Maybe it's not a bad thing that you *are* out all the bloody time. Makes the place seem less crowded."

"That's not fair."

"Anyway, since when have you been entertaining this idea?"

"I heard about a position coming up. DCI. It'd mean more money, too. Maybe fast track to superintendent. I'd be home more. Stands to reason. Smaller place, less crime."

"Where is this Shangri-la?"

"Place called Eastvale."

"Never heard of it."

"It's on the map. North Yorkshire. I'm going up there. Sort of informal interview with the super."

"When is this? You never told me."

"It's all very recent. I just haven't had time. This murder and all. . . . Couple of days, anyway. When I can get a break from the case. The weekend, maybe, if I can get away."

"But, Alan, we're supposed to be having Charlie and Rose over for dinner on Saturday. Don't you remember?"

Banks didn't. "Of course. I'll go Sunday," he said. "I can get there and back in a day if I leave really early. I don't mind the driving. Maybe you can come? Maybe we can all go?" He stood up, excited by the idea. "I'll drop you off in the town center while I go for my chat—he lives out of the town—then pick you up later on the way back. We'll have a nice drive in the country, a pub lunch."

"It's not exactly my idea of a perfect Sunday out," said Sandra. "That's a lot of hours in the car, and you know Tracy gets carsick."

"She can take a Kwell."

"They just put her to sleep. But I'll see. You must promise you'll be here on Saturday evening for dinner, though. It's Rose's birthday."

"I'll be here."

Sandra ran her hand through her hair. "Christ, your job is turning me into a bloody shrew," she said. "I never used to be like this before. It's just that I don't know where we stand anymore. All we ever seem to do when we are together is argue. And I'm not sure moving is the answer. I don't know about moving up north. I don't *know* the north. You should have asked me first."

"Nothing's been decided yet. I might not get it even if I do apply. And, of course, if you don't want to move . . ."

"I know. I know. It's just so sudden. The way you sprung it on me. It's just . . . well, I like London. I like the galleries, the parks, the pubs, the restaurants, the theaters. I just want to do it all with you, that's all. Can't you see that? You're like a stranger to me these days. Is there someone else, Alan? Is that what it is?"

Banks put his arm around her. "Of course not," he said. "Of course there's no one else. It's the job, love. It's just the job."

There were no developments over the next few days. One possible lead— a man Pamela had been seen talking to a couple of times in Naughty Nites—got everyone excited, then fizzled out when it turned out that he was in Barcelona on business at the time of the murder. The other girls Pamela worked with were interviewed, along with Micallef's nominees and employees, then club owners, bouncers, johns, pub managers and local shopkeepers, all to no avail. Pamela Morrison had met her death in a cramped room in Soho and nobody seemed to know a thing about it. Except her killer.

The psychologist Banks and Albright spoke with didn't have much to add at such an early stage, either, but he stressed the ritualistic element and that however odd the actions seemed, the killer would be able to justify them to himself. The killer was controlled, too, he said, and the way the body was posed not only accorded with his idea of innocence but hid the reality of what he had done from himself. In a way, he couldn't face his acts. There was a strong chance, the psychologist said, that the killer could unravel before long, but there might be other victims first. The press was kept briefed and up to date, but Hatchard was as good as his word and careful not to let slip any of the unusual details: the posing of the body, the Sellotape, the makeup wiped off.

Saturday's dinner was a success, and Banks was only three-quarters of an hour late. He had a nagging hangover early on Sunday morning when they set off through the deserted London streets toward the M1. Brian was quiet, gazing out of the window, and Tracy was sleepy after taking her Kwell. The old Cortina moved along smoothly and Banks slipped in a cassette of *Bags Groove*. Miles Davis, Monk and Milt Jackson. Nice music for a peaceful, sunny morning in London. It could have been a sound track for the opening of a movie. Tracy didn't stir and nobody else complained, so Banks left it on. Soon, he felt worlds away from Soho, Pamela Morrison, Jackie Simmons and Matthew Micallef.

The journey up the M1 was easy enough, not so many lorries, but a few Sunday drivers slowing down the lanes, crawling a mile or two from one junction to the next to visit their children or grandchildren. Banks had a bit of trouble negotiating the stretch between the M1 and the A1—he left the motorway too soon—and he found himself passing road signs to Normanton, Featherstone, Pontefract, Castleford and Knottingley. He passed through some small mining communities and realized he was in Pamela Morrison's part of the world. None of them had ever been farther north than Peterborough before, so everyone was very excited, the kids with their noses pressed against the car windows.

But soon everyone became quiet.

Banks hadn't really known what to expect; he had only seen images on the news, usually of miners fighting pitched battles with the riot police. The reality was grim, even in the sunshine of a beautiful summer's day, from the rows of grimy back-to-back terrace houses to the newer redbrick council estates put up in the sixties and already shabby, and the weed-covered patches of waste ground where groups of children organized makeshift games of football, using their jackets to mark the goalposts. He drove past rows of shops, most of them boarded up or advertising closing-down sales, the rest selling second-hand clothing or market-stall-priced household cleaners and utensils.

There was an aura of gloom about the place, but it was the gloom of poverty and despair, not lack of sunlight. The same bright sun shone on the soot-blackened civic buildings up here as it did on the majestic architecture of Westminster or the dome of St. Paul's. The few people Banks noticed on the streets seemed to shuffle along, hands in their pockets, heads hung low, avoiding eye contact with anyone else. Across a field, Banks saw a still pit-wheel silhouetted against the blue sky and a slag heap covered in weeds. In the distance, smoke poured from the huge cooling towers of Ferrybridge power station.

Banks couldn't imagine anyone wanting to be a miner. Certainly the long hours, claustrophobic conditions, the danger and filth of it put him off. But people did it. Generation after generation. And they fought long and hard for such basic rights as showers at the pit-head and permission to use them after their shifts. Now it was gone, wiped out. You could argue all you wanted about the economic necessity of closing the pits, he thought, but none of that took into account the level of human misery it caused in some of these communities. It was more than just the loss of jobs, of income, as if that weren't bad enough. It was the loss of a community's identity, its way of life, traditions, history and culture. He felt as if he were driving through a vanishing world.

Banks found the A1 just beyond Fryston and Fairburn and carried on north past Wetherby, turning off just north of Ripon. Nobody had spoken much since the detour through industrial West Yorkshire, but the general consensus was that lunch was in order. Banks stopped at the first village they came to on the Eastvale road. He had arranged to go and see Detective Superintendent Gristhorpe at his home in a village called Lyndgarth at two thirty, which gave them plenty of time to enjoy a pub lunch in the country.

They sat at a wooden bench outside a seventeenth-century limestone pub, looking out over the village green and enjoying the sunshine and fresh air. Beyond the green and the houses on the other side, Banks could see the beginnings of the Dales, humpbacked hills that rolled into the hazy distance like giant frozen waves.

Because he was driving and attending an interview, however informal, Banks was off the booze for the day, and he drank warm fizzy lemonade instead. The kids had the same, while Sandra asked for a half pint of cold lager. It was good to see her relaxing and unwinding for a change, Banks thought. Years of care seemed to slip off her shoulders as she smoked a rare cigarette and smiled mischievously at him, sipping her lager and gazing at the view. She even got out her camera and took a few photos.

When they had finished their roast beef and Yorkshire pudding, they set off for Eastvale. It seemed like a pleasant market town, with a cobbled square, church and ancient market cross, a ruined castle looming over it all, a sign pointing down a hill to the river. It was worlds away from what they had seen in West Yorkshire. None of the shops were boarded up, and those that weren't open were closed only because it was Sunday. The darkness that had swallowed up much of the rest of the country beyond the Home Counties didn't seem to have cast much of a pall up here.

There were quite a few tourists about, many kitted out for walking. The outside tables at the pubs were busy, and it was impossible to find a parking spot in the square. Banks just dropped Sandra, Brian and Tracy off outside a Tudor-fronted building that appeared to be the police station, and said he'd pick them up at the same spot in a couple of hours. They waved good-bye as he drove away. Just like a real family.

Banks pulled up outside the isolated farmhouse at the end of the rutted drive and turned off his engine. He got out of the car and stood for a moment and just took in the countryside, silent but for the sounds of the birds and someone hammering in the distance. The farm stood outside the village of Lyndgarth, about halfway up the northern daleside, and it commanded a magnificent view down the slope toward the winding, wooded river, then across and all the way up the other side, green fields marked out into odd shapes by drystone walls—a teacup, a milk churn, a teardrop. Sheep grazed on the lower pastures, and higher up the green paled to a dry brown, and outcrops of limestone broke through the rough grass. At the very top was a long limestone scar, which gleamed like a row of giant teeth in the sunlight. Banks thought he could see a line of walkers moving along the top, tiny dots in the distance.

Banks next took in the façade of the house. Built of limestone, with cornerstones and lintels of gritstone, and a flagstone roof, it was a bit austere for his taste, perfectly symmetrical, with two downstairs and two upstairs windows on each side of the red door. Over the doorhead a date and some initials had been chiseled into the stone: ADH 1779. Banks could imagine a farmhouse in such a wild and isolated place needed to built like a fortress. It was probably windswept and lashed by rain for much of the year.

"Three foot," said a deep voice beside him.

Banks turned, startled. He hadn't heard anyone approach him, had been so lost in his contemplation of the view and the house that he hadn't noticed the man come around the side and stand by the corner.

"I mean, if you were wondering how thick the walls are," the man said. "And the initials are the original owner's, the date probably when the house was built, or the commemoration of an important family marriage. It's also the year that state prisons were first authorized, but I don't really think that has a lot to do with the owner's reason for carving it there, do you?" He walked over to Banks and rubbed his hands on the sides of his jeans. "I'm Gristhorpe, by the way."

They shook. His hand was dry and calloused. "Alan Banks."

"Good journey?"

"Excellent." Banks gestured around him. "I've never been . . . I mean, I hadn't realized how beautiful it is up here."

Gristhorpe laughed. "You should pay us a visit in December before you make your mind up about that. Or talk to one of the local farmers."

"I suppose so."

"Come round the back. You'll probably be wanting a drink?"

"No thank you," said Banks. "I'm driving."

"Most admirable, but I was thinking of tea. You wouldn't believe how refreshing it is on a hot day."

"Tea would be fine," said Banks, following him around the side of the house to the back.

Two fold-out chairs awaited on a stone patio beside the back door. Beyond stretched Gristhorpe's garden, or "acreage" as they would probably call it up here. It was certainly too big to be a garden, though there was a vegetable patch next to one of those drystone walls that seemed so common in the area. This one seemed to have collapsed in a couple of places.

"I'll ask Mrs. Hawkins to rustle up some tea for us. She won't mind."

Gristhorpe disappeared for a moment, then came back and sat opposite Banks. He was a tall and solidly built man of about fifty, well padded some might say, with a shock of unruly silver hair, a ruddy pock-marked complexion and a bristly gray moustache. The most disconcerting thing about him, Banks thought, was not so much the dungarees and collarless striped shirt he was wearing, but his eyes. Set under bushy eyebrows, they were wide, deep blue and guileless, like a child's. It would be hard lying to this man, Banks sensed immediately, or at least it would be hard to believe that he would believe your lies.

Even though they were outside, Banks asked for permission to smoke and Gristhorpe granted it. "I see you've had an accident," Banks said, gesturing to the wall. "Storm?"

Gristhorpe followed Banks's gaze and frowned. "No," he said. "Practice. It's a hobby of mine. I build a wall, then I take it down again and build it differently."

"So it's not a wall around anything, really?"

"That's right."

"Or to keep anything out?"

"No."

"And it's not really going anywhere in particular?"

Gristhorpe beamed at him. "You've got it."

Banks was beginning to wonder what sort of weird yokel he'd got here. A man with baby blue eyes who builds walls that don't go anywhere and don't wall anything in. Were they all like that north of the Trent? Or the Wharfe? Maybe it was something in the water.

Mrs. Hawkins came out with the tea on a tray, along with a plate of scones. Banks was still full from lunch, but he had learned to eat when it's offered, so he took one. It was still warm. He made appreciative noises as Gristhorpe poured the tea. That done, the superintendent said, "So what is it that makes you want to come and work up here?"

"Well," said Banks, searching for the answer he had prepared in his mind. "It seems to me that in today's force, if a man is at all ambitious, he has to move around. You know that promotion within the same station, even region, is discouraged. This is a great opportunity for me. A step up."

Gristhorpe hadn't been looking at Banks while he was talking. Banks fancied he'd been staring at his drystone wall and wondering where to put the next stone. The silence stretched, then Gristhorpe said, "So you'd say you're an ambitious man, would you? I must admit, you do have that lean and hungry look, but I put it down to deprivation rather than overweening ambition. Missing too many meals, I'd say. Eating on the run."

Banks wasn't quite sure what he meant, but he realized the interview, or conversation, was taking off in a direction he hadn't reckoned on. "Well, you know what it's like," he said "The job. Sometimes you just forget to eat."

"So it *is* hunger, rather than ambition? Have another scone."

"Sorry, sir? No, thanks, I'm full."

"Hmm," said Gristhorpe. "I don't see advancement within the Met as a problem. It's big enough, surely, to offer all the variety and specialization you need on the job these days?"

"Well, yes, I suppose so, it's just . . ."

"Yes?" Gristhorpe stared at him with those guileless blue eyes.

Banks felt himself wading deeper into the quicksand. "I fancy a change, that's all, sir. I heard about DCI Varley retiring and . . . well . . . I thought I'd give it a go. A change is as good as a rest."

"So you need a rest? A holiday?"

"No, sir. I was speaking metaphorically."

"Ah, I see. That's admirable," said Gristhorpe. "Of course, you know it's not up to me, don't you?"

"Well, yes, sir, but I rather thought . . ."

"Yes?"

"Well, as it'd be you I'd be working for directly . . ."

"That with us being such a small and insignificant outpost, I could put a word in, and the chief constable would just rubber-stamp it?"

"No. No, sir, I didn't mean that at all."

"Then what did you mean? Why are you here?"

Banks put his cup and saucer down. "I told you, sir. I fancy a move and a promotion. I thought I was here for an informal job interview," he said, starting to stand up, "but I—"

"Oh, do sit down," said Gristhorpe, waving his hand impatiently.

Banks saw the ghost of a smile on his face and sat down. "Sir."

Gristhorpe leaned back in his chair, which seemed dangerously close to falling over, linked his hands behind his head and contemplated Banks, brows furrowed. "Let me tell you what I think, Alan, if I may call you that?"

"Of course."

"I don't get the impression, either from reading your personnel files or from meeting you in person, that you are an especially ambitious person. You're an old-style copper, and you probably always will be. That's why a move to a rural backwater like this for the sake of moving up one grade, from DI to DCI, doesn't make a lot of sense to me. I think what we've really got here is a case of burnout. Or near burnout. Look at yourself, man. You're chain-smoking, your fingernails are bitten to the quicks, you've got bags under your eyes big enough to pack for a six-week holiday, and I'd bet a pound to a penny you've got a drink problem, too. I think you're after a spot of gardening leave, but you don't want it to read that way on your service record. Am I close?"

"Not at . . ." Banks started to answer but tailed off, noticing Gristhorpe's expression. There was no point trying to bullshit this man, he realized. He might as well leave right now. But something about the place, the view, the birdsong, the useless drystone wall, and about Gristhorpe himself, kept him sitting where he was. There were other reasons he wanted this change. Yes, a lot of what Gristhorpe had said was true, but he hadn't known until he had driven up north just how much he wanted to get away from what his life had become in London.

"Well? Cat got your tongue?"

Banks lit another cigarette, self-conscious that he was doing so. "You're right in a way. It would be hard to deny that I've come to a sort of turning point and I need to make some serious choices. But this is one of them. I can do the job down there. I could stay and carry on just as I am now. Maybe in six months or a year I'd crack up, run off and join a private security firm, whatever, or maybe not, maybe it would just pass. But I don't think I'd realized until a few days ago, and especially not until today, just how much I want the change."

"Why? We must lead pretty boring lives up here compared to those action-packed days you blokes have in London."

"I don't know about that, sir," said Banks.

"And if it's gardening leave you want, or a desk job—"

"No," Banks protested. "I want to do my job. I'm a detective. A good detective. That's what I want to do. I want to work cases. I don't want to just sit behind a desk."

"You can do that down in London, just as you are doing now."

"I know. But it . . ."

"We don't get a lot of murders up here, but we do get the occasional missing sheep or post office robbery. A lot of your work would probably be routine."

"It already is," said Banks. "But as long as I can get out on the streets . . ."

"Country lanes. No mean streets here." Gristhorpe smiled. "Well, maybe one or two in Eastvale."

"Right. As long as I could get out, get among people, try to sort out the villains from the rest, follow leads . . ."

"You'd be at a bit of a disadvantage, being a Londoner."

"I'm from Peterborough."

"Same difference up here."

"People are people everywhere."

"Aye, they are that, all right. But they're a rum lot around these parts."

"I can do the job. I *want* to do the job."

Gristhorpe held his gaze and Banks sensed his own resolve strengthening for the first time since he had considered moving, becoming real, solidifying into a need to come here, to prove himself to this insufferable, all-seeing, inscrutable detective superintendent sitting placidly in the chair opposite him as if butter wouldn't melt in his mouth.

"Aye," said Gristhorpe. "Mebbe you do. Got time for a walk?"

"Sir, you'd better come quick. There's been another one. There's a car waiting outside."

Banks had only been back from Yorkshire for three days when Albright came over to his hutch at two o'clock on Wednesday afternoon. It had just stopped raining and the traffic was still a nightmare. Banks sweated even with the window open as he sat in the back and smoked, getting the scant details from Albright as the car crawled up Regent Street: a woman's body found in a flat off Charlotte Street by a cleaner. Scene secured.

At least his hangover wasn't too bad, he thought, as they went outside and got into the waiting car. After another evening in the clubs following leads in the Pamela Morrison case that twisted into thin air and disappeared like smoke, he had rung Linda and, getting no reply, had gone to Ronnie Scott's alone, sat at the bar and sipped a double Scotch while he listened to the last set by an up-and-coming American jazz singer he'd never heard of. He liked the intimacy and warmth of Ronnie Scott's, the small stage surrounded on three sides by tables, the soft lighting, plumes of smoke, a long bar stretching across the back. The singer was good, a slightly husky voice, expressive phrasing and a good range. She also sang some of his favorites: "Fine and Mellow," "Summertime," "I'll Look Around," and a version of "The Other Woman" that sent shivers up his spine.

At Oxford Circus, the driver went straight on, toward Broadcasting House, but turned right on Mortimer Street. They finally arrived at the flat, one of six in a narrow three-story building, signed in with the officer guarding the door and went inside, careful to follow the route mapped out by the SOCOs, who had got there just before them, along with DCI Roland Verity.

The actual crime scene was in the bedroom, but police tape had also been fixed across the door to the flat and across the front and back doors of the building itself, sealing off the whole place. For the moment, nobody but the SOCOs and the photographer, Harry Beckett, were allowed in the bedroom. A young police surgeon also stood in the living room looking pale, as if this were his first dead body. He told them that he had certified death, most likely caused by asphyxiation, and taken the body temperature, which indicated that she had died between midnight and three in the morning. The rest would be up to Dr. O'Grady, who was otherwise occupied in performing a postmortem, but would take over when the body reached the mortuary. It was the property of the coroner now, and when the various experts had finished, he would give the order to take it away.

Banks sent Albright to talk to the other tenants in the building, if any of them were home, and find out what he could about the victim's comings and goings, and especially if anyone had noticed anything between midnight and three in the morning. Then he turned to Verity.

"Roly," he said. "What brings you out here?"

"I was on a call across the street," Verity said, "and I saw all the activity. Copper's curiosity."

The SOCOs were as territorial as usual about the crime scene and all Banks and Verity were allowed to do was stand at the bedroom door behind the tape and watch them at work. Banks cursed under his breath. Though he wasn't supposed to do it, he always enjoyed a quick look at the scene, alone if possible, or at least without the officious presence of the technical support experts. Still, you couldn't fault them on their work. There wasn't much they missed.

The flat itself was certainly bigger and better appointed than the one where Pamela Morrison had been found, and Banks guessed that the victim probably lived here. It was nicely furnished with a leather-upholstered three-piece suite, drinks cabinet, glass-topped coffee table and sheepskin rug in front of the fake fireplace. She had an expensive TV and stereo system, a collection of pop LPs—Culture Club, Style Council, Duran Duran and Depeche Mode, among others—alongside some late-night romantic jazz—Sarah Vaughan, Frank Sinatra, Tony Bennett. A call girl, perhaps? Certainly a step up from Pamela Morrison and her tiny room off Old Compton Street.

Whatever the case, she lay there very much as Pamela had, and just as young, covered by a white sheet up to her neck, hands together in an attitude of prayer over her chest, pale face and dark hair, no makeup, her eyes staring up sightlessly at the ceiling. Beside her was a crumpled pillow smeared with black and red marks. Banks was also willing to bet that under her clothes they would find her pubic hair shaved and a strip of Sellotape between her legs. But that was for Dr. O'Grady to discover later.

Banks wandered around the living room and opened the door to the bathroom. It was spacious, sparkling clean, with gold-plated taps and pink porcelain. The bath was big enough for two and was surrounded by colored candles in heavy cut-glass holders. Banks sniffed at one of them. Musk.

In the washstand lay a damp facecloth. Banks didn't touch it, but he could see that it was smeared with mascara and lipstick. A woman's disposable razor sat beside the tap, hairs curling from under its blade. He went back out and mentioned it to one of the SOCOs, who responded immediately by taping the bathroom out of bounds, too.

"It'd probably be pretty quiet around here between midnight and three on a Wednesday, wouldn't it?" Banks asked Verity. "With all the pubs and restaurants closed."

"There's a few clubs," said Verity. "And University College isn't far away. Students seem to be up at all hours."

"We'll canvass the area, as usual. It's amazing how nobody sees anything."

"They don't want to get involved," Verity said. "Happens all the time in Vice. People don't even want to be remotely connected with anything that smells of Soho gangsters and kinky sex, let alone a loony bloody murderer on the loose. Can't say I blame them."

"Doesn't help us much, though, does it?" said Banks. He nodded toward the bed. "Know her?"

Verity bristled. "What do you think I am, a fucking john?"

"No, Roly, you're a Vice Squad cop. It's your job to know what's going on, put names to faces."

"I'll ask around."

"Do we know her name?" Banks asked the room at large.

One of the SOCOs heard him and came over with an envelope in a plastic bag. "Maureen Heseltine, according to this," he said, then produced another bag. It held a book of matches from the Bunch of Grapes Club, showing a large-breasted woman holding a bunch of plump, ripe purple grapes, her tongue out, as if to lick them suggestively. Banks hadn't heard of the place. "There was also a drawer full of condoms, all shapes, flavors and sizes. Ribbed and plain. Lager and lime and curry seemed to be her favorite flavors. French ticklers, too. And sex aids. Butt plugs, cock rings, dildos, handcuffs, vibrators. And you should see some of the outfits in her wardrobe. Leather, studs, satin, silk."

"You know your sex aids," Banks said.

"Comes with the territory." The SOCO grinned and walked back to join the others.

"Bunch of Grapes," said Banks to Verity. "Know it?"

"I know it. It's pretty new. We're still keeping an eye on it. Could go either way."

"Looks like it's already gone one way to me."

"That book of matches might have nothing to do with what happened here. It could have been lying around for weeks."

"It was beside the ashtray," the SOCO said over his shoulder from the bedroom. "And there are fresh tab ends."

"Even so," said Verity.

"Any connection with Micallef?" Banks asked him. "The Bunch of Grapes?"

"He's been known to drop in on occasion. But he drops in at lots of places. How do we know for sure she's a working girl?"

"We don't," said Banks. "And maybe she isn't. Maybe she's just not fussy about where she picks up her men, or her matches. Or maybe the bloke she brought back here gave her them. But I'd say there's a good chance she is. Either way, there's a connection. Dead girl made up to look like a virgin. Bunch of Grapes Club. Matthew Micallef. It merits another chat, at any rate."

"Christ," said Verity. "Surely you can't think Micallef's behind this?"

"I don't think anything yet, but he is connected. And I'm damn sure he knows a lot more than he's saying."

"We're done here, lads," said the head SOCO. "You can go in now."

"Maureen Lillian Heseltine from Oldham, Lancashire," said Banks to Jackie Simmons in the back room of the Dog and Duck, a small, narrow, Victorian-style pub at the corner of Frith and Bateman streets. "Do you know her?"

It was six o'clock, and Jackie had said on the telephone that she had to head into the West End to work, so they had picked somewhere on her way. The usual crowd milled around the bar, or outside, drinking, smoking and sharing jokes about their day at the office. The sky was still overcast and the humidity lingered. Banks's shirt clung to his skin.

"What? Just because we're all whores from up north you think we know one another?" said Jackie.

"I'm trying to find connections," Banks said, sipping his Timothy Taylor's Landlord. The pub was all dark panels and smoked glass, most of the tables occupied by noisy groups. Nobody paid any attention to Banks and Jackie in their intimate corner at the back.

"Sorry. I didn't know her." Jackie swept a long tress of hair back and stuck it behind her ear. She had tiny, pink ears, Banks noticed, delicate, the skin translucent where the light shone through. She had applied some makeup, but it didn't quite cover the smattering of freckles, or the darkening bruise beside her left eye.

"Who did that?" Banks asked. "The club owners used to fine girls for coming to work with bruises."

She put her hand to her cheek self-consciously. "Walked into a door."

"What was this door called?"

Jackie shook her head. Banks could swear her eyes filled with tears, but they were gone as soon as they came, reabsorbed into the sponge of flesh. "An unsatisfied customer," she whispered.

"I can't imagine you having any of those."

Jackie regained her composure, tilted her head to one side and almost smiled at him. "Are you flirting with me?"

Banks flushed. "No . . . I . . ."

Then Jackie laughed and patted his arm. "That's sweet of you to say, very *gallant* of you to defend a lady's honor like that, but you don't really know, do you?"

"Have you thought any more about what we talked about last time? Odd clients. Violent. Disturbed. A little crazy?"

Jackie pointed to her eye. "Like the door that did this?"

"Yes."

"He's a nonstarter, in more ways than one. But I did think about it."

"And?"

Jackie frowned. "Well, as I said before, you get a lot of weird people in this business. You expect it, learn to deal with them. And some of them are weird in a nice way."

"Like what?"

"Oh, they fall in love with you, want to marry you, take you home to meet mother. Take you on a cruise around the world. You name it. But the point is, they're harmless."

"Not the man who killed Pamela and Maureen."

"OK, no, I get your point. All I'm saying is just because a john's weird it doesn't mean he's likely to be violent. You have to go a lot on instinct in this business, on gut feelings."

"It didn't do Pamela or Maureen much good, did it?"

"They probably realized too late."

"Is there anyone—"

Jackie held her hand up. "Please, let me finish." She lit a cigarette and swigged some lager from the bottle. "You have to develop a sort of built-in radar if you're to survive." Then she smiled and touched her cheek. "And even that doesn't always work. But this was normal. I don't expect you to understand, let alone accept, but it's an occupational hazard."

"As is murder?"

"Not quite. I know it seems the air's full of it right now, but it's really very rare, even in our business. So my radar's tuned in such a way that if I feel a shiver up my spine, if my breath catches in my throat, if I just feel for no obvious reason that I have to get away, get as far away from a john as possible, money or no money, then I follow that instinct."

"And has this happened recently?"

"It was a few weeks ago. Long enough before Pam's death that I'd put it out of my mind. You have to move on, don't you? But when you asked me to think back, and when I found myself dwelling on what had happened to Pam, well . . ."

"You remembered."

"Yes. There was a bloke. Ordinary bloke. Perhaps a cut above the average. A gent, you might say. Nice tailored suit. None of your off-the-rack trash for him. Handmade leather shoes. Posh accent. Polite. Gentle, even. Anyway, to cut a long story short, afterward he just didn't want to leave. He was talking about innocence and stuff, telling me I should stop being a whore and become innocent again, that he could help me. I told him it was probably a bit late for that, but he wasn't having any of it. He said it's never too late. He could show me. Perhaps I'd like to see him again and he would show me how my innocence could be restored. That's the word he used. *Restored*. Well, you get a pretty high creep factor in this job, but quite honestly this bloke was freaking me out. It wasn't anything he did, or even what he said—as I told you before, I meet plenty of johns who want to save me and reform me—but it was something about the *way* he spoke, the soft, insistent voice. Have you seen that film about Reginald Christie?"

"Ten Rillington Place?" said Banks. "Yes. Ages ago."

"It was like that. His voice. The way Richard Attenborough says, 'Just a little gas,' as if it's the nicest, most natural thing in the world. It was his icy calm and that one track way he just wouldn't let go that started giving me the signals. Innocence. Purity. Virginity. As if they were holy mantras or something. Anyway, we'd finished our business—"

"Was that—"

"He didn't have any problems, no. Except he didn't want to use a condom. I insisted and he didn't like it, but I gave him no choice. He wasn't violent or forceful in any way."

"Pamela—"

"Pamela was a fool. Just because she was on the pill. I'm sorry if that sounds a bit harsh, but . . . It's not as if it's only the clap you have to worry about these days, is it? You hear about that new one, AIDS, and it doesn't sound as if there's a cure."

"How did he react when you contradicted him?"

"That's just the thing," Jackie said. "He never got angry. He would just . . . he had this sort of faraway smile . . . and his manner would get even milder. He would chastise me like you'd tick off a wayward child, but gently, out of a desire for correction, not anger. I think that was what set off my warning bells in the end. That he just didn't get angry."

"What happened?"

"Nothing. I'm still here, aren't I? In the end, he left. I'd agreed to see him again just to get rid of him, but I had no intention of ever being alone in a room with him again."

"Did you see him again after that?"

"Once or twice. Around the clubs. But he left me alone."

"Did you see him go with any of the other girls?"

"No. But I wasn't watching."

"Pamela?"

"I never saw them together."

Banks leaned back in his chair and lit a cigarette. "Another drink?"

"Sure," said Jackie. "But will you be much longer? I have to go soon."

"As long as it takes you to have one more drink." Banks made his way to the bar and picked up another lager and a pint. He noticed it was raining outside now and most of the people had come in.

When he got back to the table, he asked Jackie to describe the man. About medium height, she told him, not much hair, and what there was, fuzzy around the ears and sides, was silvery. He was perhaps a little overweight, a bit of belly, and she would put his age at around fifty, maybe a little older.

"Distinguishing features?"

"Yeah, he was hung like a horse."

Banks gaped at her.

"Only joking. No, none. I don't even know if a horse is hung or not."

"Do you know his name?"

"No. He never told me, and if he had I wouldn't have believed him. They all lie."

"How did you meet him?" Banks asked finally.

"I didn't. I mean, not before, you know, in the room."

"So what made him choose you? Was it just blind chance?"

"It's rarely that. Unless that's what the john wants."

"Then what?"

Jackie examined the dregs of her bottle, stubbed out a cigarette and finished off the lager. Her eyes darted around the pub before she leaned slightly forward and looked Banks in the eye. "He's a business colleague of Matthew's," she said finally. "He saw me dance and wanted to meet me. Matthew said to be nice to him."

"Mr. Micallef," said Banks. "Good afternoon."

Micallef swiveled in his chair. "It's you again. Inspector Banks, isn't it? Nice to see you. And your sergeant, too. That'll be all, Benny. You can leave us alone now. What can I do for you this time, gentlemen?"

They weren't in the Chinese restaurant, but in Micallef's office above a music shop on Denmark Street. The building was old, but the second floor had clearly been gutted and refurbished. One of those new Macintosh computers sat on Micallef's desk. Banks had read about them in a Sunday supplement but didn't know what he would do with one if he had one. He supposed it was useful for running a business. He could see Albright's eyes practically bulging out of their sockets at the sight of it. On the wall were framed, signed photographs of Micallef with a showbiz personality, Micallef with minor royalty, Micallef with a championship heavyweight boxer, and Micallef with a lot of people Banks didn't recognize.

"The wall of infamy?" he said.

Micallef laughed. "I'd hardly say that, Inspector. Some of those people are pillars of the establishment."

"I've often thought the establishment was built on very shaky ground."

"Well, that's very interesting, and it would make a fascinating argument sometime, but I'm a busy man. What do you want? Do I need my solicitor?"

"Not unless you're going to confess to murder, sir," said Albright.

"Very funny, Sergeant. That's definitely not in the cards."

"Just another friendly chat," said Banks.

"About?"

"Maureen Heseltine."

Micallef feigned a frown. "I'm afraid I don't recognize the name."

"Well, it's a strange coincidence," Banks said, "but her body was found in yet another building you own just off Charlotte Street."

"I own several buildings. I don't know my tenants personally."

"Nor would I expect you to know the name of every girl who works for you," said Banks. "But it's getting to be a bit of a habit, isn't it? Girls getting murdered in your buildings. Perhaps one may be seen as simple bad luck, but two . . . ?"

"What happens in my buildings isn't my problem."

Banks reached for his briefcase, pulled out a photograph and dropped it on the desk in front of Micallef. "Maureen Heseltine. Perhaps this might serve as an *aide memoire*."

Micallef glanced at the photograph. It showed Maureen when she was alive and smiling. "She does look rather familiar," he said. "A dancer, you say?"

"I didn't say, but I do believe she tripped the light fantastic from time to time, between entertaining men in the flat she rented from you."

"Then it's possible I came across her in a business capacity," said Micallef. "You know I have an interest in several local clubs as a property owner. But I certainly don't recognize her."

"Where were you yesterday?"

"I've been out of town," said Micallef. "Just got back this morning. I had some business in Paris."

"How long were you away?"

"Three days. Why? Does that give me an alibi?"

"If it can be verified."

"Oh, it can. Besides, I don't believe you would see me as a suspect anyway, given the kind of accusations you bandy about. If I'm what you say I am—which I very strenuously deny—then I'd hardy be likely to kill my own girls and Sellotape their cunts shut, would I?"

The expression had a familiar ring to it, thought Banks. Hadn't Roly Verity used exactly the same words just a few days ago? Still, it was part of Verity's job to hobnob with villains like Micallef, and a man like Roly Verity would probably be so proud of coining such a phrase that he would be bound to go around repeating it to all and sundry. "Nobody's accusing you of anything of the kind," said Banks. "We all know exactly what you are and what you do, so why don't we just cut the crap and you answer some questions?"

Micallef looked at Banks through narrowed eyes and made a steeple of his fingers, then he glanced at Albright. "Is he always like this?"

"Almost always when a young girl gets murdered, sir," Albright replied.

Banks dropped another picture on the desk in front of Micallef, this one a photofit re-creation of the man Jackie Simmons had described. "Recognize this man?"

"I don't know him," said Micallef.

"Well dressed, posh, not short of a bob or two."

"Still don't know him."

"Mr. Micallef," Banks said slowly. "We believe that this man indicated an interest in one or more of your girls, and that you set him up with dates. We're trying to find him in connection with two murders. Right now, he's about the only lead we've got. If you can help us at all, then I think you should seriously consider doing so."

"I'm sorry I can't help you. I would if I could. But I don't have any girls, as you put it. I don't even know what you could possibly mean by that. And I don't recognize this man. Maybe it's just a poor likeness, or maybe your witness was mistaken? I'm sorry. I wish I could help. Is there anything more?"

"I don't think so," said Banks, putting away the photos. "Not for the moment."

"Another whiskey?" Linda asked.

"Please," said Banks. It was late. He had spent the evening with

Albright and Roly Verity going around the clubs and bars showing the photokit to dancers, doormen, bouncers and managers. If anybody did know who the mystery man was, they were saying nothing. One or two thought they had "seen him around," but that meant nothing. They could say that about Banks, too. Nobody admitted to seeing him with Micallef or with either of the murdered girls, and that was a problem. Even if Banks could identify the man, he still needed a witness to tie him to Pamela and Maureen.

There was one weak link, a frightened hostess at the Cat & Mouse. She knew something, Banks was certain; she had either had an experience with the man, like Jackie, or she had seen him with Pamela or Maureen. She wasn't talking, but Banks thought a little more pressure, even if he felt like a bully exerting it, might loosen the floodgates.

Linda came back with the whiskies and sat on the bed beside him. "It's getting to you, this one, isn't it?" she said.

"How did you guess?"

"You're distracted."

"How we can let someone like Micallef go about doing the things he does when we *know* exactly what he is and who he preys on?"

"It's always been like that," Linda said. "You know as well as I do. It's the devil you know. That's the way Vice likes to think of it. With Micallef in place, they know what's going on. He feeds them scraps and gets to operate without interference. All to Micallef's advantage, of course, but to ours, too."

"You scratch my back . . . ?"

"Exactly. And if we took him down, we'd create a vacuum, and God knows what would get sucked into that. You can be sure there'd be a turf war, bloodshed, mayhem. Just like the old days."

Banks lit a cigarette. "You're right, of course. We've all heard stories about the old days. Jack Spot, Billy Hill, the Sabinis, the Messinas. Nobody wants those days back again. I think maybe if I could just get to the bottom of these murders I'd be satisfied, but I'm going nowhere fast. I don't think Micallef's the killer, but I'm damn sure he's got a good idea who is. Either he's protecting someone, or it's someone he hired in the first place. Maybe there was a reason he wanted these girls dead?"

"From what you've told me," Linda said "it sounds more like someone with serious psychological problems."

"It could just be made to appear that way, a nut job?"

"Could be, I suppose, but that's not the way it sounds to me. What about forensics?"

"Slow," said Banks. "We've got a print from the Sellotape at both scenes, and it matches, so we know we're dealing with the same killer. We just don't have it on file. And he shaved this one himself. Used her own disposable razor."

"Patience, Alan. Patience." She refilled his glass. "In the meantime, tell me all about Yorkshire. Is it really as primitive as they say it is? Do they all have orange teeth up there? Will I be losing you soon?"

Banks touched her cheek with his palm. He knew he had to leave her. Not just because he felt so guilty every time he left her flat, but because . . . well, it just wasn't fair to carry on. Not fair to Linda. Not fair to Sandra. Not fair to the kids. Not fair even to himself. But it was hard. She had become a big part of his life this past while, the long hours, the seediness, the sadness, the clubs, the late nights, the alienation from his family. Sometimes he thought she was the only thing that kept him sane. He put his glass down and reached for her. "Not yet," he said. "Not for a while yet."

Banks didn't like being driven through the London streets without any clue as to where he was going or what he was to expect when he got there. At least he knew where he was as the driver went past Marble Arch on to Bayswater Road. Not that that helped him a lot. It was one of the better days of the week, and Hyde Park and Kensington gardens were busy with people flying kites, throwing sticks for their dogs, sailing model boats on the Serpentine, or just lying on the grass reading in the sun, lovers touching and kissing. Ordinary things. Why did Banks always feel there was an invisible screen between himself and these ordinary things of life? It was another world, slightly blurred, and he couldn't get into it no matter how loud he hammered at the glass. Nobody heard. He was outside. Nobody inside paid him any attention. He'd had dreams like that and woke up in the early hours sweating, heart pounding.

The car continued on as Bayswater Road became Notting Hill Gate, then Holland Park Avenue. Finally, it turned down a broad, tree-lined street of elegant Victorian houses, and into a narrow mews, where the old coach houses and stables had been converted into small homes, most of them with whitewashed exteriors livened up by the occasional splash of bright color on a door, a garage or window frames. Some of the houses had hanging baskets or window boxes of red, yellow, purple and pink flowers.

The car came to a halt and Banks got out. The uniformed officer on guard opened the door and a familiar figure beckoned Banks inside. It was Superintendent Hatchard, pipe firmly clamped between his teeth, but not lit. When Banks's eyes had adjusted to the dim light in the neat, tiny living room, he saw there was someone else present.

"I'd like you to meet someone, Alan," Hatchard said, after removing his pipe. "This is Detective Superintendent Burgess. He's Special Branch. Or something like that." It was clear to Banks that Hatchard didn't approve of whatever Burgess stood for, but that his hands were tied in the matter: he was only obeying orders. As for Burgess, he didn't seem overly concerned with such delicacies. He wore a leather jacket over his open-neck checked shirt, despite the heat, blue denim jeans and white trainers. He was about six feet tall, in good shape, handsome, in a macho sort of way, with a strong jaw, slightly crooked teeth and cynical gray eyes. He can't have been much older than Banks, but his hair was touched with gray at the temples.

"Banksy, pleased to meet you," he said, as if they were old friends, sticking out his hand.

Banks shook. He was sure he had seen Burgess before and was trying to place him when the man himself did it for him. "About two or three years ago. Recent Falklands veteran, bit of a war hero, got himself into a scrape at a nightclub."

"Beat up one of the girls and stabbed a doorman, you mean?"

"That's the one. Can't have our heroes looking like villains in the national press, can we? Especially when they're shell-shocked."

"So you're the one they send around when they need a cover-up?"

Burgess laughed. "Very good. Very astute of you." He put his hand on Banks's elbow. "Come with me. I've got something to show you. Soon as that's done we'll get the team in and head down the road for a nice drink, just you and me."

Curious, Banks followed him up the stairs, along a corridor and through the door into the bathroom. It was just about big enough to hold the two of them.

It was obvious to Banks the moment he crossed the threshold that something was terribly wrong. The blood spatter on the cream tiles certainly wasn't part of the decor, and there was a cloying smell, as if something sweet had been marinating for too long. Before Banks even saw the corpse in the bathtub, he knew what he was in for.

Burgess just stood there as Banks took in the scene: the balding man with silvery wisps of hair around his ears, a deep gash visible in the wrist that rested on the side of the bathtub, the murky red-brown water up to his neck, the empty bottle of pills beside the almost empty bottle of whiskey on the floor.

"The doc's been, confirmed death, and the photographer's finished. We're still waiting on the SOCOs, so don't touch anything. His cleaning lady found him like this two hours ago."

"Who is he?" Banks asked.

"The Right Honorable Norman Stafford, MP," said Burgess. "This man's a member of HM Government, Banksy. Was. Not one of the high-profile crowd, the ones you see on the telly, but a backroom boy. A hard worker, tireless supporter of his constituents, aggressive committee man, nonetheless. Nobody's heard of him, nobody would recognize him in the street, but they also serve . . ."

"Suicide?"

"Oh, yes, I would say so, wouldn't you?"

Banks shrugged. "These things can be arranged."

"Cynic. Follow me. There's more. Had enough? Ready to move on?"

"I'm ready," said Banks. He followed Burgess back into the corridor and they crossed over to the master bedroom.

"He wasn't married, Mr. Stafford," said Burgess. "Not anymore. Married to his job, you might say. This is where he slept."

Banks gazed around the room. There were framed prints and photographs everywhere, each and every one of them showing the pure, the innocent and the virginal. Joan of Arc. The Virgin Mary. Saint Bernadette of Lourdes. Saint Margaret of Antioch. There were actresses playing parts—the young Nastasia Kinsky in *Tess* and Brooke Shields in *Pretty Baby*—and countless unrecognizable photos of young innocent girls clipped from magazines and newspapers, their pure, trusting eyes burning into him, making him squirm.

On the bedspread lay a handwritten sheet of paper.

"Read it, Banksy," said Burgess. "Read but don't touch."

Banks read. " '*To Whom It May Concern, I, Norman Archibald Stafford, wish to confess to the murders of two young girls in Soho. So there may be no mistake and no doubt as to the sincerity of this confession, I will outline in exact detail what I did and how I did it.*' " And he did. The ritual washing, the shaving of the second victim, the Sellotape, the posing. All the elements that only the killer could know. The only thing he didn't explain was why. The closest he got was the mention of the first time he felt the strong urge to kill to preserve the innocence of a young woman. He had no Sellotape, he wrote, and imagined there would be none in the small room, so he hatched the plan to equip himself and come back later. Somehow or other, the same girl knew to avoid him, so he chose someone else. Banks realized that the girl was Jackie Simmons, and that Stafford's next choice was Pamela Morrison.

So it was over. No need to push the frightened dancer any further or make Jackie Simmons go over her story again. Or was it?

"I'd say he had a bit of an obsession, wouldn't you, Banksy?"

"Seems that way."

"Word has it that he was married once. They had a beautiful daughter. Age-old story. She fell in with a bad lot. Drugs. Sex. Crime. Ended up a prostitute in Glasgow and died of a drug overdose. It doesn't explain it all, but it gives you a context, I think."

"He wanted to re-create innocence, virginity in his victims."

"Even after he'd had sex with them," added Burgess. "I've read the case file. Aren't people just endlessly fascinating? And mostly unknowable? Anyway, none of that really matters," he went on as they walked back downstairs. "Bit of an anticlimax, really, isn't it?"

Hatchard was still waiting in the living room, staring into space, having obviously seen it all before Banks had. "Well?" he said.

Burgess put his arm around Banks's shoulders. "Let's me and DI

Banks here go for a nice drink, get the taste of death out of our mouths and see if we can work out a satisfactory solution to this little mess. Bernard, I take it you know what to do now?"

"I know." Hatchard gave Banks a sheepish look, stuck his pipe back in his mouth and slunk out of the door.

Burgess hammered on the locked door of the pub on the corner.

"I told you, they're closed," said Banks. "Won't be open for another hour or more."

Burgess ignored him and kept on knocking. Eventually, a young man appeared behind the glass, scowled and pointed at his watch. Burgess thrust his warrant card in his face. The door opened.

"Important police business, sonny," Burgess said. He pointed to a corner that couldn't be seen from the street. "We'll sit over there. And I'll have a pint of lager. Banksy?"

"Bitter, please."

"Got that?"

The boy nodded, mouth open.

"Can't drink that real ale stuff, myself," Burgess said, putting his hand to his stomach. "Gives me gas." He shouted after the boy. "And bring us a packet of salt and vinegar crisps and some pork scratchings!"

They settled in the corner with their drinks and snacks, Burgess smacked his lips and took a long swig of ice-cold lager. "Ah, aren't we just living in wonderful times, Banksy?" he said. "Can't you smell the change?"

"All I can smell is last night's stale cigarette smoke," said Banks, lighting up.

Burgess took out a Tom Thumb cigar and lit it. "You've no imagination, that's your problem," he said, thrusting the cigar in Banks's general direction. "It's all there. There for the taking. And don't think I was born with a silver spoon in my mouth, either. I came up the hard way. My old man was a barrow boy. I've got no time for all these whiners and moaners. If you can't do well for yourself in this day and age, then you're well and truly fucked. Great times to be alive, Banksy."

"Bollocks," said Banks. "We're midway through the eighties. All we've had so far are race riots, a pointless war and a long miners' strike. Even the music's crap."

"It's all a matter of perspective. You're just not looking at it the right way. We won the race riots, we won the war and we won the fucking miners' strike. *That's* the way to look at it! And what's wrong with Madonna, apart from those hairy armpits?" He gestured over to the boy, who was hovering nervously by the bar. "Another two of these," he said, raising his glass. "And put some Madonna on the jukebox."

Oh, God, not again, thought Banks, when "Into the Groove" started up. "Let's agree to differ," he said. "Why have you brought me here? Not that it isn't a pleasure to drink fine ale and argue politics on a summer afternoon. With a body lying in a bath of blood round the corner."

Burgess tilted his head and narrowed his eyes. "You have a way of putting things, Banksy," he said, "that could put a bloke right off his stroke."

"Norman Stafford, MP," Banks reminded him. The barman scurried over with two more pints and apologized for spilling a drop of Burgess's lager.

"It's all right, son," Burgess said. "You can make it up next time. And . . ." He gestured to the boy to lean in and lowered his voice, "we're depending on you to keep an eye open. Nobody gets in until we've finished here, right? Hush, hush."

The boy returned to the bar like a man with a mission.

"It'll give him something to talk to his mates about," Burgess said with a wink. "Now, where were we?"

"Stafford."

"Ah, yes." He tapped a length of ash from his Tom Thumb.

"You believe it's suicide?"

"I do," said Burgess. "And the police surgeon agreed, too. I'm sure the forensic evidence will confirm it."

"So there *is* to be an investigation?"

"Of course. Where do you think we are? Russia?"

"Only I got the impression there were certain things you wanted to hush up."

Burgess rubbed the side of his nose. "As I said, Stafford wasn't a major player. Mostly he worked behind the scenes. Committees. Planning. That sort of thing. Very important job these days, nonetheless, what with all the new developments in and around the city. But he was an MP and I think even you would agree that the last thing we need right now are headlines in the papers screaming, 'Tory MP in Soho sex murder scandal!' or something along those lines. Especially in the aftermath of all the bad press the government's been getting over the miners' strike."

"So what do you propose?"

"A simple solution. Your case goes down as solved. You know who did it. I know who did it. The public at large just knows that a minor MP has committed suicide. Been suffering depression on and off for years, ever since his daughter died and his wife left him. That sort of thing. Get him a lot of sympathy. Apparently it wasn't his first suicide attempt, you know."

"Only his first successful one. But how will the public know the case is solved? How do the girls know to stop worrying? How do they know justice has been done?"

"Interesting concerns," mused Burgess. "I'm not saying I'd voice them myself, but interesting."

"And?"

"Well, strictly speaking, you won't have a name to name. That's a given. But it won't be the first time, will it? Remember when everyone thought Freddie Mills killed himself because he was Jack the Stripper, the bloke who killed all those prossies in the midsixties?"

"A bit before my time," said Banks.

"Mine, too. But don't you know your history? The point is, officially he didn't leave a note, but there's a myth around the Met that he did, and that he confessed to the killings."

"That doesn't help us, though, does it? Not if you're going to whitewash Norman Stafford."

"Oh, don't be so awkward. As I said, you won't have a convenient name to tie a hidden confession to, but don't underestimate the powers of rumor, Banksy. Word of mouth. Especially around Soho. All it takes is for word to get out from someone in the know that we were on to chummie and he fled to the continent, where he committed suicide, or got shot by the Froggy police or whatever. People love conspiracy theories. It wouldn't be five minutes before everyone in the Soho porn trade breathed easy and felt all self-righteous again."

"That's preposterous," said Banks. "We've got our killer—if the note can be proven to be authentic. Why not go public with it?"

"Haven't you been listening to a word I've said?" Burgess gritted his teeth in anger. "Come on, Banksy, I'm giving you a chance here. You can claim hush-up as long as no names are named. You can use it to your advantage."

"Do you think people are so stupid that they won't link Stafford's suicide to your proposed cover-up?"

"Yes, I do. Who was it said nobody ever went broke underestimating the stupidity of the British public?"

"H. L. Mencken," said Banks. "And it was underestimating the *taste* of the *American* public."

"Smart-arse."

"So back to my original question. How are you going to do this?"

"I'm not, Banksy. You are. In fact, it's already done. Signed, sealed, stamped and delivered. This is just me being polite and treating you to a couple of drinks. As far as we're concerned, that's the Metropolitan Police, including your boss and his boss, all the way up to the assistant commissioner, and as far as the home secretary is concerned, too, it's a done deal. Norman Stafford committed suicide while the balance of his mind was disturbed due to depression, and he will be duly mourned. They're already printing off the results of the coroner's inquest. The nut job who murdered two prostitutes in Soho has disappeared overseas under hot pursuit, is believed dead, and can't be named for legal reasons. Never the twain shall meet. By the time you get back to your office, West End Central will be buzzing with the rumor." He finished his drink, stood up and loomed over the table. "And if I were you, Banksy, I'd have my end-of-case celebration tonight, just like normal, get pissed as a newt and forget all about it. Hell, I might even drop by for a pint, myself. I could do with a night on the town."

And with that, he was gone. Banks lit another cigarette and swirled the remains of his drink. It wasn't so bad, he supposed. There were worse things than a little misdirection. Plenty went on that the public didn't know about, and it wouldn't necessarily do them any good if they did. He balked at it in principle but, in his way, Burgess was right; it didn't matter. The important thing was that the killer was dead and the killings would stop. Justice had been served, even if it hadn't been *seen* to be served.

Banks liked to think himself a champion of the truth and justice, and it irked him that Norman Stafford's responsibility for the crimes wouldn't be made generally known for political reasons. Stafford had been a committee man, Burgess said—planning, developments—and Micallef, among other things, was a property developer, so perhaps that was how they had come into contact? What more natural but that Micallef might offer the man with the power a bit of female company, an escort, dancer or club hostess, for example, perhaps in the way of a bribe? And maybe that was exactly what had happened.

But who was to know of Stafford's sickness? Banks thought of the images in Stafford's bedroom, remembered what he had done to the girls—the ritual cleansing, the symbolism of the Sellotape—and he knew that it was because he was a deranged killer, not because he was out to ruin Micallef or had some sort of grudge against him. Stafford might have met Micallef through his committees, might have accepted a sweetener, but in the end it was his own perverse fantasies he had acted out.

But did Micallef know? Had he introduced Stafford to Pamela Morrison himself on the night she died? And the second girl, Maureen Heseltine? Banks doubted it. Micallef would try to distance himself as much from the pimping, once he had turned the girls, as much as he did from owning the knocking shops and flats where some of his girls lived. But had he suspected? Perhaps. The most likely scenario was that Stafford had noticed the girls and let Micallef know he was interested, just as Jackie had said. After that point Micallef would have arranged things without any direct contact. But it still made him guilty as sin in Banks's eyes. Especially if he had known after Pamela, the first one, and let it happen again.

Banks came out of his reverie and noticed the boy hovering. "Yes?"

"Are you done, sir?"

"What? Oh, yes," said Banks, stubbing out his cigarette.

"Only it's past opening time and there are people waiting at the door."

"Fine," said Banks. "Better let them in. I'll be off, then. Thank you for being so obliging."

"Er . . . who's going to pay, sir? For the drinks. Only the other man didn't leave anything."

Banks sighed and reached for his wallet.

Banks had told Sandra he would be late home, and she had made some sarcastic comment about that being nothing new. He hadn't replied because he hadn't wanted to start another row, but he had left the house in a thoroughly bad mood.

Now it was nearly two in the morning and the taxi was pulling up outside his flat. Banks was a little the worse for wear. Linda hadn't answered her phone, and the other revelers had disappeared, so he had gone on to a club with Ozzy Albright and Burgess, where they had drunk expensive Scotch and flirted with the scantily clad hostesses. Burgess had picked up the tab, or so Banks believed. That certainly made up for the afternoon.

He took his shoes off and tiptoed into the flat as quietly as he could, but the door creaked, and so did the floorboards. He paused in the hall to listen for anyone stirring but heard only soft snoring sounds from the main bedroom.

He went into the living room and headed for the drinks cabinet. Another Scotch would finish off the evening nicely. Laphroaig, this time. Once he had poured himself a generous measure and the merest splash of water to bring out the flavor, he flipped through his LP collection looking for something suitable. He didn't feel like jazz or classical, so he dug back into his rock collection. Finally, he picked Nick Drake's *Five Leaves Left,* put on his headphones, stumbled briefly over the footstool, then settled down on the sofa to "Time Has Told Me."

It had been a subdued celebration, Banks thought as he stretched out and lit a cigarette, balancing the ashtray on his chest, perhaps because there would be no public recognition that they had caught their killer. Still, it had been fun. Hatchard had stood a round and even Commander Bickley, normally known as having short arms and deep pockets, had treated the team. Albright had tried to chat up the barmaid, whom everyone except him knew happened to be a bloke. A drunken cop groupie had lifted her T-shirt and shown everyone her tits. One of the DCs had drunk too much too fast and disgraced himself by being sick on the table. Everyone had cheered, then his mate helped him to the toilet to get him cleaned up, ready to resume the celebrations. Someone had tossed a glass of wine in someone else's face.

All in all, a good time had been had by all before things got hazy at the nightclub. Even then, Banks vaguely remembered, Burgess had been all hail-fellow-well-met and turned out to have a cache of jokes neither Banks nor Albright had ever heard before.

"Time Has Told Me" segued into "River Man" and the next thing Banks knew he could hear the telephone ringing in the distance. He opened his eyes. His Laphroaig was half drunk on the table beside him, Nick Drake had finished ages ago, and his cigarette had gone out in the ashtray on his chest, smoldered down to a length of gray ash. Banks put it on the table beside his drink.

Struggling to his feet, he slipped off the headphones. The phone *was* ringing. As quickly as he could, he made it over to the stand and picked up the receiver.

"I was just going to hang up, sir," the voice said. "Sorry for waking you." It was the night dispatch officer at the station.

"What is it?" Banks mumbled. His tongue felt thick and furry, his mouth full of dead caterpillars.

"They want you down Soho, sir. Alley off Sutton Row, back of the Astoria."

"I know it," said Banks. "What is it?"

"Wouldn't say, sir. Only that it's urgent. There's a car on its way."

Banks had taken four Paracetamol, drunk two glasses of water, brushed his teeth and cleaned himself up as best he could in the ten or fifteen minutes it took the car to arrive. Luckily it was just after dawn and there wasn't much traffic about. Though he wasn't a particularly literary type, even in his hungover state he found himself thinking of the poem Wordsworth composed on Westminster Bridge when the car drove over Vauxhall Bridge. He had had to learn it by heart at school and still remembered it, even now. The city really was wearing the beauty of the morning "like a garment," the soft early light orange and blue on the slow-moving Thames, and the "ships, towers, domes, theatres and temples" catching a ray of sun here or hiding in a mantle of shadow there.

But the effect didn't last for long. Soon they were heading through Piccadilly Circus, where there was quite a bit more traffic, heading for Shaftesbury Avenue, Cambridge Circus and Charing Cross Road.

Sutton Row was blocked off at both the Soho Square end and at the Astoria theater, so Banks got out and walked down the narrow street. Just to his right, behind the Astoria, was an alley that turned left into a dead end. There, among the dumped rubbish, the overflowing dustbins, empty bottles, cigarette ends, soggy cardboard boxes and the smell of piss, lay a body. Pale faces turned to Banks as he approached, and he recognized Hatchard, tired but still sober; Albright, who lived nearer to the scene than Banks did and was definitely the worse for wear; and a couple of other team members, including the young DC who had been sick in the pub.

"Street cleaner found the body an hour or so ago, sir," said Albright. "I'm sorry, sir."

Banks looked down at the crumpled shape then fell to his knees beside it.

Jackie Simmons lay on her back, hands spread out at her sides, legs at crooked angles. She wore a knee-length plaid skirt and a pearl blouse, open at the collar. That was where Banks could see the dark, thick bruising across her throat. Her eyes were open, fixed on the sky but seeing nothing, and her skin was pale, dry and cool to the touch.

Someone had placed a broad strip of Sellotape across her mouth.

Banks turned his head to look up at the others, clustered around him. Their faces blurred, started to spin. He got to his feet feeling dizzy and staggered as far away from the body as he could before throwing up against the wall. He felt a comforting arm on his shoulder and saw Albright towering over him.

"You all right, sir?"

"I'll be fine," said Banks. "Just give me a minute." He took a few deep breaths and steadied himself against the wall. "Can anyone rustle up some coffee?" he called out.

Albright glanced at one of the DCs, who disappeared in the general direction of Oxford Street.

"Make it strong and black," Banks shouted after him.

The rest of the morning passed in a haze. There was paperwork to be done, files to be opened. Hatchard organized the incident room, called the meetings and handed out the actions. Even Roly Verity came by and pitched in. Banks did his bit, too. Hungover or not, he had helped get a murder investigation rolling so many times before that he could do it in his sleep. Except the circumstances were different every time. And it wasn't usually someone he knew.

Hatchard invited him into the inner sanctum at noon for an update, a pot of fresh coffee sitting on his desk, and a plate of chocolate digestives beside it.

"What have we got so far?" Hatchard asked.

"The police surgeon estimates time of death somewhere between midnight and three," Banks said. "Dr. O'Grady's tied up most of the day, but he'll get to the postmortem as soon as he can. Preliminary findings indicate death due to strangulation." He paused and glanced over at Hatchard. "It appears as if someone came up behind her and hooked his forearm around her throat."

"Was she killed where the body was found?"

"Seems that way, sir, according to lividity. We'll know more later."

"Any signs of defensive wounds?"

"She got in a few scratches, broke a fingernail or two. We bagged her hands."

"You knew her, didn't you?"

Banks paused and helped himself to coffee and another biscuit. "I wouldn't say I knew her, sir," he began. "I interviewed her informally on three occasions about the murder of Pamela Morrison. They were friends and flatmates. You can see the notes I wrote up in the case files."

"I've seen them. I know it's all aboveboard. There's obviously a connection with the other murders, given the Sellotape and all. What do you think it is? What did she tell you?"

"She didn't really know anything, sir, but she did help put me on to Stafford. I mean, she described a man she had taken to her room who had acted in a frightening way and gone on about regaining innocence and purity, about being able to restore it to her, though he didn't actually harm her in any way. She was able to give a decent physical description. I like to think it would have helped us catch him if things hadn't turned out differently."

Hatchard put a match to his pipe and a cloud of cloying blue smoke filled the air. Banks almost retched again, but he buried his face in his coffee instead. It helped. "You think this man was Stafford?" Hatchard asked.

"Yes, sir. I'm certain of it."

"But Stafford is dead. Why do you think the girl was murdered? It could hardly be to shut her up, as she'd already spoken, and besides, it no longer mattered."

"I think she was killed as an example, sir, a warning."

"A warning?"

"Yes. By Micallef."

"But—"

Banks held his hand up. "Please listen to me, sir. Micallef is in the property development business, among other things, and Stafford was chairman of an important government steering committee on development issues. I think that's how they met, and I think Micallef made his . . . er . . . other services available to Stafford."

"You think he knew? I mean, what Stafford was like?"

"No, sir. I don't think so. At least not at first. I doubt that Micallef would stand for someone killing his girls like that, if only from a business perspective. I think he kept that part of the transaction at arm's length. Stafford could meet the girls through the clubs, which is how I think it happened, and they would be made available to him in the usual manner. Micallef didn't get his hands dirty with the actual pimping. But I do think that after the second one he was starting to realize there was something wrong. Maybe he thought someone was targeting him. Or maybe he guessed the truth. Either way, he was getting paranoid. And the girls were getting understandably jumpy."

"What about Stafford's suicide?"

"This is where it gets a bit nebulous, sir," Banks admitted. "I think that Micallef realized it was Stafford soon after the Maureen Heseltine murder and went to visit him. We did get a vague description from a neighbor of a man leaving Stafford's house around the time he probably died. Tall, fair-haired, smartly dressed."

"But the witness didn't see his face."

"No, sir. That's why I said it gets a bit nebulous."

"But you think Micallef killed Stafford?"

"I think Micallef went to talk to him and one way or another persuaded him to commit suicide. It's possible that Stafford was already on the verge. He'd tried it before. He'd also just got a prescription of sleeping pills a couple of days previous to his death. I think Micallef tipped the scales. I doubt that he actually killed him, but he pushed him to it. Anyway, there's nothing can be proven there. Stafford goes down as a suicide. Micallef carries on as normal."

"But there's more?"

"Yes, sir. I think that Micallef also found out that Jackie Simmons had given me the description. It's probably my fault, sir. I did talk to her on a number of occasions, and perhaps I wasn't discreet enough. He must have seen us together, or someone did who told him."

"You can't blame yourself for this, Alan."

"I wish it were different, sir. I should have been more careful. I . . . dammit, I liked the girl. I even told Micallef that Stafford, whose identity we didn't know at the time, had scared one of his girls. Maybe he put two and two together and knew it was Jackie who'd told me that. Christ, maybe I even did want to reform her, save her. I don't know. But I liked her. And it's my fault."

"You think Micallef strangled her?"

"Him or one of his minions. First thing we did this morning was run down his alibi, and as expected, it's as solid as it usually is. He was playing cards with five respectable citizens in a flat near Mayfair. They could be lying. More likely he got Benny or maybe one of his Chinese Triad pals to do it."

"Micallef's in with the Triads?"

"As far as they'll let anybody be. His hang-out is a Chinese restaurant on Gerrard Street known to have connections with 14K. I think it's a drug connection but I don't have anything to back that up."

"But why kill the girl? What possible threat could she pose to him with Stafford dead, a suicide?"

"A statement. A warning to the others." Banks shrugged. "A man like Micallef . . . it's the way he operates. Fear."

"So what next?" Hatchard asked.

"The usual. Keep asking around, searching for witnesses. I'll have another friendly chat with Micallef, which will get us precisely nowhere. We'll pull in Benny, which will get us just about as far, and maybe have a word with some of our paid informants in the Triads, see if they got wind of anything."

"Christ, I remember things used to be a lot simpler in Soho," said Hatchard, resting his pipe on the ceramic ashtray. "We used to know who all the villains were and *where* they were most of the time."

"Ah, but that was before the city cleaned it up, sir," said Banks.

"Hair of the dog, sir?" said Albright.

It was half past one and they were approaching the Pillars of Hercules down the alley beside Foyle's, the arch ahead of them. "Why not," said Banks.

They went inside, got a couple of pints and sat at a quiet table in the back.

"There's this stuff called DNA they can use to identify people," Albright said, out of the blue. He was always doing that, Banks realized, coming out with stuff he'd read. "I read an article about it in a forensics newsletter," he went on. "Apparently this DNA is different in everyone. Completely unique. Like the body's signature. Once you get a sample from a crime scene, you can match it against a sample from the suspect."

Banks had heard about DNA, but he hadn't really given it much thought. It seemed to belong to a world of the future, and he wasn't sure he had a future. "How do you get a sample from the crime scene?" he asked.

"Trace evidence. Blood, saliva, skin, semen. Even a hair, if it's still got the root."

"And from the suspect?"

"You take some of his blood, semen, saliva, skin, a hair or whatever. I suppose saliva would be easiest, come to think of it. Maybe you could just use a toothbrush or something? I mean, you wouldn't want to be taking a semen sample from a bloke, would you?"

"Jesus Christ, Ozzy, you do come up with the oddest bloody ideas."

"Not my idea, sir. It's science. Trouble is, it takes a long time to process, but they'll streamline that. It'll be all the rage soon, you mark my words. Make our job a lot easier."

"Hmmm," said Banks. "Get anywhere with Micallef's alibi?"

"Just about where I expected to get," said Albright. "They all agreed he was at an all-night card game in Mayfair, won about three hundred quid, too, from what I can gather."

"Lucky bastard. What about his gambling companions?"

"A couple with form, the others 'respectable.'"

"Meaning we haven't caught them yet?"

"Something like that, sir."

Banks downed half his drink and wiped his lips. "Pity."

"Well, it was a long shot, sir. We never really thought he did it himself. Not his style. I don't think he's got the bottle."

"Only for women."

"Sir?"

"Never mind," said Banks "Just a story somebody told me a long time ago. I think we're pissing against the wind here."

"I agree, sir, unless we can find an eyewitness."

"And eyewitnesses can be bribed, or scared off. It's not as if we can offer witness protection like they do in America."

"I could always hide her away at my house, sir, especially if she's a good looker."

Banks laughed. "Good idea, Ozzy. Good idea." He finished his pint. "And I've got an even better one. My shout."

———

In retrospect, Banks thought it might have been a mistake going to see Micallef after three pints of Beck's, but then he realized that hindsight is only reliable after the event. And what was there to lose? Feeling a little better for the hair of the dog, the two of them headed along Greek Street toward Shaftesbury Avenue. It was another fine day, and the tourists were out in Soho in force, Americans mostly, Banks noticed by the accents he overheard. People were sitting outside at coffee shops and enjoying the march of humanity back and forth. It was a long way from the area at nighttime and a world away from twenty years back.

They darted between the taxis and buses on Shaftesbury Avenue and headed into Chinatown. The odds were that Micallef would be holding court there, as usual.

When they got to the restaurant, he wasn't there, and the maître d', of course, knew nothing. Banks and Albright walked along Gerrard Street to the corner of Macclesfield and pondered what to do. It was then that Banks noticed the car pull up across from the restaurant. The driver got out, checked the street like a minder, and opened the back door. It was Benny. And there was Micallef, resplendent in his Hugo Boss suit, lock of blond hair flopping over his eye.

"Come on, Ozzy," said Banks. "No time like the present." And he headed down the street, Albright a few paces behind.

Micallef saw Banks as he was crossing the street to the restaurant. He paused on the pavement, glanced over, then smiled and ran his forefinger across his lips as if to seal them with Sellotape.

Banks ran the last few yards and he hit Micallef hard in his midriff before Benny even knew what was going on. The two of them hit the pavement, Micallef underneath, and Banks punched at his kidneys, gut and, when he got in position, at his face. Micallef for all his height and ranginess wasn't much of a street fighter, and he flailed to protect himself. Already the blood was flowing from a split lip and broken nose. Banks could see only red, only Jackie's crumpled body left in the alley like a piece of garbage, the bruise on her throat and the Sellotape across her lips. He knelt on Micallef's chest and punched and punched.

After a while, he became vaguely aware of someone kicking him, first in the ribs, then a jarring blow to the side of his skull, and another. He fell over on his side. People were shouting now, someone trying to get ahold of him. Micallef had his knees drawn up to his stomach and his hands defensively covering his bleeding face, whimpering on the pavement.

Banks struggled, but it was no good. The hands holding him were strong and sure. At one point, he thought he heard Albright say, "Forget it, sir, it's Chinatown."

He gasped for breath as Albright helped him to his feet, and the more air he got, the more he calmed down, came out of the red mist and was able to understand what was going on. Benny and Albright had scuffled at first, but in the end they had decided to try and separate Banks and Micallef. Now Banks leaned against a lamppost and felt the side of his face all wet and numb, and the blood was pounding in his head.

Micallef sagged in a heap on the pavement and held his stomach and groaned. Then he glared up at Banks, features twisted in pain. "You're dead!" he shouted through blood and broken teeth. "You hear me, Banks? You're a dead man for this!"

Maybe I am, Banks thought, and maybe it doesn't matter. The thing was, he felt like a dead man already.

"Well, mate, you've certainly been in the wars, haven't you?"

Banks instinctively put his hand up to the side of his right eye. He could feel the rough, uneven row of stitches. Eight of them. And his ribs still ached where they were taped. "The doc says I might have a scar."

Roly Verity brushed his hair back out of his eyes. "I'm sure it'll look good on you. I'm told some ladies like a scar."

"Not my wife," said Banks.

It was ten days after the attack on Micallef and the kerfuffle had more or less settled down. Micallef had declined to press charges, more out of fear of losing face than from any benevolent feelings toward Banks. Nobody had seen anything, anyway. They never did in Soho.

"You were lucky you didn't get suspended, you know," said Verity. "Young Albright did a damn good job of keeping your chestnuts out of the fire."

"Don't I know it."

He gestured toward Banks's glass. "Another?"

"Why not?"

They were in the Three Greyhounds at the corner of Old Compton Street and Greek Street, and Banks was nursing the last of a pint of bitter. It was just after dark, raining outside, and the place was crowded, noisy and smoky, mostly with a young crowd. The neon signs along the street were blurred through the rain sliding down the pub windows, and from the open door Banks could hear the occasional hiss of a car splashing through a curbside puddle.

Verity returned with the pints. "What on earth were you thinking about?" he went on.

"You know damn well what I was thinking about," said Banks.

"I know you were frustrated. Aren't we all? It's just something we have to live with."

"He did it," said Banks. "Jackie Simmons. Either that or he had it done. And he played a big part in Stafford's suicide, too."

"You know he did it and I know he did, but it's what we can prove that counts, and we can't prove a fucking thing. There are no witnesses, and he's got five people to say he was playing cards with them. No forensics worth a damn. No prints. Blood type shared with 45 percent of the population. Including you, for all I know. . . . And the victim was just another tom. What's the point in beating yourself up over it?"

Banks paused, started his fresh beer and said, "It would hardly be in your interests anyway, would it, Micallef going down for murder?"

Banks sensed Verity stiffen beside him. His tone hardened as he said, "What do you mean by that?"

"Proof, Roly, proof. I don't have any. Not of anything." Banks tapped the side of his head. "But I think I know what happened. I think I know what's been going on."

"You're talking in riddles, man."

"I just want to know how deep you're in with them, that's all."

Verity put his drink down hard and some of it spilled over the sides. He scraped his chair back. One or two of the young drinkers gave them the once-over but averted their gaze quickly when they caught Verity's evil eye. "I don't have to listen to this crap."

"True. You don't," said Banks. "But you want to know how much I know, don't you? Calculate the threat level?"

Verity picked up his glass again. "One of those hypothetical discussions," he said, smiling through crooked and stained teeth.

"You can put it that way, if you like." Banks lit a cigarette. "The way I see it, though, Roly, is that you've been playing both sides against the middle, haven't you?"

"Who was it put you on to Micallef in the first place?"

"I've thought about that," said Banks. "It was you. Right from the start, just down the street from here, after Pamela Morrison's murder."

"And?"

"You had to, didn't you? It was a smart move. You knew we'd get on to him eventually, either through the girls, the club or the building, so why not come out with it up front? You're a cop, after all. You were supposed to be helping us. I can't say you did a great deal after that, though. Not for us, at any rate."

"What do you mean?"

"I got the impression that Micallef knew we were coming, that he had time to prepare his story. I think you warned him."

"Bollocks. He'd have known anyway. A prossie gets killed in Soho? Course he'd expect a visit from the peelers."

"Maybe. But it goes a bit deeper than that, doesn't it?"

"I don't know what you mean."

"Oh, stop playing the bloody innocent, Roly. I know you blokes at Vice. Sometimes you get so close to your villains you become one yourself, or as good as. A free taste of pussy now and then, the odd bottle of bubbly, a carton of cigarettes. I know how it goes."

"Them's the old days. That's—"

"Nothing's changed that much. Not when it comes down to graft and corruption. I can understand why you want to keep in with him, because he drops a useful crumb of good information your way once in a while. If you protect him, he'll give up his competitors and any newcomers trying to muscle in. It's a dangerous game, Roly, and a dodgy one, but I can understand it. I can see why you want to do that, and I applaud you for it, I really do. It's a fine balancing act. But you've gone too far this time."

"I don't follow."

"Norman Stafford."

"He was a killer and a pervert. And he committed suicide."

"All true, more or less. But I think he committed suicide with a little persuasion from Matthew Micallef. Micallef was seen leaving his house."

"*Possibly* seen. Anyway, so what if he did? Saved us a lot of paper-work."

Banks laughed. "That's true. And he's no great loss. But the point is that at some point before that, Micallef must have *known* it was Stafford killing his girls, even if he didn't personally set up the dates. And if he knew, why didn't you know? And if you *did* know, why didn't we know?"

"This is all too complicated for me. Nobody told me anything."

"So it was a one-way street, was it?"

"What?"

"The information. The second time I talked to Micallef, he used the phrase 'Sellotaped her cunt shut.' I remembered it because it disgusted me the first time as much as it did the second, and the first time I heard it was from your mouth."

Verity raised his hands. "Fine, you don't like the way I talk. So wash my fucking mouth out with soap."

"You're missing the point, Roly." Banks counted on his fingers for emphasis. "First off, how did he know the killer used Sellotape on his victims? It wasn't in the press, or on the telly. We kept it hush-hush. And second, why did he use that exact same phrase? Word for word. Unless he'd heard it somewhere before?"

Verity sat quietly for a moment, thinking and fidgeting with his drink. Banks smoked and watched him patiently. "I suppose you're going to tell me?" Verity said finally.

"Well, there's only two ways it could have happened," Banks said. "Either he heard it from one of the team, or he was there at the scene of one, or both, murders. Take your pick."

"Micallef didn't kill those girls."

"Which leaves the team. It wasn't me, it wasn't Albright, it certainly wasn't Hatchard, and I doubt very much—"

"All right, all right, so I told him. *Mea culpa.* So what? It was tit for tat. I was hoping he might give me a lead, a name, anything."

"But he didn't?"

"He didn't know anything at that point."

"And that's another thing, Roly. You were awfully quick on the scene at the Maureen Heseltine murder. You weren't on a call across the street. I checked. How did you get there so fast?"

"What? I . . ."

"Let me tell you how I think it happened. Micallef tipped you off, didn't he? Either Stafford came unstrung and went crying to him, or he figured it out for himself. Maybe he did arrange the dates, or at least the second one. But he wanted you on the spot. You're in bed with him, Roly. I just want to know if you go all the way together or not."

"That's rubbish."

"Is it? How did you get there so quickly, then?"

"It's my job, or maybe you hadn't noticed?"

"How?"

"I got the call, just like you. I got there before you, that's all."

"You ran all the way?"

"Don't be an idiot."

"So why did you lie about it?"

"Is this some sort of interrogation? A trap? Are you wired? Because if you're trying to fit me up—"

"Relax, Roly. I'm not wired. Pat me down if you want, though you might raise an eyebrow or two."

Verity shifted in his seat "All right," he grunted. "I believe you. I told you, it was always give-and-take with Micallef. We tolerated each other."

"I think it was more a matter of give on your part and take on his. We got nothing out of this, Roly. Nothing. What did you get?"

"I resent that."

"I daresay you do. But you know what really gets me? It's not Micallef. It's not even Stafford. You can argue he deserved what he got. It's the girl."

"Which girl?"

"You know damn well which girl. Jackie Simmons."

"Why? Soft on her, were you? I've heard tell you—"

"Enough, Roly, enough," said Banks. "Jackie Simmons told me about a weird client she'd had, one who went on about restoring her innocence, and she gave me a good description. We got her in and produced a passable photokit. We were getting close to Norman Stafford. But you know all about that, don't you? Now, whether Micallef didn't want us talking to him because of their property dealings, or whether he simply wanted him out of way because he'd killed two of his girls, I don't know. I'd say for a man like that it's probably as easy to replace an MP as it is a girl, so let's say he *suggested* suicide—"

"You can't prove any of this. It's nothing but idle speculation."

"Speculation, yes, but not so idle. And the question remains: How did Micallef know that Jackie Simmons gave me a description of Stafford? How did he know she'd talked?"

"Someone must have seen the two of you together. God knows, you were practically—"

"You knew, Roly. You were in and out of the office like you belonged. You saw all the case files, had access to all the leads as soon as we got them. What did you do? Make a copy of the photokit and show it to Micallef so he could plug his leaks? Including Jackie Simmons? You told him about her, didn't you? You signed her death warrant, Roly, and that's what I can't forgive you for."

Verity stabbed Banks's chest with his finger. "You're so fucking holier than thou, aren't you? Just take a look at yourself, Banks. You're pissed half the time, hungover the rest. You go off half-cocked at Micallef in the street in broad daylight. You chat up his girls, and everybody knows you're screwing—"

"Stop right there," said Banks. His voice was soft but the level of menace was high, and Verity picked up on it. "Stop right there. You don't bring me or my personal life into this. Get it? This is between you and me."

"Oh, really? Well, I don't give a fuck. Do you want to know the truth, Banks? Do you want to know what people think around here, what they're saying behind your back? You don't fit. I might as well tell you. Word is getting round. You're a hothead. A throwback. You're not a team player. This city needs a different kind of detective for these times. One who knows the value of good intelligence. Of not rocking the boat too much."

Banks snorted. "And that's you, Roly? Because if that's the case, I'd rather be somewhere else. Anywhere else, for that matter."

"Well, why don't you take the chance if it comes your way? You can't win the war, you know, only the occasional battle."

"Maybe so, but at least I don't have to be a collaborator."

"Are you calling me a rat? Is that what you're calling me?"

"Forget it, Roly," said Banks. "You're right. We both know Micallef did it. He's got away with it. One day we'll get him for something else. Everything comes around."

"What do you mean by that?"

"Karma, Roly, karma." Banks stood up, gave him a little salute and said, "Be seeing you."

And that was it, really. Over twenty years ago. Banks had walked out of the Three Greyhounds that day *knowing* that he was right, that Roland Verity had passed on information to Micallef that had sealed Jackie's fate.

Matthew Micallef was shot by an underage Russian prostitute called Olga Chevenko in the alley beside the Nellie Dean in November 1996. In her defense, she said she was jealous because he had been sleeping with another woman. DCI Roland Verity came under investigation on corruption charges around the same time, something to do with smuggling illegal, and often unwilling, young girls from Eastern Europe for the purposes of prostitution. He took early retirement. Word had it that he was living the life of Riley on the Costa del Sol.

Over the years, Banks had thought often of Pamela Morrison, Maureen Heseltine and, especially, of Jackie Simmons, but he had put the rest of the business out of his mind and got on with his new life in Yorkshire. He might not have found as much peace as he had hoped for when he took the transfer, but things had been better, for a while. His marriage to Sandra had even blossomed for a while, though it eventually ended in divorce.

Like everyone else in the know, he had assumed that Pamela's and Maureen's killer had delivered his own judgment and carried out his own sentence on himself, with or without a little help, and that Micallef had either killed, or ordered the killing of, Jackie Simmons as a warning to the rest of the girls, though Banks couldn't prove it.

And now, as he stood looking out on a new day in Eastvale market square, he held in his hands something that he knew might change everything he had believed. The radio was tuned to some atonal piece on Radio 3, Schoenberg or Berg, but it seemed quite fitting.

Banks opened the envelope.

It was from Commander Oswald Albright, of the London Metropolitan Police, and the rather stiff, formal note told him that as a result of a recent "cold case" reinvestigation of the Jackie Simmons murder, which had always remained officially "unsolved," a warrant had been issued for the arrest of former Detective Chief Inspector Roland Verity, and an extradition request had been sent to the Spanish government. The Spanish authorities had already been extremely cooperative in arranging for a DNA sample and were expected to throw up no barriers to Verity's eventual extradition.

What comes around. Karma.

Banks wondered what Verity looked like now. Sunburned, wearing shorts and a Bermuda shirt, no doubt, probably run to fat. Did he still have that ridiculous mop of hair that used to flop over his face like a careless schoolboy's?

Curious about a few points, Banks turned off the radio and picked up his phone. After a few minutes, he was put through to Commander Albright.

"Sir," said the younger man, now at a higher rank than his old boss.

"Call me Alan, Ozzy. And shouldn't I be calling *you* sir?"

"I think we can dispense with the formalities, don't you? Do you remember a conversation we once had in the Pillars of Hercules many years ago? I was telling you about an article I'd read on DNA, and you—"

Banks laughed. "All right. All right, Ozzy. You were right. You were ahead of your time, and I was a dinosaur, even then."

"Well, it just goes to show, doesn't it, after all these years?"

"That's what I was wondering about," said Banks. "You're a bit scant with the details. Why? How?"

"Well, it wasn't down to me, if that was what you were thinking. I just got the team's results and thought you'd want to know. It's funny the way these cold case things work. Not my department. God knows if it's alphabetical or by year, or whatever system they use. Anyway, the Jackie Simmons case came up for investigation. You liked her, didn't you?"

"Yes," said Banks. "I did. She was a beautiful, spirited, intelligent girl, no matter what, and she didn't deserve what happened to her. She had her problems, but don't we all?"

"Too true. Christ, I'll never forget the day you went for Micallef in Gerrard Street. I thought you were going to kill him."

Banks fingered the scar beside his right eye. "I might have done if you and Benny hadn't stopped me," said Banks. "Not my finest hour. Back to the cold case investigation."

"Oh, yes. Well, anyway, one of the team got suspicious when he started checking out the personalities involved and saw Roly Verity's name. As you might know, Verity left the Met under a bit of a cloud. Nothing proven, nothing serious, at any rate, but even so . . . This was in the nineties, a bit after your time. We couldn't have known, not back in eighty-five."

"How deep did it go?"

"A lot deeper than people had originally thought. He had serious gambling debts at the time of the Soho killings, and it turns out Micallef had bought some of them. We know Micallef himself had an alibi for Jackie Simmons, and so, it turns out, did Benny Fraser, his chief enforcer. The alibis could have been manufactured, of course, and there were others who could have done it, including the Chinese, but the young lad, a fresh pair of eyes and all, decided to have a closer look at Roly. The thinking was that he'd done it at Micallef's request to get out of his debts and, from Micallef's point of view, it put Roly in his power ever after, tied them together. They were already close enough, and this was the clincher. Of all the people involved, it turns out that Roly Verity didn't have much of an alibi. He'd been at the celebration party with us, on and off, but remember he didn't come on with us to the club, that was just you, me and . . . what was his name?"

"Burgess," said Banks. "Dirty Dick Burgess."

"Ah, yes. Burgess. How could I forget? I wonder what happened to him."

"Counterterrorism," said Banks. "Very hush-hush."

"I'd never have thought it," said Albright. "Anyway, once our bright spark found out that Verity *could* have done it, he started going over the forensics. And that brought us to the DNA. You remember the lab got skin samples from under Jackie Simmons's fingernails? Anyway, she'd scratched her killer as he strangled her."

"Will the DNA sample the Spanish took from Verity stand up?"

"The CPS says it will. All aboveboard, agreed to, witnessed, signed for, the lot. Between you and me, he didn't have much choice. He didn't know why they were doing it, but he thought his future on the Costa del Sol depended on it."

"Well, in a way it did, didn't it?" said Banks. "Well done. Good work, Ozzy."

"As I said, it wasn't me. The only fear is that he might not survive the journey. According to the Spanish authorities, his heart's just about conked out."

"Roly's heart conked out years ago," said Banks. "Anyway, Ozzy, you're the bearer of good tidings. Thank you. We must get together sometime when I'm down your way."

"Indeed," said Albright. "I don't drink now, so it'll have to be Starbucks, I'm afraid. Oh, before I forget, I bumped into someone who said to say hello to you. Part of the cold case team, as it turns out."

"Oh?"

"Yes. A DCI called Linda. Linda Jameson. Says she used to know you."

Jesus Christ. *Linda.* Banks felt a jolt through his chest. He tried to keep the emotion he felt out of his voice. "Yes, I believe I knew her once," he said. "Done well for herself, then?"

"Very. She's head of the cold case Psychological Profiling Unit. One of the few actual cops doing the job. Went to university part-time and everything. Got all the degrees."

"Good for her," said Banks. "I always thought she was a bright lass."

"Course, back then we laughed at all that stuff."

"Not you, Ozzy," said Banks. "You had more foresight than the lot of us put together. Look, I'd better go now. Thanks for the good news. Hope to see you soon."

Albright said his farewells and Banks put down the phone. *Linda.* Well, he had once told her that she ought to be a psychologist or something, and now she'd gone and done it. Had he treated her badly? He didn't think so. He remembered their last meeting at her Waterloo flat, his home away from home. She shed a few tears, they had a bit too much to drink, a long good-bye kiss, too long, really. . . . It was all so many years ago, and they had never been in touch since. For a moment, he thought he could smell chamomile tea and hear the rustling of a silk kimono.

A coach pulled into the market square and disgorged its cargo of tourists. Banks remembered that he had been thinking about getting away for a while, just for a break, somewhere different. He reached for his phone to ring his travel agent and find out what was on offer, but before he could dial he heard a tap at his door.

"Yes?" he called.

The door opened and Annie Cabbot stepped in, looking good with her new short layered haircut, a few highlights here and there, tight jeans and a simple mauve top. She frowned at him. "Something wrong?"

"No," he said. "Nothing. Just an old case. Brings back memories. What is it?"

"Stabbing on the East Side Estate. Are you interested, or do you want me to take Winsome?"

Banks looked out at the clear blue sky through his window, then back at Annie. He smiled. "I'll come with you," he said. "Memory Lane gets a bit stuffy sometimes. I could do with a breath of fresh air."

Afternotes

"**Going Back**." This novella has never been published before in the U.S. It appeared first in the Canadian and U.K. expanded editions of *Not Safe After Dark and Other Stories*. I wrote it early in 1999, so it falls between *In a Dry Season* and *Cold Is the Grave* in the Banks chronology. At that point, I didn't know that I was going to send Banks back home to deal with his old school friend's disappearance in *Close to Home* (2003), and I wanted to show him interacting with his family and responding to the place where he grew up. In manuscript, it reached 106 pages, too long for any of the magazines or anthologies that regularly published my stories, and too short for separate book publication. And so it sat there gathering dust until I came to write *Close to Home*, when I incorporated parts of the novella into the novel—mostly details about the street where Banks grew up, his relationship with his parents, the music he listened to and the books he read in 1965. When the story was first published, I made some revisions to shift it chronologically. Now it sits somewhere between *Close to Home* and *Playing with Fire*. I also tried to avoid too much repetition of details I had cannibalized for the novel without spoiling the original conception. I haven't touched it since.

"**Cornelius Jubb**." This grew out of researching and writing about the Second World War in *In a Dry Season*. When Karin Slaughter came up with the idea of a series of stories linked through time by a charm bracelet, she asked me to set mine in this period, and it became the second story in *Like a Charm*. It's really about the title character and racial injustice. By naming him Cornelius Jubb and making him a black American GI stationed in Yorkshire in the Second World War, I was able to stress both the differences and the similarities between him and the locals. He might seem strange and exotic, but he has a Yorkshire name. Naturally this perplexes the local people. I had also written a couple of stories featuring

Frank Bascombe, as "Special Constable" in the war, and this was intended as a third, though I couldn't use his name in the anthology for copyright reasons.

"The Magic of Your Touch." For some reason this is one of my favorites, though I have always felt a little guilty that it was probably not quite as long as editor Robert J. Randisi had hoped for. It would be hard to see how it could be longer. This is an example of a story that really had no genesis other than the desire to sit down and write something to do with music, as the anthology was called *Murder and All That Jazz.* I had no idea where it was going. Obviously the variation on the Faustian "deal with the devil" (Robert Johnson at the crossroads!) was in my mind, as was the nature of obsession, and the corrosive nature of guilt, as in Poe's "The Tell-Tale Heart." But I didn't know any of that at the time I started writing. All I knew was that a man was wandering lost in an urban landscape that resembled something out of David Lynch's *Eraserhead.* What he would do, what would become of him, I had no idea until several hours later when the story was finished. Another thing I like about it is that it contains elements of horror and the supernatural that do not usually appear in my work. I have always thought that if I didn't write crime I would write horror, so I was pleased to be able to include at least a little touch of it here.

"The Eastvale Ladies' Poker Circle." When Otto Penzler asked for a story connected with poker for *Dead Man's Hand,* I balked, knowing little about the game and certainly never having won any money at it! But it's not easy to say no to Otto. Part of the challenge was finding ways around these inadequacies, of course, and my initial research showed me that the game was quite popular with British women. It wasn't a long stretch from that to the idea of the "poker circle," where a group of career women get together once in a while for an evening's fun. After that, it was the getting together that came to matter to the story, and the personalities involved, not the game of poker itself. They could have been playing cribbage for all I cared! I also got to venture into one of Eastvale's more privileged and exclusive areas for the first time, an area that became even more important in the recent Banks novel, *All the Colors of Darkness.*

"The Ferryman's Beautiful Daughter." Though the title is a homage to the Incredible String Band's 1968 album *The Hangman's Beautiful Daughter,* the ghost of Syd Barrett haunts this story. The order, from editors Claudia Bishop and Don Bruns, was rather taller than usual. Not only did they want a short story for their *Merry Band of Murderers* anthology, they also wanted a song to go with it. As it turned out, I had just finished *Piece of My Heart,* set partly in 1969, and I had invented a rock band called the Mad Hatters. It seemed to me that they could do double duty here, so I ended up writing a song by a rock band I had invented! Don Bruns set the words to music and recorded it for the CD that went with the book.

The sound I wanted was a cross between Nick Drake and the late 1960s pastoral Pink Floyd's *More* sound track and "Grantchester Meadows" from *Ummagumma*. Ethereal organ, flute and acoustic guitar. Because I was still stuck in the 1960s time warp, one thing I wanted to write about was the clash between a very straitlaced traditional community and the new hippies, with their revolutionary ideas and communal living. An island in the Pacific Northwest seemed an ideal place to play this out, as it is a fairly remote and self-contained region. Originally, I was going to tell the story from Mary Jane's viewpoint, but I soon found that Grace was a more natural storyteller. Mary Jane was a bit too flighty and would hardly have stuck to the point, but the song is about her:

> Morning mist is drifting on the surface of the water
> All the children are asleep except the boatman's daughter
> And Mary Jane is dreaming
> Of oceans dark and gleaming,
> Where she breathes the water cold,
> A mermaid blessed with scales of gold,
> And flows where the tide will take her.
> Larks are rising from the fields and scattering the air with song.
> Children dance upon the green in summer now the days are long,
> But Mary Jane is dreaming
> In her ocean dark and gleaming.
> Kaleidoscopes of fish spin by
> She hears their colors, tastes their signs
> And flows where the tide will take her.
>
> Night is day and day is night
> Truth is dream and dream is right
> Follow Mary Jane and see
> Just what the depths can teach you.
>
> White is black and black is white
> Real is wrong and wrong is right
> Follow Mary Jane and see
> Just where these words can lead you.

Darkness falls upon the woods and stars are shining in the sky,
The moon floats on the water like a fallen angel, pale and dry,
But Mary Jane is dreaming
In the ocean dark and gleaming
New friends whisper in her ear
The truths she doesn't want to hear
She flows where their words will take her.

"Walking the Dog." The request for this story for *Toronto Noir* reached me while I was on a cruise around South America. Somewhere between Cape Horn and the Falkland Islands, I could hardly have been much farther away from Toronto, or from the sort of atmosphere I associate with noir. I must admit that, at first, the whole idea of Toronto and noir didn't seem to work for me. I generally see noir as a story about lust and greed in which most people get exactly what they deserve and nobody cares. They are usually not stories with a "hero," like a private eye or a cop (unless he's a bent one!), though there are some exceptions, and many people seem to use the terms noir and "hard-boiled" interchangeably. However gritty and violent the Banks novels become at times, they are never noir, so it is also not the kind of style I'm used to writing.

I also think of movies more than books when I think of noir, of spare dialogue, a certain kind of lighting, use of shadows, atmospheric music and unusual camera angles. Movies like *The Postman Always Rings Twice*, *Laura*, *Out of the Past*, *Double Indemnity*. Of course, certain authors spring to mind, too: James M Cain, Cornell Woolrich, Jim Thompson. But on the whole, I find the term is overused and little understood.

Anyway, reminding myself that the whole business of writing a short story should involve exploring new territory, I agreed and set about it almost right away, asking only that I be allowed to set the tale in my own little part of Toronto, the Beaches, which is about as noir as a Yorkshire Dales village! We spent a number of days at sea traveling vast distances between ports, and I would sit every morning with my laptop, looking out over the limitless ocean ahead and tap away. I'm pleased with the story, yet it turned out not quite so much pure noir as a bit of an homage and a bit of a parody, and those with some interest in the subject may find some pleasure in spotting the book and movie references.

"Blue Christmas." Doug Greene from Crippen & Landru asked me for this as a gift for friends of the publishers at Christmas 2005. It was published in a special edition of 353 copies. Doug wanted an Inspector Banks story without violence or bad language. A tall order for me! But a challenge. In the end, I came up with a Banks story without a murder, and I enjoyed writing it very much.

"Shadows on the Water." This one was for John Harvey's anthology *Men from Boys*. I had been writing quite a bit about the Second World War and had even touched on the First in a story called "In Flanders Field." When I was trying to think of something that might be a defining moment in a young man's life, the point at which a boy becomes a man, I thought of this childhood betrayal and of what its effects might be in later years.

"The Cherub Affair." This story has a long and unusual pedigree. In 1985, I took a year off teaching and decided it was make or break time as a writer. I had already become interested in crime fiction and attempted one or two novels that I quickly consigned to the basement. I wanted to write about Yorkshire, partly because of nostalgia, partly because I knew it far better than I did my new country, Canada, and partly because I liked the sort of regional English detective story that uses crime and its detection to look at the character and foibles of a particular area of the country.

I had recently finished *A Dedicated Man*, which was with a publisher, and decided first to write a follow-up, *Gallows View*. They were eventually published in reverse order. After I had finished *Gallows View* my "sabbatical" wasn't quite over, so I began another novel, this time a private eye novel set in Toronto.

I had to travel quite a long way to teach, and on one of those bus journeys I remembered passing every day a small private investigation office above a strip mall. I could see a few dusty cabinets and stacked files through the window as the bus passed by, but I never saw who worked there. That made very fertile ground for the imagination, and so "Jones Investigations" was born, Old Jones being the grizzled old founder who was usually too drunk to investigate but passed on all he knew to his young protégé Colin Lang, an English student with a PhD who couldn't get a teaching job and didn't want to drive a taxi.

Around the time I finished the novel, called *Beginner's Luck*, I heard that the Inspector Banks series—at least the first two—had been accepted for publication. After that, it seemed, nobody was interested in a private eye novel written by me and set in Toronto, so *Beginner's Luck* languished in the bottom drawer of my desk. I occasionally dusted it off, and even had vague ideas for a sequel, but Banks occupied all my time, so nothing ever became of them.

When the *Toronto Star* asked for a story they could serialize over a week, I thought again of *Beginner's Luck*. While writers might dream of turning a short story into a novel, here I was turning a novel into a short story. In the end, it was easier simply to retain the key plot elements and main characters and dump everything else—subplots, minor characters, a lot of background and exposition. I don't think I even mention the detective's name in the short story! It was published in seven installments, each one with at least a minor cliff-hanger to heighten anticipation for the next. In a small way, I got to feel a bit like Charles Dickens must have felt writing his works for serialization, though I already knew how my story was going to end. I have inserted an eighth part for this edition, a scene I particularly liked in the novel but wasn't previously able to use because of length restrictions.

"The Price of Love." Written for a Mystery Writers of America anthology called *The Blue Religion,* edited by Michael Connelly, this story was another big challenge for me to do something different. The anthology was meant to deal with the "burden of the badge" that is a policeman's lot, and as most of the contributors were American crime writers, I expected a high-testosterone mix of tough guys and action. As it turned out, that isn't the case, and the anthology is full of variety in everything except its quality. Not a bad one in the bunch. Anyway, I still wanted to shy away even from Banks and his feelings about being a cop, so I decided to use a different kind of hero and a different kind of badge.

"Birthday Dance." Some of the subjects for these themed crime anthologies can be most challenging, and I have been involved in a number of such projects, including poker, American football, Shakespeare and, in this one, the Bible, for Anne Perry's *Thou Shalt Not Kill.* Well, the Bible is certainly full of murder and mayhem, but again it was a matter of avoiding the obvious, or putting an unusual twist on something. I had recently seen Strauss's opera *Salome,* so that story was fresh in mind, and when I started to research its origins I found more doubt and obscurity than I did certainty, which suited me just fine. Writers thrive much better on doubt and uncertainty than on facts and self-evident truths. Nobody was even sure how old Salome was, or whether she was old enough to perform the dance of the seven veils for which she is so infamous! The idea of a sort of innocent Salome appealed, and in the end the story turned out as a sort of cross between a Bible story and an episode of *The Sopranos.*

"Like a Virgin." My publishers asked me for a new Banks story for the collection, and I wrote a novella. This is it.

Credits

BOOKS BY PETER ROBINSON

IN THE DARK PLACES
Hardcover, Large Print, and eBook

CHILDREN OF THE REVOLUTION
Trade Paperback, Large Print, and eBook

WATCHING THE DARK
Trade Paperback, Large Print, and eBook

BEFORE THE POISON
Trade Paperback, Large Print, and eBook

BAD BOY
Trade Paperback, Large Print, and eBook

THE PRICE OF LOVE AND OTHER STORIES
Trade Paperback and eBook

ALL THE COLORS OF DARKNESS
Trade Paperback, Large Print, and eBook

FRIEND OF THE DEVIL
Trade Paperback and eBook

PIECE OF MY HEART
Mass Market and eBook

STRANGE AFFAIR
Mass Market, Large Print, Audio CD, and eBook

PLAYING WITH FIRE
Trade Paperback, Large Print, and eBook

THE FIRST CUT
Trade Paperback and eBook

CLOSE TO HOME
Mass Market and eBook

AFTERMATH
Trade Paperback and eBook

COLD IS THE GRAVE
Mass Market and eBook

IN A DRY SEASON
Mass Market and eBook

BLOOD AT THE ROOT
Mass Market and eBook

INNOCENT GRAVES
Mass Market and eBook

FINAL ACCOUNT
Mass Market and eBook

WEDNESDAY'S CHILD
Mass Market

PAST REASON HATED
Mass Market

THE HANGING VALLEY
Mass Market

A NECESSARY END
Mass Market

A DEDICATED MAN
Mass Market

GALLOWS VIEW
Mass Market